BEAR HUGS

James D. Navratil

Copyright © 2023 by James D. Navratil.

Library of Congress Control Number: 2023903212
ISBN: Hardcover 978-1-6698-6836-1
Softcover 978-1-6698-6837-8
eBook 978-1-6698-6838-5

All rights reserved. No part of this book may be reproduced or transmitted in any form or by any means, electronic or mechanical, including photocopying, recording, or by any information storage and retrieval system, without permission in writing from the copyright owner.

This is a work of fiction. Names, characters, places and incidents either are the product of the author's imagination or are used fictitiously, and any resemblance to any actual persons, living or dead, events, or locales is entirely coincidental.

Any people depicted in stock imagery provided by Getty Images are models, and such images are being used for illustrative purposes only.
Certain stock imagery © Getty Images.

Print information available on the last page.

Rev. date: 02/25/2023

To order additional copies of this book, contact:
Xlibris
844-714-8691
www.Xlibris.com
Orders@Xlibris.com
850367

Prologue

It had been a beautiful day in Antarctica, and now the sun was starting to set as Professor John James Czermak; his graduate student, Alex Pushkov; and some of their fellow shipmates prepared their camp spots on Hovgaard Island. They had to dig a level place in the snow to place their sleeping bags, and James had selected a secluded spot near the top of the hill overlooking the entrance to the Lemaire Channel and a glacial mountain range on the mainland that reminded him of the Grand Tetons in Wyoming. The expedition leader had suggested James put a big rock at the foot of his camping equipment to prevent him from accidentally sliding down the hill. The equipment consisted of an outer waterproof cocoon cover (bevy bag) with an inside sleeping bag and foam pad.

After watching a colorful sunset about ten o'clock over the sea, James turned his attention in the opposite direction towards the red glow on the mountains reflected in the channel containing numerous ice floats, a few icebergs, and their ship, the *Akademik Abraham*. The stars were starting to come out as James took off his boots, waterproof pants, and jacket and zipped himself into the sleeping bag and outer cocoon cover. As he watched the number of stars increase around the Southern Cross, he spotted a satellite slowly crossing the sky. Next, he saw a falling star and made a wish. The last time he had come close to seeing this many stars was camping out at Yellowstone National Park in Wyoming or perhaps on his property in Nederland, Colorado.

His mind raced back to Nederland and how wonderful it had been to have his "Pine Shadows" summer home at 86 Doe Trail, bordering Boulder County Open Space, with stellar views of the Barker Reservoir, Continental Divide, the town, and Eldora Ski Area. They joked about Doe Trail as the Department of Energy, not a female deer, as it was ironic that '86 was the tragic year that he had lost his DOE security clearance and ensuing trouble with the FBI. Shortly after he and Margrit had purchased the land in 1993, the Norwegian who had built the home four doors up on Doe Trail had died, and his son had him cryogenically preserved along with his father's deceased friend from California in hopes they could be brought back to life once medical science had advanced to that point. The townspeople, primarily a mixture of old miners, hippies, and new agers, started to hear stories about the two frozen dead men being stored in Nederland and held several town meetings on what they should do about the bodies that were starting to attract national publicity. One weekend, at the height of the public attention, Cable News Network (CNN) televised the event, including a sign put out by the local baker which stated, "What is the big deal about two Norwegians in the freezer? I have six Danish in the oven." The town finally accepted the bodies and now capitalizes on the publicity by having an annual "Frozen Dead Guys Day." James had missed the event this year where there were frozen dead guy look-alike contests, coffin races, and more.

James's thoughts returned to the Antarctic, and he reflected on the day. Indeed, it had been a wonderful day. James was an early riser, and with a coffee cup in hand, he made his way back to his usual spot, the middle rear of the lower deck near the cargo gate. There he watched a spectacular sunrise over the mountains between six and seven as the ship made its way to the Yalour Islands after crossing the Antarctic Circle the previous day; it had indeed been a wonderful crossing. After breakfast, they had zodiac cruises in the morning along the mountainous coast. The weather had been pleasant as the ship crossed Waddington Bay, passing through lots of brash ice and some beautiful icebergs. They spotted more humpback whales and some crabeater and leopard seals and made a few stops in the zodiacs to watch Adélie penguins, with the icy mountains in the background. After lunch, they visited Vernadsky Station, a Ukrainian research center once owned by the British and called Faraday Station.

They toured the station and were informed that its scientists were mainly performing upper atmosphere studies and were instrumental in discovering the ozone hole. James gave a short talk on his environmental radioactivity studies at Clemson University to a small group of Ukrainian scientists. The station was colorful, with a bar and homemade vodka, pool table, dartboard, and souvenir shop. They also visited Wordie House, a small museum preserving part of the early British base, and ended the visit with a walk to the top of a nearby snow hill to enjoy the view, followed by sledding down on their bottoms. Then they went back to the ship for dinner. Following their meal, they were treated with a super display in the bay by a pod of eight killer whales, including a mother and calf. There were also humpback whale sightings as fifteen campers were being transported to Hovgaard Island for their campout.

James was pleased that he had the night off from his surveillance of the Argentinean nuclear scientists and whoever was suspected of trying to pass nuclear weapons technology to them. James really thought that Brazil, or even Venezuela, would be a more likely country, but of course, Argentina was having economic problems and might be starting down the road to nuclear blackmail like the North Koreans. Only one of the Argentineans had opted for the campout. Despite terribly missing Ying, James was not going to pass up an experience of a lifetime and stay aboard the ship to continue his covert government assignment. At least this way, he would not have to worry about another attempt on his life and could hopefully get a good night's sleep.

But James was mistaken as he was awakened in the middle of the night by a sharp jar to his sleeping bag and found himself sliding fast down the hill, cocooned in his sleep equipment, and heading for a high ledge over the icy channel. As James was frantically trying to unzip the bag and cocoon, all he could think about was "Is this the same feeling his wife, Margrit, had experienced when she lost control of his car going down Black

Canyon in the Santa Susanna mountains in California?" Margrit's death was no accident as the brakes of the car she was driving had been tampered with. As James was sliding down the hill, he too knew this was no accident, but another attempt on his life.

Chapter 1

I

The US Central Intelligence Agency was founded in 1947. Its headquarters are in Langley, Virginia, and its agents collect, analyze, and evaluate security information from around the world for the president and cabinet. The agency also carries out and oversees covert action at the request of the president. The main priority of the CIA is counterterrorism, followed by nuclear weapon proliferation and counter- and cyber intelligence. CIA stations are generally part of US embassies overseas, and agents are managed by a station chief. Some missions by the agency have dealt with regime changes in foreign governments not friendly to the United States, participation in assassinations of foreign government leaders, arming insurgent groups, and illegal domestic spying on US citizens. The CIA also uses US citizens who travel widely to assist in collecting information pertinent to their mission.

One such citizen is Dr. John James Czermak, a nuclear scientist who assisted in the development of the neutron bomb when he worked at the Rocky Flats Plant near Denver, Colorado. The plant made parts for nuclear weapons. Besides being a nuclear researcher, he was a retired US Army Chemical Corps officer teaching biological, chemical, and nuclear warfare to officer cadets. Czermak also taught at universities in Australia, the Czech Republic, South Carolina, and Colorado. He traveled to conferences around the world and made first-time visits to many countries, some not friendly to the United States. He has many friends around the world, including Afghanistan, Brazilian, Chinese, Iranian, Iraqi, North Korean, and Russian scientists. In both Colorado and South Carolina, CIA agents debriefed Czermak following most of his travels about things he observed that could assist the agency in its mission. Several times on Czermak's travels, there were attempts on his life while he was collecting information on nuclear proliferation and chemical and biological warfare.

John kept a diary most of his adult life. The following is what John wrote on his way home from Vienna:

In late June, I resigned from the International Atomic Energy Agency and planned to return to Rocky Flats from my three-year leave of absence. The movers had taken all our household and personal items for shipment to Arvada. Eric, Lorrie, Margrit, and I, along with four suitcases, took an early morning Austrian Airline flight to East Berlin. Immigration was easy since I still had my United Nations passport. After a walk around a small part of East Berlin, we crossed over at checkpoint Charlie into West Berlin. Then we toured the city and spent the night at the Berlin Hotel.

From West Berlin, we flew to Oslo, took a short train ride into the city, and then a taxi to the Thom Hotel Bristol. Following check-in, we went to our room with two single and one double bed. Later, we had a walk around the area and came upon a beautiful church near the train station called Dome church. Between the church and the hotel is a nice walking mall where some young guys were doing everything from playing music to standing as a statue of someone famous. Of course, they wanted some money. The city has lots of colorful old buildings, and I took lots of pictures.

On Sunday, a tour bus picked us up for our ride to the airport. Our guide told us some facts about Oslo and Norway that were quite interesting. Their taxes are quite high, but they have free medical care and good retirements. They have large oil reserves offshore, and the people are well off. The population is small for the size of the country. The highest mountain is only 7,000 feet, but they do have lots of ski areas, lit up of course, for the long, dark winter days. The high rate of alcoholism is blamed on the winters. Last night between ten and eleven, it was still light outside.

From Oslo to Longyearbyen I had a window seat. During take-off, I saw that Oslo is relatively spread out, has many parks, and a port full of boats and ships. Outside Oslo there are some patches of farmland as well as many forests. The SAS flight was three hours with about 140 passengers.

Spitsbergen is the largest and only permanently populated island (about 2,600 people) in Norway. It borders the Barents, Norwegian, and Greenland Seas. Its administrative center is Longyearbyen, the most northerly city in the world. The island was first used as a whaling station, and later for coal mining. Now research and tourism have become important supplementary industries, featuring among others the University of Svalbard and the Global Seed Vault. The island has an arctic climate, many glaciers, mountains, and fjords. It also supports polar bears, reindeer, and marine mammals. The highest elevation is 5,600 feet. There are four months of total darkness and four months of complete sunlight. Last night we left Spitsbergen on the Akademik Abraham to the open waters of the Greenland Sea and started traveling to a large fjord system known as Isfjorden.

The Akademik Abraham, designed for polar research, is a modern, comfortable, and ice-strengthened ship. It is a Russian-flagged vessel and has a library, lounge, bar, dining room, conference room, swimming pool, sauna, exercise room, and gift shop. It was built in Finland in 1980. There are 63 staff and crew, and our cruise has 61 passengers. Eric and I are sharing a cabin that has a bunk bed, and Lorrie and Margrit have the adjoining cabin separated by a small, shared bathroom with a toilet and sink, and shower that empties onto the floor.

On Monday, at about 10 a.m., we were in the Isfjorden fjord system and saw a couple of calving events from several glaciers, and lots of beautiful snow, ice, and some blue ice floats. We then went up the coast north to Krossfiorden that has glaciers.

On Tuesday, we entered the narrow Sorgattet to cruise and search for wildlife. After breakfast, we anchored off a small island, Amsterdamoya. In the afternoon, we went to Smeerenburgfjorden, which translates into "blubber town." The area is famous from the 17th century whaling period. Instead of a stop, our afternoon consisted of a cruise up the northern waters through lots of ice to try to see polar bears. We did see several seals and a few walruses. In the late afternoon, the ice broke up a lot and it started to snow. Earlier the ship had many hard knocks on the ice to break through. Right after dinner we finally saw our first polar bear. It was close to the ship at first, and then went walking in the direction of a seal. About halfway to the seal, the bear started running and the seal ducked into the water. We were so far north that there was no darkness.

On Wednesday, we went over the tip of Svalbard with the ship hitting big chunks of floating ice. At times it seemed like the ship would split open. We ended up in a fjord called Woodfjorden. There we saw a couple of polar bears and three walruses lying on separate pieces of floating ice. In the afternoon there was a Zodiac cruise of the area.

On Thursday, the ship went back the way it came, through packed ice, going south along the area of Spitsbergen known as Albert Island. We then went into a bay called Kongsforden. After dinner, we docked at Ny Alesund, a village where scientific research is being performed by about 150 scientists. The winter population of the village is forty. It has a rich history of coal mining. There is also a gift shop and place to buy and mail postcards. Margrit sent some to the U.S. from the most northerly post office in the world. A monument of the famous Norwegian explorer Roald Amundsen is also located there.

Before dinner, there was a call for people who wanted to join an elite group who have jumped into the Arctic Ocean above 80 degrees latitude. I had not used my long red flannel underwear that I got at a surprise birthday party from my nutty brother, so I decided to put the underwear on (as a joke) and go to the place where seven crazy folks were jumping into the icy water. Margrit and the kids thought I was nuts to be wearing the underwear. I only wanted to show off and had no intention of jumping in. At the last minute, after the seven brave souls had jumped and gotten pulled out of the freezing water, I joined the elite group. However, I decided to dive in whereas the others had just jumped into the sea. My dive was a belly flop. All the onlookers, Margrit, and the kids had a good laugh as a crew member helped me out of the icy water a few minutes later.

On Friday, we were at sea all day, sometimes being tossed around by the rough seas. All four of us started the day off at 7:30 with an exercise class led by the professional masseuse Claire. She is from the Philippines whereas the rest of the staff and crew are all Russian. I had a massage and sauna in the late afternoon. During the trip, all the Russians were very cordial and talked with us. There was one crew member who avoided me. Felex was a big, rough looking guy, resembling Jaws from the James Bond movie.

We had another day at sea on Saturday. Margrit and I started the day with half an hour of exercise in the lounge followed by breakfast with the kids. Later that morning, Ankha, one of the technical staff members, gave an excellent talk on public speaking. Then all of us had a nap before lunch. In the afternoon we attended a lecture on sea ice and how the environment is affecting it. Ankha told us that he thinks one reason sea levels are rising, besides glaciers melting, is the depletion of ground water sources. After the talk, we took another nap followed by dinner. I made a faux pas at our dinner table. I asked Kelly (good-looking blonde schoolteacher) if she took the pill. I meant a motion sickness pill since the ship was bouncing along. Everyone at the table, including Kelly and Margrit, looked strangely at me thinking I meant the birth control pill, and then I said, "motion sickness pill."

Late that evening, I was alone at my usual place at the stern, next to the cargo gate. Suddenly, I found myself falling overboard. I managed to grab the bottom of the swinging cargo gate and quickly pulled myself up. I then saw a crew member running off in the distance. He looked like Felex since most of the other crew members were much shorter. In the morning Margrit urged me to tell the captain. Captain Putan thought the gate must have been unlatched and as I leaned against it, it opened. I did not see Felex for the rest of the voyage.

On Monday, we found ourselves in the northwest corner of Iceland in the large expanse of Isafjorden. Later we anchored near Vigur Island which is only about a mile long and less than half a mile wide. Vigur is one of the few privately owned islands in the country with only a handful of residents, but thousands of birds including Eiders and Puffins. There are also historic buildings there including the sole surviving windmill in Iceland and the smallest post office in Europe. We went ashore at 9:30 a.m. for a short visit. In the afternoon the ship went across the fjord to a calm location where we went ashore. We ended up docking at the Port of Isafjordur. Isafjordur is the largest of all the towns in the northern part of the west fjords with about 3,000 inhabitants.

The next day started with a sunrise at 02:52 a.m. and ended with a sunset at half an hour after midnight. Before breakfast, we cruised near the cliffs of Latrabjorg, which is one of the largest seabird nesting colonies in Europe with a spectacular, rugged landscape. It is about eight miles long and has sheer cliffs 440 yards high with an east-west direction on the northern coastline of Iceland's second largest bay, Breidafjordur. It provides nesting sites for millions of birds including approximately 40% of the world's population of Razorbills.

In the afternoon, we sailed further into Breidafjord as the bay contains thousands of small islets and skerries. Our last landing was at one of the largest islands called Flatey. The island played a significant part in trade around Iceland during the Middle Ages. A monastery that was founded during the late twelfth century resulted in the island being the center of culture and education for the country at that time. That evening, there was the captain's dinner. Afterwards, we packed our bags and placed them outside our cabin for pickup.

The next morning, we disembarked and boarded buses for a tour of Reykjavik. We stopped at a church with a statue of Leif Erickson in front, and then had a 30-minute walk in the area. Later we went to the Blue Lagoon that has large thermal baths that appear blue. There is a swimming area there, but we just took a walk on a path through lots of volcanic rocks. In the distance are several mountains as well as an inactive volcano. We were told that there are several active volcanoes beyond the mountain range. Iceland sits on the mid Atlantic Ridge, and sometime in the future, Iceland is thought to be split in half because of the few periodic earthquakes.

Following our lagoon adventure, we were transported to Reykjavik airport. It was about an hour drive through an interesting volcanic landscape. The crowded Reykjavik airport was built by the U.S. Military in World War II and until 2006, there was a strong American presence in the region. Following a non-stop, eight-hour flight on Icelandic Air, we landed in Denver to resume our lives in the U.S.

Even though his office is behind the thick concrete walls of the plutonium processing building at Rocky Flats, Dr. John James Czermak was pleased to be back. His new job is manager of Plutonium Chemistry Research and Development. In this position, he reports to the director of R & D, his old position that was filled during his three-year leave with the IAEA. Aligning the walls of his office are glass-fronted cabinets containing a host of awards, books, manuals, and *Rockwell News*. On the concrete walls, award plaques and safety posters abound, including a replica of the slogan used by the former management company for the RFP, Dow Chemical, "The life you save may be your own." On a hook beside the door is a white lab coat, along with safety glasses and a respirator.

The move back to Denver was good for him and Eric, but very difficult for Margrit and Lorrie. Amy had returned earlier to start her university studies. John was pleased to be back at their home in Arvada that they had rented during their stay in Vienna and especially happy to resume a close, loving relationship with Margrit that had been badly damaged in Vienna. He was also glad to be getting back into his old routine of working out at the gym in the weight room and swimming pool, as well as jogging several miles every morning and doing yoga. John had continued with his gymnastics, where he could easily do backflips—one of his favorite things to show off. He also enjoyed eavesdropping on people speaking French, German, or Spanish. One time he was boarding a flight in Los Angeles, and there were two Germans in front of him. One asked the other what time it was, and the other said in German he did not know. John piped up and told them the time in German and continued to speak in German, asking where they were from, what they did for a living, and more depending on their replies. In addition, he always enjoyed getting to know the people sitting next to him on flights or people he met at hotels and on tours.

John also resumed his activities with the Rocky Flats Toastmasters' and Speakers' Club. The latter was an organization whose members went out into the community to give talks at clubs and schools. John's favorite topics were water treatment and taking care of the environment. He talked a lot about what one could do to slow down climate change. One thing he always mentioned was that the wife of his PhD advisor preached that our greatest problem is overpopulation. John would then comment that we all must train and take a test to get a driver's license, but anyone can have a child without a single course on child-rearing.

John continued to travel a lot, mainly to conferences around the world and to Vienna and Moscow to have meetings with his coauthors, Oleg Yakushin and Dmitri Frolov, on a series of books they were writing for the IAEA. At the conferences, he always presented papers and even organized a few sessions, mainly at American Chemical Society (ACS) meetings. On the trips to Moscow, one of his Russian friends always arranged a dinner at their home. On one trip with Margrit, a funny thing happened at dinner in Boris's apartment. Margrit asked Boris where the bathroom was and, with a puzzled look on his face, asked her to follow him. He opened the door, and it was indeed a bathroom without a toilet.

Then she said, "I need the toilet."

Boris said with a laugh, "I did not think you wanted to bathe."

Margrit told Boris she knew that most of the bathrooms and toilets are separated in Europe, but it was a habit to ask for the bathroom.

Boris jokingly said, "Why do you sometimes call it a restroom in the States? You don't go in there to rest?"

John visited his laboratories a couple of times each week and spent time with each member of his group to see how their work was going and if there was anything he could do to assist. The group members were very happy with their work and working conditions. Once a month, John would hold a safety meeting and a few times off-site in Boulder at a bar and restaurant called the Dark Horse. The place is unique as there are antiques and junk hanging from the ceiling and hooked to the walls. The group met in an upstairs room that they had to themselves. Of course, most of the group members had a beer with some snacks while discussing the monthly safety inspection of their laboratory and having a general talk on one aspect of safety. These meetings and John's leadership and rapport certainly created dedicated and happy employees.

Several months after John and his family returned from Vienna, he received a phone call from a gentleman who introduced himself as Tim Smith of the CIA, and he asked John to meet with him in Boulder the next day for lunch. At lunch, sitting at a booth in a quiet corner of the restaurant, Tim first showed John his credentials and gave him his business card with only his name on it. John thought to himself that Tim sure looked a lot like the movie actor James Steward.

Tim said, "Of course, that is not my real name on the card."

Tim asked a lot of questions about John's recent trips to Russia. Tim wanted to know everything John knew about the Russians and his previous contacts with them. He told John that he had read his IAEA trip reports during his tenure in Vienna as the American embassy always received copies. John then relayed to Tim about his first meeting with Boris at a solvent extraction conference in Toronto and that, at the IAEA, it was rumored that he was the head KGB agent. John also told Tim about the meetings with other Russians at several IAEA meetings and technical conferences over the years and about the series of review books that he and two Russian scientists, Dmitri and Oleg, were authoring for the IAEA and that the agency had paid the expenses for several trips to Vienna and Moscow to work on the books. Tim then offered to pay John's expenses to go on an expedition on a Russian ship to Greenland and the High Arctic to see if any nuclear materials and/or radioactive wastes were being smuggled into Canada for use in dirty bombs in the United States. The semiannual trip was sponsored by a Canadian adventure group.

John agreed to cooperate and serve his country as best as he could.

Tim said, "Specifically, John, just keep your eyes and ears open and make as many friends as possible, especially of the crew. Also, have a clandestine look around the ship and use this miniature portable nuclear detector to see if there are any signs of radioactive material on board. Take some water samples of the ship's wastewater that is used to wash the ship and bring the water samples back for very sensitive radiochemical analysis. But please be careful as the trip could be dangerous."

At the end of the meeting, Tim swore John to secrecy, never to discuss their meetings, his CIA assignments, or his relationship with him to anyone, including his wife, family, and friends, as well as DOE Security and the FBI.

Travel funds arrived for John two weeks later from the Penny Group in San Francisco, CIA's financial front. After explaining to Margret and the kids that he had received funds for travel to Greenland and the High Arctic for an eight-day expedition to sample water, John left Denver two weeks later using his vacation time at Rocky Flats. John loved to use his camera and see new areas of the world; thus, he welcomed this opportunity to see the High Arctic for the first time.

First, he flew to Cartwright, Canada, via Detroit and Quebec, where he boarded the *Akademik Abraham* along with about forty tourists. John was surprised that the ship was the same one he and his family took on their Spitsbergen trip.

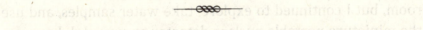

Two weeks later, John met Tim at a different restaurant in Boulder to give him a debriefing of the trip. John told Tim, "The ship's home port is Kaliningrad, located on the Baltic Sea between Lithuania and Poland. Kaliningrad was formally a Prussian city, but after World War II, it became a part of the Soviet Union. The *Akademik Abraham* and an identical sister ship, both ice strengthened, were built in Finland in 1980. The ships were radar/sonic spy ships during the cold war built to follow US submarines. Now they are used to perform acoustic research for the Russian Academy of Science's Institute of Oceanology and to serve part-time tourism. However, it was thought by my cabin mate, Don Cunningham, that the ships are still being used to keep an eye on our submarines. Surprisingly, my family and I were on the same ship on our return to Colorado from Vienna.

"I was lucky to have such a great guy sharing a cabin. Don, tall and Hollywood handsome, was retired from the Canadian government. Later in the cruise, especially after Don had a few drinks at dinner, he would loosen up and start talking about his previous work. He told me that he worked in the intelligence branch. At the end of the trip, I was sure he was a Canadian government contractor trying to get the same information that you sent me to get. That's all I know about Don.

"Tim, let me continue about the trip itself and about Don and I getting shot at and almost killed."

Tim got a surprised look on his face and said, "What?"

"Well, I will tell you about that in a few minutes. The first day after leaving Canada for Greenland and crossing the Davis Strait, I had a long walk around the ship following a lifeboat drill and lunch. Usually, during the evening happy hour, when everyone was upstairs drinking, I would have another look around at different areas of the ship. A couple of times, Felex, a crew member who was on the ship during my last voyage, reminded me not to go into certain rooms, especially the engine room, but I continued to explore, take water samples, and use the miniature portable nuclear detector anyway. I did manage to get water from various places, trying to take as many samples as possible. Probably the best sample was some drain water on the lower deck. Later on the cruise, I took more samples, and they are all in this bag. The sonic equipment is still on board and located in the mud room where we would put on heavy coats and boots for landings in the Zodiacs. There are also laboratories on the lower deck which are inaccessible as most of the rooms in the lower deck are locked.

"By the way, Tim, I had a near-death experience on my first voyage on the ship. I fell overboard at the stern and managed to save my life by quickly grabbing the swinging cargo gate. As I pulled myself up, I saw Felex running off in the distance. I think Felex pushed me, but when I reported the incident to the captain, he said I must have leaned against the gate that was usually latched. I did not see Felex the rest of that trip. I will tell you more about Felex in a couple of minutes.

"I do not require a lot of sleep, so I was awake when we arrived early the next morning at the entrance to Kangerlussuaq Fjord, the longest one in the world, on the way to the Sisimiut coast town of Kangerlussuaq. On a walk outside of the town on soft tundra, we spotted an arctic fox and observed some ringed seals sunning themselves on rocks near the shore. Following a visit to Kangerlussuaq, we returned to the Sisimiut coast and went north to Itilleq that has the second-largest system of fjords. There are dozens of deep fjords carved into Greenland's west coast. The glaciers are fed by the ice cap that covers 80 percent of the country. Unfortunately, they are starting to disappear because of climate change. The ship maneuvered between the soaring icebergs at the mouth of the Itilleq Icefjord, a UNESCO World Heritage Site. Here we saw a polar bear floating on an iceberg. The next day, we took a Zodiac cruise among the towering icebergs of the Itilleq Icefjord. We went ashore at Itilleq, a small fishing village that has an interesting museum. Next, we went to Sisimiut, a former whaling port, and visited the museum and wandered amid a jumble of wooden eighteenth-century buildings. We also had an exciting walk outside the village on soft tundra to the Sermermiut Valley."

Tim commented, "John, you sure have a remarkable memory, and I appreciate hearing the details as I would like to take the same trip someday."

"Thank you. So far, the things that really watered my eyes were seeing the mass of glaciers; different varieties of seals, whales, and other wildlife; and icebergs floating out in the middle of the Davis Strait, hundreds of miles from any shoreline, with polar bears resting on a few of them. It was remarkable to see them and wonder how they survive out there. When we climbed a glacier and saw the massive cliffs with waterfalls, it reminded me of Yosemite National Park.

"So far on the trip, I had befriended several of the Russian dining room staff and had an opportunity to practice my Russian.

I did not overhear any discussions from any of the Russians concerning nuclear materials.

"The next day, we went across Baffin Bay to Qeqertarsuaq Island and Disko, Nunavut. On the way, we saw a couple of humpback whales. Then we went to Uummannaq and Karrat Fjords, with rocky peaks and lots of icebergs as well as marine life nearby. On the crossing, I had more time to explore the ship but did not find anything new.

"We started our exploration of the Canadian High Arctic the next morning with a visit to the small Inuit community of Pond Inlet, Nunavut. We explored some beautiful bays and inlets along Baffin Island's Lancaster Sound, the eastern gateway to the Arctic Archipelago. The group and I enjoyed seeing the ragged coastline in Zodiacs and spent part of the day looking for ringed seals, arctic foxes, walruses, polar bears, and bowhead whales. We also had a brief visit to Devon Island, the largest uninhabited island on earth. This was the most northerly part of the trip. There we had a long walk with the ship's archaeologist to learn about the Thule people, ancestors of the modern Inuit, who once inhabited this region. Our group got to see the stone dwelling once inhabited by the Thule people. Shortly after leaving the island, the ship got stuck in the ice. Later, a Canadian icebreaker came to our rescue and pulled us about a mile out of the broken ice.

"The next day, we went ashore on rocky Philpots Island to hike in the tundra. Felex came along with a rifle in case we had an encounter with a polar bear. It was a long walk, and on the way back, Don and I took a nearby lower trail. A little later, we heard a shot and saw a bullet hit a nearby big boulder. Then it happened again, and we ducked and yelled to stop firing. Our fellow passengers ran over to see what had happened. Felex came and said that there was a bear nearby and he shot at him. However, both Don and I said we did not see any bears in the area. I think Felex was trying to kill me since I was exploring the ship and asking too many questions."

"John, I will try to find out more about Felex in the CIA's database."

"At the end of the trip, we flew out of Arctic Bay on Baffin Island to Quebec. After my goodbyes to Don and a few others, I continued on another flight to Detroit and then Denver. In conclusion, I think that the ship, in addition to being used for scientific expeditions and tours, could easily be used for smuggling nuclear materials. It will be interesting to see what your laboratory finds in the samples I took."

"Well, John, you had quite a trip. I wish I could have been along. Anyway, I will pass these notes on to my superiors. Let's keep in touch. Thanks."

"Tim, I almost forgot to tell you, but next month, Margrit and I are going to Vienna. I will attend another IAEA consultants' meeting on our book. Following the meeting, Margrit will stay with friends, and I will fly to Vladivostok via Zurich and Moscow and then take the Trans-Siberian train back to Moscow and then return to Vienna. I have always wanted to take this trip as I love traveling by train, but Margrit was not interested in going on the adventure."

"Well, John, let's plan on meeting here shortly after your return from Europe as I am very interested in what you discover in Russia."

A week after John and Margrit returned from Europe, John met Tim at a restaurant in Golden. Tim asked John, "How was the trip?"

"It was educational, interesting, and enjoyable."

"Please give me a detailed account after we order our lunch. I would like to take the trip someday. If you do not object, I want to tape-record your story so I will not have to take notes as I did last time."

"Well, Tim, if you really want all the details, I will begin by saying that our meeting in Vienna at the IAEA headquarters was all business, without anything to report that would interest you. However, I think what I discovered on my train trip was very surprising since it may be related to the future leadership of Russia. By the way, Tim, did you find anything out about Felex?"

"We got his full name, but unfortunately, he was not in any of our databases. Sorry."

After ordering lunch, John started telling Tim about his trip. "To begin, exactly three weeks ago, I was on an early morning Swiss Air flight to Zurich. On the flight from Zurich to Moscow, a nice young blonde Russian was sitting next to me. She was going home for a couple of months to rest in her hometown in Western Siberia. She had just quit her job in Boston where she worked for a small chemical engineering consulting firm. She had chemical engineering training from Moscow State University and plans to start working on an MBA at Columbia University in the fall. I told my new Russian friend, Tanya, the French guillotine joke. I also related to Tanya that Margrit and I had a lot of Russian friends and that Margrit spoke Russian well. She asked if Margrit had once worked for the CIA since she had two good friends who spoke Russian but were laid off from the CIA Translation Section since the downfall of the USSR. Tanya was going to stay in Moscow for a few days to see old friends and was disappointed that I was catching my flight three hours after our arrival in Moscow for Vladivostok."

Tim interrupted John, "Please tell me the French guillotine joke."

"Okay, but it is funnier when I tell it to a mechanical engineer. There were three men sentenced to die on the French guillotine, a chemist, a lawyer, and a mechanical engineer. They lay the chemist down and pull the rope. The blade comes down and stops just short of the chemist's neck. The French say, 'This is an act of God, so you can go free.' Then they lay the lawyer down, and the same thing happens. The French say, 'This is an act of

God, but since you are an attorney, you will not die but spend ten years in jail.' They finally lay the mechanical engineer down, and as they get ready to pull the rope, the mechanical engineer says 'Wait, I think I see the problem.'"

Both Tim and John laughed.

John continued, "We landed at the Sheremetyevo Airport, one of the four airports in Moscow. The airport is very nice, but the runway is rough. My contact was waiting at the exit to customs to give me my airline and train tickets. I exchanged some money after she sent me in the direction of check-in. There were five lines for check-in, and it seemed like we had returned to the dark ages, with passengers rudely crowding in line. I finally got to the check-in agent to find out that my only small suitcase was over the weight allowance for carry-ons. So I checked the suitcase in and got my boarding pass. Because of the hurry, I stupidly left my kit bag with medicine in the suitcase. I began to worry if the bag would arrive full and non-violated since everyone seemed to be checking in bags that were wrapped in sheet plastic to prevent anyone from opening them.

"The flight was delayed two hours. The plane was a Boeing 767, with 2-3-2 seats, but it seemed old. Both on takeoff and landing, everything would shake because of the bad runways. The flight took about eight hours, and it never got dark outside, but the sun did go down for about an hour. We were apparently flying over the Arctic Circle. The land looked very flat, and I periodically saw lights of remote houses.

"During the flight, I discovered that my train tickets from Ulan Ude to Irkutsk and Irkutsk to Novosibirsk were missing, and I wondered if I dropped them at the chaotic check-in. Upon arrival in Vladivostok at 9:30 a.m. there was no one to greet me. I had already paid for the tour package that included train tickets, hotel transfers, hotel stays, and tours. I waited for my host while being hounded by a taxi driver who said he would take me to town for one hundred dollars, and later he came down to fifty dollars. After waiting about an hour, I walked over to the nearby airport hotel, and the desk clerk kindly ordered a taxi for me that was 600 Rubles, which is about twenty dollars. The airport is about twenty five miles from the city.

"After arrival in Vladivostok, I checked into the classy Versailles Hotel and then took a walk down to the beach. It was Sunday, and the streets were very crowded. Almost everyone was carrying around a beer—maybe the children had beer in their milk bottles."

Tim laughed.

"There were many sailors in town, and most of the women were nicely dressed and beautiful. There were mostly families out, with some swimming, sunbathing, and enjoying the sea and the amusements, such as the Ferris wheel, merry-go-around, horse and reindeer rides, as well as having their pictures taken with monkeys and more, a very nice place for kids."

"Wait, John, our lunch is here. Let's eat and then you can continue with your detailed narrative."

Following lunch, Tim turned the tape recorder back on, and John continued with his story.

"My host and tour guide for Monday afternoon did not show, just like at the airport, so I had to give myself a walking tour. A map was a big help in finding all the key sites, so I managed to see most of these places on my own. There were many Russian warships in the harbor, and it seemed like they were ready for war."

Tim interjected, "Indeed, Vladivostok is a strategic naval outpost and was closed to most of the world since World War II."

John gave Tim copies of some pictures of the Pacific War Memorial, the steamboat *Krasny Vympel,* and some of the warships, as well as a picture of him with a group of Russian sailors.

"The next morning, the hotel taxi took me to the nearby brightly painted railway station where I caught the train to Ulan Ude. I had a two-person sleeper carriage all to myself in first class. The first night on the train was rough as the train swung side to side. I had trouble sleeping but did get to see all the stars, including the Milky Way, after we got out of the marine layer. We must have stopped at a dozen towns during the night. I finally managed to get some sleep after the sun rose at 6:30. I woke at nine and had a nice breakfast in the dining car.

"During the day, I saw many Siberian settlements near the tracks, village after village of wooden houses, all with vegetable gardens. Between settlements were rolling hills of wildflowers, green grass, small ponds, and aspen trees. In the evening, the sun was to the left of the train, and we were still heading north. That night, there was an attempt on my life."

Tim interjected, "What?"

John continued, "The adjacent carriage was occupied by a big, bald Russian. He had a key to his compartment, unlike me and the other passengers I met, and would lock his compartment upon leaving. During the evening and probably into the night, he kept his door open and watched people passing by. At about 4:00 a.m., I was awakened by someone turning my doorknob from the outside, and before I knew it, the bald Russian had entered and tried to suffocate me with a pillow. I fought him off and then woke, realizing I had a bad nightmare. The next day, I noticed that the bald villain was part of the train staff."

Tim joined John in a good laugh.

"During the morning of the second day on the train, it appeared we were finally heading west. There were lots of small mountains and trees in the area. Some of the trees in the forest had moldy black lower trunks and were sitting in water. We went by an abandoned prison with double outside fencing. Later, the terrain was more rolling hills of grass, but no trees.

"We arrived in Ulan Ude the next morning. Irena and the driver met me at the station and took me to their offices where I met Svetlana, the owner of the tour agency. Their offices were in a hotel, and I was thankful Svetlana had my missing train tickets. One was for me to go to Irkutsk by a later express train, arriving about the same time as the one I was scheduled to ride.

Dark-headed and brown-eyed Irena then took me on a walk in the old city where we saw lots of beautiful old buildings and a couple of magnificent churches.

"Very early the next morning, the train left Ulan Ude and arrived in Irkutsk a few hours later. Irkutsk was an important Siberian outpost established by the Cossacks in 1652. In the early nineteenth century, many Russian artists, officers, and nobles were exiled there for their involvement in the Decembrist revolt. Friday in Irkutsk was spent relaxing in the morning at the Baikal Hotel. Following lunch, my guide, Alex, collected me for a four-hour city tour. We visited several major churches and went to the town shopping area. At six, I returned to the hotel.

"Tim, please let me know if I am getting too detailed in the account of my trip."

"No, no, please continue."

"The next morning, Alex, driver Alexander, and I went by van to Lake Baikal. About halfway, we stopped at a village that contained a collection of classic Russian and Siberian cottages, a mill, shops, and a reconstructed church that had been saved from being left underwater after the nearby reservoir was filled. We then went to Lake Baikal, which holds about 20 percent of the world's unfrozen freshwater and is the deepest lake in the world. After visiting the visitor center and observing some freshwater seals, Alex and Alexander took me to catch the train to Novosibirsk that was to leave at about 3:30 p.m.

"I awoke early on Sunday morning to find that we were now on Novosibirsk time, three hours ahead of Moscow. The car stewardess brought cookies and coffee for me. We traveled past some villages and a beautiful countryside of rolling hills covered in forest. An hour later, we stopped in Krasnoyarsk, a major city with a large river flowing through it. I arrived in Novosibirsk late in the evening and was met by Olga and driver Kate who took me to my hotel.

"On Monday morning, Olga and Kate picked me up after I had a great breakfast. Novosibirsk is Siberia's largest city, very busy with 1.5 million people and broad streets. We saw Lenin Square, the largest opera house in the world, a couple of churches, and a few monuments. We also went to a technical university and then out to the Academic city about forty minutes from Novosibirsk. We went by the Olo River and drove over the dam of the very large Olo Lake. A village had been submerged in the reservoir when it was filled, just like the village near Lake Baikal. We had lunch at the Academic city's conference center, where a meeting was taking place. The afternoon tour was rushed since we took so long at lunch.

"Olga seemed very communistic in nature with her opinions and did not wear a scarf during the church visits. However, she said that the politicians were getting too rich while pensioners were living in poverty. She and her husband were caring for her mother and sister's daughter who is an invalid after a car crash that killed her sister and her husband about four years ago. She said life is hard, but she lives each day to the fullest and likes to develop her mind by reading and learning languages. Olga's great-grandfather had a lot of land at one time and was very rich but lost it all when Lenin took power. She thought some of the land should be returned to her. Instead, she had to buy her two-room flat.

"That evening, I left Novosibirsk for Yekaterinburg. I hope I am not getting too detailed about the trip."

"No, I find it very interesting, and it still amazes me how you can remember all these details."

"Well, Tim, I do keep a diary, and I reviewed it before our meeting today. Maybe in the future you may want me to make a copy of my diary for you."

John continued, "I arrived in Yekaterinburg early afternoon of the next day. No one was there to greet me, and after waiting half an hour, I took a taxi to the Red Star Hotel some distance away. I checked in and, after unpacking and washing my socks and underwear, arranged for a hotel taxi to take me on a drive through the city and to the Asia–Europe dividing line. At that point, Anna showed up apologizing for not meeting me at the train—she thought I was arriving in Moscow time, two hours later. Alexander, our driver, took us around the city, from its two highest buildings, main streets, Kremlin building, a nice walking street, a dam on a river, an area with ornately decorated wooden houses, and then to the cathedral that was only completed a couple of years ago. It stood on the site of the demolished home where the tsar, Nicholas II, and his family were executed and then taken out of town and dumped in a ravine where there is now a monastery. We also went to a place in the Ural Mountains where the rainwater runs west to Europe and east to Asia. Anna took a picture of me with one foot in Asia and the other foot in Europe.

"With Anna's help, I boarded the train for Moscow the next morning. An elderly gentleman, Oleg, was my cabin mate. He spoke excellent English and is a professor at the Organic Chemistry Institute in Yekaterinburg and a member of the Russian Academy of Sciences. Later in the conversation, I told him the names of the Russians I knew. I realized what a small world it is when Oleg said he knew my Russian friends. In fact, Oleg is a good friend of Boris and made macro molecules for him to test. Oleg said that Boris will have a conference in his honor at his seventy-fifth birthday party in September in the Black Sea city of Sevastopol. During our conversations, I also had time to view the lovely scenery passing by. The Ural Mountains are not too high in this area of the train route but are full of evergreen and juniper trees and lots of wildlife. I joked with Oleg about his dacha, which is about forty kilometers west of Yekaterinburg. I said, 'So you go to Europe every weekend to chop and saw firewood—that is how you stay in shape?'"

"Oleg said, 'I suppose a lot of people live near the dividing line between Europe and Asia and visit each place every workday.'

"He also told me about life in this area during the war. Stalin moved whole industries to the Asian side of the Urals, and there were many hardships. They had no electricity most of the time, and he was always cold and hungry. In grade school, they each received half a piece of bread at lunch. His father tried to enlist in the army but was refused since he worked in a vital food industry supervising only women.

"Tim, I think you will especially take note of what I am going to disclose to you next. Oleg told me in confidence that the Russian Academy of Sciences may run the country soon. Oleg was trained in the military school that is part of the Academy of Sciences. He was a reservist and served every summer for two weeks, learning how to drive and operate a tank that was very hot, crowded, and especially noisy. Oleg said that the Academicians run institutes of thousands of professors and scientists, teach, and have students worship them for life. The Academicians meet regularly, confer, and represent almost all facets of society. They have the real brain and political power of the country and are highly respected by the average university-educated Russian. Oleg said there may be a coup by the intelligentsia someday soon, especially since our leaders are so corrupt.

"When we arrived in Kazen on Wednesday night, Oleg got off the train as he was to lecture the next morning at a European conference for mainly PhD students.

"The next morning, the train arrived in Moscow. An elderly lady was waiting for me with her driver, and they took me to the Rossia Hotel. I got lost in the 'world's largest hotel' trying to find my room. Once in the room, I received a call from Boris saying he would pick me up in thirty minutes and take me to lunch. Traffic in Moscow was very bad, and we waited and waited to get out of the Red Square area. Finally, Boris's driver started driving down the sidewalk for about half a block. We went to see Boris's office at the Academy of Sciences, an old palace next to a park. He has a lovely corner office, and I got my picture taken below a picture of Mendeleev. Boris showed me their meeting room where the leaders meet and electronically bring in the Far East, Ural, and other divisions. Then we went to the Academy of Sciences high-rise building for lunch. Boris mentioned that the Myack nuclear accident site was south of Yekaterinburg, between another large city and Yekaterinburg. They are studying the site and evaluating water treatment methods. The government had plans to treat all the radioactive water, but after Perestroika, the funding stopped.

"Following lunch, we took the elevator to the twenty-second floor where there was a bar under construction. I got some nice pictures of the city there. Then we went to the Vernadsky Institute to see Boris's lab and meet his wife, Tamara, and some of her students. They took me on a tour of the labs. Boris stated that he was responsible for the lab getting its first computers, and I said the most important improvements were the modern toilets with toilet paper. Twenty years ago, I had to use newspaper for toilet paper in dirty old toilets."

Tim laughed.

"Boris then went back to work at about four, and his driver brought me back to the hotel.

"On Friday, I checked out of the hotel and took a taxi to the airport for my flight to Vienna. I had a wonderful reunion with Margrit at the Wandl Hotel, and we both spent the day telling one another about our adventures. The next day, we returned to Colorado.

"I would be happy to send you copies of the important pictures I took after leaving Vladivostok."

"John, please do. It appears to me that this was indeed a trip of a lifetime, and I hope I can do it someday, but without the interference of Russian security. Anyway, my superiors are going to find my written summary of this tape very interesting, especially the part concerning the Russian Academy of Sciences getting involved in political matters."

II

During the early 1950s, a Republican United States senator from Wisconsin, Joseph Raymond McCarthy, gained worldwide attention by charging that communists had infiltrated the government. Such widely scattered fear became known as McCarthyism, and phrases such as "Better dead than red" and "Don't be caught with a red under your bed" swept the land. As a result, a goodly number of patriots were accused of disloyalty, even treason, many of whom suffered horrific hardship. One of the best-known casualties of this parody was physicist J. Robert Oppenheimer, the man who designed the atomic bomb.

In 1980, with the inauguration of Ronald Reagan as the fortieth president of the United States, McCarthyism leaped from the grave. For, almost immediately after being sworn in, Reagan began to level derogatory charges against the Soviet leaders and their form of government. A witch hunt soon ensued to ferret out any American remotely suspected of sympathizing or collaborating with a communist agent.

Even though, practically speaking, the cold war was over, and amicable relations currently exist between the United States and the former Soviet Union, no actions have been taken to alleviate the sufferings of those Americans and Russians unjustly accused of treasonous acts during the Reagan era. And, without doubt, there are several of them, as there were in the dark days of McCarthyism.

In 1983, the Russians shot down a commercial South Korean airliner that had accidentally entered Russian airspace, killing all aboard. At the same time, John was attending an international scientific conference in a downtown Denver hotel that he had assisted in organizing. During the reception, he got caught up on what his many friends had been doing. Three Russian professors, who were good friends of the Czermaks, were also attending the meeting. Misha was the chairman of the nuclear department of Moscow State University, and Dimitri and Oleg were in the same department. Dimitri and Oleg were also John's coauthors on a series of books they were writing for the IAEA. That evening, a group of close friends, including the Russian scientists, joined John and Margrit for dinner in the Brown Palace Hotel, a Denver landmark.

Halfway through the conference, one day was allotted for tours. John and Margrit took the occasion to entertain their Russian guests by taking them to the mountains, first to Echo Lake, then up Mount Evans for a walk, and to have a grand view of the city. Their final stop was to the old adjoining mining towns of Blackhawk and Central City where they had a Bratwurst lunch at the Blackhawk Inn and a walking tour of historic Central City. Margrit was always looking for fun, so she excused herself and disappeared into a shop that published newspapers with headlines of one's choice. She had one printed, which read "Soviet Spies Arrested in Central City." Luckily, the Russians had a good laugh, and Misha happily accepted the gift. They ended the day at the Czermak's home in Arvada for dinner. Before dinner, Misha enjoyed seeing Margrit's vegetable garden. John snapped a photo of him pulling up some carrots for dinner. He also got a nice picture of the group admiring his Ford Model T that he was restoring.

Before the conference resumed the next day, Misha took John aside in a corner outside the conference room where no one could overhear their conversation. He told John that he thought of him as a very good friend and that he was only delivering a message from the KGB. They wanted information from John on the production of the neutron bomb. Misha brought out a small picture of Svetlana Isenova making love to John, with Vasilenko, a known KGB agent, taking part in the sexual act. Svetlana was also a KGB agent enlisted to blackmail John. This horrific event had been filmed and photographed on the Russian ship during a

Russian Club dinner on the Danube when the Czermaks resided in Vienna. Of course, John did not recognize the embarrassing event as he had been drugged and had passed out. Misha said that if John did not cooperate with the KGB, the picture would be sent to the FBI. John flatly refused to cooperate even though Misha continued to try and convince him that the picture would get him into a lot of trouble, even losing his job. John told Misha that he never wanted to hear from him again on the matter.

Meantime, unbeknownst to John, the FBI had underway an investigation of the Czermaks. The same day that John had been approached by Misha, Margrit was asked to appear at the FBI headquarters in Denver.

She told John in the evening, "I had no choice but to comply with the FBI request to submit to the interrogation. Otherwise, I was sure I would have been judged guilty of the charges leveled against me—the charges being that I had been seen passing secret documents to a suspected KGB agent. In the days preceding the interrogation, neither the security officer from Rocky Flats, Meg Showman, nor the FBI agent, Phil Gilbert, had confronted me with the charges. My immediate reaction had been one of disbelief. For this reason, I'm afraid I was initially quite belligerent."

Margrit continued, "Once at the FBI headquarters, I was informed that I would be interviewed and given a lie detector test. Leaving my purse in the anteroom, I asked if it would be safe there, which I thought was very funny. Meg, who looked a little like an overweight Marilyn Monroe, greeted me and introduced me to her colleagues, one from the DOE and the other a representative of the FBI, Phil. I was informed that a background investigation had recently been conducted on you to assist the DOE in determining your continued eligibility for a DOE security clearance. Certain matters had been raised because of that background investigation.

"The interview began rather comically when I was asked if I was Margrit Czermak. No, I answered. My name is Margrit

Grayson Czermak. I was next asked when and why I had gone to Vienna. I told them. Then I was asked if I had worked while in Vienna. I said I had for the United Nations Industrial Development Organization. I explained that most American wives who wanted to work had to work for a UN agency. I was writing a novel, but I needed to get out and be with people. So when UNIDO called me and asked if I would like to come in for an interview, I did. I was subsequently hired by Taniaka in the Department of Technology Transfer.

"I was next asked about my friendships while working for UNIDO. I replied that they were with Michael Prince, an English Austrian, and Andrei Pushkin from Estonia. I told them that Prince worked in the IAEA Library and that Pushkin was a staff officer for UNIDO. I said that we were a friendly group, and everyone in our section got to know each other well. 'And how did you and Pushkin become friends?' I was asked. 'He helped me with my Russian,' I answered. It was about now that I noticed Meg had a copy of the last book I had written, *The Bare Essentials*.

"I was asked if I was now or had ever been a member of the Communist Party. That brought a chuckling no from me. I was asked if I was now or had ever been a member of an organization sympathetic to the doctrine of the Communist Party. 'No,' I replied. Next, I was asked if I had ever contemplated passing sensitive information to a foreign agent. I told them that I had not myself but that my character in the book I was writing did. So I went on to explain that the main woman in the book and I were inseparable: Her thoughts were mine, mine were hers, and I spent days thinking of what information she could pass to her lover.

"And then we went through the whole rigmarole again—only yes or no answers this time. I was subsequently asked if I ever meet clandestinely with a Russian national, to which I replied yes and no. I explained that Pushkin was indeed a Soviet national.

"During the five-hour 'interview,' John, I did not lose my characteristic sense of fun. Never mind that I had been subjected to the polygraph examination thrice. Thrice the same questions had been propounded. For what seemed forever, I was asked to identify photographs of Soviets, most of whom I had never seen before. Each time I did recognize an individual, I was asked if I felt that person could be suborned. The entire episode caused me to feel intimidated and used. I was angry, insulted, and, lastly, embarrassed by the Neanderthal mentality of my own countrymen.

"John, I am sorry, but they asked me to tell you they want you at the FBI's Denver office at nine tomorrow. The FBI wants you to submit to polygraph tests and answer questions concerning the three visiting Russians."

After the first FBI interrogation, the lie detector testing continued several more times at the FBI headquarters for John, once after returning from a trip to Moscow with a stack of business cards and many photos and notes that he had taken for Tim. John thought that these assignments were the primary thing that contributed to him failing the FBI's polygraph tests. John thought it seemed like Meg was trying to find all the incriminating evidence she could to make herself look good. Of course, she passed all this information on to Phil. After the last polygraph, Phil showed John the incriminating picture that Misha had shown him. John told Phil that he did not remember the sexual entrapment and thinks he was drugged.

On Good Friday, Meg came to John's office with a guard and demanded that he give her his security badge as his clearance had been suspended. He was told to remove personal things from his office. Then he was escorted out of the security area and told to go home and that his supervisor would be in contact with him the next day. That night was one of the worst John had ever endured, especially since he was told that he could be faced with horrendous legal fees if he attempted to exonerate himself. The next morning, his manager told John over the phone to take a few days off and that he could understand how embarrassed and angry he must be.

Several agonizing days later, John went to work in an unclassified area of the plant. The first thing he did was apply for a three-year leave of absence. A few days later, it was approved since Rockwell management was sympathetic to his troubles. John then accepted an invitation for an academic position at the University of New South Wales (UNSW) in Kensington, a suburb of Sydney, Australia, as head of the Department of Mineral Processing and Extractive Metallurgy.

The last month before the Czermaks left for Australia, they sold their cars and house in Arvada. During this time, the FBI continued to bug their phone and dig through their trash. All of John's mail at the plant was being opened and read. Both John and Margrit agreed it was a dreadful month but were excited about a new life in Australia, just like it had been when they went to Austria. The children were already settled in their own lives. Amy was happily married, and both Eric and Lorrie were attending the University of Colorado and living in dormitories. John and Margrit's plan was to have Eric and Lorrie come down for the summer and for Amy to bring Dave for a visit anytime they could come.

Later, John found out that Tim seemed quite pleased by this turn of events since it would be much easier for him to send John on assignments, especially to Russia and Eastern Europe, without the interference of the FBI and/or DOE Security. John would also be asked by Tim to try and take trips to China, Iran, Libya, North Korea, and South Africa related to nuclear proliferation. They were to communicate mostly by phone. At the time, John wondered if the CIA had any role in turning over the incriminating picture to the FBI.

III

Tim's first telephone call to John in Australia: "John, I am sure you have heard of Dr. Kahn, father of the Pakistan Nuclear

Program, who has been exporting nuclear technology to Iran, Libya, and North Korea. Everyone knows that terrorist groups would like the bomb, or nuclear materials to make one, and/or radioactive materials or waste to make a dirty bomb. Thus, we hope to send you to these countries to find out as much as possible about their nuclear programs. We also hope you can go to South Africa to verify their removal of nuclear weapons. However, I do understand that it will take some time before you feel at home 'down under.'"

It was spring, and Sydney was green and lush. It reminded Margrit a great deal of southern California when she was a girl. Sydney put John in mind of Florence, Italy, or San Francisco, Florence because of the red tiled roofs and San Francisco because of its endless hills and the ocean. From their modest apartment, they could look out on the Tasmanian Sea, with its extraordinary aqua color, and see the waves crashing against the rocks. It took about fifteen minutes to walk to the sea from their flat, about the same amount of time John needed to walk to his office. At the seaside, there is a path that winds along the cliffs and provides a wonderful view of the sea and gives one an exhilarating climb. Despite its size, the Czermaks learned that Sydney is a safe city and that most Australians are friendly and pleasant.

John had adjusted to life in Australia much faster than Margrit, probably since he spent most of the day at a job he liked and had use of a university car. He was supervising ten faculty members with the help of a secretary and teaching a mineral separations course. The only thing that initially annoyed him was the large number of students talking while he was lecturing. At first John stopped his lecture and tried to wait until the chatter stopped. It did quiet down a little but picked up later. After a couple of weeks of this, John gave up as he found out from his first exam that most of the students were indeed learning about the separation of minerals.

John also had time to look after six graduate students and do some consulting and traveling. He had one postdoc, a nuclear scientist from Libya. Ala had his family with him, and during their year's stay in Australia, the Czermaks became such good friends with them that John referred to them as his godfamily.

Because Margrit had a hard time adjusting to the new life, John became almost desperate in his desire to find diversions to amuse her. One of the things John did was take Margrit with him to Melbourne where he was going to give an invited lecture at the university. The drive down was lovely since they took the Princes Highway along the coast. Because there had been a lot of rain along the coast, everything was very green, and of course, it was great to see the lovely seascapes that appeared from time to time. It took two days driving to Melbourne. They were staying near the university, and Margrit got out and explored the neighborhood while John visited the university. They also had dinner one night with his host and a couple of old friends whom they had not seen since the conference in Denver. Before their return to Sydney, they visited the nearby Twelve Apostles.

John and Margrit's first trip out of the country was to South Africa, where John was to present an invited paper at an international nuclear waste meeting; the conference organizers paid all their travel expenses. The following is a letter Margrit wrote to Lorrie:

Dearest Lorrie, please do not throw this letter away. I'm going to tell you all about our trip so far and would like to have this to refresh my memory someday. I thought you would like the lions on the heading of the paper; in fact, that's why I bought the stationery. We first went to Kruger National Park on a flight from Johannesburg and stayed in a hut for three nights. We saw lots of animals on several game drives.

Then we flew to Livingstone, Zimbabwe via Johannesburg. There we took some short trips to Victoria Falls National Park and Chobe National Park in Botswana. At Victoria Falls we were staying at a hotel within walking distance of the falls. The first night at the hotel the fire alarm went off. Your father walked out into the hallway and saw that no one was leaving the building. He decided that we should also remain put as there might have been some kidnappers outside who were the ones who set off the alarm. The first morning, as we were having breakfast at the restaurant outside, a mother baboon with her baby hanging on came running over and jumped on our table, stole some bread, and ran off. Every time we walked to the falls there would be several baboons blocking the walkway, so in fright we had to walk around them in the bush.

In Chobe National Park, our tour consisted of a boat ride on the Chobe River between Botswana and the Namibia Caprive Strip. On the boat ride we saw some hippopotamuses on the shore and in the river. Suddenly, a hippo came up under our boat and nearly capsized it. In the afternoon we had a ride around the park in a Safari vehicle and came upon a pride of lions. Chobe has one of the largest concentrations of game in Africa. Later the skies opened, and we had to find shelter from the terrific rainstorm as the vehicle had open sides.

After we arrived back in Johannesburg, our friends, Jan and Janice, picked us up at the airport. We went to their home in Hartbeesport. The next day we visited the Ann van Dyk Cheetah Center that was established in 1971. We saw lots of cheetahs that had been saved, as well as falcons, vultures, wild dogs, and a few wild cats. We got our picture taken petting Chaka, one of approximately twenty king cheetahs at the Center. On Sunday we went to nearby Pilanesberg National Park and saw eleven rhinos, two elephants, many giraffes, warthogs, impalas, wildebeest, ostriches, dung beetles, and a few hippos in the lake, but no lions or cheetahs or leopards. Afterwards we went into a gold mine to see how gold is mined; it was very interesting and fun. We also saw Zulus dance and they were good. Such rhythm! Jan and Janice are a delightful couple, and it was great to reminisce about our days in Vienna. We had lunch with them at their home. Janice prepared a typical South African meal for us which was scrumptious! It included mutton pie, chicken of some sort, baked peaches, potatoes, veggies, plus a yummy dessert. Janice's home is very European. You would have loved it. She was a stage actress before marriage and is very striking. We've found the South Africans to be very clannish and friendly. I love to hear Afrikaans sung; it is so soft and calming.

The next day your father went with Jan to the Pelendaba Nuclear Site, which means in English to leave or get out. Your father gave a talk on nuclear waste treatment, and later he and Jan drove around the site, which, by the way, is the same place where South African scientists clandestinely constructed several nuclear weapons during the Apartheid days.

At noon they returned to get me and Janice and we went into Pretoria for lunch. Afterwards we visited the monument to the Boor's War and saw how the country was developed (covered wagons like ours). Later Jan dropped us off at the Protea Hotel Manor in Hatfield. That night we went to the Conference Center for the Mine Water Conference reception. Kathy, an old friend, showed up to greet us. The next day your father went to the meeting to give his talk, and later came back so we could have a walk around the neighborhood. The University of Pretoria is directly across the street from the hotel (approximately 50,000 students), and on campus and around town there were lots of Jacaranda trees with their beautiful purple blossoms. That night we attended the conference banquet. The highlight of the banquet was that everyone got to play their own drum along with the band via their instructions – great fun! The next day we flew to Cape Town.

Now we're at the Inn on the Square and it's elegant! We've only been in Cape Town a couple of hours and just had time to settle in. Dad has gone to the Cape Sun Hotel where the conference is being held. He's going to come back soon to give me a report. The reception is being held there tonight and tomorrow the conference begins.

It's Tuesday morning and now I'll continue this communication to you. Dad has gone to the conference; he gives his paper this afternoon. Tonight, is a reception with the Mayor of Cape Town; should be lush. The one last night was first-class. One joke that Bret told me was about a mayor giving a talk to his constituents after he won the election; the mayor said, 'I thank everyone from the bottom of my heart and my wife also thanks you from her bottom.'

Tomorrow we may go to see Table Mountain as well as the Cape of Good Hope, which is quite near and has lots of Baboons in the area. We toured the nuclear facility and a winery. They've had specially labeled wine prepared for the "Radwaste" conference. Thursday I may take a tour of the botanical gardens. I'm told it's very worthwhile. You won't believe the flowers here, Lorrie; they are so exotic and breathtaking in their beauty!

We had such a good time with Bret and Elda. Your father went to the University of Port Elizabeth during our first day there and met Bret's students. He told me that one of the students' name is Pardon. Now if you think Pardon is a curious name, he does too. Asked how it came to pass, he said several stories circulated. One was that the doctor asked his father (who was hard of hearing) what he wished to call the baby. His father replied, 'Pardon?' "Pardon it is," declared the doctor, and he's been Pardon ever since.

I loved their home in Port Elizabeth that overlooks a long canyon with a few monkeys about. We then went to Storms River. They told us we would be staying in a hut and must rough it, so naturally we assumed it would be a grass hut with no amenities. Lo and behold, it was a modern cabin complete with maid service. We teased them to no end about this. Bret did some fishing and made us South African cheese sandwiches with tomatoes for lunch. There we took a nature hike - 'twas fun! The most fun though was our visit to an Ostrich farm following our stay at Storms River. We learned a good deal about this fascinating bird; we visited their homes, and petted babies. The Ostrich egg is so hard it must be opened (by man) with a hammer, yet this tough young critter bursts it open when he/she is ready to be born. (I even sat on an Ostrich egg.) Both the father and mother bird sit on them - the mother during the day, the father at night. Ostrich couples' mate for life and usually live to be about forty. Ninety-five percent of the world's Ostriches live in the area we visited. Each family has its own plot of land. We'll have to revisit with you; you'll love it. Oh, Dad and I got to sit on an Ostrich and watched the Ostrich races. They were a riot! Take care, my darling daughter. You mean everything to me. Love and kisses, Mom.

At the end of the conference, the Czermaks flew back to Sydney via Johannesburg and Perth. Shortly following John's return, Tim called John and wanted a short report about his visit to South Africa's Nuclear Research Center. John told Tim about his one-day visit where he toured the laboratories and gave a lecture.

"Jan, who manages a chemical research group, was my host. Jan talked about the country destroying its nuclear arsenal and signing the Nuclear Non-Proliferation Treaty. He told me that one nuclear weapon was tested and six were turned over to the IAEA, France, and the United States. However, Jan said that there was a rumor that an eighth warhead was produced but missing and not destroyed. Jan would like to investigate this more and write a novel about it someday. He thinks the missing bomb might have been clandestinely shipped to Israel for a lot of money for a select few."

The following is another letter Margrit wrote to Lorrie:

Hello darling. This is the last day of November, and I can't believe it! The month has flown by. How has it seemed for you? I talked to Eric earlier today and he told me he would be going to Fort Collins for the big CU-Colorado State University game this weekend. I hope you will see it and that you will both enjoy it.

We have no plans to leave Sydney, aside from our visit to Colorado during the holidays, because Dad has another year of his three-year leave of absence from Rockwell to go. For the most part, he is happy here with his work and is making a name for himself as a professor and consultant.

And Sydney is a lovely place; there is no two ways about it. And it's quite exciting. Yesterday culminated week-long festivities sparked by the Bicentennial Naval Review. Russia wasn't invited to the Navy celebration but was here anyway. There is an enormous Russian cruise ship (Alexander Pushkin) docked at the harbor; such a coincidence, we think. Of course, we're certain it is here to spy on the other ships. It's so obvious. The review, which began at noon and lasted for three hours, included steam-pasts from the visiting warships. There are fifty-three ships from sixteen countries here, including our own battleship New Jersey, for a total of 17,000 visiting sailors. Thereafter, there was a fly-by from visiting naval aircraft, including jets and helicopters, and then the giant 747 of Qantas and Australia Air's airbus. The entire display was most impressive, and we highly enjoyed seeing it.

Ying Hsu, Dad's graduate student from China, has been trying to teach me a few words of Chinese so I won't be a total loss during our upcoming trip to China. Ying is very nice, beautiful, speaks English well, and lots of fun. She was telling me about a friend of hers who recently arrived in Sydney and had been talking with an Australian woman while waiting for the bus one morning. The elderly lady had asked her where she was going, and she said to school. Then my friend asked her where she was going, and she said, 'I am going to hospital to die.' She was aghast and questioned, 'You're going to hospital to die?' And she smiled and said, 'Yes, I am going to hospital to die.' When my friend got to school, she told me about this healthy-looking woman, and I laughed and laughed. Ying told her friend that 'to die' is the way Australian's pronounce 'today.' I really got a chuckle out of this. Dad is keeping very busy, as usual. Love, Mom.

The first week in November, Margrit went to the Chinese consulate to collect their visas. The following weekend, the Czermaks left for Beijing. The Chinese covered all their expenses, even the airfare. They had a fantastic time in China. Their hosts in Beijing were extremely kind and courteous. Their main activities were climbing the Great Wall on Margrit's birthday and visiting the Forbidden City, Temple of Heaven, Ming Tombs, and Summer Palace.

In Shanghai, the Czermaks stayed at the Fudan University Guest House. John was very impressed by the beautiful university grounds as well as the many changes that had occurred in China since his first visit in 1979. The highlight of the stay for Margrit was a three-hour cruise on the Huangpu River, which runs into the Sea of China. During the visit, John presented six lectures at different institutes, and Margrit presented one about life in America and Australia. After their return to Sydney, John summarized the trip to Tim in a telephone call and promised to send him a trip report.

Margrit thought to herself as she discovered John's China trip report, *Why did he write a report?* She suspected he did the same thing following his trip to the USSR. Why? Was it for our government? Did John give reports of visits to communist countries for the CIA? Margrit concluded that it was not a good idea to broach the subject with him, especially since she should not have been reading his report. Anyway, he would probably deny everything since she was sure he was sworn to secrecy just like he could not talk about his work at Rocky Flats.

A week after the Czermaks returned home, they attended a reception at the Chinese embassy in Sydney to celebrate the Chinese Spring Festival. The following Saturday, John spent the better part of the day conducting an experiment along with three of his students, Anthony, John, and Ying. He had on loan six identical cars from the university, and they took temperature readings of the heat buildup in each car under different conditions: the first car had an expensive sunscreen next to the windshield inside the car, the second an inexpensive cardboard sunscreen on the inside, the third an expensive sunscreen on the outside of the windshield, the fourth an inexpensive cardboard one on the outside, the fifth no sunshield, and the sixth no sunscreen but with the windows cracked. Their conclusion was that an expensive sunscreen on the outside of the windshield with the car windows cracked keeps the car the coolest. A reporter and photographer from *The Sydney Morning Herald* saw that the event made the newspaper. The work of John's research group also made the newspapers a couple of other times, which made his superiors very happy.

The Czermaks were caught, as were those around them, in a labyrinth of shoving tired individuals who had just disembarked from various transatlantic flights and were waiting to pass through immigration at Milan's airport. John had forgotten, until they now reoccurred, that he had sworn never again to fly through Milan. His travel agent, however, had assured him it would provide the best connection between Sydney and his ultimate destination of Tripoli, Libya. Now that sanctions against Libya had been reduced, John had been requested by Tim to visit Tripoli at their expense and to try to confirm if Qaddafi had eliminated his nuclear program as claimed. John had hoped that his dear friend Ala, a doctor of nuclear science, could assist him since he was employed at the Libyan Nuclear Research Center. Ala had worked for John as a postdoctoral fellow during John's first year at the UNSW. John and Margrit had been scheduled three hours between flights. They had already been waiting almost an hour to pass through immigration. Glancing at his watch to note the time, John was beginning to wonder if they would make their connection to Tripoli.

Upon arrival at the Tripoli airport, the Czermaks were immediately ushered through passport control and customs and directed to baggage claim to be greeted by the joyous faces of Ala's wife, Mimara, and their three children, Abdul, Salan, and Mary. The older boy, soon-to-be eleven-year-old Abdul, was truly overcome as he exclaimed again and again, "Uncle John, is it really you? Are you really here? Oh, I'm so glad to see you!"

While waiting in the shadows equally as boisterous was his younger brother, Salan, who quickly clasped his godmother's hand and was not to be released. Two-year-old Mary, who was born in Australia and initially (thanks to Margrit) spoke only English, was now chattering away in Arabic, one minute coyly flirting with John, the next shyly hiding behind her mother. The boys looked magnificent in matching outfits that their parents had purchased for the festival following Ramadan. Little Mary was in a multicolored dress, with lace at the sleeves and throat, that Margrit had purchased for her the previous year. They could see how much she had grown since that time. Mimara, glancing about for Ala, was modestly attired, her head covered with a colorful shawl.

When Ala and his family arrived in Sydney more than two years ago, neither of his sons could speak English. Neither could his wife. Before the term was out, both boys were on the honor roll at Kensington Elementary School. English became their first language. For the next year, the Czermaks shared not only Christmas, but Easter, Thanksgiving, Ramadan, and other holidays, both Christian and Muslim, with Ala's family.

After John claimed their two large suitcases, one filled with gifts for their godfamily and the other with clothes to tide them over for five days, Ala took the Czermaks to their hotel in the heart of the city. After checking in and getting settled in their room, they made an early night of it following supper.

On Christmas Eve morning, John and Margrit took a walk near the hotel. On the walk, they stopped to peek inside St. Francis Catholic Church. There was joyous music coming from the front of the church. They had not intended to participate in the mass, but rather just to look at the interior, but, lo and behold, they were propelled in by loving hands and ushered to the first pew of the overflowing church. The ceremony was the most moving they had ever experienced. A bishop from Rome said mass in English and was assisted by priests from India, Korea, Africa, and Sri Lanka. Beautiful hymns were sung in cadence in native tongues by the many Africans, Indians, and Asians.

On Christmas, the Czermaks went to their host's home and celebrated the joyous holiday. Everyone exchanged gifts following a wonderful meal that Mimara had fixed. After spending the day at their home, John and Margrit returned to the hotel for some rest.

The next day, the Czermaks and their host family visited the other two cities that formed the African Tripolis, Sabratha and Leptis Magna. On the last day of their visit, Ala took John to the Libyan Nuclear Research Center for a tour and for him to give a talk to a group of nuclear scientists. The day was very interesting, especially what Ala told John in his office about their nuclear weapons program.

"Well, Ala, we had better return to the hotel so Margrit and I can get ready for our departure in the morning. Thank you for your kind hospitality, and it was wonderful to spend this week with you and your lovely family." After an emotional goodbye, Ala took John to the hotel. Since Ala had to work in the morning, John and Margrit took a taxi to the airport to catch their early-morning flight home via Milan.

Following their return from a wonderful time in Libya, John phoned Tim and gave him a report on what he had found out during his visit to the Libyan Nuclear Research Center. It seemed like Kaddafi had fooled the world into thinking they had developed nuclear weapons, but according to Ala, he only had a nuclear power program underway. John also told Tim about his next trip to attend an IAEA-coordinated research program meeting in Kiev, Ukraine. All expenses for the trip would be paid by the IAEA. At the end of the meeting, the attendees would visit Chernobyl and observe the progress of the decontamination of the nuclear reactor facility. Following that meeting, John would travel to Baku, Azerbaijan, to give an invited lecture at Baku University.

Several months later John started making arrangements to return to Rockwell since his three-year leave of absence would end. One of the professors in the department would take over his management duties as well as continue to supervise his remaining graduate students. Before leaving Sydney, John and Margrit arranged to have their personal items shipped, sold their furniture, and checked out of their apartment. They stayed in a hotel before catching their flights two days later.

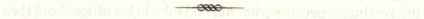

Long before the Czermaks' return to the states, the FBI had been investigating Rocky Flats about unsafe conditions at the site because of disinformation Phil Gilbert had received from a couple of disgruntled employees. The continued search for information at the time probably was related to Phil's further investigation of John. Because of Phil's reporting, the FBI started clandestinely flying light aircraft over the area and noticed that the incinerator, which was not permitted to operate, was apparently being used late in the night. After several months of collecting evidence both from workers and by direct measurements, they informed the DOE that they wanted to meet about a potential terrorist threat. When the FBI agents arrived at the plant, the DOE manager was served with a search warrant.

The FBI then raided the facilities and ordered everyone out. They found numerous violations of federal antipollution laws, including massive contamination of water and soil, though none of the original charges that led to the raid were substantiated. Rockwell was charged with minor environmental crimes and paid an $18.5 million fine. Rockwell was then replaced by EG&G to operate the plant. EG&G started an aggressive work safety program and cleanup plan for the site that included the construction of a system to remove contamination from the groundwater at the site.

Thereafter, a new name was assigned for the plant, the Rocky Flats Environmental Technology Site, reflecting the changed nature of the facility, from weapon production to environmental cleanup and restoration. The cleanup effort was contracted to the Kaiser-Hill company, which proposed the release of 4,100 acres of the buffer zone for public access. The cleanup of contaminated sites and dismantling of contaminated buildings continued with waste materials being shipped to the Nevada Test Site, the Waste Isolation Pilot Plant in New Mexico, and the Envirocare Company in Utah. After all the weapons-grade plutonium was shipped out and the last contaminated building removed, the cleanup was declared complete but remained under DOE control for ongoing environmental monitoring. Two years later, the Environmental Protection Agency (EPA) announced it had certified the cleanup that started the conversion of the site to a wildlife refuge.

IV

When John returned from his leave of absence to Australia, he reported to another DOE laboratory in the Santa Susanna Mountains north of Los Angeles that was managed by Rockwell. Although John's title was chief scientist and supervised the research of only three technicians and two chemists, he readily accepted the position to resume his years of service to the company. John did not need a security clearance at this DOE laboratory.

The Czermaks moved into a townhouse on the west end of Simi Valley after temporarily staying at a hotel in Chatsworth. One of Margrit's letters to Eric and Lorrie describes their initial days in California:

Dear Eric and Lorrie, Dad and I are getting our townhouse in order, and it looks pretty good. One more Saturday and it should be there. Since we work all week, we don't get much done around here, and it all falls on the weekend. Dad is busy with his work and happy to be back with Rockwell. He has a lovely work location atop a mountain between the Santa Susana Mountains and the Simi Hills. Many animals, such as bobcats, deer, raccoons, and rabbits, are in the area. We have also seen the tracks of a mountain lion here in Simi Valley and on occasion can hear the coyotes. Today we're having rain again - another deluge! Believe me, when it rains in California, it pours. It's supposed to keep up until Wednesday. Only five days until Amy's birthday. Wow, I'll bet she's excited. Love, Mom.

The Czermaks took a trip back to Colorado to join Amy's birthday celebration and see her and Dave's new baby son. On the way to Colorado, they did a bit of sightseeing in southern Utah, which is, without a doubt, one of the most beautiful spots on the face of the planet. They stopped in five state parks: Zion, Bryce, Capitol Reef, Canyonlands, and Arches. This was their first visit to any of these parks and was amazed at their magnificence. After their arrival in Colorado, they had a cookout at John's brother's house, and most of the family was there. John also had a meal with his Rocky Flats friends. The Czermaks spent four days in Colorado and then headed to Texas to see Margrit's sister. On their way to Texas, they visited John's younger brother at his cabin in West Cliff, and they had a great time with Margrit's sister and her family in Wichita Falls. On the Czermaks' return from Texas, they drove through Arizona, where they visited the Painted Desert/Petrified Forest and saw the cliff dwellings at Walnut Canyon National Monument and the Meteor Crater caused by a giant meteor that struck the earth about fifty thousand years ago.

Monday, November 4, 1991, began as any other perfectly glorious day in Simi Valley—with one exception: Today, the day of the Ronald Reagan Presidential Library Dedication, would be the largest gathering of presidents and presidential families ever to be assembled, and John and Margrit, who were to be part of it, were excited.

The Czermaks were both up before six. An hour later, they arrived at the press parking lot, a stone's throw from their townhouse in Simi's Wood Ranch, to catch the shuttle to the library (known as 40 Presidential Drive), which is located atop the mountain directly north and opposite Wood Ranch on Madera Road. There, along with the other members of the press, cameras, purses, and other paraphernalia were subjected to a brief airport type of security before everyone could enter the grounds.

After everyone found their way to the press section, where countless other photographers were jammed in, they were lucky as they got a place in the first row of the press photographers' section next to the main aisle and approximately one hundred feet from the red-white-and-blue-bannered stage. A chest-high metal railing separated them from the section in front, in which celebrities would be seated. Also, members of the library staff were positioned in the aisle to their left to prevent members of the press from crossing the imaginary line established by the railing. To the right of the Czermaks were photographers from the Catholic News Service, Ventura County Star Free Press, Simi Valley Comcast, and the Santa Paula News. Directly behind the Czermaks on a raised platform, getting their monstrous cameras in place, were the privileged photographers from the presidential news staff, *Newsweek*, *Time*, Reuters, and so on.

The center aisle separated the press on the left from honored guests. The section ahead of them was reserved for the VIPs, who, upon arriving, were hustled through the growing (and somewhat unwieldy) crowds. Even though the press was crammed together, they did not have to worry about pickpockets.

Despite all the shoving as newly arrived photographers tried to find a spot, the Czermaks managed to retain their spots on the aisle. They had an excellent opportunity to see celebrities entering the arena. Event director and former deputy chief of staff Mike Deaver, busying himself next to the stage, was one of the first VIPs everyone recognized. Once Margrit spotted Casper Weinberger, former secretary of defense, she asked him to say a few words to scientists around the world for her tabloid *The Professional Blabbermouth*. He said, "I think a great deal has been done to advance science during the eight years of the president's administration, and I think that will be reflected in the library. I think that the Strategic Defense Initiative is one of the major advances that draws upon science and calls upon science to reach the frontiers, and I think it will be demonstrated that we can do that. Also, many of our weapon systems that worked so well in the Gulf were scientific achievements of the first order."

When Charlton Heston arrived, cameras worked overtime, including John's. The arrival of Arnold Schwarzenegger, who looked terrific, caused even more of a stir, especially amongst the ladies. Calls of "Arnold, Arnold," including Margrit's—who was hoping to get an interview—rang through the air. He took a seat in the row in front of the photographer's platform. Wheelchair-bound James Brady, former press secretary, who was crippled by a would-be assassin's bullet meant for Reagan, received a round of applause as he came down the aisle.

Many of the people in attendance were surprised to see Secretary of State James Baker, who had just returned from the Middle East peace talks in Spain. Also in attendance were James Watt, who resigned as Reagan's secretary of the interior; singer-turned-politician and now mayor of Palm Springs, Sonny Bono; somewhat-overweight Merv Griffin with his beautiful wife, Zsa Zsa Gabor; Steven Spielberg; and more. Bob Hope's arrival caused quite a stir. Margrit commented that he still looks good despite his advanced age. Next to arrive was Edwin Meese, former attorney general.

Just prior to the time the official ceremonies began, Meese, along with the other honored guests, were escorted to the right side of the stage. Other dignitaries, including John Kennedy Jr., Caroline Kennedy Schlossberg, and Colin Powell, who received a loud round of applause, were escorted to the left side of the dais. A few minutes later, also to a loud round of applause, the first ladies entered in a group, causing quite a stir. Then shortly thereafter, to the music "Hail to the Chief," the five presidents emerged, followed by thunderous applause. It was a most impressive sight to see these five distinguished men standing before everyone, who, as if by magic, appeared larger than life.

Charlton Heston opened the ceremonies by speaking of the presidential office, the men who had held the highest position in the land, and this great land of freedom. Summarizing the words of Martin Luther King, F. Scott Fitzgerald, Thomas Paine, Samuel Eliot Morrison, William Faulkner, Thomas Wolfe, and Abraham Lincoln, he said about Americans, "I have a dream. I refuse to accept the end of man. I believe he will endure, he will prevail, and he is immortal, not because alone of God's creatures he has a voice, but because he has a soul, a spirit, and is capable of compassion, sacrifice, and endurance." About America, "where miracles not only happen, but they happen all the time."

Thereafter, Lodwick Cook, chairman of the board of trustees, extended a welcome to all. This was followed by the invocation given by Reverend Donn D. Moomaw, senior pastor of Bell Air Presbyterian Church and friend of the Reagans. To the music of the combined bands, the colors were presented by the Joint Armed Services Color Guard. The Pledge of Allegiance was led by General Colin Powell, chairman of the Joint Chiefs of Staff. The US Army's SEC Alvey Powell led everyone in the national anthem, following which the colors again passed in review. Lodwick Cook then asked that the board of trustees and their spouses stand for a round of applause. Pete Wilson, the governor of California, began the introductions of the dignitaries: Mrs. Anwar Sadat, Lady Bird Johnson, Pat Nixon, Betty Ford, Rosyln Carter, Barbara

Bush, and Nancy Reagan, each of whom was greeted with a round of applause. Wilson stated that this was a historic event: the first time four presidents have come together to honor one.

Former President Richard Nixon was the first speaker to honor Reagan. Still looking good, albeit somewhat aged, he joked, "Speaking as a politician, I think you should know that I am much more impressed by the fact that there are four people here who served and were elected to governors of their states. Over the past forty-five years, I have been elected to the House, I have been elected to the Senate, I have been elected as vice president, and I have been elected as president. I never made it for governor." He also spoke of his meeting with Nikita Khrushchev in Moscow thirty-two years ago, at which time Khrushchev jabbed his finger into Nixon's chest and said, "Your grandchildren will live under Communism." Nixon responded, "Your grandchildren will live in freedom." Nixon drew a chuckle from the crowd with "At that time, I was sure Khrushchev was wrong, but I wasn't sure I was right." His concluding statement "Khrushchev's grandchildren now live in freedom" brought hefty applause.

Gerald Ford remembered an old line from General Douglas MacArthur in his farewell address to Congress: "He may have been right about old soldiers, but you can be sure that old presidents don't just fade away."

Of the presidents, only Carter was a Democrat. "The Republican side of the program has four times as much time as the Democratic," said he who arrived in California last night from Zambia after monitoring that country's first free elections. "You all have another advantage over me: At least all of you have met a Democratic president. I've never had that honor yet." Carter also paid tribute to James Baker for his efforts to obtain peace in the Middle East.

President Bush, who complimented all the former presidents, was most adroit in his tribute to Reagan. "He may have been born February 6, but his heart was born July 4. He was a politician who was funny on purpose." He reminded us of Reagan's unfailing sense of humor of that day in March 1981 when he looked at the doctors in the emergency room and said, "I hope you're all Republicans."

"The Old Gipper," who, despite his eighty years, still looks like Peck's Bad Boy, could not forbear such quips as "Although we presidents don't get together very often, when we do, well, as you can see, it generates quite a bit of interest. At one time or another, I've run against most of these gentlemen, and they've run against me. Yet here we are.

"It is said that after leaving the White House, Harry Truman once came into his living room to discover his wife, Bess, tossing their old love letters into the fireplace. 'Think of history!' said a horrified Mr. Truman. 'I have,' said Bess.

"In my eighty years . . . what I prefer to consider the forty-first anniversary of my thirty-ninth year . . ."

At the conclusion of his speech, Reagan presented the key to the library to Don Wilson, archivist of the National Archives, as a symbolic gesture of turning the Ronald Reagan Presidential Library over to the American people.

The program was concluded by singer Lee Greenwood, who brought a tear to many an eye and caused a lump in many a throat and many a heart to swell with pride with his beautiful "God Bless the USA."

"And I'm proud to be an American where at least I know I'm free. And I won't forget the men who died, who gave that right to me. And I'll gladly stand up . . . 'Cause there ain't no doubt I love this land. God bless the USA."

One of the most captivating moments of the day occurred in the next instant when there was a flyover of four US fighter jets in formation. The stands then cleared of the military pomp of John Philip Sousa's "Three Cheers for the Red, White, and Blue." John and Margrit made their way toward the stands where lunch was being served. They chose two kinds of salad, some hot pasta, and a slice of sausage pizza. Taking their plates to a nearby tent, they joined members of the Secret Service, members of the press corps from around the world, and other guests to enjoy the delicious fare. Thereafter, they drifted toward tents where vendors were selling souvenir golf caps and commemorative T-shirts.

By the time John and Margrit left the grounds that afternoon, they realized that being a member of the press is no picnic but hard work. Despite it, they were keenly aware that they were most fortunate not only to have been granted the privilege of attending the dedication but also to have been part of a good, patriotic rally. They also knew this was a day they would long remember and often think about.

Once again, Simi Valley was in the news with the arrival of former Soviet president Mikhail Gorbachev and his wife, Raisa, who visited former adversary Ronald Reagan. Gorby's visit officially opened the Reagan Center for Public Affairs, an international center that focuses on the study of individual freedom and the promotion of global democracy and foreign affairs. Following a day spent at the Reagan ranch in Santa Barbara, our former president presented his fellow former president with the first Ronald Reagan Award for Freedom. How the world turns!

Margrit was currently writing a series of mystery stories about a forensic scientist here in Simi Valley. "It's good fun, it keeps me out of the male brothels, and I'm happiest when I'm writing," she told John after he had arrived home from the office.

He told Margrit about his day. "My group at the lab is making good progress on our projects. The most interesting one is trying to use electrolysis to make oxygen and water from simulated moon rocks for future long-term explorations on the moon. Once the process is perfected, we will be receiving a small amount of actual moon rock that was brought back from the moon during the Apollo mission. It is nice that Rockwell has some connections with the National Aeronautics and Space Administration (NASA). As I told you following my first day on the job, there is rocket testing for NASA on the site. I will never forget the ground shaking during that first day when I did not know about the rocket testing. The ground shook, and I first thought it was an earthquake, but minutes later, my coworkers told me about the rocket testing. We are also making progress on the project using molten salt oxidation to destroy nuclear waste. The Department of Energy is very pleased with what we have reported so far, and they want to fund a pilot plant demonstration.

"They also want to fund me to spend three months at the Czech Nuclear Research Institute (NRI) to learn about their new solvent extraction process to separate the fission products, cesium and strontium, from spent nuclear fuel. Once the fission products are removed, uranium and plutonium would be purified and recycled to make new nuclear fuel. The fission product waste would then only have to be stored hundreds of years instead of thousands of years."

"John, I hope you accept that assignment since you know how much I love living in Europe. I would of course accompany you. I also wish I understood more chemistry so I could ask more questions about your work."

Since first getting a glimpse of the Czech countryside while living in Vienna, John and Margrit had long dreamed of a day when they could tool around the country to view its magnificence. That was the main reason John had accepted DOE's offer to send him to Prague to work with the Czech scientists at the NRI, near Prague, for three months. All expenses would be paid by the DOE. Tim was also pleased with John working there. Tim told John that they needed verification that their two research reactors were only being used to develop the Czech nuclear power reactor program and not nuclear bomb material.

The institute adjoins Rez, a small village next to the Vltava River. The train tracks between Prague and Dresden parallel the river most of the way and pass by Rez, about twenty miles from

Prague. Rez is about a thirty-minute drive from Prague and a little longer when going by train. Workers getting off the train to the institute must cross over the Vltava River on a pedestrian bridge to get to work. The institute is surrounded by a high fence with barbed wire on top, and the cafeteria is outside the fence near the entrance where guards check workers' badges.

John had the pleasure of working with Miroslav Curie and his small group of chemists and technicians. As John assisted in the research, he acquired detailed knowledge of the new solvent extraction process, from laboratory scale to pilot plant operation. Discussions with site workers and visits to the reactor areas during his tenure at the NRI provided John with the information that Tim wanted. Some of the workers first spoke with John in Czech only to find out he did not understand them. They assumed that he was Czech since he had a Czech name. John also interacted with Vera Vedakova at the Technical University and gave several lectures there.

During the three months spent in Prague, the couple took car trips on most weekends to see the country. During the last week of their stay, John received a phone call from Boris, who, with a contingent of Russians, was visiting Řež. Professor Bob Beld from Clemson University also arrived to look at the facilities at Řež. Bob had been participating in a DOE-sponsored program, along with John's group. Bob told John that they had received funding from the DOE for a new professor position and that he would be perfect for the position. At the end of the week, the Czermaks filled their suitcases, turned in the house keys, returned the rental car, and went to the airport to board a Delta Air Lines flight to the States via Frankfurt.

Clemson University, located in the upstate of South Carolina, is a land-grant institution founded in 1889. The 1,400-acre campus is near the foothills of the Blue Ridge Mountains and sits next to Lake Hartwell, a 17,500-acre Clemson Experimental Forest, and the towns of Clemson and Pendleton. The forest is used for education, research, and recreation. This public university is the second-largest one in South Carolina, with more than twenty-five thousand undergraduate and graduate students.

A couple of days following the Czermaks return from Prague, John got a call from Tim about his stay in the Czech Republic. John told Tim that he had learned all about their new solvent extraction process and that he would send him a copy of his trip report that he had submitted to the DOE concerning his research at Rez. He told Tim that he toured the site several times and spoke with many workers during his three-month stay, so he was confident that the Czech nuclear program was only for nuclear power and not weapons. John also received a call from the head of the Department of Environmental Engineering and Science at Clemson University asking him to fly down to the university for an interview the following week. The Department would pay his and Margrit's expenses. On the flight back to California following the interview, Margrit and John discussed the interview trip.

"John, I was very impressed by the university and the nearby towns. I especially liked Pendleton. I also had a good time at the dinner hosted by the dean of engineering and science and the department head. It was nice to talk with Bob about his activities since his visit to Prague. I sincerely hope you get the job as I am tired of generic Simi Valley, being stuck out in suburbia and not having a house with a big yard. If you get the offer, please call the realtor that showed us the lovely new home on Golden Pond in Pendleton and tell him we will take it."

"I also had a good time at the dinner and found out a lot more about the position I might be offered. I would start in about two months and would not have to start teaching until the fall semester. I would have three graduate students who are ready to start their research. From Ying's last email from Australia, I know she is looking for a postdoc position in the US, so maybe I could also get her in my group as I would start with enough funding to financially support her and a couple of other students for at least two years. I got a good laugh out of the dean when he started talking about the Clemson Tigers. I piped up and said, 'Clemson has a football team?' By the way, Margrit, I arranged for an appointment for your car to be serviced and worked on tomorrow, so you will have to accompany me to work and use my car to run your errands. After you pick me up in the late afternoon, we can stop on the way back and get your car. Hopefully, Mike can complete the work in one day."

A little after they arrived back at the townhouse, John told Margrit, "I just received a call from the head of the department, and I have the job. Let's celebrate!"

After opening a bottle of cold duck and toasting, Margrit asked John, "Are we going to ship our cars or drive mine to South Carolina?"

"Well, Margrit, I am sorry, but I want to sell your car. I will also have to spoil my surprise and tell you that I bought that smart car you looked at when we were in Clemson. After I accepted the job at Clemson, I phoned our realtor to say that we wanted the house on Golden Pond in Pendleton. I also asked him to contact the car salesman and have the car waiting in the garage for you."

"Oh, John, what a lovely present." She thanked him with a long, romantic kiss.

About noon the next day, Margrit received a very puzzling phone call. The caller said in a Russian accent, "Hello, is this Margrit Cermak?"

"Yes" was her reply with a puzzled look on her face. "Who is this?"

"Please do not be too shocked or offended, but this is Andrei Pushkin."

"What?" she said in a strained voice. "You can't be Andrei as he died over six years ago."

"Yes, it is me, Margrit, and if possible, I would like to meet you this afternoon and explain what happened to me and where I live and work now."

Margrit did not believe that this caller was really Andrei, but she agreed to meet him at a local restaurant mainly because she was curious who this man was. As Margrit arrived at the almost-vacant restaurant, she went to a table in the corner of the room where a man was seated with his back to the entrance.

Margrit said, "Andrei?"

He stood up and faced her with tears in his eyes. As she recognized Andrei, Margret started to hysterically weep and cried out, "It is you." After several minutes of trying to get over the shock, Andrei helped her sit down. Margrit was still weeping as she quietly asked in a shaking voice, "Andrei, I am so happy that you are alive. Please tell me what happened and why you are here."

After the two calmed down from their emotional reunion and ordered coffee, Andrei began to tell Margret his story.

"Margrit, I am so sorry I put you through so much sadness and heartbreak. Just before my faked suicide, I realized the futility of our relationship and the times we unsuccessfully attempted to terminate it. I continued to suffer self-debasement, realizing I was destroying our families. In this state, I seriously considered suicide, but my good Russian friend Mikhail Romanov talked me out of it. He then somehow got a dead body to use as a decoy for the car crash and fire. He also arranged a new life for me in Canada with a passport and job. I now work for an aircraft parts manufacturer in Toronto. I am here on business with Rockwell and have been at their Santa Susanna site, where your husband works, for the past two days. I return to Canada tomorrow. I followed your lives over the years on Facebook since your husband accepted me as a former friend at the IAEA where I used my friend's identity. I also found out that my wife married someone else and that my older son works in Moscow. I did contact him and Alexander, but only Alex wanted to join me in

Canada. The boys agreed never to tell anyone about my faked death and where I am. Alex has finished his master's degree in chemistry at the University of Toronto and plans to go to graduate school in the US for his PhD. He will return to Moscow in two weeks. Since that time, I continued to love and miss you dearly. I had hoped someday to start a new life with you, and that is the only reason I go on living."

A shocked Margrit told Andrei that she continued to think about him over the years and how she suffered for many months after she received the terrible news of his death.

"It would be different if I was divorced or a widow. Then indeed, I would consider a new life with you, Andrei. However, I am very happy with my life now. John and I have reconciled our past problems and have a very amicable relationship and a wonderful life together. We have so many memories of traveling together, attending events in California, making new friends, and having wonderful visits with family. I do not want to jeopardize my marriage and my relationship with my children and friends. I am also very excited about John and my future. We will move to South Carolina in a couple of months, where John will teach at Clemson University, and I can enjoy the academic environment and help students. Andrei, you will always have a place in my heart."

Following their conversation and coffee, Margrit told Andrei that she must go as she has John's MR2 and must pick him up at the site. Andrei accompanied Margrit to the car, and they said their very emotional goodbyes with a long embrace.

After picking up John and driving to Mike's car service, Mike apologized to John that Margrit's car was not ready but would be completed by the next afternoon. Since Margrit had a doctor's appointment the next day, she planned to accompany John to work and use his car again.

As they were driving up the narrow, steep, and winding Black Canyon Road the next morning, Margrit asked John, "Do you ever get tired of driving up and down this dangerous road every workday?"

"I seldom see another car, and almost all the workers come up at other times or drive up from the San Fernando Valley on a much better road. I also enjoy pretending to be a race car driver and time the drive. The first hairpin curve at the top is known as Dead Man's Curve. Our secretary describes it as, when you turn on that sharp curve, the back of the car kisses the front."

"Do you still see lots of wildlife on the site, John?"

"I do see some wildlife early in the morning, especially deer and raccoons. One morning, I even saw a bobcat. About the same time, I witnessed a beautiful sunrise. As you know, we need some rain, Margrit, but not by the bucketsful as what happened last month. Because of the flooding, this road was quite literally washed away in places, and a newly formed 'river' ran at the bottom, making it perilous for me to get to work. Nor were most parts of Ventura and the San Fernando Valley spared, as raging waters created chaos and destruction throughout the Southland. Of course, as you know, since that time, we've had forest fires, a hurricane, and several major earthquakes—the mightiest registering 7.4, which occurred near Joshua Tree National Monument. Remember it jolted us from our beds!"

After arriving at the outside parking lot and parking the MR2 in his usual place near the road, John and Margrit went through the guard station to the nearby plant cafeteria. Over a late breakfast, Margrit told John that she is so happy with her life with him and that she loves him more than any other time in their marriage and looks forward to moving to South Carolina. After finishing their coffee, John took a five-minute walk to his office, and Margrit went through the guard station to the car.

A few minutes later, the guard saw lots of smoke coming from Black Canyon Road and called the site fire department. They found a red MR2 upside down and on fire in a steep ravine below Dead Man's Curve. After putting out the fire, they discovered Margrit's dead body nearby.

Following John's return from a very nice but sad memorial for Margrit in Colorado, the Simi Valley police summoned him to headquarters. They again questioned him about Margrit's death. The police captain told John following his questioning, "You are not a suspect because of information from the front gate guard observing both you and Margrit leaving the car together to come on-site and her leaving alone. We also have confirmation from a fellow worker that you left Margrit in the plant cafeteria and went to your office. The guard had also observed a black car leaving the parking lot and going down the other way into the San Fernando Valley just before Margrit came back to the car and drove down Black Canyon Road. Following our investigation after the fire was put out and Margrit's body removed, we found that there was a trail of brake fluid from the parking lot to the wrecked car and that the brake line had been cut. Thus, we concluded that the person in the black car had cut the brake line, resulting in the murder of your wife. Since that person did not know that Margrit would be driving the car, we assume that person was trying to kill you. John, do you know anyone who has a grudge strong enough to try and kill you?"

John was flabbergasted as he slowly thought about the question. "Well, I did hear from one of my friends at Rocky Flats that FBI agent Phil Gilbert, who was investigating me for disclosing classified information to the Russians, was later fired for providing false information to his superiors about me. Meg Showman was also fired by the DOE for her mishandling of the investigation of me and that I should have never lost my security clearance. Meg let me know about this in an apologetic letter."

Two weeks after Andrei returned to Toronto, he was devastated to find out about Margrit's death via John's Facebook post. He had cut the brake line, and the car crash was meant for John and not Margrit. Andrei was beside himself with grief and kept saying, "My life is over with no hope for a life with my beloved Margrit. I have no reason to live."

At that point, he started drinking glass after glass of vodka and then pulled out a revolver from a drawer in his modest home, shot himself in the chest, dropped the gun on the floor, and barely managed to push it under the couch with his foot. His son was upstairs, getting ready to go to the airport and return to Russia. He ran down to his father's side when he heard the shot. Alex immediately tried to stop the blood coming from his father's chest.

With difficulty, Andrei spoke to his son. "Alex, I have told you about Margrit Czermak before. Well, I accidentally killed her, and I meant to kill her husband, John, who has ruined my life for the past ten years. I had hoped that after his death, she and I could have a life together. But instead, he just left here after shooting me. I have no reason to live now. Please do not call anyone. Pack your bag and return to Russia as soon as possible. Please make a promise to me that you will apply to Clemson University and study under Czermak." Next, Andrei whispered another promise for Alex to keep before his heart stopped.

V

After an agonizing fortnight of final work in California, John accepted Tim's offer at government expense (via the Penny Group in San Francisco) to go on a mission to North Korea. John had always wanted to take the train across China to Tibet, and he planned on doing that following the dangerous CIA assignment. John also planned to meet Ying in Beijing to discuss her coming to Clemson as a postdoc in his research group. He had hoped that the travel would help him cope with his loss.

Following John's return from his trip to North Korea and China, he phoned Tim to give him a summary of his visit to North Korea. He told Tim that he was sending him a copy of his diary concerning the North Korea trip and copies of some of the many photos he took. He informed Tim that he traveled with six other

Americans and a Korean guide and driver and that the main things they did were visit the infamous Demilitarized Zone and attend a parade following a speech by the son of Kim Jong-il, Kim Jong-un, marking the 100th anniversary of the birth of his grandfather, Kim Il-sung.

On John's return to California, he made a couple more short trips before the movers came and transported his household belongings to the newly purchased home on Golden Pond in Pendleton that Margrit loved. On the last night in Simi Valley, John slept in a sleeping bag in the townhouse's second-floor bedroom. He was awoken at 4:31 by a 6.7 earthquake that had its epicenter in Northridge, about ten miles away. He thought the devil himself had come to call. After the shaking stopped, he got dressed, packed his remaining personal items, and headed to Denver in Margrit's car. After spending a few days visiting the kids and family, he continued his drive to South Carolina. After the furniture arrived and the home arranged, he started his new job at Clemson's Research Park, about ten miles from the main campus. At the university, he started using his middle name instead of his first name, one way to start a new life.

Professor Czermak was to start teaching an environmental actinide chemistry course in the fall but had the spring and summer semesters to get his graduate student's research underway, attend a few conferences, and get more research funding. At the time, he was trying to expand his research group. One of the things he did was to arrange for Ying to come and work for him as a postdoc. James was glad to have her in his research group since she was hardworking, extremely intelligent, and full of ideas. She was also very cooperative and pleasant to be around since she had a wonderful personality. Ying arrived about a month after James had started supervising the research of his three graduate students, Shana Sharp, Jerry Crow, and Chris Brown. When the fall semester started, James got a fourth graduate student, Alex Pushkov, who had received a bachelor's degree in chemistry at Moscow State University and a master's in environmental chemistry from the University of Toronto.

At the first meeting with his research group, James brought up the topic of them attending technical conferences. He emphasized that they were good learning events where they could give papers, interact with other researchers, and perhaps make some new friendships. Of course, he said, "There were limitations of time and money." He went on to say, "I have been invited, all expenses paid by the Egyptian Atomic Authority, to give the plenary lecture about our environmental nuclear studies next month. I would like one of you to participate. I suggest we put your names in a hat and see who gets to accompany me. For the next meeting, the person going this time would not be permitted to participate in that drawing. Does this seem fair?" Everyone agreed. Then the professor added, "I am sorry, but next week, I head to Iran and Afghanistan. In Iran, I will attend a conference at their expense, followed by a humanitarian mission in Afghanistan for the government. I may also attend a conference in India and make a few stops in Northern Africa. Otherwise, I will return in about two weeks and will try and stay in touch via email. I assume you all will continue to work hard on your coursework and do some reading on your planned research projects."

A letter to Tim after James returned from his travels:

I left Kabul yesterday morning at nine and got back home last night at six via London and Atlanta. The humanitarian mission to Afghanistan was very interesting (thanks for arranging the funding) as well as the 3-day water conference at the University of Shahrood, about a 6-hour bus ride north of Tehran and surrounded by beautiful mountains on three sides. The Iranian people were so wonderful and kind and want better relations with the USA. I sent the attached letter to our president on the matter:

Dear President Obama, two weeks ago, I attended an international conference on water resources at Shahrood Technical University, Iran. Shahrood is north of Tehran (six hours by bus) and has a population of about 300,000. There were over 300 participants at the meeting, but only five foreign guests out of an expected 30: two from India, one each from Brazil and Spain, and me. The mayor and university president hosted a dinner for the foreign guests the first night, and we were treated like celebrities. I urged the mayor to invite you to his beautiful and hospitable city. Three dear students from the University of Shahrood gave me a picture and a card that they had signed, and on the card, they wrote a Shakespeare quote, "This life is too short even to love . . . I don't know how people find time to hate." I spent the last day of my trip in Tehran with two graduate students from the University of Tehran who showed me around the city, including the university, major museums, and parks. The Iranian people I met were all very kind and helpful, and some of them expressed concern that most Americans thought badly of them. I returned from the trip knowing that we urgently need to normalize relations between our countries. Let them have their peaceful nuclear program if they allow IAEA safeguards. Inform the 75 million Iranian people that we trust their leaders' words that their nuclear program is for peaceful purposes only. Similarly, South Africa clandestinely built several nuclear weapons but gave them up once apartheid was over. Sincerely, Professor John James Czermak, Clemson University.

Tim, per your request, I have mailed to you a copy of my diary writings about my trip to Afghanistan. I assume the information above on Iran is sufficient. For your information, next Saturday, I will board a plane to London and then fly to Vishakhapatnam via Bangalore and Hyderabad. I will be attending a nuclear conference there for five days, and then I will go to Casablanca via London. If my visa arrives, I will visit my godfamily for a few days in Tripoli. Otherwise, I plan to visit Marrakech and Tangier and then fly to Timbuktu via Bamako. There I plan to join an excursion by camel caravan to visit a Tuareg camp on the dunes (I hope I can stay on a camel for the 2-hour journey). They tell me it is too dangerous to go farther out into the desert because of al-Qaeda. If all works out, I will also fly to Mopti and sail on the Niger River, then onto Djenne and Segou for short visits. I can send you a copy of my diary entries if you wish. I hope your work goes well in Denver. Let me know if you want to meet with me before I head back to South Carolina. Best wishes, James.

The following is a copy of John's diary regarding the Egyptian trip that he mailed to Tim:

My student Jerry Crow and I left Atlanta for Luxor via Paris and Cairo on Thursday night. We landed in Luxor on Saturday morning. At the airport, the conference bus came and collected us and several others. On the bus, I had a nice conversation with a lady from Brazil who was accompanied by her husband, also a chemist, and their two children.

At the hotel and after a long check-in process, Jerry and I went to our rooms. We had breakfast before the opening of the conference. After that, we returned to our rooms for a couple of hours of sleep. Following our naps and lunch, we went to the conference room where I gave my lecture. There were about thirty people in attendance out of approximately 300 attendees at the conference. That night, we experienced a wonderful sunset over the Nile.

On Sunday morning, we walked around the city and visited the Palace of Luxor and the Valley of the Kings. That night, there was another beautiful sunset over the Nile, with boats going up and down the river. After the sunset, we heard the calling for prayer from a couple of Mosques. The next morning Jerry and I walked up to Luxor Palace, and then I had a TV interview about our research.

In the evening we watched a display of lights and narrative history of Karnack Temple that was spectacular, just like in the James Bond movie. We returned to the hotel for dinner. Following dinner, there was a great singer and lots of old folks dancing.

The next day, we returned to Atlanta via Cairo and Paris. Tim, let me know if you have any questions. Best wishes, James.

During James's travels, he had been preparing lectures for his actinide chemistry course for the fall semester as well as making proposals to the DOE, EPA, and IAEA for funding research projects. Tim had promised to find some research funds that would be part of a CIA mission. While on campus, James planned to continue having periodic meetings with his students to review their research. Shana, Jerry, and Chris were also taking a couple of classes and were financially supported by the department. Ying was serving as a laboratory assistant for her paycheck, Jerry had started his research on uranium removal from a drinking water project, and Chris was examining methods to remove arsenic from drinking water. James told Chris that there is a three-day meeting on drinking water methods in Washington DC next month. "I would like you to attend. I think it would be very useful, and there are funds in the grant for your expenses."

James had just returned from a Thursday afternoon chemistry seminar when he received a call from a Mr. Johnson in the US Department of Homeland Security. Mr. Johnson stated that James had been recommended to him as one of the world's leading nuclear sleuths. He wanted to know if James was interested in coming to Boston for a few days of consulting to assist in a dirty bomb threat to the city. Mr. Johnson stated that they had received intelligence reports alleging that two Iraqis had smuggled dirty bomb material into the country from Canada and were heading to Boston. James told Mr. Johnson that he would be pleased to do what he could for his country. James never had trouble accepting these types of government assignments when they would give him a chance to visit relatives, friends, or new places.

He was also concerned about his younger daughter who was now attending Boston University and residing in Waltham, a suburb of Boston. In fact, James had discussed the threat by phone with his daughter and advised her of appropriate measures.

Early the next morning, James left Pendleton for the two-hour drive to the Atlanta airport. He had left behind very mild weather in South Carolina and was advised to dress warmly for Boston since there was a forecast of a big snowstorm Saturday afternoon. As the plane started its descent into the Boston area, James could see previous snow on the ground through the partly sunny sky. He was met at the airport by Mr. Johnson, who promptly took him to the State Emergency Center. The two joined a small group of nuclear and radiological experts in a secure conference room. They were asked to review an emergency plan and how to respond to the dirty bomb threat. The usual scenarios were discussed, mainly dealing with the detonation of nuclear material in a strategic location to contaminate as many areas and people as possible. It was James who brought up the possibility of terrorists just walking into the front entrances of airports, hospitals, public buildings, and/or schools and casually dropping a small amount of radioactive material on the floor and letting the building employees and the public be the vectors to spread it around. For example, this could cause all the major hospitals in Boston to be evacuated and not usable for some time. The approaching snowstorm would add to the problems of a nuclear incident.

VI

Near the end of the fall semester, James received word that he has been awarded a grant from the National Science Foundation to study radioactivity in Antarctic ice layers formed since 1930. Tim also notified the professor that the CIA was providing additional funds through the Penny Group. Tim described his assignment for James and informed him that this is their last communication because he is retiring. He thanked John for all his time in assisting the CIA and ended the call by saying his replacement will be in touch with him following the trip to Antarctica.

The grant and Penny money would cover the entire trip cost for him, two graduate students, and a postdoc. Chris and Jerry have already been on trips, and in addition, they cannot come because of family matters and the fact that the trip will start after Christmas. James plans on spending Christmas in Colorado with all his family.

Several days after Christmas, Shana, Alex, and Ying came to James's office for a meeting on the trip. James gave each of them a list of things to buy for the expedition. "Be sure and bring me the receipts so the university can reimburse you from project funds. The most important things on the list are motion sickness pills, sunglasses, sunscreen, knee-high waterproof boots, a warm parka with a waterproof poncho, waterproof gloves with separate liners, and waterproof pants that would go over long underwear and regular pants. Buy a sweater and stocking hat if you do not have one. I will take the ice coring tool with me and am sure I can borrow a hammer aboard the ship."

James asked Ying to stay after the meeting. He told her how much he had enjoyed working with her in Australia and the past year and thanked her for all her hard work. He said he admires her very much for her cooperation, intelligence, and good work. Then he concluded, "How about having dinner with me tonight at the Old Plantation House in the Pendleton Town Square?"

"Thank you. That sounds wonderful and romantic, Yim. Please excuse the 'Yim,' but that is your new nickname with your students."

The evening was so nice for James that he asked Ying to accompany him the next evening to a concert at Clemson with dinner afterward. One could tell they were in love.

A few days later, James, Shana, Alex, and Ying waited in the Atlanta airport for their flight to Ushuaia via Buenos Aires. During their wait for their flight, they watched on TV a program reviewing the news on the exposure of Dr. Khan, the father of the Pakistan nuclear program, for exporting nuclear technology to Iran, Libya, and North Korea. After the broadcast, James told the group that even though a country may not use a weapon, they may sell it to another country or group. Of course, terrorist groups would like the bomb, or nuclear materials to make one, and/or radioactive materials or waste to make a dirty bomb.

James then thought about the assignment Tim had given him. He was requested to keep his eyes and ears open on a small group of scientists from the Argentinean Nuclear Energy Agency located near Buenos Aires. James was to find out if nuclear weapons information, the type that Dr. Khan was selling around the world, would be passed to Argentinean nuclear scientists during the trip. He was not told anymore as had been typical of his previous assignments.

On the group's flight from Atlanta to Ushuaia (the most southerly "city" in the world) via Buenos Aires, James could not sleep as Alex, Shana, and Ying were doing. He thought of Margrit and the last time they had been in Buenos Aires. One of the highlights of Margrit's first visit to Argentina included a conference-sponsored trip to Iguacu Falls.

James's three traveling companions woke on the descent into Buenos Aires. After immigration and customs, the foursome went to the gate for their flight to Ushuaia via a short stop in Rio Gallegos. On the flight, there were two beautiful young children sitting next to James, with their mother across the aisle. He started talking to the mother, who was fluent in English. James had to refrain from speaking with her in Spanish despite understanding the children's Spanish. He did not want anyone on the plane to know he was fluent in Spanish since there might be someone going on the same vessel to Antarctica. Aboard the ship, he was planning on eavesdropping on the conversations of the Russian crew and the Argentinean scientists. James almost slipped a couple of times in trying to talk with the two children. The mother let James practice his favorite hobby, photography. The children would laugh when they saw their images in James's digital camera. At the short stop in Rio Gallegos, the family got off. The plane arrived in Ushuaia less than an hour later. The foursome took a taxi to the hotel, and after check-in and a meal in the hotel restaurant, they all went to their individual rooms very tired. At breakfast the next morning, James summarized his past two trips on the Akademik Abraham for his students. He did not mention the encounters with Felex. Then the foursome had a walk around the beautiful city that is surrounded on three sides by beautiful snowcapped mountains, did some shopping, and enjoyed a meal. In the afternoon, they joined some of their future shipmates, as well as some who had just returned from the Antarctic, on a short tour of the national park. It had been a beautiful and relaxing day.

The passengers were transferred to the *Akademik Abraham* around four, and everyone went to their assigned cabins. James and Alex were cabin mates, as were Ying and Shana. After unpacking their luggage, many of the passengers explored the ship's facilities and enjoyed the scenery and wildlife as the ship moved down the Beagle Channel. James also took a walk around the ship and met several of his shipmates, including the group of Argentinean nuclear scientists. Later, James met Ying, Shana, and Alex, and they all went to one of the upper-most places on the ship to take some pictures and have a last look at Ushuaia. It was a beautiful sight, a glacier off to the west and a high mountain range to the north.

At around six, everyone assembled in the dining room where the expedition leader, Phil Daily, gave a safety briefing and an overview of traveling aboard the ship. After Phil's presentation and dinner, there was a mandatory lifeboat drill. About that time, the ship passed the most southerly town in the world, Puerto Williams, on the Chilean side of the Beagle Channel. At midnight, the Argentinean pilot left the ship via a small speedboat. It was where the Beagle Channel ended and the Drake Passage of the Atlantic and Southern oceans began.

In contrast to the trip to Greenland and the High Arctic that turned out to be quite dangerous with an attempt on his life, James thought that this trip would be a vacation since he was not asked to take sensitive radiometric equipment along to detect nuclear materials or radioactive contamination on the ship or collect water samples. Instead, his only duties were to supervise Alex, Shana, and Ying on the ice sampling and observe six Argentinean scientists who might be receiving nuclear weapons technology from someone else aboard the ship, especially a Russian crew member from Kaliningrad. He did recognize several of the crew members from the last trip on the ship and exchanged greetings with each of them in Russian. He was more acquainted with friendly Swetlana who worked in the kitchen and dining room. Felex, the Russian who had shot at him during the last trip on the Abraham, did not exchange any greetings with James.

The next morning, the passengers woke to the motion of the surrounding seas as the ship made its way steadily south. Sunrise was a little after six. Crossing the Drake Passage was unusually calm, and several of the crew referred to it as crossing the "Drake Lake." Following breakfast, the educational presentations began with a talk from Rinie, one of the technical staff members, who introduced the Antarctic Convergence. Robert, another expert, presented a summary of the history of the Antarctic Peninsula and an interesting and informative talk about Ernest Shackleton's *Endurance* expedition and the lengths that Shackleton went to ensure his men made it back alive. In the afternoon, the presentations continued, with Sean describing the marine mammals that everyone may encounter on the voyage. He also gave an introduction to seabirds that were flying around the ship. Graham gave a few tips on photography that he knew would come in handy over the next week or so as the passengers try and capture the great white continent on film or with digital images.

After these excellent presentations, everyone made their way into the dining room for another fabulous Akademik Abraham meal. After dinner, Robert gave a lecture on climate change; he discussed the significance of Antarctica as a barometer for the rest of the world. Following Robert's talk, Scott hosted a wine tasting party in the library for interested passengers. Some of the group adjourned to the bar immediately afterward to join Graham for the Liars Club—a fun competition between Rinie, Robert, and Sean. The drinkers returned to their cabins at sunset and were all rocked to sleep once again on the Drake Passage.

The sunrise the next morning was a little before seven, and after breakfast, everyone attended a mandatory talk from Phil and Robert on the International Association of Antarctic Tourism Operator's regulations and how to stay safe in zodiacs which everyone will be doing a lot of very soon. Phil also presented the trip's itinerary, and Sean explained the plight of the graceful Albatross and the effects that longline fishing is having on this majestic bird. Everyone knew they were in Antarctic territory when the first iceberg was spotted at latitude 63 degrees south before lunch. Another spectacular sight was a pod of humpback whales feeding just off the Port Bow. They also observed the first Adélie penguins on an ice float and some fur seals and minke whales. The crowd on the bridge was very excited to be seeing the first real evidence of the continent.

Captain Putan announced at lunch that because of our smooth crossing of the Drake, the ship was going to head farther south and cross the Antarctic Circle. The educational presentations continued while waiting for the crossing of the circle. Toni gave a great talk on the life of her father, Frank Hurley, and Sean talked more about humpback whales. Following the talks, all the passengers and most of the crew went to the bow deck to celebrate the ship's arrival at 66° 33'—the Antarctic Circle. Although visibility was low and the air temperature was zero degrees Fahrenheit, excitement was high among everyone. South of this line of latitude is where there are periods of twenty-four-hour daylight or darkness depending on the season.

As everyone on deck was assembled in front of Captain Putan, James asked Ying to accompany him to join the captain. There James got on his knees and said, "Dear Ying, I love you so much. Will you marry me?"

A surprised Ying said, "Yes, yes" with a big smile and tears in her eyes.

"Ying, the captain was aware that I was going to ask your hand in marriage, and he agreed to marry us if you accepted my proposal."

The captain then conducted a short marriage ceremony. With music playing, everyone had a toast to the couple with special hot chocolate. Then most of the attendees gave them congratulations with handshakes or hugs. Shana had tears in her eyes, and she and Alex gave them their best wishes. Both told the newlyweds that they were surprised that they got married on the ship but knew that they were in love with each other and that eventually they would marry. Later, James made a short speech thanking the captain and everyone for traveling this long distance from their homes to attend his and Ying's marriage. The crowd laughed and applauded. In the evening, the newlyweds had a special dinner seated with the captain and his officers.

James was an early riser, and with a coffee cup in hand, he made his way back to his usual spot, the middle rear of the lower deck near the flimsy cargo gate. There he had watched a spectacular sunrise over Detaille Island. James then went back to his cabin and woke Ying. Shana had agreed to let Alex move into her cabin since there were separate beds. Later, the four of them went to the dining hall for breakfast and sat at their usual table within earshot of the Argentinians so James could overhear their conversations.

There was an exciting start to most of the passengers' adventures following breakfast as the backdrop of the Antarctic Peninsula was getting clearer. The brave ones first cruised in the zodiacs, with some humpback whales alongside. Later, they went ashore at Detaille Island where they visited the abandoned British base N. It was a great opportunity to stretch their legs after being on the ship for several days. James and his threesome took some samples of ice on the island. On the way back to the ship, everyone saw more Adélie penguins, skuas, and sheathbills. They also spotted more humpback whales and some crabeater and leopard seals and made a few stops in the zodiacs to watch Adélie penguins with the icy mountains in the background.

After lunch, most of the passengers went ashore on the mainland and visited Vernadsky Station, a Ukrainian research center once owned by the British and called Faraday Station. The foursome took some ice cores before they joined the others to go back to the ship via zodiac for dinner.

Over a delicious dinner, the captain had studied the weather conditions and charts and concluded that it was a good night for anyone wanting to spend sleeping on the snow and ice. Following dinner, they were treated to a super display in the Lemaire Channel by a pod of eight killer whales, including a mother and a calf.

James and Alex decided to join the campers. As James was packing the necessary clothing for the campout, Ying said, "Do you really want to camp on the freezing ice and snow on the coldest and harshest continent in the world?"

"Yes, it will be one of the most unique experiences of my life besides making love to you."

The zodiacs were loaded with supplies, and the anticipation was ripe among those who had chosen to camp. As the fifteen campers, Phil, and three Russian crew members were being transported to Hovgaard Island, there were sightings of several humpback whales. Once on the island, James, Alex, and the other campers prepared their camp spots.

James was awoken in the middle of the night by a sharp jar to his sleeping bag and found himself sledding fast down the hill, cocooned in his sleeping equipment, and heading for a high ledge over the icy channel. As James was about to go over the high ledge of the ice-covered hill into the freezing waters of the Lemaire Channel, he managed to roll over and got stopped by grabbing on to a large rock and hitting a snowbank. A few seconds later, Alex, then Felex, and the Argentinian arrived and asked James if he was okay.

They got James up, and he asked, "What happened?"

Felex did not say anything, but the Argentinian said, "You must have turned over in your sleep and rolled off the rock holding you in place."

James knew that it was not the case as he always slept on his back.

"It is a good thing you got stopped by the snowbank you hit," said Alex.

James told them he was okay, and the four returned to their camp spots to try and get some sleep.

Of course, James was unable to sleep the rest of the night. James suspected the Argentinian and/or Felex of wanting to kill him by removing the rock holding his sleeping bag in place. During the night, he recalled that in his youth, he and his friends would sled down a snowy hill on an air mattress that was tied to them. If they needed to stop, they would just flip the mattress over. Fortunately, the rocks in James's path ripped open the outer cocoon cover, allowing his arms free so he could flip over and get stopped, just like he had done in his youth.

The campers all came back on board at seven for breakfast. Most of the campers said they had a great night with spectacular views of the stars, albeit a little chilly. When James got back to his cabin, Ying asked, "How was the camping on the freezing snow last night?"

James responded, "Well, it had its bad aspects." Then he told Ying the whole story of his near-death experience and who he suspected of removing the rock.

Ying asked, "What are you going to do now?"

"I am not sure since there is no proof of the Argentinian and/or Felex trying to kill me. I will just have to be very cautious for the rest of the trip."

The landing the next morning was on a black volcanic beach on Deception Island in bad weather that later turned into a real blizzard. The visitors split into several groups for different walks. The group that included James and his students headed along the beach to Neptune's Window to first look at all the old water boats and remnants of whale oil barrels. When they reached the Window, they could see a little into the distance, but the snow kept falling. They also walked past some fur seals and marveled at their ability to move along on land. Next, they had a tour of the historic British Antarctic Survey buildings with large metal tanks and processing equipment from the whaling era. The last stop was the hangar, where there was still a single Otter plane on-site. Before the group headed back to the ship, several of the brave ones, including James and Alex, went for a "soak" in the relatively warm plunge pool constructed with volcanic sand by Robert.

The sea was choppy as the visitors left the island. After returning to the ship and going out of the harbor, the ship made its way to Livingstone Island where most of the group went ashore for more walking and penguin watching at Hannah Point. Later, the ship went to the Bulgarian Research Station where some scientists boarded for their journey home.

The passengers awoke the next morning to discover that the ship was going north across a calm Drake Passage. That night, at dinner, as usual, the foursome sat together. Shana told Ying and the professor that Alex will join them in a few minutes. She said, "I'm so happy to be sharing the cabin with him. He is such a gentleman and so interesting to talk to since he has lived in

Russia, Austria, and Canada. He has many stories to tell, and some are so funny. I like him so much."

Ying stated, "I also like my roommate and that we also have a lot of fun together."

James said, "The only annoying thing is sometimes I get up in the middle of the night and find that our Australian friends in the next cabin have locked us out of the bathroom we share. I must then go out in the hallway in my pajamas, knock on their door, and ask them to go and unlock the bathroom door on our side."

Everyone laughed as Alex came to the table. After dinner, Sean gave a special presentation in the library about cleaning up disused Antarctic stations. Scott challenged a small group with trivia in the bar.

The Drake Passage was getting rough but rocked James and Ying to sleep. The next morning after breakfast, Phil recapped the journey. James had skipped the talk to write his report to Tim's replacement concerning the Argentinian scientists. In the evening, with rough seas, everyone carefully headed to the dining room for a special captain's dinner. As usual, James and Alex were seated together with their ladies. In a soft voice so as not to let the others overhear, James asked Alex, "What were you doing on the campout just before my accident since you were the first one to arrive where I had rolled over and stopped? Do you know why the Argentinian and Felex immediately followed you down the hill?"

Alex replied, "I think they must have heard my yelling and came running after me. Can we meet after dinner at the stern where you always have your after-dinner cigar?"

"Certainly," James said.

Following the captain's dinner with drinking and dancing and despite the weather changing and the sea getting very rough, most of the passengers headed out on the decks to see if the mainland was starting to appear. Although it was overcast, one could make out the outline of the landmass and Cape Horn.

Instead of joining James and Ying on deck, Alex and Shana went to their cabin. Alex told Shana that he was in love with her. After exchanging loving emotions, Alex told Shana all about his past, his father, and the promise he had made to his father. He told Shana that he now plans to someday be a professor like James and wants to marry her when they arrive back in South Carolina. He promised to change his life and make amends. She said that he should go down and tell James everything he told her and ask for his forgiveness.

Later, James was on the bottom deck at the stern where he usually went to relax, looking at the stars and smoking a cigar since usually there was never anyone about. It was a grand night as it had just gotten dark around eleven, but the sea was very angry. The ship was tossing back and forth, and large waves were hitting the ship as it was starting to go around Cape Horn. They would be disembarking the next morning. James was not feeling any pain since the dinner with lots to drink. Ying was not feeling well and went to their cabin. Shana quietly went to the second deck, above where Alex would be talking with James, to overhear what they both discussed.

Alex joined James, and James said, "You had better hold on to the railing as the sea is really getting rough."

After some discussions on the joyous evening, Alex started a conversation about how much he had enjoyed his graduate studies, how great an advisor James was, and how he wanted to follow in his footsteps. He also stated that he was so lucky to have found Shana and that soon they would marry. John smiled as Alex spoke. However, as Alex continued to talk, James's smile turned to the opposite with a look of surprise and astonishment. Alex said that his real name was Alex Pushkin, and his father was the one who had a love affair with Margrit in Vienna. He related to James that his father had faked his death, tracked him and

Margrit down in California, and tried to renew his love affair with Margrit by killing him.

"Professor, it was my father who caused Margrit's death. He told me that it was meant for you to die in the car crash, not his love, and wanted me to kill you."

James was shocked as Alex admitted that on the camping night, he was the one who kicked the rock that was holding him in place. Alex told James that he was immediately sorry for what he had done and that as James started to slide down the hill toward the ocean, he ran after him, trying to stop him, but that James had managed to stop himself at the edge of the hill by turning over and grabbing some rocks. Alex said, "My father told me in his dying breath that you had shot him and that I should kill you." James sternly told Alex that he did not kill his father and had an alibi. "Yes, Professor, yesterday, I received word that my father had actually committed suicide as the police found his gun under the couch where he was sitting and it had only his fingerprints on it." Alex told James that he was extremely sorry that he had tried to kill him. At the end of the conversation, James said, "Under the circumstances, I forgive you and know that you will turn out to be a great professor and husband to Shana. Come here, big guy, and give me a bear hug." Alex happily jumped over to give James a hug, but they both fell against the unlocked fragile cargo gate. It opened, and they accidentally went over the back of the ship into the rough, freezing ocean.

Chapter 2

I

Cape Horn, located on the small island of Hornos, is the most southern part of Chile. It is where the Pacific and Atlantic oceans meet. This area is very hazardous because of strong currents, high winds, and large waves, making it dangerous for ships transporting goods around the world prior to the building of the Panama Canal. Today, cruise ships, yachts, and small sailing vessels use the channels north of the Cape, between Wollaston and Hermite Islands or between Tierra El Fuego and Isla Navarino, to avoid the dangerous seas around the cape.

Puerto Williams, located in the middle of the north side of Navarino Island, faces the Beagle Channel and is the most southerly city in the world. It is located two hundred and forty miles south of Punta Arenas, one hundred miles from Cape Horn and almost five hundred miles from Antarctica. Settlements have existed there since the nineteenth century. Puerto Williams was founded in 1953 and was established initially as a base for the Chilean navy. Now it has approximately three thousand inhabitants, half of which are non-naval citizens that work in artistry, commerce, fisheries, public administration, scientific research, schools, tourism, and shops. The city has an airport, fire and police stations, several hostels and bed-and-breakfasts, four restaurants, two small supermarkets, two bars, a bakery, two churches, a museum, a tourist agency, a kindergarten, an all-grades school, a university center, and a naval hospital. Navarino Island is mostly covered by beautiful mountains and has one of the densest concentrations of archeological sites in the world. The island attracts tourists for its aquatic birds, botany, fishing, geology, hiking, and mountain climbing.

An unpaved, fourteen-mile road that parallels the Beagle Channel leaves Puerto Williams to the east and ends at Puerto Eugenia. One occupied farm is located there as well as the beginning of a hiking trail that ends in Puerto Toro where some fishing boats dock for king crab catching. In going west out of Puerto Williams, the thirty-two-mile unpaved road ends at Puerto Navarino where a hiking trail to Caleta Wulaia begins. There is a ferry that travels between Ushuaia and Puerto Navarino, a shorter route than between Puerto Williams and Ushuaia. There were many occupied homes along this road in the past, but the homeowners moved to Puerto Williams. Now there are only two occupied farms near Puerto Navarino.

One of the farms near Puerto Navarino is owned by a retired medical doctor, Deborah Klose. She and her husband worked at the naval hospital in Puerto Williams until his heart attack and death a year ago. Thus, she retired early and sold her house in Puerto Williams because the wonderful memories with her husband haunted her. Then she moved to their weekend home. She enjoys the remote and quiet life, living off farming, ranching, and fishing.

Her nearest neighbors, Eduardo and his wife, Maria, have about the same size farm as Deborah, ten acres. Eduardo took care of Klose's ranch during their absence. Eduardo's farm has a dock for his small fishing boat. The thirty-foot wooden fishing boat has a cabin for the pilot as well as a sleeping area. The area behind the cabin is large enough for his zodiac, and under the deck are storage areas and another small sleeping area. He mainly uses the boat for fishing and travels to other towns and islands. Both farms have vegetable gardens in greenhouses and fruit trees, as well as a few chickens, cows, goats, and sheep.

Early one morning, following a violent rain and windstorm, the threesome went to the small island of Hornos in Eduardo's boat to do some fishing. At one point, they spotted a man lying on the beach. They then took the zodiac to shore to discover the man asleep. He looked awfully bad with bruises and cuts on his face and hands. They immediately covered the man with a coat as he awoke. Deborah asked him in both Spanish and English, "Are you okay?"

He replied in American English, "Yes, I am okay, but very tired, thirsty, and cold.

She then asked him, "What is your name, and how did he get washed up on shore?"

"I do not know."

Eduardo stated, "A cruise ship went by in the middle of the night heading for Antarctica, and he must have fallen off the ship."

Deborah said, "Let us put him in the zodiac where I can bandage him up and give him some water. Although it will take us the rest of the day, we need to take him to my home for recovery."

Once at Deborah's farm, she gave the injured man more water and properly bandaged him up. Deborah then asked Eduardo to put him in one of her two bedrooms to get some sleep. The home also has a spacious living room, kitchen, dining room, and bathrooms in each bedroom. From the front covered porch, one has an excellent view of the channel and forest.

Late the next day, after the stranger was rested and had a shower, Deborah invited him to come to dinner. She had given him one of her husband's robes to wear. Over a meal of fish, corn, and salad, she asked him again, "Who are you, and how did he get here?"

"I do not know, but I am still very tired."

"Please go to the bedroom and sleep as long as you want. You can also use any of my late husband's clothes that I moved from my bedroom."

About twenty-four hours later, the rescued man dressed in a fresh set of Deborah's husband's clothes met her in the dining room for another dinner. Over dinner, they talked in both English and Spanish. Deborah thought to her herself that he must have learned Spanish from a teacher from Spain. She told him about herself, "My name is Deborah, but you can call me Deb. I grew up in Santiago and am a widow and medical doctor. I took early retirement from working at the naval hospital in Puerto Williams after my husband died a year ago from a heart attack probably caused by his long hours at the hospital. I met my husband when we were in medical school at the University of Santiago. Then we did our internship at the naval hospital in Puerto Williams and continued working there."

He thanked her for taking such good care of him as he thought to himself what a beautiful, kind, caring, and intelligent lady she was and about my age.

Deborah continued, "We did not have any children or siblings, and our parents have gone to heaven. We inherited this weekend home from Richard's father. His father was the head doctor at the naval hospital, and Richard replaced him when his father passed. His mother had died five years earlier in an accident. Eduardo lives on the adjoining farm with his beautiful wife Maria. She was the one who helped me and Eduardo bring you here. Eduardo assists me around the farm. I pay him well since I have my husband's life insurance money, our savings, money from selling our big home in town, and my retirement income. All three of us are mostly self-sufficient, growing vegetables and fruit, caring for the animals, and fishing. We also go on lots of hikes, and I read a lot, especially murder mysteries. We rarely leave the farms for shopping. When we must shop, Eduardo takes Maria and I in his fishing boat to Ushuaia, Argentina, although we could drive to Puerto Williams, but it takes longer. The road is muddy after rainstorms, but the snow is plowed in the winter. I also have a piano that I play, and I usually sing. Since we have finished our meal, let me play and sing my favorite song 'The Way We Were' by Barbara Streisand."

Days later, as the injured man continued to recover, Deborah told him, "You are welcome to stay as long as you like, especially since you do not know where your home is. You can help Eduardo around both farms, tending the gardens and animals as well as fixing up the outbuildings and painting some of them. I will pay you the same amount that I pay Eduardo and will take you on a tour of my property later. Oh, by the way, since you look so much like my late handsome husband, except for the beard you are starting to grow, do you mind if I call you by his name, Richard?"

"No, of course not."

Deborah thought that Richard must have amnesia. She told him about amnesia. "Amnesia is a deficit in memory caused by disease, brain damage, or using various hypnotic drugs and sedatives. Due to the extent of damage, memory can be either wholly or partially lost. There are two types of amnesia, anterograde and retrograde. With the first one, people cannot remember things for long periods of time. The second one is what you probably have, Richard, which is you do not have the ability to retrieve information that was acquired before your accident. Retrograde amnesia is usually temporary and sometimes can be treated by exposure to the location of events prior to the amnesia. People suffering with amnesia can recall immediate information, and they can form new memories. They can also retain substantial linguistic, intellectual, and social skills despite impairments in the ability to recall specific information before the amnesia. I think we should wait before we seek professional help in Santiago since your previous memories may slowly return. Also, most forms of amnesia fix themselves without being treated.

"By the way, I called two cruise lines that were operating the night of your accident, trying to find out if any passengers were lost at sea, but the managers of the cruise lines told me that they cannot give out that kind of information. Eduardo, Maria, and I assume you must have been in your own boat when it crashed in the wild sea that night, and you managed to swim to shore. If anyone was with you, they probably drowned."

Richard started helping Deborah and Eduardo tend to their gardens, fished with them, and took care of repairs on the farmhouse and chicken coop. After about two months, Deborah invited him to go with her to Puerto Williams. There she introduced him to a few of her friends. Of course, she did not mention Richard's accident and his memory loss but just introduced him as a visiting friend. After their return from Puerto Williams, Deborah told Richard, "I love to travel, but my late husband never wanted to travel much, even around Chile. Since you told me that you seem to like traveling, let us take a trip to southwest Patagonia. I will arrange the trip with a tour company I have used before, and you can use my late husband's passport since you resemble him so much."

II

Richard and Deborah started their Patagonia adventure early on a Saturday morning by catching a flight to Puerto Natales via Punta Arenas. That night, they stayed at the Lighthouse Hotel in separate rooms with wonderful views of the Andes. After dinner at the hotel, the couple had a walk around the nice small town and came across many young folks having a good time. They continued their walk in the town the next morning, but this time, they went down to the large Fjord that was fed by the Pacific Ocean, with a lighthouse nearby. They both were very hungry, so after their return to the hotel, they had breakfast. After a delicious meal, their driver came and took them to the pier where a small ship was docked. The tour boat held about twenty-four passengers.

Their boat ride, which took about an hour, with cocktails on the way, was to the Ultima Esperanza Fjord for a visit to the Balmaceda and Serrano glaciers, which are in Bernardo O'Higgins National Park. After disembarking, Deborah, Richard, and their fellow passengers took an hour's hike around the area that was rough in places, and they even had to walk across two swinging bridges. At the end of the walk, everyone enjoyed the great views of Gray Glacier, a great ice mass, and the surrounding mountains.

At lunch, the group watched a hungry fox circling nearby and listened to their guide, Ruth, giving an excellent talk about the glaciers and why they are receding in Chile. She said after Antarctica and the High Arctic, Chile has the third largest number of glaciers. Ruth went on to say that she thinks the receding of the glaciers is from less cold and snow. She explained that glaciers are formed from falling snow and that it must be cold and snowy for a long time for ice to accumulate and become part of a glacier.

In the afternoon, the group was transferred to the area of Grey Lake to start a boat ride across the lake that was part of Grey Glacier. The boat ride gave Richard, Deborah, two Spaniards, two Brazilians, and four Russians a chance of staying at the front of the main wall of Gray Glacier, a magnificent natural marvel which is an important part of the Southern Ice Field. Later they saw more glaciers and then went to Torres del Paine National Park by van where the members of the small group went to different hotels. Richard and Deborah were taken to the Tyndall Hotel, and it reminded him of the movie *The Shinning*, starring Jack Nicholson. He was surprised that he remembered the movie. They were the only ones at the hotel besides a weird old lady cook and Jose, a strange-looking waiter, who was also the front desk clerk. The couple enjoyed the food, soup, bread, and pasta. Jose had studied at the University in Florida and had been in other US states, and the more he talked, the more worried Richard got, and the feeling that Jose hated people and seemed a little crazy. Later the couple went to their separate rooms. Richard had a restless night thinking of Jose coming into his room with a big knife.

After their breakfast in the hotel, they joined their group and went into Torres del Paine National Park by van to see more glaciers in the distance. They stopped at one overlook to admire the unmatched panoramic view of the area and later visited Nordenskjold Lake, Salto Grande, and Pehoe. After finishing the park tour, they returned to the hotel.

The second night at the hotel was not as frightening for Richard as a couple, Tim and Sarah, checked in and joined them at dinner. Sarah was a professor in Austin, Texas, and they were headed for Bakersfield, California, where Tim planned to teach. Deborah and Richard listened to Sarah describe her undergraduate studies at the University of Colorado; following her good time in Boulder, she went to Berkeley where she received her PhD and met Tim. Something about what Sarah had said brought back some memories of the University of Colorado for Richard.

On Monday morning, the couple and other visitors left the national park by bus and had a long drive about 140 miles to Punta Arenas. On the ride, Richard saw that the driver was waving at cars/buses/trucks going by, especially in leaving the national park, something he remembered about Southern folks in the United States. The country was very flat, with lots of horses, cattle, and sheep grazing on the grassland. The bus passed many farms and went through several small towns. At one point, the bus stopped at a border checkpoint where there was another road that led to nearby Argentina.

Richard and Deborah spent the night in separate rooms at a Punta Arenas hotel near the sea. The next morning, they had a walk down to the port and admired a monument on the parkway. After a late breakfast, a driver came and took them to the nice modern airport with excellent security. They left Punta Arenas in the early afternoon for home.

On the flight, Deborah had the aisle seat, Richard had the middle one, and an elderly lady had the window seat. After takeoff, Deborah fell asleep. Richard noticed that the elderly lady was carrying a small medical bag and asked if she was a doctor. She knew some English and said she was a healer. She told him that her name was Ligia Castillo and lived in Puerto Williams. Richard said he had problems with his memory. She then asked him if she could do some therapy on him. He agreed, and the first thing she told Richard was to press his thumb very hard under his nose while exhaling and do this three times. She also held Richard's hands and kept stroking his middle finger on his right hand to release his built-up stress and trouble. She did this ten times then threw the stress from her hand downward. Richard felt much better and thought that he remembered something of his childhood. Then she read Richard's hand and told him that the line perpendicular to his middle finger shows strong intelligence and that the line running from his middle finger down his palm to his wrist shows his lifeline; the middle of the line was broad and deeper, and she said it indicated a bad or hard time in his life. She then put her hand over his forehead and said she was sending him universal love. About that time, the plane started descending into Puerto Williams, and that woke Deborah.

About a month after their first trip, Deborah invited Richard to go on a pre-arranged trip to the northern part of Chile. A week later, they boarded a flight to Santiago via Punta Arenas. They spent the night at the Sheraton Hotel in Santiago in separate rooms. The next morning, they took a two-hour flight to Calama, a city near the Peruvian and Bolivian borders that was once part of Bolivia. The terrain between Santiago and Calama is very mountainous, and near Calama it looks like Death Valley in the United States, flat land with lots of sand. Upon arrival in Calama, there were strong winds resulting in a dust storm. Their tour driver/guide, Rodrigo, was waiting for the couple and said that the weather did not make it safe enough for their drive to San Pedro de Atacama. So he took them to the nearby five-star Park Plaza Hotel. There were few guests at the hotel, and the front desk clerk told them that during the weekend, most of the two hundred rooms are filled. After a first-class buffet lunch, the couple went to their rooms for a nap and later dinner. At the time, a couple from Amsterdam had just ridden their bikes from the airport. They had raincoats and were very wet and windblown. It had even started to snow.

Following breakfast the next morning, Richard and Deborah waited for their ride to the village of San Pedro de Atacama. The front desk clerk told them that the last snowstorm was in 1993. Later Deborah got a call from Rodrigo that the road had opened between the two cities and that he would be there right after an early lunch. On the way to San Pedro, which was about an hour's drive on a nice two-lane paved highway, many cars stopped along the way, with families having snowball fights and making snowmen. Most of the snowmen were placed on the hoods of the cars. Thus, as they drove along the highway, many cars were going to Calama with snowmen on their car hoods. Of course, it looked very funny. Rodrigo did most of the talking on the drive, telling the couple about the area and what they would see. He said that he has a wife and two young children and had been taking people on tours since high school.

Later on the drive, the flat terrain changed from snow covered to brown land with a few small hills. As they approached San Pedro, there were high mountains and volcanos. One volcano was even emitting smoke. As the threesome were coming into the city, they went through a series of big, slanted red rocks that the locals called dinosaur ridge. The beautiful rocks looked like the backs of giant lizards.

San Pedro is a small town of approximately 3,500 inhabitants and has an elevation of 7,200 feet. Rodrigo dropped the couple in front of the Kimal hotel. The street was muddy, as were most of the other streets in the town. They both tracked mud into the small reception area and later into the room that they had to share. The hotel was rated four stars, but it was more like an American motel of one or two stars. The room was small with twin beds, no television, and only a small shower. There was a sign near the toilet that read "No paper down the toilet" in both English and Spanish. Deborah apologized to Richard that when she made the reservations for the trip, this was the only hotel in town with a vacancy.

Later that afternoon, Rodrigo took the couple out to the Atacama Salt Flat. It was about a thirty-minute ride from town, and they passed a radio observatory rated as the most powerful one in the world. Rodrigo said that there are scientists from many countries doing research at the observatory. They also passed through the village of Tacoma. Lake Chata is situated on the expansive Salt Flats of the Flamingos National Reserve, and the threesome had a nice walk on a salt path around one of the lakes full of three different species of beautiful flamingos. In the distance were several volcanoes of the Andes Mountain chain. On the way back to San Pedro, they had a brief stop in Tacoma, renowned for its classic bell tower. Back in San Pedro, Richard had a short walk around the village on the muddy streets and saw many dogs and two black cats. He was told later by Rodrigo that most of the dogs are strays and do not have owners.

After dinner in a nearby small restaurant, the couple returned to their room. They had a long discussion about the wonderful things they had seen during the day. The discussion ended with Richard saying, "Thank you, Deb, for arranging such a fantastic trip, just like the one to Patagonia, and for taking such good care of me at the farm."

"Thank you as well for coming into my life and making it like a wonderful dream."

Then she gave him a loving hug and said good night.

Early the next morning, the couple was picked up and taken to see the Geysers del Tatio. Rodrigo had warned Richard and Deborah that it would be very cold at the geysers. The couple had only light jackets with them, so they both wore their pajamas under their pants and short sleeve shirts and put on two pairs of socks. The drive was over a washboard, narrow, and muddy road. The fast and scary drive in the dark took about an hour.

The enduring ride was worth it to see many steaming geysers, several of which were erupting boiling water several feet in the air. The 14,000-foot elevated area was mostly surrounded by volcanoes, and there were some old stone dwellings used by travelers in the past. Before they left the area, all three had a picnic breakfast in the car.

The ride back to San Pedro was slower so the couple could admire the beautiful valley along the way. They passed a few more small rock dwellings, green fields, and a stream and saw several llamas. They also had excellent views of the Torcopuri and Sairecabur volcanoes.

In the afternoon, the group had a scenic drive to Salt Mountain and Valle de Marte (Chile's Death Valley) and had a long walk up one of the picturesque canyons. In the evening, they watched a spectacular sunset in the extraordinary landscape of Moon Valley, which has one of the largest salt flats in the world.

Late the next morning, Richard and Deborah were on their way back to Santiago. After their arrival at the Sheraton, Richard told Deborah, "I think I am starting to remember some things in the past. Although I did not remember being in Santiago when we stayed here several days ago, now I think I have been to the city before, maybe several years ago. I think I attended a conference in this hotel, and I recognize some of the buildings in the city."

Deborah replied with a smile on her face, "That is great, Richard! Maybe where we go in the next few days will also help you remember more of your former life. I have arranged a ride for us to go to Vina del Mar and Valparaiso next to the ocean. First though, I want to show you around Santiago and the area where I grew up."

Following the visits, they went for a walk over to the newer part of Santiago where the tallest building in South America is being built. In the area, there were plenty of folks on the sidewalks and in the many stores.

In the late afternoon, they went by bus down to the Pacific Ocean to visit Vina a del Mar and Valparaiso. These coastal cities are about a ninety-minute drive from Santiago. The trip took the couple through the central valley, famous for its wines, fruits, and cheese. Vina del Mar was initially a land of wineries, but today, it is Chile's most important beachside city. After arrival, they checked into the Sheraton Miramar, a plush five-star hotel. They made an early night of it since they were going to have a long walk around Vina del Mar after an early breakfast.

The next day, they spent all morning touring the old part of the city. "It was very interesting," commented Richard over lunch at McDonald's.

"Yes, I do love this city, mainly because of its location next to the beautiful ocean."

After a Big Mac lunch, they noticed a lot of big stray dogs, some sleeping and others walking around. The dogs seemed to know when to cross the street with the green light. Some of them needed a veterinarian; one dog had a back leg that she could not walk on. They also saw a man picking through the trash can and eating what food he found as he continued his search for more discarded food. Later the guy found a gold mine of food in another trash can and took a seat outside to consume his find. Deborah had not eaten all her french fries, so Richard put some money on her tray with the fries, and as they were leaving for another walk, he placed her tray on the poor soul's table. Deborah told Richard that he was kind and generous.

In the early afternoon, the couple took a taxi to the adjoining town, Valparaiso, for twenty dollars. Valparaiso was declared a World Heritage Site in 2003 by UNESCO. Its buildings have unique architecture and were built on forty-one hills. It also has one of Chile's main ports. Richard and Deborah went for a long walk around the city and found out that except for a couple of long streets near the port, the other streets are narrow and steep. Richard told Deborah that it is a nice old town but he thinks Vina del Mar is better. They had an early dinner at a pizza restaurant. After dinner, there was rush hour traffic, and they had trouble finding a return taxi. After stopping several taxis, the drivers told them that they were not going in the direction of Vina del Mar. The couple finally got a taxi that was going in their direction. There were already two other passengers in the taxi. Then the cabbie picked up another passenger, but despite the crowded conditions in the car, they got back to their hotel for less than two dollars.

The next morning, after returning to the Sheraton in Santiago by bus, the couple took a bus tour of the city. They heard many interesting facts about the city. The guide's narrative started with a reminder that Santiago is ringed by the Andes Mountains and was shaped by the contributions of Chile's indigenous population and a dozen different European cultures. "Its history dates back to 1541 when it was founded by the Spanish conquistador Pedro de Valdivia. Towards the end of the nineteenth century, Santiago became a national territory supported by the wealth generated from nitrate mining. A major urban remodeling was undertaken which was greatly influenced by French and Italian neoclassical architecture. By the beginning of the twentieth century, Santiago's population was in the range of three hundred thousand inhabitants. However, during the 1950s and 1960s, the city's population jumped above two million, and urbanization expanded in all directions. Now Santiago has a population of approximately six and a half million, which represents around 40 percent of Chile's population."

On the tour, the passengers visited Plaza de Armas, which exists because when the Spaniards established cities, they always used a central point as the axis of their city plans. From the Plaza de Armas stop, the group visited some of the city's most relevant historic buildings, which included the Metropolitan Cathedral, Santiago City Hall, Central Post Office, Casa Colorada and Santiago Museum, National Congress, Royal House of Customs and Pre-Colombian Museum, Judicial Palace, and Palacio de la Real Audiencia and National Historic Museum.

After lunch, the tour continued in a van by going to Concha y Toro winery with seven others, plus a guide and driver. The winery is in the picturesque rural setting of Pirque, only an hour's drive out of Santiago. At the winery, the group learned about the growth and development of the vines and visited its ancient cellars, which included the Casillero del Diablo (Devil's Cellar), where they heard the legend that has made Chilean wine known worldwide. The group also got to see the owner's historic summer house. At the end of the tour, everyone was offered red wine to taste. All the guests, including Deborah and the guide, took a glass, except Richard. After everyone had finished toasting and drinking the wine, the guide asked Richard why he did not take his glass of wine. Richard replied that he does not drink. So the guide quickly took Richard's glass and gulped the wine down in two seconds.

Following the winery visit, the group went up to the Valle Nevado ski area in the Andes. The ride up in the small van was scary for the couple and the other passengers. The driver drove too fast, and one person got sick. The trip to the ski area was about thirty miles long with sixty-one hairpin curves. The Nevado Ski Area is nine thousand feet high, with wonderful views of the surrounding mountains. The weather was great with blue skies, and everyone only wore light jackets despite snow on the ground. The ride back to Santiago was a little calmer than the ride up.

The next morning, Deborah told Richard that she had invited an old friend to have breakfast with them. "Coni and I went through medical school together. She has worked at the main hospital in Santiago since her internship and has a husband and two grown children. I have already told her a lot about you."

"That sounds fine. I hope you only told her the good things about me."

"Yes, indeed, you funny clown."

The threesome met in the hotel lobby, and after introductions, they went to the hotel restaurant. The two ladies did most of the talking during the meal, catching up on their activities since they were last together two years ago. Following the meal, Coni went to work, and the couple took a long walk behind the hotel up Cerro San Cristobal Mountain that has spectacular views of the city. They also saw the white statue of Jesus, a beautiful church, and the zoo from the viewpoint. They then went to explore the old city center. They spent some time in the church square where plenty of artists were painting, singers were singing, and bands were playing. The morning ended in a big church where an orchestra was playing wonderful music, and they sat there for a while enjoying the music along with many others.

After lunch in the city and a cab ride to the airport, they flew back to Puerto Williams. Fall weather also arrived as the couple had to start wearing heavy coats. Richard continued his work around the farm and helped Eduardo with his chores. Deborah started playing and singing lots of new music in the evenings following the delightful dinners. She and James's loving friendship continued to grow.

One cold day, Deborah told Richard that she was ready to experience some warmer weather. She asked him if he would like to go with her for several weeks of touring a few other countries in South America. Of course, he agreed. So she started organizing the trips and making reservations.

The happy couple flew to Rio de Janeiro via Punta Arenas, Puerto Natales, and Santiago and stayed at a five-star hotel in the Copacabana area. After checking in and leaving their luggage in their separate rooms, they took a five-block walk to the beautiful Copacabana Beach. The waves were remarkably high, and there were a few surfers on the waters, a couple of hang gliders in the air, and lots of sunbathers on the beach. It had rained during their taxi ride to the hotel, but now it was sunny and warm. There were lots of street vendors on the beach selling hats, sunglasses, water, T-shirts, and a variety of other items. The couple continued their walk following a late lunch at Burger

King. Along one stretch of the street near the hotel were about a dozen homeless young men sleeping on the sidewalk on old mattresses, covered with blankets.

The next morning after breakfast, Richard and Deborah started an all-day city tour in a minibus along with ten other tourists. The group visited Corcovado Mountain where the Christ the Redeemer statue is located. One can see the Atlantic Ocean and most of Rio from the bottom of the statue.

After a buffet lunch, the group took two exciting cable car rides to Sugar Loaf Mountain. There they had a wonderful view of Rio, the Copacabana, Ipanema, and Leblon. The trip ended with a city tour passing by the downtown area, Maracana, San Sebastiao Cathedral, and Sambodomo. Their tour guide dropped the couple off at the beach near their hotel where they enjoyed watching half a dozen young boys playing soccer on the beach. It seemed like every player was trying to win as they did not form teams. It was like cutthroat pool. Richard exchanged one hundred dollars for three hundred reais at a local exchange store before they headed back to the hotel.

On their last full day in Rio, both Richard and Deborah slept in and then went down for a late breakfast. The rest of the morning was spent doing some shopping in nearby stores. In the afternoon and evening, they took a couple of long walks, one near the hotel and the other along the beach. They stayed at the beach until it got dark. There were plenty of people walking on the sidewalk paralleling the beach and lots of vendors displaying their goods for sale. Sugar Loaf Mountain was visible from the beach area and a fortress in the opposite direction. Richard told Deborah, "I think Rio is one of the most beautiful and unusual cities we have visited so far mainly because there are beautiful beaches on one side of the city and fantastic mountains on the three other sides."

"I agree with you, Richard, and the architecture of the buildings is also to be admired. Shall we return to our room now for our last night in the great hotel?"

"Okay, Deb, but are you sure you want to skip dinner?"

"You can go ahead and eat, but the late breakfast where I pigged out is enough for me. Say, I have an idea, instead of going back home, let us see some more of Brazil. I can look into flights out of Rio while you are having dinner."

"I forgot to tell you, Deb, that last night, I went to the business center in the hotel where I Googled Travelers' Century Club, the organization your friend Coni belongs to. Remember she told us about the club and that she has silver status because of visiting more than 150 countries and territories on the club list of 327. I printed out the club's list of countries and territories that they suggest for visits. The club rules state that one must only step on the ground at an airport to check that country or territory off the list. So in case we join the club someday, we should travel to some of the places on the list. The information is in my room. Please take a look at it. Maybe there are some destinations that they recommend in Brazil. Here is my key card. See you later."

They left the hotel Saturday morning and had a race car driver as a taxi driver. He drove over the speed limit, passing everything on the highway. Most traffic was going into the city. It only took twenty minutes to get to the airport. However, the ride gave them a good view of the large city with its sprawling suburbs. They checked in for their two-hour TAM flight to Salvador that Deborah had arranged the night before.

Salvador is a city of two and a half million in the state of Bahia. Bahia, a religious destination for most visitors, has more than three hundred churches and thousands of Candomblé houses of worship that make the state a powerful source of religious faith. Many destinations in Bahia are well known for their religious attractions, including Salvador, Cachoeira, Santo Amaro, Bom Jesus da Lapa, Canudos, Monte Santo, and Candeias. Salvador has a mixture of individual homes, some nice and others in various stages of construction. There are also many groups of high-rise apartments.

Richard and Deborah stayed at Cocoo Hotel, and their rooms were like cocoons. The rooms had painted concrete floors and were more like a lower-class Motel 6 in the states with twenty-seven rooms on two floors. The hotel did have a small swimming pool, restaurant, and bar. Following getting settled in their rooms, the couple took a walk down to the beach, about two blocks away on the other side of a six-lane major road that paralleled the beach. The waves were high, and numerous surfers were out on the water. There were few people along the beach, and the area was far from town, but only a fifteen-minute taxi ride from the airport. There is another motel nearby called Hotel Jaguaribe Praia. The area around the hotels is called Praia, and the first thing Richard thought of was a jaguar near a cocoon. A small shopping mall is attached to the Jaguaribe hotel, but most of its shops are vacant. There is also a gas station nearby that has a small convenience store where the couple bought a few supplies, including water.

It was raining the next morning. Camilla, the beautiful young lady at the front desk, loaned the couple an umbrella that was indeed needed. Richard and Deborah boarded a Salvador tour bus that had arrived near their hotel. There were already about ten passengers who boarded at other hotels between theirs and the airport. The bus driver made three more hotel pickups and then proceeded into the city. On the double-decker bus, the couple soon found out how big the city is. Some of the places the bus went by before an hour's break at noon were Barra Lighthouse, Castro Alves Theatre, Forte de Sao Pedro, and Campo Grande. In the historic center were more than a thousand houses, churches, and monuments built since the sixteenth century, making Salvador the greatest collection of Baroque architectural heritage in Latin America.

The hour's midday break was spent at the Mercado Modelo, a big old structure housing many souvenir shops. Deborah bought a hat and a couple of postcards. Nearby was a marina that had a naval station on the shore, and next door was a beautiful church in need of repairs.

On the way back to the hotel, the driver took the group through the rest of the historic city and into the old town. The tourists had a thirty-minute break at Senhor do Bomfim Church, which sits on Mont Serrat, a high point in the city that provides a spectacular panoramic view. The final stop was at the Memorial of Irmã Dulce, which consists of a small church and museum. As a child, Irmã Dulce or "Sweet Sister" used to pray to Santo Antonio asking for a sign since she wanted to know if she should follow the path of religious life. At the age of thirteen, she began to help the poor, the sick, and the helpless. In 1933, she joined the Congregation of Missionary Sisters of the Immaculate Conception of the Mother of God in the Our Lady of Carmel Convent in the state of Sergipe. Upon her return to Bahia, she devoted the remainder of her life to helping the less fortunate. She died in Salvador in 1992 at the age of seventy-seven.

The next morning, the couple left for Relife, the most eastern city in South America. The ride was on an Azul Airlines Embraer 190 plane. About halfway to Recife, the landscape started to get flat and barren.

After arrival in Recife and a taxi ride to the Boa Viagem Praia Hotel, Richard and Deborah got settled into their room that had a partial view of the ocean across a major four-lane road. The twin bedroom was small and not too nice. Later they had a walk about, and it seemed like there were a lot of cars that were Chevrolets.

The next morning, the couple went back to the airport and caught their Azul flight to Fernando de Noronha Island at nine. About halfway, they had an hour's stopover in Natal, a large city with a broad river running through it to the ocean. Almost all the passengers got off, except Richard, Deborah, and ten others who continued on the flight to the island.

The plane arrived at Fernando de Noronha with an extremely hard landing as the short runway that was used for landings, takeoffs, and taxiing was in bad shape. The weather was very pleasant. There are several resorts on the island as well as three old fortresses and two churches. The main feature the couple saw from the small one-gate terminal was the extinct Morro do Pico volcano and the smaller Morro do Francês volcano. Richard and Deborah did not leave the airport, and after an hour layover, they returned to Recife.

On the return flight, Richard told Deborah, "Now we can check off Fernando de Noronha on the Traveler's Century Club's list of countries and territories. At least we got to see the island from the air during the plane's landing and takeoff."

"I think we should join the club after our return to my home."

The next morning, the couple took a city tour in a minivan with ten other visitors. The guide told the group that Recife has a population of five million whereas Fortaleza has three million. Sao Paulo and Rio are in first and second place. The weather was perfect, but the traffic was terrible. The group saw much of the big city and stopped at a couple of museums. One museum had mannequin replicas of famous people, including Elvis and the pope, and the other museum had groups of native mannequins. They also stopped at a big cathedral that overlooked the city of many high-rise apartments and office buildings. At noon, the group had a buffet lunch where there were many varieties of food, from Chinese and Japanese to American and Italian. Richard loaded his big plate with numerous dishes, including four pieces of sushi. There was a line of people waiting to pay and go to a table. Meanwhile, Richard ate the sushi and found out when he reached the cashier that she weighed the plate, and the charge was by weight. Richard had gotten some free sushi that Deborah kidded him about over their meal.

After lunch, the driver took the group on a long drive near the city's edge to visit the Ricardo Brennand Institute that covered a large area, with part of it being a fenced-in antelope herd. The mile-long driveway was lined with beautiful palm trees. The museum was housed in two buildings that looked like castles. Ricardo Brennand inherited a vast fortune from his father and collected everything, from paintings and sculptures to guns, jewelry, and clocks from around the world. All these things were displayed in a very museum-style manner. There was even a small collection of old-world globes that Richard particularly enjoyed. Outside the buildings were a fountain and some statues of lions.

The next morning, they traveled by taxi to Recife airport, which was nice with twenty-one gates and even three rooms with beds where a person can sleep for a price. The couple took a TAM flight to Fortaleza that was about an hour. After arrival at the good-sized Fortaleza airport, they took a thirty-minute taxi ride to Crocobeach Hotel. The five-star hotel is across a main road from the beach, which is lined with many restaurants with outdoor tables. The ocean waves were extremely high, and many surfers were being challenged to stay on their boards.

That afternoon, Richard and Deborah had a short walk along the beautiful beach and then got a taxi ride to the nearby Rio Mar indoor shopping center. Rio Mar has five stories in a large building where there are two major grocery stores and many shops selling everything, from furniture to clothing. There are also many restaurants, including Outback, McDonald's, Burger King, and Subway. The couple had a pizza dinner at Pizza Hut.

The next morning, after a nice buffet breakfast, the couple joined a group of ten for a four-hour city tour. The city is very dense with many high-rise apartments and business buildings, just like in Salvador and Recife. The tour bus went to an old dock area where two large wooden piers, built by the English many years ago, are located. Nearby was one of the oldest houses in Fortaleza. The guide told the group that it was built by a wealthy businessman who had seven sons. After each son grew up and got married, the father had homes constructed near his home as gifts to his sons. During World War II, there was a small American base near the new dock area. The final stop that morning was at a large old open-air structure of six stories housing at least a hundred vendors in their stalls selling everything that anyone would want as well as a restaurant where the group had lunch.

The old building was across the street from a fortress, next to a beautiful big cathedral.

The next morning, the couple went by taxi to the airport to catch their TAM Airlines flight to Rio. The flight took three hours, and they almost missed their flight to Brasilia. When Richard got his boarding pass, the TAM agent told him that he had a corridor seat, not an aisle seat; he thought it was an interesting word to use. Following their arrival in Brasilia and checking into the Mercure hotel, they both took a short nap in their separate rooms. After their rest, they had a long walk near the hotel as well as around the shopping mall across from the hotel. There was an excellent food court in the three-story shopping center, which included Burger King, McDonald's, and Subway. For dinner, they both had a healthy salad at Subway.

The city is very new and planned out with lots of high-rise hotels and office and apartment buildings going up in various areas of the city. There is not a downtown, but groups of buildings with shopping malls about ten miles apart connected by four-lane highways with roundabouts at various intersections. It appeared like the bus service was good, with lots of walking paths with underpasses.

On the second day, the couple took a city tour. The ten-person tour group went in a minibus. On the tour, the group stayed at eight places for around fifteen minutes each. The first stop was at a new church. Another stop was to see several government buildings. There were also some government buildings at another stop where there was the changing of the guards. After several more stops, the last one was at the President's Castle that had a fence around it about half a block from the building. There were guards at each corner of the fence and three flags in the middle outside the fence. Their guide told the group that when all flags are up, it means that the queen is at home. Of course, the king was at work in the nearby government offices.

As the couple left the hotel on their last morning in Brasilia, there was a lot of traffic that thinned out as they got closer to the airport. Near the airport, there were some areas with single-family homes and fewer high-rise buildings. The airport was nice and new, with the domestic and international airports next to each other. At the airport, they arranged a direct flight from Manaus to Lima instead of a long flight via San Paulo. The flight from Brasilia to Manaus was about three hours. Richard was trying to get some sleep on the plane because he did not sleep very well the previous night as there were some folks in the hallway making lots of noise. He had even called the front desk and complained. To make matters worse, early this morning, one of the hotel's neighbors kept saying his prayers very loud and repeating Jesus's name. This was about five. The noise did not bother Deborah, so on the flight, she read about Brazil in the airline magazine. In Manaus, they stayed at Sleep Inn for two nights.

After getting settled in her room, Deborah booked a tour for the next morning, leaving at nine. That night, they explored a little of the city and a small shopping center near the hotel where they had dinner. The next morning, they were picked up by taxi and taken to the tour meeting place. There were twenty in the tour group, and after boarding a double-decker boat, they crossed an area where the white Amazon and brown Negro rivers meet. The guide described the area in both English and Spanish. One thing he spoke about was the two-hundred different kinds of fish in the Amazon, including several different varieties of piranhas. Later the boat docked at a small village, where the group was divided into several smaller groups for short canoe trips into the backwaters of one of the rivers. The river was surrounded by lots of trees and other vegetation. On the canoe trip, the couple's group saw a small alligator and lots of birds. During the dry months, these small rivers dry up, and boats cannot travel on them. Following the canoe ride, the group returned to the boat and went back to town. The next day, the couple flew to Lima.

The couple arrived in Lima late in the afternoon. Richard was surprised that the Lima Airport was big, modern, and busy. After collecting their luggage, they took a taxi in heavy traffic to the Gran Hotel Bolivar. The hotel is in front of the Plaza San Martin. There is a statue of General San Martin in the middle of the plaza that is a block square and surrounded by several beautiful white buildings. One of the buildings is a hospital that used to be a railroad station. Next to the square is a Pizza Hut, and to the left of the hotel is a pedestrian walkway. There is a KFC next to the hotel entrance. During their stay, the couple ate at both places, including the hotel restaurant.

The Grand Bolivar, the first major modern hotel to be built in Lima, was constructed by an American company, Fred Tilley. Its area is 4,000 square yards, and it was finished on December 9, 1924. There is a 1920 Model T Ford in the lobby. Famous guests were William Faulkner; Ernest Hemingway; Ava Gardner; President Nixon's wife; Clark Gable; Yul Brynner; and Mick Jagger.

Following breakfast the first morning, Richard and Deborah took a long walk in the inner city. It was light-jacket weather. Lima does not get much rain, but the sky was overcast. In the afternoon, Deborah arranged a tour. A taxi picked up the couple at the hotel at two and took them south across town in about thirty minutes in heavy traffic to Miraflores. Deborah took several pictures of the seaside while they waited for the tour van and guide. Two ladies from Ireland joined them as well as their guide. Jason was a nice young man who spoke excellent English. After the van came and the drive started, he told the foursome about the city and country. He said, "There are eleven million people in Lima, and it is divided into forty-three districts. Peru has a population of thirty-two million people. After slavery was abolished, many Chinese came to work here. There is even a Chinatown in Lima. The main industries in the country are mining, fishing, and agriculture."

Following the tour, the couple had a wonderful dinner in the hotel restaurant and discussed the events of the day. Richard thanked her for arranging such a wonderful trip. She said, "I have not been here since I was in college, and I do have more plans for us during the next couple of weeks. The day after tomorrow, we will go to Trujillo, then Cusco and Machu Picchu."

After dinner, Richard walked Deborah to her room and gave her a loving hug with kisses on both cheeks and his sleep-well wishes.

Following a late breakfast, the couple took a long walk to the end of the pedestrian street where the cat park is located. Deborah took many pictures of the magnificent old buildings and churches. In the afternoon, they went on another tour with Jason and the van driver. This time, their traveling companions were a couple from France who understood Spanish. The trip started in Miraflores again. The van driver first drove around Miraflores and then went south along the coast to a very deserted area where they toured the Pachacamac Citadel and the Sanctuary of the Pachacamac God, who was considered to be the creator of the universe by the ancient Andean people. The citadel has temples, pyramids, and palaces. The highlights were the Temple of the Sun, the Pachacamac Temple, and the "Acllahuasi" or Palace of the Virgins of the Sun (women were sacrificed there.) The group of six had a thirty-minute walk to the top of the Temple of the Sun, the highest point in the area. There everyone had a great view of several high hills with many homes on them. Next, they visited the historic center of Lima with its palaces, mansions, churches, and squares, as well as the monumental compound of San Francisco with its convent and catacombs. There the group saw at least a hundred skeletons, bones, and skulls. In the main square is a cathedral, bishop's palace, governor's palace, and city hall/parliament. A nearby park is home to over one hundred cats, and a large demonstration was taking place there over low wages.

That evening, after an early dinner at the nearby Pizza Hut, the couple walked from the hotel to the end of the pedestrian mall. The pedestrian walkway was packed with families out enjoying the evening as well as about a dozen street performers. There were three different guys looking a lot like Michael Jackson who sang and moved like him. Most impressive was a genie suspended in space over a teapot with no apparent props. Lots of vendors were walking around with trays of goods, mainly snacks, and some of the lady vendors had their small children on their backs. Every shop was closed, except casinos, pharmacies, a few small restaurants, KFC, and McDonald's. There were also lots of police near the government buildings at the end of the walkway. After the walk, the couple returned to their rooms to pack and retire for the night.

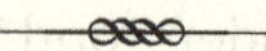

After a late breakfast, Richard and Deborah checked out at noon and took a taxi to the airport in much traffic. The airport is on the northern end of Lima and next to the ocean. The thirty-minute ride to the airport showed Richard again what a large city Lima is. Unfortunately, their scheduled flight to Trujillo was canceled, so they had a long wait until six in the busy airport for the next flight. The Avianca Peru plane landed in Trujillo a little past seven. The couple then took a twenty-minute ride in the hotel van to the very classy Casa Andina Premium hotel near the center of Trujillo.

Following breakfast the next morning, the couple started walking around the central part of Trujillo. On the walk, they passed a fellow who turned around and said, "John Czermak?"

The couple stopped and turned around. Richard said, "Excuse me."

"Don't you remember me, John? I am Durado. We went through graduate school together at the University of Colorado. Professor Harold Dalton was our PhD advisor."

"Now I vaguely remember you, and you might not have recognized me several weeks ago when I had a beard. Please excuse me, but I had a bad accident and lost my memory. Please tell me more about my life. But first let me introduce you to Dr. Deborah Klose. She is a medical doctor and saved my life at Cape Horn in Chile. Can we go somewhere and discuss this more?"

The threesome went to a nearby café and ordered coffee. Over coffee, Durado started his recollection of his friendship with John. "As I mentioned earlier, both of us went through graduate school at the University of Colorado and did our PhD research in the same laboratory. You made three visits here, the first one following a conference in Santiago, the second time when you and Margrit came before your trip to Cusco and Machu Picchu, and the third time three years ago, again following a conference in Santiago."

"Who is Margrit?" a surprised Czermak asked.

Durado laughed. "She is your wife, whom you married while in graduate school, and you have three children. At the time, you were working at Rocky Flats full-time and attending graduate school full-time. After graduating, you became the manager of Plutonium Chemistry Research and Development at Rocky Flats. A few years later, you had some hard times when you lost your security clearance. Then you went to Australia to teach for three years, followed by returning to a DOE facility in California. Your last visit here was when you worked in California. Amy, your oldest daughter, is married, and both Eric and Lorrie are studying at the University of Colorado."

"I am very shocked that I have a wife and three children. But now I am starting to remember a few things. On my last visit here, you and your driver took me to your tanning factory and out of the city to see the ruins of an old fortress. I also remember accidentally running into friends years ago, just like I ran into you today. The first time was accidentally meeting a Russian friend in a Toronto restaurant following a trip to the High Arctic. The other time was when I was waiting at a train station in a small German village. I looked across the tracks, and there was a former student of mine from Australia. We exchanged greetings before one of the trains arrived."

Deborah spoke up and said, "Richard, I mean John, has retrograde amnesia that was probably caused by accidental brain damage after being washed up on shore during the night of a violent storm off Cape Horn. We assumed he was in his yacht that sank. He did not have the ability to retrieve information that was acquired before his accident. Retrograde amnesia is usually temporary and sometimes can be treated by exposure to the location of events prior to the amnesia. People suffering from amnesia can recall immediate information and form new memories. They can also retain substantial linguistic, intellectual, and social skills despite impairments in the ability to recall specific information before the amnesia. Also, most forms of amnesia fix themselves without being treated.

"A week after John's accident, I told him that we should wait before we seek professional help in Santiago since his previous memories may slowly return. I live in a remote location on Navarino Island near Port Williams, the most southerly city in the world. My few friends call me a hermit as I have little contact with the outside world since my husband died almost two years ago. Thus, I had no knowledge of John's accident from the news. John did start remembering a few things about Santiago while we were there last week, and I am sure now that he will start remembering more about his previous life and hopefully will get his memory back with your help, but perhaps not the very unpleasant events of his past."

John told Durado, "Now I vaguely remember that I am a professor at Clemson University in South Carolina, and there I used my middle name James instead of John. I was on an expedition in Antarctica with two of my graduate students and a postdoc from China whom I married on the ship. I do not remember if Margrit died or we divorced. On the way back from the expedition, my graduate student from Russia and I accidentally fell overboard near Cape Horn during a violent storm. Since my student could not swim, I tried to rescue him, but he disappeared into the raging waters. By then, the ship was too far away to swim to, but I could vaguely see that land was closer. It was extremely hard to swim through the large waves. About halfway to shore, I was about to give up, but Jesus suddenly appeared and told me I must continue to swim ashore and not die because I still have too much to contribute to the world. The next thing I remember is Deborah attending to me the next morning on the rocky beach."

Following more discussions of Cermak's life, the threesome ordered lunch. Following a light meal, Durado said, "If you agree, let me call my driver and he can take us for a drive around the city, followed by seeing the ruins of the old fortress. Then we can return to the main square where we met this morning. John, or should I start calling you John James, we can then show Deborah the beautiful cathedral and several old buildings surrounding the park. As you may remember, James, nearby is an old church that was converted into a small university building where I received my undergraduate degree in chemical engineering. This is also where Professor Dalton taught on his sabbatical. This building is now part of the university campus where several new buildings were built."

Following the drive around the city center, Durado told the couple that he must return to work. They agreed to meet the next day at the hotel so Durado could show them his farm and home as well as his bottling company. James thanked him with a hug for bringing some of his memory back. He told Deborah that he was very tired and would return to the hotel, skip dinner, and make an early night of it. He asked her to see more of the city and do some shopping if she wished.

After a late breakfast the next day, Durado and his driver picked the couple up and went to his bottling plant for a tour. The plant produced bottled water and soft drinks. Next, they went out of the city to his farm. The farm has a small house where a couple of workers stay, several farm buildings, and a big swimming pool in the backyard. The main business on the property is raising guinea pigs for several meat markets and growing asparagus for canning. Following the tour of the large farm, the lady of the house prepared a nice lunch for them. James thought the meat was chicken, but Durado told him after the meal that the meat was guinea pig, not chicken. James replied that it was an excellent meal. The final stop in the afternoon was at Durado's home in the city. He had inherited the fifty-year-old house from his parents. The most impressive room in the home was Durado's office with a library. He must have had over a hundred books, including a couple that James had written.

The three sat at a large table, and while drinking tea, Durado and James started talking about their time at the University of Colorado. Durado said, "James, do you remember the time when you were distilling some extremely smelly liquid in the lab, and it overheated and sprayed all over the lab bench? Everyone on our floor had to evacuate because of the horrible odor of the chemical."

"Yes, I remember that well since I thought my research days were over. But I cleaned up the mess, and you and the other students returned to their laboratories. The other thing that stands out in my mind is going to an American Chemical Society meeting in Mexico City. Professor Dalton and his wife were with us as well as Margrit. We had been warned by Dalton not to drink the water. However, at the opening ceremony, they were serving Margaritas. Mine was warm, so without thinking, I went over to where they were serving drinks and asked the bartender to chip off some ice from a big block of ice and put it in my drink. After drinking the margarita, I realized the ice was probably made from tap water. Sure enough, I was sick all night and did that get any sleep." Everyone laughed.

"Durado, I think we need to go back to the hotel and get ready for our return to Santiago via Lima tomorrow morning. I can't tell you how great it was to see you and for bringing most of my memory back."

Deborah also thanked Durado as the couple got into the car for their return to the hotel.

The couple left Trujillo early the next morning for Lima. During the flight, Deborah started the conversation. "As you know, I had arranged a trip to Cusco and Machu Picchu, but with you discovering your identity from Durado, I think it is best to cancel the remaining visits so we can go to the American embassy in Santiago and arrange a passport for your return to South Carolina. I am also sorry I did not do more to help you regain your memory. I guess I wanted you to stay with me forever."

Following their return to Santiago late in the afternoon, they went to the American embassy. After a long wait, James explained to one of the officials that he lost his memory for almost a year because of an accident and now it has mostly returned. He told the official that the lady with him is a medical doctor and can vouch for his story. He then got fingerprinted and his picture taken. Since the State Department has a file on James, they gave him a copy along with a new passport.

After checking into a hotel near the airport, James planned, with Deborah's help, to fly to Atlanta the next morning. After calling Clemson University and leaving a note for Ying to meet him at the Atlanta airport, he went to the hotel's business center and Googled his name. There he was surprised to find considerable information about his professional career. He printed out a copy of several entries and took them to the room he was sharing with Deborah. He showed the Google and State Department's information to a surprised Deborah. She was amazed by his professional accomplishments and the awards he had received. He told her that hopefully his return to his family and work could bring back all his memories.

After breakfast the next morning, he sadly told Deborah goodbye and thanked her for all her help with a loving hug and kiss, saying, "I love you dearly, but I hope you understand that I have a wife waiting for me in South Carolina. I will miss you so much."

With tears in her eyes, Deborah managed to say, "I also love you and thank you for the work you have done for me as well as bringing so much happiness into my life this past year. Goodbye, my dear. Until we meet again."

III

Upon James's arrival in Atlanta, he did not have any checked luggage to look for since he had been using Richard's clothes during his stay at Deborah's. He did have a small carry-on containing some toiletries. Thus, he went directly to immigration. After the agent checked him into the country and stamped his passport, he asked James to wait a minute. He came back a couple of minutes later with another man. The other official asked James to follow him, and they went to an immigration office. There the man identified himself as an FBI agent and showed James his credentials. The agent started asking questions about his trip to Antarctica and his last night aboard the ship. After James told him of his ordeal and his stay with Deborah, the agent said that their interviews with his wife and student confirmed that the death of his Russian student was accidental. The agent thanked James for his cooperation.

Then James breezed through customs and went to the arrival hall to be met by an overjoyed and tearful Ying and Shanna. There were a few minutes of loving embrace of the couple, followed by James receiving a hug from Shanna. The ladies were overjoyed with happiness that James was alive and well and had returned as everyone had assumed he and Alex were both lost at sea.

Following the happy reunion, the threesome went to an airport café to catch up on each other's lives. After going to a quiet area of the café with their coffee, Ying started the conversation. "After our arrival back in South Carolina almost a year ago, very distraught, we tried to resume our lives. Meanwhile, we continued to make inquiries about the ship's owner and captain.

The ship officials all contended that you and Alex fell overboard without life jackets in the terrible storm and certainly drowned and were eaten by sharks. After a month back at Clemson, I was appointed lecturer in the chemistry department, and Shanna and a couple of your other students graduated. Shanna plans on continuing with a postdoc position in the chemistry department."

James continued the conversation, describing the last year with Deborah and their travels. The threesome then left the airport and returned to Pendleton in Shanna's car. James's son and two daughters surprised him at his and Ying's home, and they had a wonderful reunion, with James telling everyone about his time in Chile and the kind and generous Deborah. Ying and Shanna prepared a delicious dinner that everyone enjoyed with their lively conversations. The three young adults spent two nights at the Pendleton home before returning to Colorado.

Following the departure of his children, James drove to his department's building at the Research Park to be greeted by fellow faculty members, staff, and students. They had a long reunion, with James summarizing his year in South America. The exchange of information continued in the break room for the individuals who did not have to go to their classes. After the lengthy reunion, James went to his office to catch up on his mail and emails.

Later James found out that his remaining students had been transferred to the supervision of other professors. Late in the afternoon, the dean of engineering and science called him and welcomed him back. He told James that the chairman of the chemistry department had retired and that he would like James to take over the department. James readily accepted the change in jobs.

The next morning, as James was packing his books and papers to move to the chemistry building, a CNN representative with a cameraman and several newspaper reporters came to his office, wanting to get the story of his ordeal. In the following days, most newspapers around the world would print his story, including the Russian newspaper *Pravda*.

Following James's return, the couple resumed their leisurely routine. Periodically, they hosted a dinner party at their home for their students and a few faculty members. Of course, the two students living in their basement were always invited to these dinners. The Czermaks also participated in a dinner rotation party with their nearest neighbors. The young lady next door, who was also a faculty member at Clemson, had adopted a five-year-old Chinese girl; of course, Ying saw the girl every chance she got. Their other activities in the area were working out at the gym, swimming, and playing golf, tennis, chess, and pool. They also attended plays at the nearby Clemson Playhouse and went to some of the Clemson football games during the season. On weekends, they took short car trips or worked in their garden. James also renewed his love of photography.

Several weeks after his return to his old life, James received a letter from Deborah:

Dear Richard, I mean James (ha ha), I know you have at least four other names besides Richard and James: John, Johnny, Jim, and Jimmy. What are the others? I hope this letter finds you well and enjoying the resumption of your life with your family and job. I wrote this letter after my return from our trip together but waited to mail it since I was not sure about contacting you. After we went our separate ways in Santiago, I went onto Cusco and Machu Picchu, both UNESCO World Heritage Sites, in the hope it would ease the pain of losing you. It did help a little since the trip was great with one exciting part. The day after you departed, I flew to Cusco via Lima. The city was the historic capital of the Inca Empire from the thirteenth to the sixteenth century. After my arrival at a first-class hotel and since Cusco is 11,000 feet in elevation, I started drinking lots of Coca tea which is supposed to help with altitude sickness. I spent the first full day wandering around the beautiful city with its Inca and Spanish colonial buildings. I especially liked Sacsayhuaman, the Inca ceremonial fortress, with its stacks of beautiful large boulders of all shapes and sizes stacked tightly together. One wonders how the Incas crafted the large blocks. The greatest thing about dinner that night at the hotel restaurant was drinking a couple of pisco sours. They are sure good!

Early the following day, I went to Machu Picchu via army helicopter since a bad rainstorm had washed out the train tracks in places. The ride was quite exciting and was the first time I had been in a helicopter. Machu Picchu, a fifteenth-century Inca citadel, is breathtaking and in excellent shape. I greatly enjoyed walking through its three primary structures, Intihuatana, Temple of the Sun, and Room of the Three Windows. Most of the outlying buildings have been restored. It was fun and interesting, although the altitude was starting to get me in the afternoon. In the evening, I helicoptered back to Cusco for the night and returned home the next morning. I miss you. Please stay in touch. Love, Deborah.

Near Christmas, Deborah received a card from James that included a summary of his activities and holiday plans. He also wrote that his children were coming to Pendleton to spend an early Christmas with him and Ying. They both were excited about their visit since they did not see much of them these days.

A few weeks later, James received another letter from Deborah:

Dear James, I hope you are well and now completely settled down in your old life. I am missing you so much. One thing you did for me was to renew my interest in traveling. On that note, I just returned from a trip to Ecuador. My good friend Coni, whom you met in Santiago, invited me to go on the three-week trip that was sponsored by Global Exchange, a humanitarian, non-profit organization located in San Francisco. I took your advice and started keeping a diary. Love and best wishes, Deborah.

James wrote back, inviting her to come to Clemson when possible so he could introduce her to Ying and their friends and show her around South Carolina.

James's new office and research laboratories were on the fourth floor of the Hunter Chemistry Building that was located about the middle of campus. The first floor of the building had general chemistry laboratories, the second floor some teaching and administrative rooms, the third a mix of teaching and research laboratories, and the top floor mostly research laboratories. Besides a secretary and small staff, James supervised a dozen faculty members, including Ying. He also had two new graduate students and would teach an actinide chemistry class in the fall.

James and Ying usually drove their own cars to campus, James in a Chevy convertible and Ying in Margrit's Smart car. They both took the steep and curvy Queen Street out of Pendleton. Ying's office and laboratory were on the second floor of the Hunter Building, and she and James usually met for lunch in the nearby campus restaurant. If Ying does not prepare dinner, they go into Pendleton's old town square where there are several restaurants, including the Plantation House.

One warm and sunny morning, the Czermaks left the Smart car at Rick's garage for two days of repairs. Then they both went to work in James's convertible with the top down. After arrival in the parking lot, James discovered that the convertible top would not go up. So they left the car in the parking lot all day with the top down. At the end of the workday, James phoned Ying and told her that he needed to work late. He recommended that she went home for dinner and that he would call her for a ride home when he finished his work. It had just gotten dark as Ying went to the parking lot and started driving James's car home.

Several hours later, James tried to call Ying without success. While he was waiting to reach her by phone, he turned on his office television to hear the local news. The first story was about a hit-and-run accident near Pendleton on Queen Street. They showed a burned-out and upside-down Chevy convertible down in a ravine surrounded by trees, with a fire truck and several police cars on the road. James hysterically jumped up as he recognized his car. The newsman reported that the driver burned to death and that the accident was under investigation. With tears in his eyes, James frantically called the police about the accident. He told the operator that it was his wife who died in the car crash on Queen Street and that someone should come to his building to take him to the tragic accident scene. After arriving at the accident site by police car, James was informed that the remains of the driver were only ashes and they found the hit-and-run vehicle, a large pickup that had been stolen earlier in Anderson.

An anguished James did not get any sleep that night and found out in the morning that the fire had started with a Molotov cocktail and that the flames ignited the gas tank. The police now concluded that Ying was murdered. James spent the morning wondering who would want to kill Ying. She was liked and loved by everyone who knew her. But did she have an enemy back in China who came to South Carolina to kill her?

With tears in his eyes, James made a few difficult phone calls to his children, Ying's daughter, and several close friends to inform them of Ying's tragic death. He also told the dean that he would need to take a week or so away from campus to arrange a memorial for her. The dreadful time he had after Margrit's death was reoccurring.

Ying's and James's families came to the funeral, as well as many friends, fellow faculty members, and students. They had a wonderful memorial. The following day, James sent out the following email:

Dear family and friends, thank you so much for your thoughtful cards and emails on the passing of Ying. I received almost fifty emails and cards of condolences from loved ones and friends, and over twenty people attended her funeral and memorial. Your cards and/or presence at the memorial gave me much comfort. Of course, it was great to see at the party Ying's daughter who came all the way from Vancouver, Canada, with her family. Ying was loved by many people. Her memorial letter is attached. Love and best wishes, John James Czermak.

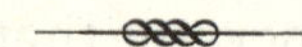

On a cold and windy Saturday night, it was unusual to find anyone in the chemistry building. Earlier, Czermak had been showing his graduate student, Igor Medvedev, how to operate the gas chromatograph/mass spectrometer systems. Now he was performing his own experiment with the instrument. So engrossed with the analysis, he was unaware that behind him, the laboratory door had opened. An unseen hand tossed a Molotov cocktail into the room, which exploded at once, shooting flames in every direction. The sea of flames created an inferno, and within seconds, fire was licking at James's feet and legs. Poisonous fumes had permeated the air, blinding, chocking, and disorienting him.

As he was crawling across the laboratory floor, he now knew for certain that the car crash that killed Ying was meant for him, just like the raging inferno around him. James managed to crawl to one of the windows, opened it, and jumped from the ledge to a nearby tree. After climbing to the ground, he saw a man running toward the street. James dashed after him but barely got to the car as it was pulling away. James did get a good look at the driver and remembered the car and license plate number. Several minutes after calling 911, a fire truck arrived along with two police cars.

After the fire was out, the police captain arrived and asked James to come to the nearby police station for questioning. At the station, James told the captain all he knew about the fire, including his conclusion that someone was trying to kill him. Then the captain got a report on the assassin's car. "It was a stolen car and was just found abandoned in Anderson just like the truck that killed your wife. We should be able to get fingerprints in the car to match up with the ones obtained from the stolen truck. However, the fingerprints in the truck did not match any in the police or FBI files."

IV

One day, James heard a knock on his office door. He went to the door and found a lady who looked a lot like Marlene Monroe. He invited her into his office. After he shut the door, she pulled out her credentials and introduced herself, "I am CIA agent Kim Carn, and I have replaced retired agent Tim Smith as your contact. I know he told you that another agent would be contacting you for your continued assistance with the CIA. I am so sorry to hear about your accident in Chile, the loss of your wife, and now the fire and attempts on your life. Is this a good time to discuss how you can continue to assist us?"

"Yes, I have some time now."

"First, here is a copy of my business card for you. As you can see, it only has my name on it, and of course, Kim Carn is not my real name. I have read the large file we have on you, and I was also briefed by Tim before he retired. You deserve a big thanks for all the work you did for us in the past. However, I want to know if you are still willing to take some government-paid trips, some that could be dangerous, to obtain certain information for us, mostly about nuclear weapons proliferation."

James agreed to cooperate and serve his country as best he could.

"Your CIA assignment on your trip to Antarctica over a year ago was to find out if someone aboard the ship was passing nuclear weapons information to a small group of nuclear scientists from the Argentina Nuclear Energy Agency. During the past year, we have obtained enough information to conclude that Argentina was not trying to develop the bomb, but now

Brazil is suspect. Thus, we would like you to take a trip to visit your friend at the Brazilian Atomic Energy site in Sao Paulo and find out all you can about their possible involvement with nuclear weapons. We know you have been to the site before as an IAEA expert, and you reported that you saw a secure area where Uranium enrichment was taking place. You are welcome to use this trip to visit your friend who saved your life on Cape Horn."

At the end of the meeting, Kim swore James to secrecy, never to discuss their meetings, CIA assignments, or relationship with her to anyone, just like he had done for Tim.

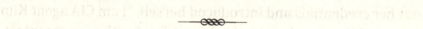

Travel funds arrived for James two weeks later from the Penny Group in San Francisco, CIA's financial front. The day after receiving the money and explaining to the dean that he needed some travel time to give an invited talk in Brazil as well as spend some vacation time in South America that may help him overcome the loss of Ying, he drove to the Atlanta airport. As he was waiting to catch the subway to the international terminal, a good-looking young lady got off the train, looked at James, and said, "Hello, John, I remember you from the Habitat for Humanity trip to the Dominican Republic."

"Katelin, what a small world to see you here."

"John, you have not changed a bit these many years, still handsome as ever. That was sure two weeks of hard work building the cinder brick home in that small Dominican Republic village for the family of six living in a shack."

"Yes, the project was a great experience, and it was rewarding to see the mother with her five young children move into the new home. I do not think today that I could carry two cinder blocks at a time for those many days."

"John, I am sorry, but I need to get to the gate to catch my flight to Los Angeles. It was great to see you. Goodbye and take care."

After a departing hug, James waved as she was running to her gate.

On the flight from Atlanta to Santiago, James had the aisle seat, and the middle seat was vacant. The young lady at the window introduced herself to James. Sara had just graduated from Florida State University with a degree in astronomy. She was heading to Machu Picchu to walk the Inca Trail in three days. She said that she would be meeting other friends there and that they hired a guide that had tents and camping gear. In the fall, she would start a PhD program in astronomy at Columbia University. Her goal was to be an astrophysicist and professor.

James asked her, "Do you know Professor Karl Chopen?"

"Well, everyone at the university knows of this famous professor of chemistry. I took his course and loved it because of his interesting style of lecturing. He always put several jokes in his talks."

After arriving in Puerto Williams via Santiago and Punta Arenas, James was met by Deborah in the small arrival hall of the airport. She was overjoyed to see him, and they both went to her car after a loving embrace. On the drive, she told James how sorry she was about Ying's tragic death. They both exchanged stories about some of their activities since James left Chile many months ago. After the couple arrived at Deborah's home, Mary and Eduardo came over for a wonderful reunion. Later over dinner, James told Deborah about his trip to see her, his plans to go to Brazil, and more about his life in South Carolina.

"Deb, since my memory has almost completely returned, I will tell you some major things about my life, some of which I have told you before after our meeting with Durado in Trujillo. Over a decade ago, I spent three years at the International Atomic Energy Agency in Vienna, Austria. Before then I worked at the Rocky Flats Plant, near Denver, Colorado, where triggers for nuclear weapons are made. In my previous work at the plant, I was a major contributor to the development of the neutron bomb. In Vienna, KGB agents were trying to get information on the bomb from me via Margrit, my first wife, who became romantically involved with Andrei Pushkin, thought by the CIA to be a KGB agent. Realizing the futility of their relationship, Margrit told me about Andrei and how they both had on several occasions unsuccessfully attempted to terminate it. Later, Andrei committed suicide, and Margrit was beside herself with grief, but that event saved our marriage. Later, I was to find out that Andrei had faked his suicide and left Vienna for Canada to start a new life. After leaving the agency, Margrit and I returned to our home in Arvada, Colorado, and resumed a close, loving relationship that had been severely damaged in Vienna. I also returned to my former job at Rocky Flats as manager of Plutonium Chemistry Research and Development.

"About this time, I traveled a lot to conferences around the world and to Vienna and Moscow to have meetings with my two Russian coauthors on a series of books we were writing for the IAEA. Following more contacts with my Russian colleagues, I was informed that a background investigation had been conducted by the Department of Energy and the FBI. This investigation resulted in losing my security clearance. I then went to Australia to teach for three years and later to work in California for four years. Andrei came to California and tried to renew his relationship with Margrit and kill me, but instead, he accidentally killed Margrit. I found out later that he committed suicide in Canada and told his son Alex in his dying breath that I had shot him.

"At that point, I wanted to start a new life and left California for a teaching job at Clemson University. As you know, I even started using my middle name. I enjoyed the academic life very much, supervising several students and teaching actinide chemistry. I even purchased the car and home that Margrit liked. The automobile is a small Smart car, and the home has three bedrooms upstairs and two downstairs with bathrooms in all the bedrooms, plus living and dining rooms, and kitchens on both floors. I rent the basement to two graduate students in my department.

"Alex joined my research group using a different last name. I did not know that he was Andrei's youngest son. In early January, I took him, Ying, and my student Shana with me on an expedition to Antarctica where we would do some ice sampling. By that time, I had fallen in love with Ying. We were married by the ship's captain as we crossed the Antarctic Circle. The following night, me, Alex, and a dozen other brave souls camped out on Hovgaard Island where I had an attempt on my life. On the last night of the trip, as we were crossing the Drake Passage and heading past Cape Horn, the sea was very rough, and large waves were coming over the front of the ship. Alex met me at the stern of the ship and with difficulty admitted that his real name was Alexander Pushkin, that his father was the one who had a love affair with Margrit in Vienna, and that his father had cut the brake line on my car in California with the intention of killing me and not Margrit. I was shocked as Alex admitted that on the camping night, it was he who had kicked the rock that was holding me and my sleeping bag in place. As I was sliding down the hill, Alex told me that he was immediately sorry for what he had done and ran to stop me but that I had managed to stop myself at the edge of the hill. His father shot himself in his home in Canada where Alex was staying, and his father told him in his dying breath that I had shot him and that he should kill me. I sternly told Alex that I did not kill his father and had an alibi. Alex agreed and told me he learned that morning that his father had committed suicide. Alex told me that he was extremely sorry that he had tried to kill me. At the end of our conversation, I told Alex that under the circumstances, I would forgive him. My last words were for him to come and give me a big bear hug. Alex happily jumped over and gave me an embrace that caused both of us to accidentally fall over the back of the ship into the rough, freezing ocean."

After finishing dinner, James told Deborah how much he missed her and that a day does not go by without him thinking of her. He then took her in his arms and gave her a long romantic kiss. Following the embrace, James said, "If you agree, someday

I would like to marry you, but first I must find out who is trying to kill me so that you do not come into harm's way. I told the authorities that one of my students is a Russian, but I have no reason why he would want to kill me. The only other persons I thought would want me dead would be Andrei's oldest son and/or Andrei's brother since they might think I killed both Andrei and Alex. The FBI did go through government records and reviewed the names of all visiting Russians the past year, but there were no Pushkins on the list."

"James, I love you so much, and of course, I want to marry you. It would be a dream come true." The couple continued to talk until bedtime when James was invited into Deborah's room for the night.

The next morning, James asked Deborah if she would like to come with him to Brazil. Of course, she agreed and started making arrangements to join him on a flight to Sao Paulo via Punta Arenas and Santiago the next day.

During the flight from Santiago to Sao Paulo, James told Deborah about his second time to Brazil when he attended a nuclear conference in Maresias, a small tourist town next to the South Atlantic Ocean. He also related to her about some other South American trips.

"As you know Sao Paulo is a large city, stretching out for miles to house its ten million inhabitants. After arriving in Sao Paulo, I boarded a bus to Maresias. The bus ride took four hours, and the highway went from eight lanes to four lanes to two lanes. The curvy two-lane road went through beautiful tree-covered hills and mountains. There were lots of palm and banana trees and even an incredibly beautiful waterfall dropping from the mountaintop to the valley below. As the bus got close to the South Atlantic Ocean, I could see a beautiful island in the distance and wonderful beaches with lots of sunbathers and swimmers. We went through one big city and then several small towns with dirt side streets. Most of the houses in the towns were made from cinder blocks, and a lot of them were partly built but still lived in. After reaching Maresias, the bus stopped in front of the Beach Hotel, and guess what, it faced the beach, but I did not get a beachfront room, but one near the main road that goes through Maresias.

"Late on Sunday afternoon, I took a walk on the beach before the reception of the conference. There were lots of sunbathers, swimmers, and surfers around. The Fourth International Nuclear Chemistry Congress was held across the street from the hotel in a conference building. I was one of twenty International Scientific Board members. Margrit and I attended the second such conference in Cancun, Mexico, years ago.

"There was a conference opening ceremony that night, followed by a reception. At the social, I met some of my friends that I have known for many years. Of course, Cecee, whom you will meet in Sao Paulo, was there. I have known her the longest, and the last time we were together was at a conference in Hawaii where Margrit was with me. The first time was when I was in Sao Paulo as an IAEA expert to visit her nuclear research site and advise her how to process americium contained on the tips of used lightning rods.

"I attended the conference talks all day on Monday with all the attendees, including Cecee, Ana, and a couple of their fellow workers. In the evening before dinner, I had a nice walk around the little village of Mareisas. The weather was great. It was hard to believe it was winter in the United States. The small town has lots of hotels and restaurants, and the main road through town parallels the beach. There were more presentations the next day at the conference.

"Wednesday was a free day, and I took an excursion with ten other conference attendees via speedboat to Ilhabela Island. It is about sixty miles around the beautiful island, and the population is about ten thousand. The occupants use to grow and export coffee, sugarcane, and bananas, but now they rely mostly on tourism and fishing. In the early days, slaves were imported to cut sugarcane.

"After arriving at a town called No Name, we had a wet boarding on a Flex boat and about an hour's rough ride on the ocean to the farthest place we would visit on the island, a cove called Eustaguio, with four houses. On the way over, we saw a whale, and a little later, the driver stopped the boat, and our guide asked if everyone was feeling okay on the wild ride. I then pretended like I was vomiting and got some laughs from my fellow passengers. At the cove, we had some snacks and climbed an embankment using a rope to see the bay on the other side. There was a young boy and a much younger, beautiful girl, playing on the beach and a small kiosk with drinks for sale. A few of the folks swam, and the couple from the Netherlands snorkeled. The rest of the group just sat around talking during the hour's stay.

"On the return to port, the driver went a little slower and stopped at several small beach areas with a few houses. I commented to the guide that it must have been expensive to bring the building materials in by boat. The driver said in broken English that most of the wood as well as the rocks were obtained from the island. One small community had a small school. Our guide told us that in the small village, there were several big rocks that made loud noises if you hit them hard. This phenomenon later saved the people one night in the past from an attacking group of pirates to ward off their surprise attack. We were also told that there was a shipwreck nearby many decades ago. The ship had the same design as the Titanic and was built by the same company in Belfast, Ireland. All were lost aboard the ship, but its sinking was not nearly as known as the Titanic disaster. When our group returned to No Name, we had lunch and a short walk around the city center and then returned to the conference center by bus.

"In the evening following dinner, there was the same singer-guitar player we had on Monday, but this time, the lady that controlled the meeting accompanied him singing. She was great, and Ana also joined her for a couple of songs. At the end, the lady asked us if we wanted to come up, one at a time, and sing a song representing our country's culture. First, she said how about someone from the US. Since I was sitting at the front table with Ana, she and the rest of the audience urged me to get up and sing a song. Reluctantly, I got up and did a wonderful dancing and singing rendition of Elvis's 'You Ain't Nothing but a Hound Dog.' My performance was a big hit as I also had the audience singing, wailing, and clapping during the end. Several other conference attendees also sang some good songs representative of their country."

"James, I did not know you were so talented, but of course, I have always enjoyed your humor."

"Part of the lady singer's job during the conference was to give the speaker a note that read, 'One-minute left.' As the singer was thanking us at the end, I passed her a note with 'One minute left' written on it. She laughed and told the audience of my antics, and everyone had a final good laugh.

"The next morning, she told me that her dad was a successful singer, and he did not want his daughter to follow him in his footsteps. Thus, he encouraged her to go into business studies, which included running conferences.

"After the closing ceremony, I left for the Sao Paulo airport via bus. The ride back seemed more spectacular. The jungle-covered mountains, some trees with flowers, and the high and long waterfall made the four-hour ride seem much shorter."

"James, that sure sounds like a wonderful trip and a great conference."

The couple arrived at the Sao Paulo airport where James's Brazilian friend Cecee and her husband, Walt, greeted them. The foursome then went to Cecee and Walt's home for a late dinner, where they got caught up on each other's activities over the past several years.

Following a night of restful sleep at their host's home and an early-morning breakfast, the foursome went to see the interesting sites in the city. After lunch, Deborah and Walt continued the city tour while Cecee and James went to her institute for James to give an invited lecture. After the seminar, Cecee took James on a tour of the research laboratories and the institute's nuclear center. The center has an experimental nuclear power reactor and an area where uranium enrichment research is being performed. On the way back to Cecee and Walt's home, James candidly asked her about activities relating to building a nuclear weapon somewhere at her institute. She assured him that no such activities were taking place and there was no intention of the government undertaking such a project. She continued, "If there were any efforts to build a bomb, my colleagues and I would know about it. Furthermore, I think if Brazil had the bomb, some other South American countries would do the same thing, especially Venezuela."

After three nights in Sao Paulo, James and Deborah flew to Buenos Aires. During the flight, James told Deborah about a trip he made to Morocco and Mali.

"The North African adventure started in Casablanca, an interesting city of seven million people. On my only day there, I had a walk around the old city center to see the main and historic sites. There is even a Rick's Café, like the one in the movie *Casablanca* with Humphrey Bogart, where I had lunch. The movie is one of my favorites. I especially like what Rick said a couple of times when toasting to Ilsa with a drink, 'Here's looking at you, kid.' Have you seen the movie?"

"Yes, of course. I also love the movie, especially Sam's singing 'As Time Goes By' and his piano playing."

"Early the next morning, I was awakened by the call to prayer. Thus, I caught an earlier train to Marrakesh. On the trip, we passed through several small towns, all between lots of green farmland with roaming cattle. Following my arrival in Marrakesh, I checked into the nice Ibis hotel. Across the street from the hotel is a large and beautiful opera house.

"At breakfast the next day, there was a guy playing the piano, and one of the songs he played surprised me. It was 'Santa Claus Is Coming to Town.' Later, I took a horse and buggy ride through the old walled city and saw many interesting buildings. A large mosque was the main attraction. In the afternoon, I took a bus tour outside the old city. Marrakesh is very modern with many new buildings. On the two tours, I saw many lovely people walking about and beautiful children playing. In general, the people seem very well off, but there was a significant amount of people asking for money, especially elderly women and mothers with babies.

"After two nights in Marrakech, I boarded a train back to Casablanca and then transferred to another train to Tangier. The ride to Tangier was spectacular. The land was very green with lots of small lakes, wheat and grass fields, wildlife, birds, farm animals, and small villages with many people slowly building their half-completed homes. Rolling hills appeared during the last hour of the ride. I stayed at the Ibis hotel for two nights.

"Following a late breakfast the next day, I had a walk around the old city and then back to the hotel along the beach. The old city was interesting. After lunch, I went on another beach walk in the opposite direction of the morning walk and saw that there were lots of new construction in this part of the city and a circus next to the train station featuring tigers that were in small cages.

"We should start a campaign for a worldwide boycott of circuses and zoos where all the innocent animals are caged. They need their natural wide-open spaces which game reserves and national parks can provide. When you come to the US, I will take you to the Wild Animal Sanctuary near Denver, Colorado."

"That sounds great, and I agree with you that wild animals need their freedom."

"Tangier is certainly not catering to tourism as in Marrakesh, which has lots of American fast-food places and clean and modern restaurants. Casablanca is in between these two cities in amenities. I had not seen any tourists, and the hotel seems to have only a few businessmen staying there.

"I had hoped to take a ferry to Gibraltar, but it did not work out, so I returned to Casablanca for the night. The next morning, I took the train to their airport for my flight to the capital of Mali. Bamako is located on the banks of the Niger River. That waterway flows for hundreds of miles, winding through the savannahs of West Africa, eventually emptying into the ocean. It serves as the main channel for travel and commerce in the whole sub-Saharan area. But Bamako itself is very unimpressive in appearance and functionality even though it is home to almost two million people.

"Following my arrival in Bamako, I left for Mopi with twelve passengers and two pilots on a two-propeller Air Mali plane. The flight to Mopi was a little over an hour. After arrival, all the passengers got off, except me. The two pilots then flew me to Timbuktu in about two hours.

"The legendary city of Timbuktu was the ancient crossroads where camel caravans carrying gold, salt, and slaves from the black kingdoms in the south connected with the Arab sheikdoms to the north. The local Tuareg people led the convoys, and Timbuktu became wealthy as the center of trade. Eventually, it declined in importance as ships supplying the coastline proved more efficient. The town still boasts the largest mud structure in the world, which serves as a huge inn and meeting place, although it does dry out and must be reconstructed every other year.

"I was met at the Timbuktu airport at noon and taken to the Grand Hotel, the only hotel in town, by Mohammed, my driver, and Sani, my guide, in a white Toyota Land Cruiser with four-wheel drive. On the ride to the hotel, Sani told me he plants trees in the summer when the tourist business stops. I was the only guest at the thirty-room hotel. The hotel manager said business had been bad since the French tourists were kidnapped a few months ago. That night, I had a restless sleep since I was the only guest in the hotel, and I kept thinking of the movie *The Shining* with Jack Nicholson."

"James, that hotel sounds like the same one we with stayed at in Patagonia."

"You are right. The next day, I visited four mosques, the museum, library, post office, and big and small shopping areas. People are nice and friendly, but extremely poor. They mainly raise livestock and transport items down the Niger River.

"The third day I went by camel, with the white Toyota following, to visit a Tuareg village on the dunes. The village was easily reached by camel and is where the villagers raise goats and some cattle. I was told that it was too dangerous to go farther out into the desert because of Al-Qaeda. At the camp, I was introduced to a local Tuareg chief. He was quite tall, dressed in the traditional deep-blue robe, and his smiling face had a dark-olive complexion. He told us in perfect English how he spent two years at the University of Colorado, where most people assumed he was Mexican. Although there was now a paved road across the Sahara, he informed me that he still leads camel caravans from the desert salt mines to the urban centers. The continuing success of the ancient mode of transport, he said, was because trucks get stuck when the blowing sand clogs their engines or large dunes block the road. Other people told me later that the camels would soon be outdated, but I prefer to believe that our Tuareg chieftain will be leading his caravans for years to come.

"The Tuareg camp elders offered me tea and then asked me very cautiously if they could show me their goods, mainly jewelry wrapped up in cloth. I told them I did not need anything. They kept saying the money would help the camp, the people are so poor, tourism was ending with the increased hot weather, and the coming rainy season lasts until August or September. Before I left, I gave them some money.

"On my last morning there, I went to the airport with Mohammed and Sani. I left Timbuktu on the same Air Mali plane I arrived in, and after a stop in Mopti, the plane landed before noon in Bamako. There I took a tour around the city. Bamako is nice, and there are big roundabouts, also known as traffic circles, on their main streets. One roundabout had a statue of a hippo in the middle, an elephant in another traffic circle, and animals of different kinds in other circles. After the tour, I walked around an open market and witnessed how they treat animals. One guy was holding six live turkeys in each hand by their legs and was swinging them wildly as he was walking around, trying to sell them. I saw others beating their animals. I really got upset when I witnessed a big watchdog on a chain that was barking at some guys as they were throwing rocks at him, so all I could hear was the dog winning between his barking.

"I left Bamako for Casablanca that afternoon on a fully loaded plane. After arrival in Casablanca, I flew to London for the night and then returned to the good old USA."

"James, it amazes me how you remember all the details of your trips, especially since you are still recovering from amnesia."

"Thank you, but that was a very memorable trip. However, your memory is much better than mine as you know all the diseases man can get and what are the options for treatments as well as knowing all the drugs and what they do and their side effects. Say, since you have never been to Buenos Aires and Iguacu Falls, let us make a couple of more quick trips there before we head back to Santiago."

"That sounds great, my dear James."

Buenos Aires Airport is some distance from the city, and it took Deborah and James about an hour by bus to the bus terminal in the city, and then they had to take a fifteen-minute taxi ride to the Apart Hotel and Spa Congreso. After dinner that evening, James checked his email at the hotel's business center.

He found out that his assistant was handling the department's administrative work fine and his graduate students were not having any problems with their research. It was the spring semester, and James did not have any teaching duties.

The next day following breakfast, the couple went out to explore the city near the hotel. They got to the main street, which was four lanes divided by a broad grass strip. There was a monument at one place that looked like the Washington Monument in DC, but not as high. They noted that Buenos Aires is a large city with a mixture of old and new buildings; some of the old ones are magnificent. On their walk, they had to safely watch for missing tiles and holes in the sidewalks. The city was clean, with only a few homeless and no panhandling to speak of.

The following day, James and Deborah got up early to catch a taxi to the domestic airport for a flight to Iguaçu. After their arrival and check-in at to St. George Hotel, they took a long walk around the small town.

The next morning, they boarded a bus to see the falls from both the Argentinian side and the Brazilian side. Then they had a nice walk to the lower falls. This area is better than the higher falls walk since one sees the whole falls instead of only the top. They loved watching the terrific amount of water cascading over the rocks. The water had a brown-tan color in places, and that disappeared by the time the water reached the bottom. On the trail, there were many coatis, animals similar to raccoons. After a couple of hours walking around the falls, they returned to the bus terminal. There a big coati ran over and grabbed a lady's plastic bag of sandwiches and ran away, with many of his fellow species chasing after him. They went back to town for lunch and then to the airport for their flight to Santiago via Buenos Aires. On the second leg of the trip, James told Deborah about some trips he took years ago.

"The trip started in Caracas, Venezuela, where I gave an invited seminar talk at their Central University. The following day, I went on a tour to Angel Falls. The first night in a campground near the falls, my host and I slept outside in hammocks covered with mosquito nets. As you can probably guess, I got no sleep. Following a campout breakfast the next morning, we went to a remote runway where I got in a two-seater, single-engine plane, with me riding next to the pilot. The pilot flew over and next to the falls several times. It was spectacular, but scary.

"The second stop on my trip was Bolivia. Upon my arrival at the La Paz airport, which is about fourteen thousand feet above sea level, I and several other passengers were having breathing problems, so we were given oxygen for about an hour. After receiving oxygen and drinking some coca tea, we were bused to the city, which was about a thousand feet lower than the airport. At the hotel that night and the next morning, I did not need any oxygen. Of course, I drank lots of coca tea at breakfast. Around noon, I started having breathing problems while eating lunch at McDonald's. To add to my lack of oxygen, everyone at McDonald's and in the nearby stores and streets got tear-gassed because the police were breaking up demonstrations of an illegal march of striking workers. Otherwise, it was a great trip seeing some beautiful mountains."

Following their arrival in Santiago, Deborah gave James many thanks for taking her to the neighboring countries. "As always, it was great fun to be with you, James, and to meet your friends in Brazil and see many new things, especially Iguaçu Falls. I look forward to our next adventures together."

"You are very welcome, and I look forward to more trips with you."

The couple had a long loving goodbye before they went to their respective gates for their travels to Atlanta and Puerto Williams. They agreed to meet again as soon as possible.

V

Following James's return from South America, he got a call from Kim, who asked him to meet with her in Pendleton Town Square the next day at their usual restaurant. At lunch, sitting at a booth in a quiet corner of the restaurant, Kim said, "Please give me a detailed account of your travels after we order our lunch. Someday, I would like to take the trip, so if you do not object, I want to tape-record your story so I will not have to take notes."

After ordering lunch, James said, "Well, Kim, if you really want all the details of my last trip, I will begin by saying that my Chilean friend and I had a great time seeing some of Argentina, Brazil, and Uruguay. My talk at the Brazilian Nuclear Research Center was well received."

"Wait, James, our lunch is here. Let us eat and then you can continue with your detailed narrative."

Following lunch, James said, "Again, Kim, I hope I am not getting too detailed about the account of my trips and the people I meet."

"No, please continue as I find it very interesting, and it still amazes me how you can remember all these details."

"Well, Kim, I do keep a diary, and I reviewed it before our meeting today. Maybe in the future you may want me to make a copy of my diary for you."

After James gave Kim his assurances that Brazil was not involved in a nuclear weapon program, he told her in detail about his and Deborah's travels. Following their lunch, she thanked him for his excellent report.

Before going their separate ways, James told Kim that he plans on inviting Deborah to the United Sates to see some of his favorite places in Georgia, South Carolina, and Colorado. He also informed her that he might be making a trip to Europe and Russia soon and will give a report to her following that trip.

James exchanged several emails with Deborah, and in the last one, he asked her if she would like to see some of America. She sent James an affirmative response and started planning the trip to the USA.

After Deborah's early-morning arrival in Atlanta a week later, James was there to meet her. On their way to the airport train station, Deborah said, "I had a nice long nap on the plane and also read a lot of nice things about Atlanta and Georgia."

"Well before going onto Pendleton in a couple of days, I have planned for us to have a short visit to the city today and tomorrow take a short flight to Providenciales, Turks and Caicos. As you know, I am a member of the Traveler's Century Club, just like your friend Coni, and the islands are on the club's list of 327 countries and territories. I want to check them off the list so I can achieve platinum status in the club. Now I am a gold member, having visited more than 250 countries and territories on the club list."

"Maybe I should also join the club, and perhaps in the future, I can attend some of the dinners of the Chilean chapter that Coni attends once every couple of months."

After taking the train from the airport to downtown Atlanta, the couple first visited the world-famous zoo. After a short walk around the zoo, with tears in her eyes, Deborah said, "James, I feel so sorry that some of the animals are in such small cages."

"Yes, I agree. As I mentioned to you before, when we go to Colorado, I will take you to the wildlife sanctuary where they have rescued many animals that had lived in small cages in circuses and zoos, mainly in South America. Now the animals can roam over acres of land."

Following a long walk around downtown Atlanta, which included going through the Coca-Cola Museum and seeing the world's largest aquarium, they returned to the airport and spent the night at a nearby hotel. At noon the next day, they take a US Airways flight to Providenciales on one of the Turk Islands.

Deborah also read a little about their destination:

The group of islands next to the Turks Islands is the Caicos Islands, and both have a combined population of thirty-two thousand and are among the British Overseas Territories. The islands are located about 650 miles southeast of Miami in the North Atlantic Ocean. The Providenciales airport is small, and its runway is for both takeoffs and landings. It is the largest city on the islands.

After James and Deborah's arrival, they took a taxi to the Turtle Cove Hotel, checked in, and had dinner at a nearby restaurant.

The next morning, the couple were on the balcony of their room, looking out over a beautiful marina. Debora commented, "John, the island is amazingly beautiful, and I am looking forward to seeing more of it."

"Yes, I especially like the green water washing up against the coral reefs in the bay. After breakfast, I have arranged for a driver and guide to take us on a tour of the island."

Their guide arrived mid-morning and was also the driver, using his own car. Ruben is a part-time pastor and does not have a parish or church but makes house calls. He took the couple to all the major sites. James thought to himself during the tour that there was nothing too interesting, a few classy hotels, nice houses, and several mini markets. The highlight of the tour was visiting the historic lighthouse and going to the top of Blue Mountain, which is a small hill. From their vantage point on the hill, they admired another beautiful green water bay that is cut off from the Atlantic Ocean by a coral reef. It was like the one they saw from their hotel room.

Ruben told the couple that there were no traffic lights on the island. He asked Deborah, "What does a green light mean?"

"Of course, it means it's okay to drive through the intersection."

Ruben then asked James, "What does a yellow light mean?"

"It means one should stop or speed through the intersection, depending on how close the car is to the intersection."

"Well, what does a red light mean?"

"It means stop."

"No, we believe that red means danger, and one should speed like hell through the red stop light, and that is why we do not have any stop lights on the island!"

All three had a good laugh.

Near the end of the tour, Ruben informed the couple that he must make a brief stop at an elderly lady's home to give her a short sermon. "I already mentioned to you that I do not have a church or parish but make house calls. You both can join us and see an example of a typical home visit."

After that, the three returned to the hotel. The couple thanked Ruben for the interesting tour. After a short walk to find a restaurant, they had a late lunch. Following their meal, they returned to the hotel where they both had a nice long nap, followed by a walk near the hotel and then dinner.

Early the next day, they returned to Atlanta and got James's Smart car from the airport parking lot. Following a short drive around Georgia Tech's campus, they started their drive to Pendleton. About an hour later and halfway to Pendleton, the couple stopped for lunch at the Chateau Élan. Following lunch at the hotel restaurant, they had a short walk around Chateau Élan, which was next to the classy hotel, admiring the beautiful large building. James told Deborah that wine was made at the chateau from the acres of grapes around the area. There was also a nearby golf course. They then drove to Helen, Georgia, for a nice walk around the German village. On the way, they had a brief stop at Toccoa Falls.

About an hour later, James stopped at the Clemson Research Park to show Deborah where he used to work and introduced her to several faculty and staff. Then he took her over to Sunny Acres, his second home that was about a five-minute drive from the research park. "I designed and helped build the two-story home that sits on five acres of woods with great views of the Smoky Mountains from one side and Lake Hartwell from the other side. I have seen lots of birds, squirrels, and chipmunks as well as a few snakes, frogs, and turtles on the property. A couple of times, I was lucky and saw deer, foxes, moles, raccoons, and a wild turkey. Let us take a short walk among the beautiful oak, pine, and spruce trees. Can you guess why I call this place Sunny Acres?"

"Of course, it is because the acreage sits on the sunny side of the property."

"You are correct, my dear doctor."

"The home and property are wonderful, especially the large decks on each side of the building. It's too bad, James, that we cannot go inside, but I will peak through the ground floor windows."

"There is one bedroom on the ground floor as well as a living room, dining room, bathroom, kitchen, and laundry room. Behind the two-car garage is a separate entrance to the stairs that go to the second floor. On that floor are two bedrooms, a bathroom, a kitchen, and living and dining rooms. The property was once part of the old Davis Plantation."

"You did a great job in designing the structure."

"Thank you. I am renting the home out to a visiting professor, who lives downstairs, and two students who camp out upstairs."

Next, they proceeded to James's Pendleton home, where Deborah received a tour of the upstairs. Later the two graduate students, who were living in the basement, brought up several dishes of food for a pleasant dinner. During the meal, the students asked Deborah about her home and career. After a short story about her life, Deborah asked the students where they were from and where did they receive their undergraduate degrees.

Mina spoke up first. "I am from Porto, Portugal, and graduated from the University of Porto."

Deborah stated, "I know a lot of Portuguese, so maybe later, I can practice it with you."

Diane told the group that she grew up in Los Angeles and graduated from the University of Southern California.

After dinner, the girls returned to the basement, and James showed Deborah the two guest bedrooms. "You have a choice of which room you would like to stay in."

With a smile on her face, she said, "I would rather sleep in your room on one of the twin beds and enjoy your Jacuzzi before night, night."

"That would be great. Let me clean up the kitchen and do the dishes. Then I will join you for a needed good night's sleep."

Over breakfast the next morning, James told Deborah that he had an attempt on his life last night.

"No! What happened?"

"Well, I was in my car at a stoplight in Clemson, and a car pulled up alongside me. I turned to look at the driver, and it was the same person I saw driving away from the chemistry building during the fire in my laboratory. Then the guy threw a Molotov cocktail through the open passenger window and sped away. Then I woke from a terrible nightmare."

"James, you had me scared to death for a minute. It sounds like a terrible thing to experience during sleep."

"I usually have at least one dream at night, but rarely nightmares like this one. Perhaps it is a warning about trouble in the future. Would you like to see my office and laboratory this morning?"

"Of course, but let me clean up the kitchen first."

Following a nice tour of the chemistry building and introductions with his students and a few faculty members, James took her on a drive around campus and Clemson and then back to Pendleton, where they have a walk around Pendleton Old Town Square and lunch at the Mexican restaurant.

After their meal, James told Deborah, "I need to go to my office and catch up on some paperwork as well as check in with the dean. Would you like to stroll around Pendleton and visit the many antique shops or go back to 102?"

"It would be interesting to look at merchandise in some of the shops. I can easily find my way back to your lovely home since it is only a few blocks away. I guess you call your home 102 because that is the part of the address. It is also clever that you call the lovely pond behind 102 'Golden Pond' since the vegetation in the water gives it a golden look. However, before you leave, I need to borrow your house key."

"Of course, here is my key. After my return later, we can go and have a key made for you. Then I will show you the Pendleton Library and two old plantation farms that are historic sites near here. After that, and if you wish, we can take a stroll around the South Carolina Botanical Gardens that are next to the university campus."

James gave her a hug before he departed.

After the events of the day and over dinner, James suggested an agenda for the next two days. "Tomorrow, I would like to take you to White Water Falls that is about an hour's drive from here. It is located just over the state line in North Carolina. The falls remind me of Victoria Falls in Africa but are much smaller of course. If you are up to it, we can walk down many steps to the bottom of the falls."

"James, that sounds great, and I am sure I can handle the walk."

"After seeing the lovely falls, we can drive through the small tourist towns of Cashiers and Highlands to Walhalla for a walk about the interesting city with some beautiful buildings and then lunch, followed by returning to Pendleton via Seneca and Clemson."

"Okay, remember I am in your hands to see your favorite places."

"The day after tomorrow, we can take a long drive through the Great Smoky Mountains National Park that is in North Carolina and Tennessee, followed by having short visits to some small historic towns on the way back."

At the end of the weekend of their travels, James surprised Deborah by telling her that he had airline tickets for a short visit to Colorado to see his children and show her some of his favorite places. Of course, she agreed and said, "James, are you sure you can spare the time away from the university?"

"Well, it is summer break, and most of the faculty are out vacationing, as well as some of my students. The ones that are remaining have their research underway, and if they have any questions, we communicate via email. I also gave the dean notice that I will take early retirement at the end of summer since I am fifty-five."

"Wow, are you sure you want to start another new life?"

"I am ready to travel more and have no more responsibility of managing the department, teaching courses, and supervising graduate students. I also want to write more, especially about my travels. Before my wonderful year with you in Chile, I had started writing a chemistry textbook that I would like to finish. I will be okay financially since I will have retirement checks from the university and Rocky Flats, my IRAs, and money from selling both of my South Carolina homes and later Social Security. I plan to move to Pine Shadows in Nederland, which is about a half-hour drive from Boulder. I have not told you about my mountain retreat, but I will take you there when we are in Colorado. Of course, then I will be close to my grown children and later, hopefully, grandchildren"

"It sounds like you have thought out plans well. I hope you include visiting me often."

"Of course, and I hope you will be able to accompany me on some of my visits to places I have never been to before."

After flying to Denver from Atlanta, James's three grown children were waiting for the couple at the airport reception area. Following the happy reunion and introductions of Deborah, Eric got his car from the parking lot and picked up everyone for the ride back to his home in Boulder where the couple would stay for several days.

That evening, over a wonderful dinner that Eric's wife had prepared, there was a discussion of everyone's activities since the young adults came to Pendleton for Ying's memorial.

James asked Deborah to tell the group about her life. Next, Eric explained about his job working for a biotech company in nearby Longmont and how he and Sylvia met. "My wonderful wife works at the same company I do, and we met at CU. We bought this house last year after we were secretly married. Sorry, you all were not invited to the ceremony, but it was only us, a preacher, and two of our mutual friends. We know the house is small with only two bedrooms, but housing is expensive in Boulder, and this is all we could afford. I do plan on finishing the basement sometime in the future. Before the home purchase, we were living in separate condos and, before that, in dorm rooms at the University of Colorado, finishing our doctorate degrees in biochemistry."

James told Deborah, "Because of their secret wedding, I had to find out about it in an email from Eric. Of course, I sent them a congratulations card with a generous check."

Amy spoke up next. "I think I can speak for both Lorrie and I since we are on the same path of studying chemistry. Although I took a long break after high school, I am now in graduate school, majoring in geochemistry, and Lorrie is a senior and planning to go to graduate school, majoring in organic chemistry. Lorrie is uncertain if she will continue at CU or go to another university. As you can guess, our father was a big influence on our studies. We both stay in student dorms."

The next day after breakfast, James and Deborah dropped Eric and Sylvia at work and borrowed their car for visits to the colorful tourist town of Estes Park, Rocky Mountain National Park, and Nederland, an old mining town. On their way back to Boulder via Clear Creek Canyon, they had quick stops in Blackhawk and Central City, old mining towns that now have lots of new hotels with casinos.

Following their return to Boulder, Deborah thanked James for the wonderful day. "I especially liked the park and seeing so many deer and mountain sheep. I had hoped we would see a bear and/or a mountain lion. I was surprised by the small herd of elk in Estes Park, and the lunch we had at the Stanley Hotel was exceptionally good. I did see that the hotel was the same one in the movie *The Shining*."

"Well, there have been several bear visits to Estes Park, Nederland, and even Boulder looking for food, mainly in trash cans."

"I also know why you call your weekend home in Nederland Pine Shadows. It is because the home is on the shady side of the acreage and covered by shadows of the many pine trees behind the house."

"As you saw, it is much like Sunny Acres, except it has a larger kitchen and a basement that houses a two-car garage, laundry room, and workshop. I like the decks with stairs at the front of the home on both the main and second floors that give one access to both floors from the driveway. Of course, the other entrances are on the enclosed stairway behind the house where there is access from the garage to both upper levels. I am also happy that the ten-acre property is next to Boulder County open space with a walking trail that goes to the other side of the mountain. I also love the views of Barker Reservoir, the town, Eldora Ski Area, and some of the Rocky Mountains. I am sorry the couple that rented the house was not at home so I could have shown you the inside. Although I have a key, it would not have been right to enter without them being there. Since tomorrow is Saturday, I will take you and the kids to the Wild Animal Sanctuary near Keenesburg, north of Denver's international airport. The sanctuary was founded forty years ago and has more than five hundred bears, lions, tigers, and wolves roaming on eight hundred acres of prairie. There is also an extension of the sanctuary that is in Southern Colorado, near the town of Springfield, which has 9,700 acres of hills of boulders and trees, a wonderful habitat for rescued wild animals. Well, it is time to pick up Eric and Sylvia from work. They suggested we eat at a restaurant on Pearl Street for dinner. By the way, Sylvia has another commitment tomorrow and will not join us to see the wild animals."

On their last full day in Colorado, the couple visited the old mining town of Breckenridge for lunch. James told Deborah that instead of mining in the nearby mines, tourism and skiing were now the main attractions. On the way back to Boulder, he told her about his many past visits there. "We had a time share condo for the first week of each year, and I would always come to Breckenridge with Margrit and the kids for skiing, ice skating, and walking around town, looking in the many shops. We would also try to eat at different restaurants for dinner. The family and I always had breakfast at the condo and would usually have lunch at the same restaurant at the base of one of the ski lifts. Breckenridge is where Margrit and the kids learned to ski. I got my ski lessons in a gym class at the university where we would spend the weekend at another ski area above Georgetown, the old mining town we stopped at coming here this morning."

"Breckenridge is truly a lovely town, and I also enjoyed our stop on Kenosha Pass as well as going through historic South Park City in Fairplay."

On their flight back to Atlanta, James told Deborah, "I am sorry we did not have time to visit my favorite national park, Yellowstone. It is the first national park in the US, established in 1872. We would have had to fly to Jackson, Wyoming, and rent a car for the drive. On my previous visits to Yellowstone, I always made a round trip of the adventure, first driving north from Jackson and going by the Grand Tetons and then by the beautiful mountains around the park. I always stayed at the Yellowstone Lodge next to Old Faithfull Geyser. After my stay at the lodge, I drove through West Yellowstone to Idaho Falls to see friends and then back to Jackson. Can you guess what my favorite number 2 and number 3 national parks are?"

"I give up, dear. There are so many parks in your country. One park I would guess is the Grand Canyon."

"Correct. That is my third favorite national park. Number 2 is Yosemite National Park in California."

A month following Deborah's visit to the United States, James received an email from his Russian friend, Misha. He was the chairman of an upcoming International Chemical Congress that the Russian Academy of Science was hosting at the Rossiya Hotel in Moscow. In the email, he formally invited James to attend the congress and deliver the plenary lecture. James knew he would probably be invited as Misha had mentioned it in a previous email. James accepted the flattering invitation where all expenses would be covered by the academy. After James sent his reply, he wrote to Deborah that he would attend the conference and asked her to accompany him. Of course, they had been exchanging emails since Deborah's visit to the United States. Deborah excitedly accepted James's offer and started making travel arrangements. A month later, they met at Atlanta airport and flew to Vienna.

On the long flight, Deborah asked James, "How do you like retirement?"

"Well, so far, it is okay, but we shall see."

James asked Deborah to come with him to the rear of the Boeing 777 Dreamliner where there was no one present. In the galley, he got on his knees, holding Deborah's hand, and said, "Deborah, you know how much I love you, and I know you love me. Will you marry me?"

"Oh, James, I am so happy to hear your words. I do love you very, very much, and of course, I will marry you. This is the happiest day of my life to have you ask me to be your wife. I will always love you and will not let you down."

"I have arranged for one of the stewardesses to bring the captain back and marry us. He has agreed to do this even though it may not be legal. I wrote the usual marriage vows that are said at most weddings on a piece of paper for him. I will get the stewardess now and ask her to bring the captain back. Of course, after we are in Vienna, my friends have arranged a wedding ceremony for us to have a legal marriage presided over by a judge. I got this idea from the movie *Casablanca* where Rick wants to marry Ilsa on a train by the engineer. Well, here is the captain to marry us."

After the short ceremony, the happy couple returned to their seats. James told Deborah about some of his proposed travel plans for them in Europe. "After we arrive in Vienna tomorrow morning and drop our luggage at the Hotel Wandl, I will take you to a friend's home. He has kindly arranged for us to legally get married in his home by a judge. Following the marriage ceremony, our hosts and a few other friends from the IAEA will have brunch with wedding cake for us. After the party, I will show you some of the must-see things in Vienna's first district. In the evening, after a dinner of Wiener schnitzel and salad at Figlmuller, we can check into the hotel and begin our wedding night. I will tell you my other suggested travel plans after our arrival in Vienna. Now let us try to get some sleep, my dear lovely wife."

VI

On their first full day in Vienna, James told Deborah over a late breakfast about his tentative plans for their stay in Europe. "Today, I will take you to see sites in Vienna's first district. Tomorrow, I will show you the place my family and I lived in the past. followed by a visit to the Vienna International Center, abbreviated VIC, to have a late lunch with Jan whom you met at the wedding. Jan is the section head at the IAEA of a group assisting Africa. In the afternoon, we can take the underground to Schönbrunn Palace. If you agree, we can spend our last day taking a day trip to Bratislava. The train ride only takes an hour, and I would like you to meet one of my best friends who is a retired university professor. We are writing a book about radioactivity and nuclear energy. Following our last morning at the Wandl, we will start our honeymoon train travels in a first-class sleeper car to Istanbul, Turkey, with a day visit to Bucharest on the way. Then fly to Moscow from Istanbul.

"After the Moscow visit and my attendance at the conference, we will fly back to Vienna. After a couple of nights at the Wandl, we will travel by train for one-day visits to Salzburg and Innsbruck and return to Vienna a different way via Graz. After one-night stays in Graz and Vienna, we will take the train to Prague and stay there for several nights and then to Warsaw. We may stop in Gdansk, Poland, if we have time before our return to Vienna for our flight back to the US."

"That sounds like a trip of a lifetime, and I am looking forward to seeing some of Europe and Russia."

"In case we do not get to visit Gdansk, you can read my diary tonight about my trip there several years ago. But first, let us start our walking tour by visiting St. Peter's Church in front of the hotel."

After their short visit to admire the beautiful inside of the church, they started their walk on the nearby Graben pedestrian street to Stephansdom. Following a short time admiring the beautiful inside of the church, James asked Deborah if she would like to climb 343 steps to the south tower.

"Of course, my dear, as long as you accompany me."

After leaving the church, they walked down the long Kärntner Strasse pedestrian street, past many shops selling everything from clothes to souvenirs, to the Opera House. After James took a few more pictures, they boarded a horse carriage for a ride around Vienna's ring street, past Parliament, Burggarten, Hofburg, Museum, Rathaus, and Burgtheater. After continuing the journey around the inner city, they returned to Stephansdom, where they left the carriage and took a short walk to Venicea,

James's favorite Italian restaurant. Over a late lunch of pizza, they discussed the morning's activities.

"James, I especially liked seeing the inside of Stephansdom, but I do not think I will climb the stairs on our next visit."

"Yes, the stair climb was challenging. I love the architecture of the old buildings in the city, and Parliament is my favorite. What you will see at VIC tomorrow will be several modern high-rise buildings. We will travel there by underground train that goes over the Danube River before reaching the UN buildings. After our lunch, Jan will take us around the IAEA building, where I worked for three years. There are other UN agencies located in the attached buildings. I always finish my visit with Jan over coffee in VIC's bar. From there, we can say our goodbyes to Jan and go up the Vienna Tower that is nearby for a unique view of the city.

"I have a funny story about the tower. A few days after my family arrived in Vienna, I took them to the restaurant on the top of the tower. My German was not too good at that time despite taking a semester of it at the university. I ordered hotdogs and drinks for everyone in my best German. Later, the waitress brought our drinks and hotdogs, and several minutes later, she brought another round of hotdogs. When the third round arrived, I told her that we only wanted one order of hotdogs. Margrit and the kids had a good laugh."

After finishing their meal, Deborah asked James, "What will we see this afternoon?

"If you are not too tired, we can first take the underground to Belvedere Palace with its beautifully landscaped garden and great views of the rooftops of the city. After our walk around the gardens, we can have a return walk to the nearby city center and visit Karl's Church. After visiting the beautiful church, we can continue our walk past the first McDonald's in the city and a hotel that was once the headquarters of the IAEA before it was moved to the VIC. We can then take a streetcar to Grinzing for a short walk and then go to Neustift am Walde to see the house my family and I lived in for three years. If you wish, we can have dinner in a Horigan. My favorite place is Hubers that has a wonderful buffet, and we can eat in their garden."

After breakfast the next morning, James started the conversation with Deborah by recalling their wonderful buffet breakfast. "I especially liked the yellow cheese paste to spread on the whole wheat rolls."

"I agree. There was lots of good food to choose from, and I was surprised they have champagne available."

"I was also surprised at the large number of tourists in the city, more than I have ever seen. Are you up for a long day in the city?"

"Of course, I can hardly wait to ride the famous giant Ferris wheel at the Prater and see where you worked and visit Schönbrunn Palace with its glamorous rooms and have a long walk in the gardens. From what I read, we could spend a whole day there, including trying to get out of the high shrub maze."

Later that evening, they went to the train station, obtained their luggage, and boarded the train for a nine-hour overnight ride to Bucharest. The Czermaks got little sleep that night even though they were in a first-class sleeper cabin. After their arrival, they stored their luggage at the station and took a taxi to the city center in search of a nice-looking restaurant for a late breakfast. Over their meal, James told Deborah about the recommended tourist sites that were the best places to visit. "This guide starts out by stating that Romania's capital is rich with a storied history and was once known as Little Paris for its elegant architecture. The guide highly recommends a stroll down Calea Victoriel, where one can see the country's monuments and grandest buildings. There are other charming cobbled streets that weave through the Old Town and are lined with bookshops, cafes, restaurants, and theaters. Nearby are city parks and museums. The map in this booklet should help us find these interesting places.

"The guide also recommends visiting Curtea Veche, an open-air museum, and the National Museum of Romanian History. The top attraction is the Palace of Parliament that has three thousand rooms. It used to be called the People's House by the dictator Nicolae Ceausescu, who used it as his family's residence and as a seat of government. Now a small portion of the building houses Romania's parliamentary headquarters and the National Museum of Contemporary Art.

"On my short visit here years ago, I remember getting lost in this enormous building. The other thing that stands out in my mind is getting called into the American embassy since I was taking pictures outside the embassy. The security person wanted to see if I was taking pictures of the embassy with my video camera, which I was not. I know never to take pictures of embassies, police stations, and military installations."

"James, it sounds like we will be spending a good part of the day in Parliament!"

"Yes, indeed. The tourist guide also advises to see the Romanian Athenaeum that is home to the George Enescu Philharmonic Orchestra and resembles an ancient Greek temple with a peristyle of six ionic columns and a 120-foot-high dome. Other must-see places are Stavropoleos Church; the Old Princely Court, Church, and Museum; Revolution Square; and the Arch of Triumph. Remember, we did see the arch on the taxi ride."

"Yes, the arch is very impressive. It was interesting what the taxi driver, who spoke a little English, told us about the arch being dedicated to the Romanian soldiers who fought in the First World War, and it continues today to serve as the central point for military parades."

"Shall we finish our meal with a little more food so we can skip lunch and see more of this interesting city? Deb, are you ready for a lot of walking?"

"Of course, but first please order me a piece of apple pie."

Following a long, wonderful day seeing the major sites in the city, James and Deborah were now in the restaurant car of the train to Istanbul. James started the conversation after they ordered dinner. "Do you agree that it was a wonderful day in such a fascinating city with so much to see."

"Yes, I agree. I wish we could have spent more time in the National Museum of Romanian History and its collections of religious and royal treasures. The open-air museum built on the site of the Old Princely Court was also worth seeing. It was interesting to hear that the Curtea Veche was once the home of Vlad the Impaler, who inspired Bram Stoker's tale of Dracula."

"Although I have been there before, I saw some new things at the awesome Palace of Parliament. I also enjoyed seeing for the first time Stavropoleos Church and reading that it was built in 1724 by a Greek monk, Loanikie Stratonikeas. The Orthodox church features fine stone and wood carvings and is surrounded by a wonderful garden courtyard filled with eighteenth-century tombstones."

"James, I am ready for bedtime. Let us make our way back to our sleeper car."

The train ride from Bucharest ended early morning in Istanbul. This time, the Czermaks slept much better than the ride the night before. They obtained their Turkish visas at the train station and then went to their hotel in the center of the fascinating city with many beautiful mosques. After storing their luggage at the hotel, James arranged an all-day tour. At nine, a van with a driver, guide, and four other tourists arrived at the hotel to pick up the Czermaks. The guide first told the group that they would see the most popular landmarks of the one-time Ottoman capital. At the Grand Bazaar, they would watch a handicraft demonstration and see the Hippodrome, where hundreds of spectators were gathered, and marvel at centuries-old attractions in the Topkapi Palace and Hagia Sophia Museum. The tour also included a multicourse Turkish lunch.

The tour began with a visit to one of the Eight Wonders of the World, the Hagia Sophia Museum, which occupies a unique place in architecture history. James especially liked this stop since he considered himself to be a part-time architect. The tour continued with a drive by the Blue Mosque. The guide explained that it is the only imperial mosque in the world that was originally built with six minarets and that it takes its name from the beautiful blue tiles in the interior. At the next stop, the guide and passengers got fifteen minutes to view the social and sporting center of old Byzantium, the Hippodrome Square. The van then went to Kapali Carsi, which was next to the Grand Bazaar, where the group received a brief handicrafts presentation. Following the presentation, everyone got some time to wander through the bazaar, followed by a delicious lunch.

After their meal, the group boarded the van for a short visit to the Haci Besir Aga Camii Mosque, followed by a tour of Topkapi Palace. The palace was home to Ottoman sultans, and on the two-hour tour, the group got to see the Baghdat Kiosk, Imperial Treasury, and collections of Chinese celadon ceramics. The palace also contained a Harem that only the sultan and his ladies could occupy. The tour concluded with a drive around more of the city and dropping each group member at their respective hotel. James and Deborah were the last to return to their hotel.

Before dinner, the Czermaks had a walk near their hotel, followed by a meal at a nearby restaurant. Over their dinner, they discussed their day. "Deb, I thought it was a great tour of a beautiful and fascinating city."

"Yes, I agree. Our best stop I think was at the Blue Mosque. It's amazing how they built such wonderful buildings during those ancient times, especially the beautiful blue ceramics."

"Well, we must retire early tonight and prepare for a dawn-rising flight to Moscow."

VII

On the plane trip from Istanbul to Moscow, James stated, "Deb, we are now flying over the Black Sea and will soon be above the North Caucasus. I hope that we will be able to see the mountains from the plane, especially Mont Elbrus, the highest mountain in Europe. We are lucky to have blue skies.

Following their mid-morning arrival in Moscow, the Czermaks took a taxi to the Rossiya Hotel. Following check-in, they had a hard time finding their room in the largest hotel in Europe. After unpacking, they went to the hotel restaurant for a leisurely lunch, followed by a long walk near the area of the hotel. They spent some time at several souvenir shops before returning to the hotel for an early dinner.

After a long dinner, they went to their room, where Deborah said, "James, I am tired and will bathe and then go to bed."

"Well, I am wide awake, so as you bathe, I will go out for a short walk to see what the area around the hotel looks like at night. On my return, I will take a shower and join you in bed, dear wife."

James took a short walk near the hotel in an area where no one was about. At one point, he heard a car coming behind him. He turned around to see a fast-moving car, with its headlights off, coming down the sidewalk at him. Immediately, he jumped into a doorway as the car sped by. He recognized the driver as the same person who started the fire in his laboratory months ago.

James returned to the hotel very shaken up. After entering their room, James nervously told Deborah what had happened. She jumped out of bed and gave him a hug. "James, I am so sorry and scared. What can we do?"

"I am also frightened and do not know what to do. Should I report this to the police and start being incredibly careful during our visit here? Maybe I will just ask Misha in the morning what he thinks I should do. He is the general secretary of the Russian Academy of Sciences and has many connections to people in high places. Meanwhile, we must be careful not to let anyone enter the room. I will put a chair against the door and make sure it is double-locked in addition to the chain being hooked."

In the morning, Misha and Sonya joined the Czermaks for breakfast in the hotel. Over their meal, James told Misha about the attempt on his life the night before and asked his advice on what he should do.

"Well, John, if you do not know this man's name, I think it's wise not to bring the police into the matter, but to do your best to be very careful. You will be in the hotel during the conference, with many colleagues around, so there should be no worries here. My driver Alexander, Sonya, and I will be with you both anytime you plan to go out of the hotel. Just phone me. On the tour of Moscow midway through the conference, you both will be with many of our friends and their wives on the tour bus, so certainly, you will also be okay that day. Of course, we will take you to the airport following the five-day conference."

After their meal, Deborah suggested to James, "Perhaps you should consider starting to use your first name since everyone here at the conference knows you as John."

"That's an excellent idea. At Clemson, I started using James instead of John. In Chile, since I did not know my name, Deborah suggested I use her late husband's name, Richard. Before I became a teenager, my folks called me Johnny!"

Everyone laughed as John agreed to a name change.

Following their meal, John and Misha went to the hotel auditorium for the start of the conference, which included John presenting the plenary lecture. Alexander came to the hotel and escorted Sonya and Deborah to the Academy of Science's car for a drive around Moscow in heavy traffic. The traffic was so bad in one place that Alexander drove down a sidewalk for half a block to get around a lane of stopped cars. They finally arrived at Tamara's university, followed by a lengthy lunch at her home.

During lunch, Sonya told Deborah about her university during the USSR times. "In the toilets, we called them Happy

Rooms, there was no toilet paper. Everyone had to use pieces of newspaper. We did not have computers either. Now we have toilet paper and computers."

After spending most of the afternoon in Sonya's apartment, they both returned to the hotel by taxi to freshen up before the conference welcome reception in the hotel's ballroom. Most of the conference attendees, some with their wives, attended the reception. There was plenty of food and drinks served buffet style, and John had numerous reunions with old friends, including Dmitri and Oleg, coauthors with John on a series of books they wrote for the IAEA. Deborah got to meet some of John's friends and their wives and spent most of the time talking with some of the wives who knew English.

The next day, the conference resumed, while Deborah stayed in the hotel to rest and do some reading. She joined John for the conference lunch where they discussed their activities of the morning. "I had a leisurely stay in the room, not doing a lot, just watching a little television and reading more of your diary. How is the conference going?"

"Well, it's nice to see some friends and hear about their research, but to be honest, science does not interest me very much these days. I would rather listen to talks about trips to faraway places. Tomorrow should be interesting for you since we will take the conference tour. Our bus driver and tour guide are supposed to show us the city's iconic sights. Our group will spend a lot of time walking around Red Square, followed by visiting St. Basil's Cathedral, the Armory Museum, and Novodevichy Convent. Following lunch, we will visit the Memorial Museum of Astronautics and the Monument to the Conquerors of Space. The day will conclude with dinner at the Rossiya Restaurant. Misha and Sonya will both be working at their institutes tomorrow, but we will see them tonight at their apartment."

"That all sounds wonderful. I am excited about the tour."

"I should return to the conference. What are your plans before dinner?"

"I will go for a walk and do some window shopping."

"Well, sweetheart, please be careful. Remember there is a murderer in the city that wants me dead, and he may want to use you to get to me."

After being picked up in the evening by Alexander, the three arrived at the apartment late because of traffic jams. At the party, there were several mutual friends of both Misha and John and their wives. The small group had a great time talking about old times over a delicious meal that Sonya had fixed. Later the Czermaks thanked their hosts and said their goodbyes to the other guests since Alexander needed to leave.

The next evening, following the tour and dinner at the hotel, Deborah told John, "Sonya will take me shopping tomorrow, followed by more sightseeing. I assume you will listen to lectures all day. By the way, who do you usually sit next to at the conference's lunches?"

"Beautiful Svetlana on one side of me and gorgeous Katarina on the other side. Just kidding! It is always my dear friends Misha, Oleg, and Dmitri. As you know, we can eat all we want from the buffet with a large variety of food. I especially like the borscht soup.""John, after our return from Europe, what are your plans for us?"

"Yes, now is a good time to start our plans for spending the rest of our lives happily together. My desire is to return to Clemson and put my two homes up for sale. After both are sold, we can move to Nederland. Perhaps we can live at your place to get away from the snow in Colorado for a couple of months each year. But of course, I want to teach you to ski. What do you think of my crazy plan?"

"Living in Colorado sounds great. I am not sure I want to keep my home. Perhaps we can decide later if I should sell it or not. I know if we keep it, Eduardo and Maria will look after it when we are not there."

"After our return to Vienna this weekend, we will have plenty of time to decide our future. Now it's bedtime."

After breakfast the next morning, John returned to the conference, and Alexander and Sonya picked up Deborah for more sightseeing and shopping.

In the evening, Alexander and the Czermaks went to a fancy restaurant for dinner. Dmitri and Oleg and their wives joined the three. After they ordered their meals, Oleg asked John, "What do you think of the conference?"

"It has certainly been nice to spend some time with you all and to have some reunions with other friends I have not seen in several years. Most of the papers were interesting."

Dmitri commented, "Your lecture was first-class, and it was great to hear about your student's research. What are your plans after you both leave Moscow?"

Deborah spoke up. "We will first return to Vienna for a couple of days, then take the train around Austria, then to Prague to see John's favorite city. We will end the trip with a visit to Warsaw, and perhaps Gdansk, then home.

John told the group that since he was retired now, he and Deborah would do more traveling. "By the way, I plan to play hooky tomorrow and skip the morning papers so I can sleep in and catch up on some writing in my diary."

The conversations continued as everyone ate their tasty food. The party ended with Dmitri and Oleg and their wives departing and the other three going to the academy car for their travels to the hotel.

Both John and Deborah were late in waking from a long night's sleep and skipped breakfast. However, they went for an early lunch before the morning session of lectures ended. Later John returned to the conference room to hear the last few papers and participate in a discussion period for the attendees to comment on the papers. Deborah had gone to their room to pack, watch television, and get ready for the evening banquet.

The farewell banquet was first-class with plenty of wonderful food and lots of drinking and dancing. After the joyous dinner and telling their friends goodbye, the Czermaks returned to their room. John urgently went to the bathroom. A minute later, there was a knock on the door. Without thinking, Deborah opened the door and was pushed back by an intruder holding a gun. Deborah screamed as the guy slammed the door shut. John came charging out of the bathroom and was shocked by what he saw.

The intruder said, "My name is Nikolai Pushkin, son of Andre Pushkin and older brother of Alex. You killed them both, Czermak! I know that you killed my father from what Alex told me on his short visit to Moscow following our father's death. I found out about your survival in Chile and you being charged for killing my brother from reading the story about you and Alex in *Pravda*, the main Russian newspaper. Before your arrival in Moscow, *Pravda* also had a story about the conference being held at the Rossiya Hotel and that you were the keynote speaker. I assumed you would be staying here and stalked you to discover you taking a walk near the hotel the first night you arrived. I am sorry I did not kill you that night. I was also the one that tried to murder you in your car during my short visit to South Carolina. I am sorry that I accidentally killed your wife and sorrier you did not die in the fire I set in your laboratory. It was easy to break into the building and turn off the water to the fire sprinkler system.

"My uncle wanted to help me kill you tonight, but I told him I did not need his assistance. I regret that I must kill your friend first, but she is a witness."

Nikolai then shot Deborah in the chest, and John cried out, "No!"

He then turned the gun on John and shot him, but John, wounded in the chest, managed to lunge at Nikolai and put him in a bear hug, trying to wrestle the gun from him. Then the gun fired a third time, and the bullet went through Nikolai's heart. The couple in the next room heard the shots and called the front desk. After phoning the police, the clerk came and unlocked the door with his master key. The couple and the clerk discovered the three bodies and tried to stop the bleeding with towels.

Ten minutes later, an ambulance and the police arrived, and the medical technicians managed to stop the Czermaks' bleeding and took them to a nearby hospital. Following a police investigation of the murder scene, Nikolai was transported to the morgue.

After the wounded Czermaks were treated in the hospital's emergency room, John was taken to a recovery room and Deborah to the morgue. She did not survive the shot to her chest. John's wound was below his heart, and he would recover.

A few days later, as John was continuing to recover in the hospital, he received a visit from Misha, Oleg, and Dmitri. John told them the whole story of the attempts on his life in California, Antarctica, South Carolina, and Moscow. "My biggest regret is that my three wives were murdered on my account. I am not sure I can go on living a normal life with the guilt."

Misha asked, "Do you have any concern that Andrei's brother might make an attempt on your life?"

"I don't know. I am being discharged the day after tomorrow and will make arrangements for my return to the US with Deborah's body so she can have a proper burial at our home in Colorado. I will also have memorials for her in Boulder and on Navarino Island in Chile. I will be careful during these days for the brother's revenge, even though I do not know what he looks like."

Misha said, "John, if there is anything we can do to help you, please let us know. I would be happy to take you to the hotel and later the airport."

"Thank you, and I really appreciate you all coming here to visit me."

During his last night in the hospital, a man quietly entered John's room and started to suffocate him with a pillow. He said, "This is for you killing my brother and two nephews." Although John was very weak, he tried to fight off the intruder but soon passed out. At the same time, a nurse entered the room and screamed. The man pushed her aside and ran from the room and out of the hospital. The nurse then called for help as she was administering CPR to the lifeless man.

Chapter 3

I

Immediately following the attempt by Andrei Pushkin's brother, Alexei, to kill John, the nurse at the Moscow hospital was successful in using CPR (cardiopulmonary resuscitation) on Czermak. The following day, John was discharged from the hospital, and his good friend Misa took him to the airport, along with his suitcase. He told John, "The police did not have any luck in finding Alexei, but they will continue to search. I tried to arrange for Deborah's body to be returned to Colorado but with no luck. The authorities suggested that she be cremated and have the ashes shipped to you via DHL or UPS."

"That sounds like a good idea. That way, I can take some of the ashes to Chile and have the rest buried in Pendleton and Nederland. Thank you, dear friend, for all you have done for me."

A very distraught Cermak arrived back in South Carolina. A few days later, he had a memorial for Deborah, which included placing some of her ashes under the big oak tree in front of his Pendleton home. Of course, he called Eduardo and informed him of Deborah's death. "Eduardo, I plan to make a trip to see you and Mary as soon as possible and bring some of Deborah's ashes with me to spread at the farm, at the central park in Puerto Williams, and on the University of Santiago campus. Then we can discuss what to do with her farm. One idea for you to think about is to make her home into a bed and breakfast (B and B). I know lots of hikers from overseas hike the trail to Caleta Wulais, and staying at her farm would be more convenient for them. Of course, we would need Mary's approval since she would be doing most of the work as a breakfast maker and room cleaner. Or maybe you could hire someone else to take care of hikers that would stay there."

The next morning, John received a call from Kim Carn who invites him for lunch. During lunch at the Pendleton Plantation restaurant, Kim told John that she was so sorry to hear about the death of Deborah. John told her about his plans to retire and move to Colorado. At the end of the meal, she thanked him for his contributions to the CIA and wished him good luck in his new life. They went their separate ways after a long hug.

A week later, John attended a goodbye party with his colleagues at Clemson and completed getting ready to move to Colorado, which included instructing his realtor to sell both of his houses. He then started his three-day drive to Denver in a new Jeep Compass. He had his Smart car shipped to Nederland.

Upon John's arrival in Colorado, he had a reunion with his grown children at Eric and Sylvia's home in South Boulder. John stayed at his son's home until the builders, whom he had contracted before his return to Boulder, completed the remodeling of his house in Nederland as well as built a detached three-car garage with a second-story apartment. With John's assistance, the builders worked on the house first by converting the three-car garage and large workshop into a living room, two bedrooms with bathrooms, a dining room, and a kitchen with cabinets and appliances, the same floor plan as each of the upper two floors of the house. There was already a laundry room, with a washer and dryer, and an enclosed back stairway to the upper two floors that were not changed. The builders continued their construction work, building a detached three-car garage with living quarters on the second floor, identical to each floor in the house. They completed the work after bathroom fixtures and kitchen cabinets were installed, along with a stove, microwave, dishwasher, and sink. A new refrigerator was also placed in the kitchen, electric heaters were installed in all the rooms, and a beautiful fireplace was constructed in the living room. A washer and dryer were delivered and installed later.

During part of this time, John made a short visit to Chile to distribute Deborah's ashes in Santiago, Puerto Williams, and on the farm and have the ownership of her house transferred to Eduardo and Maria. Earlier, Eduardo had sent John an email stating that it was not a good idea to use the home as a B and B. He wrote that most of the hikers who went by their home in the past told him that they really liked staying in town with its bars and restaurants. Also, Marie said that she would have a hard time taking care of the home and that finding help would be difficult. If Mary and Eduardo sold the property, they agreed to give John one-third of the proceeds. However, they all acknowledged it would be difficult to find a buyer. John stayed at the home for two more days, enjoying some of Mary's wonderful meals and finishing the legal work. Surprisingly, he found out that Deborah left him a sizable fortune in cash, gold, jewelry, and stocks. The visit ended with a small memorial at the farm for Deborah that her friends from the city attended.

John's house was in the old mining town of Nederland, west of the city of Boulder. After the building was completed at John's property, which he called Pine Shadows, the moving van from South Carolina arrived at the home. The movers unloaded their truck and placed the furniture and boxes of household items in the apartment above the garage. Once the boxes were unloaded and the furniture arranged, John started living in the apartment. His renters continued to live in the second and third floors of the house. He planned to rent the first level of the house.

The first Saturday after John started living in the apartment, he had a housewarming potluck party, which his family and friends attended. His longtime friends included a few former West High School classmates and some colleagues whom he worked with at Rocky Flats. After several tours of the apartment and the first floor of the house, everyone enjoyed the food. Later, John and most of the guests went to the enclosed covered patio behind the garage for several games of pool and ping-pong. A few of the guests played volleyball in the nearby tennis court next to the empty covered swimming pool. After an afternoon of partying and playing games, the visitors and family left in small groups and returned to their homes.

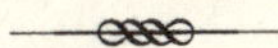

The main campus of the University of Colorado is in Boulder and was established in 1876. The first building was Old Main, surrounded at the time by a barren eight hundred acres of land. The first student body was composed of forty-seven pupils. Macky Auditorium was built in 1923 and Norlin Library in 1940. All three structures still stand today, along with at least five dozen other academic, research, and residential buildings, with more being built. Of course, sidewalks connect the buildings. Between most of the buildings are large grass areas lined with flower gardens, bushes, and trees.

There are three other campuses: Denver, Aurora, and Colorado Springs. It is a public research university and the largest in Colorado, with more than thirty-six thousand undergraduate and graduate students and about four thousand faculty. CU is composed of nine colleges and schools that offer over 150 academic programs. Twelve Nobel laureates and twenty astronauts have been affiliated with the university. CU was ranked forty-fourth among public universities in the United States by *U.S. News and World Report*. The Boulder campus was named by *Travel and Leisure* as one of the most beautiful college campuses in the United States.

The chemistry building sits across the Dalton Trumbo Fountain Court from the University Memorial Center, which houses a restaurant, bowling alley, bookstore, conference rooms, and offices for student activities and organizations. The center is located next to Broadway, one of the main streets in Boulder. The four-floor Cristol Chemistry and Biochemistry Building houses most of the faculty's offices and research laboratories.

Master's and doctoral students' research work is advised by over thirty professors in all the major fields of chemistry: analytical, atmospheric, biochemistry, environmental, inorganic, organic, and physical.

After a wonderful weekend at Pine Shadows, John visited Bob Stevens, chairman of the University of Colorado's chemistry department. Bob was a good friend of John's and was his postdoctoral advisor decades ago. He thanked John again for inviting him and Betty to the party. Then they reminisced about the good times they had during John's days as a student at CU. After more conversations, Bob offered John a part-time professorship to mainly bring in research money, supervise a couple of graduate students, and present a seminar talk once a semester. John accepted his offer on the condition to only be at the university Mondays, Wednesdays, and Fridays. He told Bob that he wanted to use the other days of the week to complete writing a chemistry textbook, work out at the gym, do some hiking, and when the snow was right, ski at the nearby Eldora ski area. He also planned to learn how to fly a small plane, host visits from neighbors and friends, make some trips around Colorado, and attend conferences in the United States and overseas.

A week after being hired by Bob, John moved into a southwest corner office on the fourth floor of the chemistry building. The office was spacious, and Czermak's desk sat against the west wall, and the visiting professor's desk was next to the opposite wall. The only window in the room was located opposite the door. The view from the window overlooked the water fountain court and the University Memorial Center, with the Flatirons in the distance. The Flatirons are five large slanted rock formations of red conglomeratic sandstone along the eastern slope of Green Mountain. The name comes from their resemblance to old-fashioned clothes irons.

John shared the office with a visiting faculty member. His present office mate was a professor from Australia, and he was due to return to the University of Sydney at the end of the fall semester. They had a lot to talk about since John had worked at the University of New South Wales, located in a suburb of Sydney, for three years.

John enjoyed a joyous Christmas and New Year holiday with his family. On the second Monday of the new year, Bob brought a beautiful tall blonde, about John's age, to John's office. "John, I would like you to meet Professor Lara Medvedev, a visiting professor from Mendeleev University in Moscow. She is on a sabbatical for a year at CU. I have already shown her around campus and our building and introduced her to most of the faculty and staff."

"Lara, I am so happy to meet you, and welcome to Boulder and the University of Colorado."

"Thank you. I am looking forward to spending a year here and sharing an office with you. Bob and Betty were kind enough to meet me at Denver International Airport yesterday, take me on a short drive through downtown Denver and around Boulder, and let me stay at their home in North Boulder until I can find an inexpensive apartment to rent. You can probably guess that Russian faculty are not paid well."

"How would you like to stay in a new apartment at my home in Nederland at no cost? The apartment is on the first floor of my house. A nice family is renting the second and third floors, and I live in an apartment above my three-car garage near the house. However, you would have to buy some furniture, especially a bed, unless you want to sleep on the floor. I would ask you to leave the furniture there after you go back to Moscow. You could ride with me to work on Mondays, Wednesdays, and Fridays and take the bus the other two days. You would have to take my second car to the bus stop in Nederland on those two days. Once you reach the main bus station in Boulder, you could walk to campus or transfer to a Boulder bus. An easier option is to just drive my car to campus on non-snowy days since my Smart car does not do well on icy and snowy roads. Before you say yes or no, let me show you the apartment on Wednesday afternoon."

"John, do you think I should buy a car?"

"I would wait a couple of weeks to see if the bus service suits you since cars can be lots of trouble but a convenient way to get around. Of course, I have already offered you the use of Whit."

"Okay, I will take your valuable advice, but I will have to get a Colorado driver's license as soon as possible. Why do you call your car Whit?"

"I like to put names on my houses and cars. I call him Whit since he is painted white. The *e* is missing."

"John, that is a truly kind and generous offer, so please consider it, Lara. Of course, I told you that you could stay at my home as long as you want, but I can understand how you want to have your own bedroom and living room and a kitchen where you can make your own meals. By the way, John, I think the name of your red Jeep is obvious."

"You are correct, Bob. Lara, please make yourself at home and unpack your suitcase full of books and papers. You can share one of my bookcases. How about the three of us having lunch at the Packer Grill in the Memorial Center? We will have to watch for ice on the sidewalks. What do you think of all the snow on the ground, Lara?"

"Well, it is warmer here than in Moscow, and of course, we do get lots of snow."

Bob agreed to meet John and Lara in his office at noon.

Over lunch, Bob did most of the talking. "Lara, I would like to tell you more about Denver and Boulder. I think I already told you a lot about CU, and I am sure during your stay you will learn much more.

"Denver was founded in 1858 and is in the South Platte River Valley on the western edge of the High Plains, just east of the Front Range of the Rocky Mountains, with an estimated population of almost eight hundred thousand according to

Wikipedia. It is nicknamed the *Mile-High City* because of its elevation of 5,280 feet above sea level. Snowfall is common from late fall to early spring, and summers can range from warm to hot, with occasional afternoon thunderstorms.

"Boulder was founded in 1858 and is located at the base of the foothills of the Rocky Mountains in a basin beneath Flagstaff Mountain. It is twenty-five miles northwest of Denver and has a population of about one hundred thousand. The city is known for its association with gold seekers and being the home of CU. Arapahoe Glacier provides water for the city, along with Boulder Creek, which flows through the center of the city. One of the most popular sections of Boulder is Pearl Street Mall, home to numerous shops and restaurants. The four-block pedestrian mall is a social hotspot in the city. The Hill, next to the southwest side of campus, is one of the centers of off-campus life for students who mainly hang out at the Sink, a popular bar and restaurant. In fact, the movie star Robert Redford worked there as a waiter during his studies at CU. I am sure John will take you there for a meal during your stay, as well as in the dining hall at Chautauqua Park. As you can see, I am using notes I took from reading *Wikipedia.*"

John interjected, "My father told me a story about the time he and his father, who ran a nursery, were contracted by the university to plant a variety of trees around the barren campus. Now these trees are fully grown or have been removed for new buildings. Also, one of the things I would like to do on Memorial Day is run in the BOLDERBoulder, a six-mile race through Boulder. It would be great if you could join me for the race. I know Bob has no interest participating in the event."

"You are correct, John. Even Betty does not have any desire to run in the strenuous race. Please tell us about Moscow and your university."

"As you know, the Russian capital is Moscow, the most populous city in Europe, about thirteen million. It was established in 1147 and is home to several UNESCO World Heritage Sites.

John, I am sure you have visited Red Square, the Kremlin, and Saint Basil's Cathedral. You probably also saw the Moskva River that flows through the city and all the greenery in and around Moscow. It has the largest forest in an urban area, more than any other major city in the world.

"Mendeleev University of Chemical Technology is a public university that was founded in 1898. It is the largest higher educational institution and research center of chemistry and chemical engineering in the world. The university has several campuses, which include two higher colleges, four institutions, and nine faculties. I teach chemical separations in the Faculty of Engineering Chemistry and Technology and even use the latest edition of your chemical separations book that was translated into Russian. You did a great job of writing the book, John."

"I need to return to work now. Please come to my office at five, Lara, and we can go to my home for dinner. If you wish, following one of Betty's wonderful meals, you can try and get more sleep to help with your jet lag."

Back in their office, Lara told John, "You sure resemble the Hollywood actor Tom Cruise, but taller. Indeed, your resemblance to Mr. Cruise is striking! You have his handsome features, enticing azure-blue eyes and lustrous black hair, extraordinary physique, and an undeniable aura of machismo."

"Thank you, Lara. Indeed, both of my parents were good-looking, and the nice body they gave me does bring stares from women of all ages. You are indeed beautiful and charming and obviously highly intelligent being a tenured professor."

"I was also fortunate that my parents are intelligent retired teachers in Moscow and that my education in Moscow was first-class. I also had a great advisor during my doctoral studies at Oxford. That is where I perfected my English and got to see a lot of the beautiful English countryside."

Later that afternoon, John took Lara to his laboratory, where he introduced her to his three graduate students whom they would be supervising together. "Larry received his undergraduate degree from Florida State University, Susan's degree was awarded at Washington State University, and Mark graduated from the University of Melbourne, Australia. All three will be doing research in using new separation methods to treat radioactive wastewater and acidic mine water containing hazardous metals. We plan to obtain some water samples from major mines in western Colorado and prepare simulated radioactive water. I also arranged to take them to the Actinide Separations Conference in San Diego at the end of March, where they will present poster papers on their research. Of course, you need to join us as I have plenty of travel funds in our Environmental Protection Agency contract."

"I would love to, especially since this is my first visit to the United States, and I want to see as much of your country as I can during my year here. I was lucky to visit several European cities during my studies at Oxford."

"Lara, maybe we could drive to California and visit some interesting cities and sites along the way. You three would have to fly since you need as much time in the laboratory as possible."

"That sounds wonderful, John."

The three students then took turns asking Lara about her university, students, and research. She ended her replies by saying that her student's research was in the same area as theirs. John and Lara then returned to their office.

"CU's campus is certainly lovely, and the Flatirons are beautiful. The nice tour that Bob gave me of Boulder and the campus showed me how lucky I am to be able to have my sabbatical here. You certainly have a lot of interesting books on the shelves. Are the large ones all theses?"

"No, some are my annual diaries. I mainly write about the trips I took each year. You are welcome to borrow some to read if you want to."

After their start on the seventeen-mile drive to Nederland through Boulder Canyon that parallels Boulder Creek, John asked Lara to tell him a little more about herself. "Well, I grew up in Moscow with an older brother and wonderful parents and attended public schools until my university studies. My father was a chemistry professor at Mendeleev, and my mother taught chemistry at a nearby high school. Both are now retired. I think I told you that I did my undergraduate studies at Mendeleev and then went to Oxford University for my PhD, doing research in chemical separations. We used the first edition of your book, *Chemical Separations*, in one of my classes. After returning to Moscow, my father arranged a postdoc position for me at Mendeleev and later a position as a lecturer. Over the years, I worked my way up to full professor. During this time, I had a short marriage to Ivan Medvedev, who was a police officer. He was a very jealous and violent man, and after two years of his abuse, I divorced him. For many months after the divorce, he continued to harass me and even threatened to kill me. He said on many occasions that I would always be his wife. Finally, he left me alone after I got a restraining order. It was indeed a very dark time in my life. I used to refer to him as Ivan the Terrible to my friends. Since then, I have avoided getting serious about a second marriage. I also moved back to my parents' apartment to help them.

"My travels are just a small fraction of the number of your trips. Of course, I have seen some of western Russia, and when I was in England, I toured the countryside near Oxford and London. The highlight was seeing Stonehenge. I also enjoyed visiting Paris, Brussels, Amsterdam, Luxembourg, Frankfurt, and Northern Ireland. I will tell you about the Ireland trip on our return to Boulder."

"The summary of my life so far is a little longer than your story. I grew up with wonderful parents and two brothers and two sisters in a two-bedroom home in West Denver. I attended elementary and junior high schools near our home and West

High at the edge of downtown Denver. In high school, my grades dropped since I became more interested in cars and girls than education. I also worked at a supermarket part-time. I dropped out of high school during my senior year to work more but went back the following year and graduated. I then started college studies at CU Denver part-time and started working full-time at Rocky Flats as a janitor.

"The Rocky Flats Plant was between here and Golden off Highway 93. Parts for nuclear weapons were made there for many years, but now the plant is no longer there. It was decontaminated and demolished several years ago. Now the area is a national wildlife refuge.

"During the next three years at Rocky Flats, I was promoted to laboratory technician and continued part-time studies at CU Denver, majoring in chemistry. I then took a two-year leave of absence from Rocky Flats and attended classes full-time during my junior and senior years on the Boulder campus. Following being awarded a bachelor of science degree in chemistry, I returned to Rocky Flats as a full-time chemist in the research and development department and continued going to CU Boulder full-time for my master's, doctoral, and postdoctoral studies. After my university studies, I was promoted to manager of a group in the department and later director of the department.

"I met Margrit Hoffman when I was in graduate school. We only had a three-month courtship before we were married. She was a beautiful, wonderful lady, and we were lucky to eventually have three great children, Amy, Eric, and Lorrie. I am sure you will get to meet my adult children sometime soon. Margrit was killed in an automobile accident when we lived in California."

"John, I am so sorry to hear that. Please continue."

"Over two decades ago, I spent three years at the International Atomic Energy Agency in Vienna, Austria. In my previous work at Rocky Flats, I was a contributor to the development of the neutron bomb. In Vienna, KGB agents were trying to get information about the bomb from me via Margrit.

She became romantically involved with Andrei Pushkin, thought by the CIA to be a KGB agent. Realizing the futility of their relationship, Margrit told me about Andrei and how they unsuccessfully attempted to terminate it. Later Andrei committed suicide, and Margrit was beside herself with grief. Later I was to find out that Andrei had faked his suicide and left Vienna for Canada to start a new life. After leaving the agency, Margrit, our three children, and I returned to our home in Arvada. Margrit and I resumed a close, loving relationship that had been severely damaged in Vienna. I also returned to Rocky Flats as manager of the Plutonium Chemistry Research and Development Group.

"About this time, I traveled a lot to conferences overseas and to Vienna and Moscow to have meetings with my two Russian coauthors on a series of books we were writing for the IAEA. Following more contacts with my Russian colleagues, I was informed that a background investigation had been conducted by the Department of Energy and the FBI. This investigation resulted in me losing my security clearance. I then went to Australia to teach for three years and later work in California for three years. Andrei came to California and tried to renew his relationship with Margrit and kill me, but instead, he accidentally killed Margrit. I found out later that he committed suicide in Canada and told his son Alex in his dying breath that I had shot him.

"At that point, I wanted to start a new life and left California for a teaching job at Clemson University in South Carolina. I even started using my middle name, James. I enjoyed the academic life very much, supervising several students and teaching actinide chemistry. I even purchased the car and home that Margrit liked.

"Alex joined my research group using a different last name. I did not know that he was Andrei's youngest son. In early January, two years ago, I took him, two other graduate students, and Ying, a postdoctoral student from China, with me on an expedition to Antarctica where we would do some ice sampling. By that time,

I had fallen in love with Ying. We were married by the ship's captain as we crossed the Antarctic Circle. The following night, me, Alex, and a dozen other brave souls camped out on Hovgaard Island where there was an attempt on my life. On the last night of the trip, as we were crossing the Drake Passage and heading past Cape Horn, the sea was very rough, and large waves were coming over the front of the ship. Alex met me at the stern of the ship and, with difficulty, admitted that his real name was Alexander Pushkin, that his father was the one who had a love affair with Margrit in Vienna, and that his father had cut the brake line on my car in California with the intention of killing me and not Margrit. I was shocked as Alex admitted that on the camping night, he was the one who had kicked the rock that was holding me and my sleeping bag in place. As I was sliding down the hill, Alex told me that he was immediately sorry for what he had done and ran, trying to stop me, but that I had managed to stop myself at the edge of the hill above the sea. He also said that his father shot himself in his home in Canada where he was staying and his father told him in his dying breath that I had shot him and that he should kill me. I sternly told Alex that I did not kill his father and had an alibi. Alex told me that he was extremely sorry that he had tried to kill me. At the end of our conversation, I told Alex that under the circumstances, I forgive him. My last words were for him to come and give me a big bear hug. Alex happily jumped over and gave me a hearty embrace that caused both of us to accidentally fall over the back of the ship into the rough, freezing ocean."

John then told Lara about Deborah saving his life, his year in Chile, falling in love with Deborah, getting his memory back, and returning to South Carolina. "Upon my return to the US, Ying and I resumed our lives together, and I went back to teaching at Clemson. But later, Alex's brother arrived in Clemson, trying to kill me, but instead killed Ying in a similar manner as Margrit's death. A week later, he also attempted a second time to kill me but failed.

"In trying to get over my loss of Ying, I slowly renewed a loving relationship with Deborah, and we started traveling in South America. Several months later, while back in Clemson, I was invited to speak at an international conference in Moscow. I invited Deborah to join me, and we first went to Vienna where we were married. After our arrival in Moscow and my attending the conference all week, Deborah and I enjoyed the banquet on the last night of the conference. After returning to our room that night, Alex's brother surprised me and Deborah with a gun and shot both of us. Immediately after being shot, I jumped over to the brother, giving him a bear hug, trying to wrestle the gun from him. During the scuffle, the gun fired a third time, killing him.

"The police and ambulance came and took Deborah and me to the nearby hospital where we were operated on to remove the bullets and then placed in intensive care. I survived, but Deborah did not.

"After Deborah's passing, I had another attempt on my life in the hospital that nearly succeeded, but I had a good nurse that did an excellent job of CPR on me. I knew it was Andrei's brother that tried to kill me, and I told that to the police.

"After returning to Clemson, I had several email exchanges with Misa, my best Russian friend. He wrote that the police continued their search for the brother, but with no success thus far, and he would continue to keep me informed. I also arranged for a realtor to sell my two homes in South Carolina and, when I was ready, for movers to come and load my furniture and personal things for transport to Nederland. I then drove to Colorado so I could start a new life here."

"John, I am so sorry about the death of your wife and the attempts on your life. Do you have any concerns about another attempt?"

"Hopefully not since I do not think Andrei's brother knows where I work and live now."

As they passed an intersection on the right, John said, "That is the road to the old mining town of Gold Hill that consists of a restaurant and bar, store, and a few homes. There are two roads going out of Gold Hill, one to the Peak-to-Peak Highway and the other one back to Boulder."

A little further up Boulder Canyon, they passed a road on the left. Lara asked, "Where does that road go?"

"That road eventually ends in Nederland. Near the west end of the road, which is called Magnolia Drive, is where the Boulder County Open Space trail from Pine Shadows ends.

"I have told you about the several trips I have made to Moscow and my train trip from Vladivostok to Moscow, but let me tell you about the trip I made to Kamyshin, Russia, a small city on the Volga River between Volgograd and Saratov, where my mother's father emigrated from in 1910. I do not know much about my mother's mom, except that she was also of Russian ancestry.

"I flew into Sheremetyevo Airport from Berlin and then transferred to a flight to Volgograd. I stayed in Volgograd at the Ruefa Hotel for three nights. The first morning, I arranged for a taxi to take me to Kamyshin, a four-hour drive. The landscape was beautiful on the drive. The highway paralleled the Volga River about half of the time. Kamyshin is a nice compact city with a long bridge going over the Volga River. We went to the town's historical museum, but I did not find any information about my mom's father or grandfather. After two hours in Kamyshin, we headed back to Volgograd.

"I spent most of the next day taking a long walk around Volgograd. There is a beautiful church near the hotel that has unique architecture. As I was there, the bells of the church started to ring, so I went inside the church named Kazansknu Cobor, and a service was just starting. It was a different type of service. People were just standing around as the choir was singing and the organ playing. There were two priests walking around, spreading incense, and the people would bow at different times. Some would kiss pictures on the pillars. All the women and children were wearing scarves. The inside of the church is beautiful, and the service was divine. The next morning, I flew back to Moscow and stayed there two nights before flying to Berlin and then home."

"Wow, John, I think you have seen more of Russia than I have."

John then told Lara a little about Nederland. "During the 1850s, the town started as a trading post between European settlers and Ute Indians, and in 1874, it was officially established. The town's first economic boom started with gold, silver, and tungsten discoveries in Eldora, Caribou, and east of the town. I plan to take you to see Eldora, Caribou, and the Eldora Ski Area. The town's name came from the Nederland Mining Company, headquartered in the Netherlands, which bought the Caribou Mine."

"What is the elevation and population of Nederland, John?"

"The town's elevation is 8,234 feet above sea level, and the population is almost two thousand. The Continental Divide is eight miles west of Nederland, and Barker Reservoir is on the east side of town. Boulder Creek runs through the reservoir, supplying Boulder with its drinking water. The Peak-to-Peak Highway goes through the town from Blackhawk to Estes Park, some of the towns I would like to take you to see if you are interested."

"Yes, of course."

"The main recreational attractions for visitors to Nederland are the nearby Indian Peaks and James Peak Wilderness areas and the Roosevelt National Forest. The town's cultural events are an annual music and arts festival, Miners Day celebration, and Frozen Dead Guy Days. The latter commemorates a Norwegian immigrant freezing his father cryogenically to bring him back to life once medical science reached that point. The desire to leave his father in a frozen coffin gave the town a lot of publicity, including CNN televising a baker holding a sign with the words 'What Is the Big Deal about a Norwegian in the Freezer, I Have Six Danish in the Oven.'"

John smiled as Lara laughed.

"Of course, later the town capitalized on the situation by having Frozen Dead Guy Days with coffin races, dead guy look-alike costumes, and other crazy and deadly activities. By the way, the frozen guy is just four doors west of Pine Shadows on Doe Trail."

"Why do you call your home Pine Shadows?"

"It is because the house sits on the shady side of the mountain and is mostly covered by the shadows of the many pine trees behind the house."

As they were starting to drive past Barker Reservoir, John said, "Can you see my house and garage now? It is the highest one on the north side of the mountain."

"Yes, your big white house is easy to see, and it sure stands out among the smaller homes west of your home."

They drove through Nederland and made a left-hand turn onto Big Springs Drive and then another left turn onto Alpine Drive to Doe Trail that ends on the southeast corner of Nederland. The almost three-mile ride is on a gravel road. "I think it is interesting that my house has the address '86 Doe Trail' since I lost my DOE Security Clearance in 1986."

"When did you start building the house?"

"It was several years after I purchased the land when I had more money."

Upon arriving at Pine Shadows, John and Lara walked to the garage and climb the steel and concrete stairs to the front deck. After admiring the wonderful westerly view of the Continental Divide, Eldora Ski Area, Barker Reservoir, and Nederland, they went through a patio doorway into John's living room. Lara said, "This is a beautiful large room with a nice dining area and spacious kitchen. I love your furniture and the fireplace."

John then showed her both bedrooms with bathrooms as well as the laundry room and stairs that are behind the kitchen. "John, I find all your maps, pictures, and awards on your walls very interesting."

"As you can see, both bedrooms have patio doors that go onto the large front covered deck that also serves as the roof of the carport for three autos. Whit, Red, and Gail's car rest in the garage, and Randy parks his Jeep Wrangler in the carport behind Gail's car since he is usually the first to leave in the morning and the last one to come home. There is a large workshop and storage area in front of where the three cars sit, as well as a door leading to the covered patio where I have my exercise machine and weights, a jacuzzi, some outdoor furniture, and a ping-pong/ pool table. The patio has windows around the top half of the walls and a patio door in the middle of the east side. A little farther east is my tennis court and swimming pool. Do you play tennis or shoot pool?"

"You will have to teach me tennis, and I am not good at playing ping-pong or shooting pool. I do love to play chess though. Do you?"

"That is one of my favorite games, as well as a card game called Crazy Eight. I also like to play scrabble. Let me show you the first floor of the house now where you will hopefully be living."

After taking the short walk to the house that faced northwest, John explained, "The house is much like the rental home I designed and helped build in South Carolina, except it is larger. The upper two floors are identical to this floor and my apartment over the garage. You could use the second bedroom as your office. As you saw, my office has a desk, bookcases, and a sleeper couch for overnight guests.

"Both the house and garage have fire-resistant siding and solar collectors on the metal roofs. There are also sprinkler systems in all the rooms as required by the county building code. The code also requires a large open area around structures. As you saw, I have rock gardens in those areas. I especially like the southern colonial appearance of the house with the four large white pillars holding up the extended roof that covers the top-floor deck. The extended roof also keeps the second-floor deck and front patio dry. From all three levels, one has the same lovely views as from the apartment deck. There are dormers above each of the three patio doors on the top floor. The ten-acre property is next to Boulder County Open Space, with a walking trail that I mentioned to you. By the way, my renters have invited us for lunch."

After John showed Lara the other rooms, they went out the front patio door onto the concrete patio and admired the view. After several minutes there, they walked up the outside steel and concrete stairs to the second-floor deck. After a knock on the middle patio door, Randy came and let them into the living room. John then introduced Lara to Gail and Randy. Then they all sat down, and John started the conversation by asking Randy and Gail to briefly tell Lara about their lives.

Randy started by saying, "We moved here from Boulder shortly after John built this house. We love the home and the area, especially since it is close to my job. I am a climate scientist working at the University of Colorado Institute of Arctic and Alpine Research Field Station at 9,500 feet and about seven miles north of Nederland on Highway 72, also called the Peak-to-Peak Highway. After reaching the turn off to the institute, one must drive west a little over a mile on a gravel washboard road to get there. The institute has two main buildings. The largest building contains offices and classrooms, and the other one houses research laboratories. I have worked there since graduating from CU over two decades ago. You are welcome to come for a visit anytime."

Gail then briefly told the group about herself. "I am a realtor in Nederland and can work from home a lot. We have two teenage boys that attend Nederland Middle and High School. I also love the area and this home. The whole family snowboards at Eldora a lot, and we hike the trails on many summer days. The adjoining trail as well as the other one closer to town are our favorites. Every once in a while, I see the same pair of deer in the nearby woods. Once there was a bear trying to dig up some of our garbage that Randy buried in the vegetable garden. We do put our trash in a bear-proof bin. We also got rid of our bird feeders since we were told they also attract bears. John's good friends the Cochins told us they get deer, elk, and sometimes a moose in their backyard. They have a big, lovely home on twenty acres a few miles north of Nederland that we got to visit a few times."

Following Lara telling the group about herself and having lunch, Gail gave Lara a tour of the second and third levels while John and Randy chatted in the living room. Their two boys who shared the top floor were in school. John and Lara concluded the visit to the house by thanking Randy and Gail for the lunch. They then took a short walk around part of the property where the snow had melted."How would you like to see Nederland now and some of the surrounding area?"

"That sounds great, John. I certainly love the apartment, and your home and property are wonderful, especially the large decks on the front of both buildings with great views. I look forward to living here for a year. I hope I can move in as soon as possible."

"Why don't we go and pick out your furniture at a store in Boulder later so we can hopefully have it delivered tomorrow while I am at home? You will need to buy a bed, dresser, sofa, desk, and table and chairs. As you saw, all the kitchen appliances are already installed, as well as the washer and dryer. Friday night, you can move in with your luggage."

"I will call Bob and let him know I will not be back for dinner. Perhaps we can eat somewhere before I buy the furniture."

"If it's okay, I can help you select the furniture since I am sure you will leave it behind after you return to Moscow."

"Of course, John. I will be buying the furniture for you so I can have a lovely furnished apartment for a year. Of course, as you offered, the cost of the furniture will be in exchange for no rent money."

"Before we head back to Boulder a different way, via the mining towns of Blackhawk, Central City, and Idaho Springs, let me show you briefly around Nederland now."

After a walk down the three blocks of Nederland's old town and short visits to Eldora Ski Area and the old mining town of Eldora, they traveled to Blackhawk. During the twenty-minute drive, John told Lara about some of his boyhood days with trips to the area with his friends and friends of Bill, his older brother, who had cars. "We did a lot of fishing at lakes and streams and took many hikes on the trails in the mountain valleys, looking for minerals. I could name most of the minerals we found. At the time, I had quite a mineral collection that I displayed in my one-room chemistry laboratory that Bill and I built. It was in our backyard, and I used to do lots of experimenting there. My interest in chemistry first started after receiving a chemistry set on my tenth birthday. A couple of years later, we used the lumber from the one-room lab and some I had to buy to build a larger two-room laboratory. At the time, I was buying more and more chemicals and laboratory equipment with the money I earned from cutting lawns."

"It sounds like your love for chemistry started at an early age. My interest in chemistry was sparked by doing chemical experiments in my high school chemistry class. Of course, my parents were a great influence on my career in chemistry."

"After I started driving my own car and joining a hot rod club, my interest in chemistry faded but came back after I started working at Rocky Flats as a laboratory technician. Then I was determined to become a chemistry professor someday and started attending evening classes at CU's Denver Center."

After reaching Blackhawk and parking Red, they strolled around the gambling town and took short visits to two casinos. After a short drive to the adjoining historic town of Central City, they went into one of the casinos that John suggested since he had some good luck at the slot machines in the past. However, Lara lost some money on the machines. Next, they drove to Idaho Springs so John could show Lara another mining town. On the way, he told Lara about the time he and Margrit hosted three Russian friends who were in Denver to attend an international solvent extraction conference. "We took our three friends to the top of the highest paved mountain road in the US, Mount Evans, followed by showing them Central City. As I was taking my friends on the town tour, Margrit had a newspaper printed in a souvenir shop with the headline 'Soviet Spies Arrested in Central City.' Our friends got a lot of laughs over the newspaper, and Margrit gave the paper to Misa to take back to Moscow."

"Well, John, I am glad you did not have a newspaper printed for me. If you would have, what would have been the headline?"

"Maybe 'Beautiful Russian Professor Loses Lots of Money at the Slot Machines.' Or maybe 'Slot Machine Beats Beautiful Russian Visitor.'"

"John, you sure are lots of fun to be with. I am so happy that we are office mates and that we will also be neighbors."

"Thank you, and I am also pleased that I get to spend some time with a very remarkable lady. Maybe you can help me improve the little Russian that I know. By the way, how would you like to join me for a meal at my son's home on Saturday, followed by a visit to the Wild Animal Sanctuary north of the airport?

"Well, I will have to cancel many engagements with my numerous friends, ha ha. You are the only real friend I have since the other faculty members I have met all spend their leisure time with their families."

"As you know, I have been invited for breakfast at the Stevens on Friday morning, where, of course, you will be eating. Following breakfast will be a good time to put your luggage in my car for transport to Pine Shadows after work. We will have another faculty meeting on Monday, where you will have to discuss the research you have underway. I think Bob will want you to give the seminar talk a week from Friday."

"Thank you for the warning. It will be easy for me to talk about the research, and at the seminar, I will discuss the work I have done at Mendeleev as well as my planned investigations in your laboratory. Of course, most of my research will be related to the students' work that you have asked me to assist you with."

On their drive back to Boulder following their short visit to Idaho Springs, Lara told John about her trip to Northern Ireland. "I arrived in Belfast on an early morning flight from London. One of the city's principal landmarks was seen upon arrival, the two Harland and Wolff Cranes, nicknamed Samson and Goliath. It was there that many great ships were built, including the *Olympic*, *Britannic*, and the *RMS Titanic*. After a tour of Belfast, our tour group proceeded to the town of Carrickfergus by bus for a short photo stop, and then the bus took the coast road north through the picturesque fishing village of Carnlough. We continued passing the coastal villages of Glenariff, Cushendall, and Cushendun. There were stunning views of the sea to the right and the mountains to the left. Most impressive were the spectacular views of the Mull of Kintyre, Scotland. Moving inland, we came to the town of Ballycastle, home to Ireland's oldest town fair. Our next stop was at the famous Carrick-a-Rede Rope Bridge. Its construction facilitated the local fishermen's access to Sheep Island, where there is excellent fishing. The walk to the swinging bridge was up a hill and then down on stone steps. Going over the bridge was quite scary. We then headed for Dunluce Castle for a photo stop before arriving at the Giant's Causeway. There are about forty thousand interlocking basalt columns there, caused by a volcanic eruption. After leaving the Giant's Causeway, we returned to Belfast, taking a different route."

"That sounds like you had a great trip, Lara. Years ago, I had a short visit to Belfast that was very enjoyable. I especially liked the Titanic Museum."

After their return to Boulder, they had dinner at the Dark Horse, Lara's first visit to the unique restaurant and bar with lots of collectibles hanging on the walls and from the ceiling. John told Lara about the place and how he used to have safety meetings there when he worked at Rocky Flats. After the meal, they went to a nearby furniture store and picked out the furniture for Lara. "John, I am so happy you liked the pieces I chose. I am also pleased that the furniture can be delivered in the morning while you are at home."

"I am happy that you are happy. Now it is past my bedtime, and I will drop you at the Stevens."

On Friday, John arrived at the Stevens' home for breakfast. Over the meal, John told Lara and the Stevens, "Lara's furniture arrived safely yesterday at Pine Shadows and was arranged on the first floor of my house where she will be living this year."

"Thank you so much, John. I think Nederland is great, and your home is superb. I sure like the furniture we bought."

"By the way, Lara and I have been invited to have a meal at my son's home tomorrow and visit the Wildlife Animal Sanctuary near the Denver airport. Have you been there?"

"Bob and I have not, but it is on our to-do list."

"Your meals are so delicious, Betty. I will certainly miss your wonderful cooking. You and Bob have been so kind to put me up since I arrived in Colorado."

"Lara, it has been our pleasure, and perhaps someday we will visit you in Moscow, where you can return the favor. Please put your suitcases in John's car now since I need to get to the office."

John and Lara gave their thanks to Betty for a wonderful breakfast and departed for campus.

II

John and Lara left their office early on Friday afternoon, did some grocery shopping, and drove to Pine Shadows. As John was bringing Lara's luggage and food into her apartment, she started touring her new home. "John, the furniture is perfect in all the rooms." She then walked over and gave him a hug. "Thank you for providing such a wonderful place for me to live this year."

"Well, if you need anything, just call and I will walk a mile, ha ha, to assist you. I need to run some errands now. I think you have enough food for dinner."

"Please come by when you are finished and have dinner with me. Then you can see how good Russian food cooked by me tastes."

On Saturday morning, John and Lara traveled to Eric and Sylvia's home in South Boulder. Since the foursome had late breakfasts, they went directly to the Wildlife Animal Sanctuary.

After their visit to see all the wonderful animals at the sanctuary and a short walk in downtown Denver, they returned to Eric and Sylvia's home for dinner. Amy, Dave, and Lorrie arrived, and the five young adults spent most of the time exchanging information with Lara over a wonderful meal that Sylvia had prepared. After dinner, John and Lara thanked their hosts for a wonderful day and returned to Pine Shadows.

Following Sunday morning breakfast, John took Lara to Eldora for her to try some snow skiing. She was excited to learn how to ski. After John rented some skis for Lara, he showed her the basics of skiing before they took the lift to the top of the beginner's slope. Lara slowly skied next to John and made it downhill with only one fall. They continued this routine several more times with no more falls.

After a good time skiing, they went for an early dinner at the Black Forest Restaurant in Nederland. John told Lara that this was his favorite Nederland restaurant since they had excellent Wiener schnitzel and bratwurst. My other favorites are Back Country Pizza, Kathmandu Restaurant, and Neds Restaurant. I usually do my grocery shopping in Boulder, but there is a nice supermarket in Nederland called B&F Supermarket. Years ago, Margrit and I have stayed at the Boulder Creek Lodge a couple of times."

"Thank you so much for taking me to the slopes and teaching me how to ski. I really enjoyed the day and have fallen in love with the sport. I look forward to more of the same."

"I am so happy you like skiing as I think it makes the winter go by faster. Maybe next weekend we can go to Breckenridge to ski. As you saw, I have my own skis. I also have a snowboard that

I usually use on the slopes. Maybe after a few more trips to the slopes, you can try snowboarding. I also like to cross-country ski on the trails around Pine Shadows, but if you join me for that, you will need to buy your own skis."

After they return home, Lara gave John a thank you with a hug. John said, "I will see you in the morning about eight so you can ride with me to the office. Now I need to do my chores around the garage and apartment. Good night."

At the staff meeting the next day, Lara told the faculty about her planned research on treating mine water using some unique methods. John gave a summary of his students' research and announced that he was successful in one of his proposals to the National Science Foundation. Other proposals with the DOE and the EPA were pending. He also informed the faculty that his students would accompany him and Lara to the Actinide Separations Conference in March.

After John and Lara arrived back at Pine Shadows in the early evening, John told Lara, "Remember, I will take you to the Nederland bus station at 7:45 so you can catch the eight o'clock bus to Boulder. You can phone me when you arrive back to Nederland in the late afternoon. Sometime this week, I will take you to get your driver's license so you can start driving Whit to the bus stop or just drive directly to the office if the roads are not icy."

"What are your plans for tomorrow?"

"I will work on my chemistry textbook in the morning, followed by doing some cross-country skiing on the trail next to Pine Shadows even though the snow is starting to disappear."

John and Lara spent most of Wednesday in the laboratory with their students, and Thursday's activities were about the same as they were on Tuesday, except for John helping Lara get her driver's license. She also received a small package at CU from Moscow containing a shot-size plastic bottle of Russian Standard vodka made in St. Petersburg. There was no return address on the package, and she was surprised that the seal on the bottle cap was off. Lara assumed it was from her folks or brother and sent them thank-you emails.

Following Lara's excellent seminar talk on Friday afternoon, John told Lara in their office, "Your talk was very interesting, and you did an outstanding job in telling everyone about your work in Moscow and your planned research. Your use of the English language is first-class."

"Thank you. I do enjoy my research here and your wonderful company."

"Would you be interested in seeing the eastern part of the Rocky Mountain National Park and Estes Park tomorrow?"

"Certainly, that sounds great."

"Since the highest continuous paved mountain road in the US is closed for the winter, we can only drive through part of the eastern side of the park. Be sure to wear a heavy coat and bring along a hat and gloves. After the park visit, we can go to Estes Park and have lunch at the Stanley Hotel. Following our meal, we can take a walk around the interesting tourist town and then head back to Nederland. If you agree, we can go skiing on Sunday in Breckenridge."

"That sounds like a wonderful weekend."

"Although Randy uses a snow blower to clear the driveway after snowstorms, he usually does not clear the tennis court. An exception was the time I had an open house party after I moved into my apartment. When the snow disappears in the early spring, I will teach you how to play tennis. Maybe when the Boulder Golf Club opens, we can play some golf. I am impressed that you are so good at playing pool, and I do love playing chess with you despite losing about half of the games we have played. Before we drive to San Diego next month, I would like to show you on the weekends some of the places on the northern front range, such as Colorado State University in Fort Collins and maybe even Cheyenne, Wyoming. We can visit Garden of the Gods, Pike's Peak, Colorado Springs, and Pueblo on our trip to

San Diego. On our return from California, we can stop at Grand Junction, Glenwood Springs, Aspen, and Vail."

The next day after breakfast, James and Lara visited the colorful tourist town of Estes Park, followed by a drive through the eastern part of Rocky Mountain National Park. After their return to Nederland, Lara thanked James for the wonderful day. "I especially liked the park and seeing so many deer and mountain sheep. I had hoped we would see a bear and/or a mountain lion. I was surprised by the small herd of elk in Estes Park, and the lunch we had at the restaurant of the Stanley Hotel was exceptionally good. I did see that the hotel was the same one in the movie *The Shining*.'"

"There have been several bear visits to Estes Park, Nederland, and even Boulder looking for food, mainly in trash cans. After the road through the park is cleared of snow in a few weeks, we can take a drive through the entire park and return to Nederland via Grand Lake, Granby, Winter Park that has a ski area, Idaho Springs, and Black Hawk."

Early the next morning, the couple traveled to the old mining town of Breckenridge. James told Lara on the way, "Breckenridge was founded by prospectors mining in the nearby mountains. Tourism and skiing are now the main attractions. When the kids were young, Margrit and I had many visits to Breckenridge. We had a timeshare condo for the first week of each year, and I would always take Margrit and the kids to ski, ice skate, and walk around town, looking in the many shops. We would also try to eat at different restaurants for dinner. The family and I always had breakfast at the condo and would usually have lunch at the same restaurant at the base of one of the ski lifts. Breckenridge is where Margrit and the kids learned to ski. I got my ski lessons in a gym class at the university where my class would spend the weekend at another ski area above Georgetown, the old mining town we stopped at coming here this morning."

After a wonderful day of skiing and during the drive back to Nederland, Lara thanked John again for taking her to Breckenridge. "The lovely old mining town is certainly interesting, especially with its original buildings, and the ski runs are great, maybe a little better than Eldora."

The following Saturday, Amy and Dave hosted a day-early birthday party for John. Lara and the whole family, including John's older brother, Bill, and his wife, Kay, attended the festivities. It was a fun party in Aurora, where John received lots of gifts. Everyone enjoyed the food and birthday cake as well as the family reunion. The party ended with Amy telling everyone that she was going to have a baby in about eight months. The visitors all congratulated the couple and gave their thanks for a wonderful time as they slowly departed. On the drive back to Nederland, Lara asked John, "I thought you had two sisters?

"They died of cancer several years ago and are now in heaven with my folks and relatives."

"I am so sorry, John."

The next day, Lara invited John, Randy, and Gail for an early dinner to celebrate John's birthday. Following the meal and cake, Lara asked everyone what they would like to drink for a toast to John. Gail and Randy said they preferred a shot glass of brandy. Lara said, "I will have the same. John, since this is a special occasion, I think you should have a Russian drink. How about a shot of vodka?"

"You know that I do not drink, but since this is my birthday, just give me half a shot glass of the vodka. After the toasts and expressions of gratitude to Lara, John returned to his apartment, and Gail and Randy went upstairs for the night.

Ten minutes later, Randy received a frantic call from John saying that he was extremely sick and needed his help. Randy ran over to the garage to attend to John and found him passed out on the floor of his bathroom, with his face in a pool of vomit. He moved John to a dry spot in the bathroom and turned him over to see if he was still breathing. After making sure he was alive, Randy immediately called 911 and briefly told the operator about John's condition. Ten minutes later, a Nederland Fire

Rescue EMS vehicle arrived. The paramedic started to attend to John. Gail and Lara heard the siren and rushed to John's side, where they asked Randy what happened. "All I know is John called me and asked for help. I came down and found him here on the floor unconscious."

John was rushed to the main Boulder hospital. Randy, along with Gail and Lara, drove to the hospital. They anxiously sat in the waiting room. About an hour later, the doctor came in and told the three that they had stabilized John after stopping the internal bleeding and pumping out his stomach and intestinal tract. "His digestive tract contents are now in the laboratory for analysis. What did John eat for dinner?"

Lara spoke up. "We all had the same food, but John had a half of shot glass of vodka while we had brandy for a birthday toast."

"Is there any vodka left so we can have it analyzed?"

"Yes, I can bring it back to you later."

"We will keep John stabilized and see what the analysis shows. Meanwhile, there is no need for you all to wait here. I will call you if things change. But please get the bottle of vodka to me as soon as possible and on your way out ask the nurse for a sample jar to place some of John's vomit in for analysis."

After the three returned to Pine Shadows, Randy volunteered to take the half-full bottle of vodka and a sample of the vomit to the doctor.

Late the next morning, Lara received a call from the doctor. "The analysis of John's stomach and digestive track contents, the vomit, and vodka all show high levels of arsenic. John is slowly recovering and should be allowed to go home tomorrow. He might not have recovered if he had drunk a full shot glass of the vodka. Where did you get the vodka?"

"It arrived about two weeks ago from Moscow, and my parents and brother wrote that they did not send it. I do not know who would have sent it, but it appears like the sender wanted to poison me."

Late the next afternoon, Lara picked up John from the hospital and took him home. On the way, she told him what the doctor told her about the analysis and their discussion on the origin of the vodka. "Do you think Ivan, your ex-husband, could have sent it?"

"Yes, he did try and kill me after our divorce."

After they arrived home, he thanked her for bringing him home and asked her to give his appreciation to Randy for his kind help. "I now want to spend the rest of the day and tomorrow in bed and probably the rest of the week at home. Please inform Bob of my situation when you go to campus tomorrow. We should be thankful we are having some nice weather."

As John was resting in bed, he wondered if Lara could have tried to kill him. She could have easily lied about the bottle of vodka coming from Moscow and got some arsenic from the lab to put in the vodka that she had purchased at a liquor store. *I think I will now be more careful around her in case my hunch is true. I will ask her the next time we are together if she has any relatives named Pushkin.*

John's thoughts about Lara trying to kill him were reinforced the next morning. He had had a terrible nightmare about Lara killing him in their office with a hunting knife.

That evening, Lara came to John's apartment and asked him if he needed anything. He told her that he would confine himself to his apartment for the rest of the week and the weekend and did not need anything.

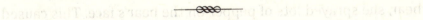

The following Monday, John returned to his routine of driving to campus with Lara and his activities in the chemistry building. On the first morning of driving to campus, John asked Lara, "Do you have any relatives with the name Pushkin?"

"John, that is a common name in Russia. But I do have a distant cousin with that name. She married a Pushkin, and he was a very violent and crazy man, worse than Ivan. She divorced the abusive man after only being married six months. Why do you ask?"

"I was curious if you had any relatives that were related to Andrei Pushkin, Margrit's lover in Vienna that I told you about. I had a graduate student at Clemson named Igor Medvedev. He was from Moscow. Since I know Medvedev is a common name in Russia, I am certain that he is not related to your ex-husband."

As John still considered Lara was trying to kill him, he did not do any weekend traveling with her and continued to stay at home most days. Bob had agreed to his working at home if he continued to communicate with his students about their research.

A week before the conference in San Diego, Lara asked John if he would like to hike the trail next to Pine Shadows with her since she has not been on the trail before. He agreed and said, "We have had a very mild winter so far with little snow. Today, it is almost like spring maybe because of climate change. However, the trail may be covered in snow in a few places. Since the county placed wood chips on the trail last year, we do not have to worry about mud."

During their walk on the narrow trail, Lara was behind John. At a turn in the trail, Johns saw a bear ahead. He frantically told Lara to run back to the garage. John closely followed her, but the bear caught up to him and knocked him down. As John was fighting off the bear, Lara ran back to help him. On the way, she pulled an aerosol can of pepper spray out of her backpack that she had recently purchased. When she reached John and the bear, she sprayed lots of pepper on the bear's face. This caused the bear to let go of John. Then the bear ran up the hill and disappeared. Lara kneeled and asked John, "Are you okay? I see blood running down your arms."

"No, I am hurting."

She helped him take off his coat and shirt. "There are several deep puncture wounds on your upper arms and shoulders." Lara then ripped John's shirt into strips. "I will try and stop the bleeding with these pieces of your shirt."

After getting most of the bleeding to stop, she helped John return to her apartment, where she washed his wounds and properly bandaged him. She told John that he needs to go to the hospital to get some of his wounds stitched.

As Lara was driving to the hospital, John thought about how wrong he had been about Lara wanting to kill him. *If she wanted me dead, she would not have rescued me from the bear attack.* He then told Lara how grateful he was for her saving his life and commented, "I was lucky you had some pepper spray with you. How did you find out about its use against bear attacks?"

"Gail told me about a bear she saw near the house last year and advised me that it would be wise to buy some pepper spray. She said that I could also use it against an evil man attacking me."

"It is unusual to see a bear so early in the year, but the snow is almost gone, and the young bear must have been very hungry after hibernation all winter."

After getting treated by the emergency room doctor, they returned to Pine Shadows. John then told Lara that he would go to bed and get some rest. Before they separated, John took Lara in his arms and thanked her again for saving his life.

"John, I would go to the end of the earth to save your life. I love you and never want anything or anyone to hurt you."

After a loving hug, John said, "Thank you, but now I will spend the rest of the weekend in bed. I will see you on Monday morning for our ride to school."

As John was resting in bed, he thought more about how wrong he had been about Lara trying to kill him. If she wanted me dead, she would only have had to keep running away from me and the bear. The arsenic-laced vodka was most likely sent by her ex-husband since she told me that he had tried to kill her after she divorced him.

Upon reaching the chemistry building on Monday, they invited their students to come to their office and give them a review of the posters that they will present at the meeting next week. John told the students that he and Lara would ask them some questions that they would probably be asked by the conference attendees who viewed their posters. He also told them that he has arranged their travel and hotel accommodations. "Lara and Susan will share a twin-bed room, as will Larry and Mark. Since I snore, I will have a one-bed room. You all will fly directly to San Diego on Sunday morning, and Lara and I will go in my Jeep so I can show her some of the southwestern US."

After the students left their office, John told Lara about their travel plans. "We will leave Nederland early tomorrow morning and spend the first night in Santa Fe, New Mexico, and the second next night in Albuquerque so we can have dinner with a high school friend of mine and his wife. Thursday morning, I would like you to meet a couple I worked with at Clemson over breakfast. That night, we will get a hotel in Farmington, Arizona, and visit the Grand Canyon. The following morning, we will drive to Kingman and stay there overnight. On Saturday afternoon, we should reach San Diego. Following getting checked into the hotel, we can have a walk around the center of the city. After Sunday's breakfast, we will need to go to the airport and pick up our students. After they check in and unpack at the hotel, we can all go for lunch, followed by attending the opening ceremony of the meeting in the hotel's conference center. Sometime during the meeting, I need to find a doctor who can remove the stitches in my shoulders and back."

III

John and Lara departed Nederland the next morning before the sun started to come up so John could avoid the sun in his eyes on the ride on HY-36 to Denver. A little after they started going south on I-25, there was a beautiful sunrise. Before they reached Colorado Springs, John pointed out to Lara the Air Force Academy next to the mountains. John suggested they drive through the Garden of the Gods to Manitou Springs and take the cog rail train to the top of Pikes Peak. John remarked, "Because of the mild winter, the train had just started operation a week ago. The drive through Manitou Springs, known for its mineral springs, is nice since the beautiful old buildings are much like the ones in Central City. After we reach the summit of Pikes Peak, we can have coffee and donuts. We need to eat the special donuts there because I was told if we take them with us, they will collapse at the lower altitude. There is an annual car race and marathon up the mountain. The peak is 14,114 feet above sea level and is one of Colorado's fifty-three mountains above fourteen thousand feet."

After the train ride and going through Manitou Springs and Colorado Springs, Lara said, "The train ride was great and what a view from the top of Pike's Peak. I was surprised to see that the red slanted mountains at the Garden of the Gods are just like the Flatirons in Boulder, so beautiful and breathtaking."

"There are similar groups of mountains in Denver's Red Rocks Park near Morrison and at Roxbury Park south of Denver. A good friend of mine lives in a subdivision next to Roxbury Park. I should take you there sometime."

About an hour later, they got off I-25 and had a short stop in Pueblo. Over lunch, John told Lara a little of what he knew of the city, including that their main industry is steel making.

After the couple's visit to Pueblo, they got back on I-25 and had a brief stop in Walsenburg, a small western town, and then proceeded to Trinidad, a good-sized city with some picturesque mountains nearby. They had a short walk around the downtown area, and Lara noted that the most interesting thing about Trinidad was the red bricks laid in some of the downtown streets instead of concrete or asphalt. They both liked the architecture of some of the old buildings. Next, they had a brief stop in Las Vegas, New Mexico, and a walk around the old city center. The couple got to Santa Fe at about six and checked into two adjoining rooms at the nice Chimayo Hotel next to the Old Town Plaza. After getting settled in their rooms, they had a nice dinner at a packed restaurant called The Shed and then took a walk around the old town square with its beautiful buildings of Spanish Pueblo style. After breakfast the next morning, they headed to Albuquerque.

Before arriving in Albuquerque, they made a detour to see the nuclear museum in Los Alamos. John explained to Lara that Los Alamos is the home of a national laboratory that was instrumental in the development and building of the first nuclear bombs. "Now the Lawrence Berkeley National Laboratory near San Francisco and the Hanford site in Washington assist the Los Alamos laboratory to produce the nuclear warheads. Rocky Flats was part of the nuclear weapon production complex before it was closed. I had spent some time in Berkeley when I worked at Rocky Flats assisting them in the development of the neutron bomb."

Following their short visit to the museum, they went to the Kasha-Katuwe Tent Rocks National Monument. The road near the monument was like a roller-coaster ride as they had to slowly go over many dips in the road where water flowed during rainstorms. The mountains in the area were white, with many smaller peaks that looked like upside-down ice-cream cones. John explained to Lara that the cone-shaped tent rock formations are the products of volcanic eruptions that occurred six to seven million years ago and left pumice, ash, and tuff deposits over a thousand feet thick. Precariously perched on many of the tapering hoodoos were boulder caps that protected the softer pumice and tuff below.

In Albuquerque, they stayed at the Holiday Inn Express. That night, they met with John's high school friend and his wife at Applebee's next to the hotel for dinner. The men talked about their last time together, boyhood antics, jobs, and what they were doing now. Bill still donated his mornings to helping his church and, in the afternoon, wrote on various topics.

The next morning, they had an early breakfast at the hotel with one of John's former students and his former postdoc. The two got married after leaving Clemson. They talked about Brian making homemade beer with a colleague at work, Brian's job, and what Shanna was doing at the University of New Mexico now. Before leaving Albuquerque after breakfast, John and Lara had a brief visit to the Old Town Square where the oldest church in Albuquerque, San Felipe de Ner, is located. Old Town is right next to the famous Route 66 highway.

After their visit to Albuquerque, they resumed their drive west on HY-40. One of the funny things they saw was a recreation vehicle pulling a small airplane with its wings detached. Most of all the other RVs they passed were pulling cars. They got off HY-40 at Thoreau, New Mexico, and headed north on HY-371 to Farmington. After reaching Farmington, they went east a short way on HY-64 to HY-550 and then to HY-57 to visit the Chaco Culture National Historic Park, which is now a World Heritage Site. They walked down to Pueblo Bonito, the core of the Chaco complex, and the largest great house. It was built by Chacoans in stages between the mid-800s and early 1100s and is four stories high with over six hundred rooms. They also went to Chetro Ketl, another of the largest great houses, that has an immense elevated earthen plaza. Later the couple returned to Farmington and checked into the Red Lion Inn. They had a late dinner at the Olive Garden across town since John was craving some tortellini.

Following an early breakfast the next morning, they traveled to the nearby Aztec Ruins. The Aztec structures were built in the late 1000s to the late 1200s by the ancestral Pueblo people who lived there centuries before the Aztec empire prospered. The settlement included large public buildings, smaller structures, earthworks, and ceremonial buildings. After the short visit, John and Lara got back on HY-64 and stopped at Four Corners, where Colorado, New Mexico, Arizona, and Utah meet. Lara got her picture taken by John where she had her knees in New Mexico and Colorado and her hands in Utah and Arizona. Both laughed a lot during the picture taking.

They then got on HY-160 to HY-64, heading toward the southeast rim of the Grand Canyon. Before they arrived at the

Grand Canyon, they stopped for a quick look at the Canyon of the Little Colorado River. The Little Colorado Gorge, comprising 379 thousand acres, was established as a Navajo Tribal Park in 1962. The park lies in the extreme western portion of the Navajo nation, adjacent to the eastern boundary of Grand Canyon National Park. The park straddles the Canyon of the Little Colorado River at its confluence with the Colorado River. Although not nearly as wide as the Grand Canyon, the deep, precipitous cliffs of the gorge are colorful and spectacular. The park affords an excellent westward view of the Grand Canyon itself, revealing some of the most completed geological sequences ever to be found in the world.

Next, they went to the beautiful and spectacular Grand Canyon. John told Lara a little about the canyon. "The story of the Grand Canyon stretches back almost two billion years. Evidence of every geological period from the Precambrian to the end of the Mesozoic can be observed."

Lara told John following the canyon visit, "I was a little nervous standing on the glass platform. But it did provide an excellent view of the canyon below."

The couple then traveled to Kingman, Arizona, via HY-64 and HY-40, arriving late in the day. They spent Friday night at the Ramada Hotel. Kingman is a good-sized town with Walmarts on both ends. After breakfast the next morning, they went south on HY-95, which parallels the Colorado River, and then caught HY-1, which goes past La Paz, a ghost town. The area is an Indian reservation with many farms.

Near the junction of HY-1 and I-10, they caught HY-78 to Julian, California. Although the speed limit was 65 mph, John had to go much slower since there were many dips in the road where there were gullies. Lara said she would not take the road during a rainstorm. The road got better as they approached a large sand dune with nearby mountain ranges. They then went by the Salton Sea into Julian. Julian is a small historic town with old buildings on about three blocks, housing souvenir shops and a couple of restaurants. The road in and out of the town is a curvy mountain road with lots of wineries. All of them were advertising free wine tasting. John told Lara, "If anyone stopped at just a few of the vineyards, they would arrive in San Diego drunk."

After reaching San Diego, they checked into the Hilton Garden Inn, where the Actinide Separations Conference would be held. After a long walk around the area of the hotel and dinner, they retired to their separate rooms for the night. On Sunday morning, they went into Old Town San Diego, where they had breakfast at Café Coyote. The town had about four blocks of old buildings with souvenir shops and a few restaurants.

Over breakfast, John told Lara about some of the things he did when he and Margrit lived in Simi Valley. "I would love to show you where I worked in Simi Valley, but because of Margrit's death there, I do not want to ever visit that place again. If we had more time, we could drive to Yosemite, my second favorite national park."

"What is your favorite?"

"Yellowstone. Number 3 is the Grand Canyon. I propose that we skip the last day of the meeting and visit Disneyland with the students. After we take them to the airport on Saturday morning for their early flight back to Denver, we can drive to Los Angeles and spend most of the day at Universal City. Then we can drive through Malibu, have a short visit to the Reagan Library, and find a hotel in Thousand Oaks for the night. On Sunday morning, we will leave for Las Vegas."

"John, promise me I will win more money than I lose at the slot machines."

"I will try. By the way, the meeting organizers have also arranged tours of San Diego for Wednesday afternoon. I have signed all of us up for one of the city tours. Now we need to drive to the airport and pick up our students. In the afternoon, we can attend the opening of the conference."

The next day, John, Lara, and their three students continued attending the conference. John had brought twenty copies of his book *Actinide Separations*, and the free copies went fast. He also had a flyer posted advertising free electronic copies of the latest edition of *Separations Chemistry*. Of course, he knew most of the attendees and got caught up on some of their activities since the conference a year ago. His student's posters drew a lot of interest, and the five found most of the talks educational.

That evening, they went to the Gas Light District. After a walk around the area, they had dinner. The group's discussions were mainly about the meeting and what they would hear the next day. Lara told the students, "You all did an excellent job during the poster session. I noticed you had a lot of visitors with many questions. I am sure you learned a lot from these chemists. I also liked seeing the other posters and the company exhibits."

John added to Lara's comments, "I agree, and you three are to be congratulated on your presentations. I also enjoyed the company exhibits and seeing many old friends."

The three students took turns expressing their favorable views of the meeting. Later they enjoyed the desert.

John then asked the students to tell everyone about the places they had visited in the past. Susan said, "Since I grew up in Washington, I got to visit a lot of the northwestern US numerous times and even took a vacation to Vancouver, Canada, with my parents. When I was about fourteen, we had a good time at Disneyland."

Larry remarked, "I was in California one time as well as all the states in the southeast and made a couple of trips to DC and New York. I grew up in Miami."

Mark explained, "I have seen all the major Australian cities growing up in Perth and even made a trip to New Zealand when I was going to the University of Melbourne. This is my first visit to the US, and after getting my PhD, I plan to see more of your country."

Before they returned to the hotel, John told them a little about living in Simi Valley. "After living and working in Australia for three years, Margrit, my first wife, and I returned to the US and lived on the west end of Simi Valley, across from the Reagan Library. My job was at the Rocketdyne site in the Santa Susanna Mountains at the east end of Simi Valley. After I arrived at the site on the first day of work in the nuclear part of the site, the ground started to shake extremely hard. Of course, I thought it was a major earthquake and jumped under my desk. My boss had seen my actions, laughed, and told me the other side of the site is where rocket engines are tested. He said when the rocket engine blasts, the whole site shakes. I worked on several different research projects during my three years with Rocketdyne. Unfortunately, there was a 6.8 earthquake during my last night in California. The shaking scared me so much I had a hard time getting out of bed and taking shelter in the bathroom. However, the movers had an easy time the next day packing our pictures since everything on the walls was lying on the floor. Please do not worry about an earthquake since I think they are rare in San Diego. But if the ground starts to shake, seek shelter away from windows immediately."

Following their return to the hotel, they sat in the lobby for a while, where John told the group about one of his trips to Mexico. "I took six of my Clemson students for a short trip to Juarez following the environmental design contest at New Mexico State University in Las Cruces. They had participated in the contest and won first place for their project on the treatment of wastewater. We took a walk around the old part of Juarez, had lunch, and did some shopping. I have a great picture of the group wearing Mexican sombreros. I am sorry we do not have time to make a short visit to Tijuana. Anyway, I think Professor Medvedev would need a Mexican visa to get into the country."

The next day, the group attended the meeting all day, followed by dinner in the hotel. Everyone enjoyed the tour of San Diego on Wednesday, and after the talks on Thursday, they all had a good time at the conference banquet. The group of five did not attend the last day of the meeting but traveled to Anaheim for a day at

Disneyland. At dinner that night, the group mainly talked about the good time they had at Disneyland. Lara said, "The Pirates of the Caribbean was my favorite ride, but I was a bit scared at the beginning of the boat ride when we went down that waterfall."

John remarked, "I also liked that ride, and it was fun to take it twice. The Big Thunder Mountain Railroad was also quite exciting."

The three students all agreed that they liked the Splash Mountain ride the best since they thought it was the most exciting one of the day.

After an early breakfast the next morning, the group checked out of the hotel and went to the airport. After their arrival at the airport, the students said their thanks and goodbyes to John and Lara and walked to the departure hall. John and Lara then traveled to Universal City. They had a long walk around Universal Studios and rode the studio tour train. As the train passed the Bates Motel, Lara was startled when the actor playing the crazy Norman Bates chased the tour cars, swinging a big hunting knife. The man-eating shark, Jaws, coming out of Jaws Lake, also scared Lara.

After touring the studio, taking a ride on the Flight of the Hippogriff, and going through Jurassic World, they left the park and had a late lunch at a nice restaurant overlooking the ocean. Then they went to the Getty Museum for a short visit, followed by driving up the coast, through Malibu, to Simi Valley to visit the Reagan Library. John told Lara that he was impressed by the large piece of the Berlin wall that was displayed behind the museum. Lara commented that the view of Simi Valley from the library was terrific. They ended the day at the Holiday Inn in downtown Los Angeles.

After breakfast on Sunday morning and a short walk near the hotel, John and Lara checked out of the hotel and headed for Las Vegas, a five-hour drive. On the drive, Lara said, "I sure enjoyed our visits to Disneyland and Universal City. I am looking forward to winning at the slots in Vegas."

In Las Vegas, they stayed at the MGM Grand, where the Ms. America contest was being held. The couple got to meet Ms. Colorado and had their picture taken with her. That evening, they had dinner with John's cousin and his Colombia-born wife. After dinner and arriving back at the hotel, John coached Lara in playing five-card draw, and she won thirty dollars. Then John played and lost twenty-five dollars.

The next day, they had an early breakfast with a West High friend of John. Following the meal, they headed to eastern Utah, going northeast on I-15 and east on I-70 to Arches National Park. Surprisingly, there were not a lot of tourists there. The couple agreed that the park was spectacular. John told Lara later that Arches now moved Grand Canyon National Park to fourth place on his list of favorite national parks.

At about eight in the evening, they reached Grand Junction. Before dinner at an Italian restaurant, they had a short walk in the old downtown area that had lots of souvenir shops, restaurants, and a few street entertainers. They spent their last night on the trip at Knights Inn.

After an early breakfast the next morning, they took a twenty-mile ride through beautiful Colorado National Monument. This was John's first time through the fascinating red rocks that had been weathered into beautiful sculptures. They continued the trip with short visits to Grand Mesa, Glenwood Springs, Aspen, and Vail.

On the way, Lara said, "John, I wish I could see some of Canada, but just like Mexico, I think I would need a visa."

"I wanted to surprise you, but I will tell you now that I have arranged for us to take a cruise on Glacier Bay, in western Alaska, after the spring semester ends. There you will see similar scenery as in the western part of Canada.

"That sounds great, John. By the way, what is the answer to your question 'Why is a river so rich?'"

"It is because a river has two banks."

Lara laughed.

"Another question for you. Do you know how to spell Mississippi with only one I?"

"I have heard that before," she answered as she covered her left eye and recited each letter of Mississippi.

This time they both laughed.

IV

After their return to Nederland, John and Lara continued their usual work activities, mainly working in the laboratory with their students. They also attended faculty meetings on Mondays and seminars on Fridays. After work, John sometimes took Lara on a drive to Chautauqua Park for walks up to the Flatirons, dinner at the park's Dining Hall, and meals at the Pearl Street Mall, the Sink on the Hill, the Dark Horse, and other restaurants in Boulder, as well as his favorites in Nederland.

Of course, they had several dinner parties with John's children, Randy, Gail, and the Cochins and Stevens. They also took weekend trips around to some of the places in the Colorado mountains that Lara had not seen.

At the end of the spring semester, the three students returned to their homes for several weeks of vacation. John discussed his plans for the summer. "Lara, I plan to attend a solvent extraction conference in Sweden at the end of next month, mainly to see old friends and take some tours. I will not give a paper at the conference. Would you like to join me?"

"Of course, John. Maybe we could go to Moscow after the meeting so you can meet my folks and brother."

"Well, I will have to be careful since Andrei's brother is still somewhere in Russia and would like me dead. But it will be nice to meet your parents and brother and have reunions with a few of my dear friends in Moscow."

"Of course, John. We can keep the information about our visit just between us, my relatives, and your friends so you will not have any concerns about Andrei's brother."

"Before we leave for Europe though, I would also like to take you to my favorite national park, Yellowstone, for several days. However, I would like to drive Red there instead of flying to Jackson. It will be a long car trip. How does that sound?"

"Great. I do love your car trips since I can see more of the countryside and towns we drive through, unlike flying. How about we leave this Thursday since I need a couple of days to finish drafting the journal article on our research for you to edit?"

"Okay. I have another question. I have registered for a National Geographic expedition to see some of the sites in western Alaska. You are welcome to join me if you do not mind sharing a cabin with me. The cruise leaves from Juneau."

"That would be wonderful, John, and I know you are a gentleman and lots of fun to travel with. What is the cost of the trip?"

"Do you mind paying half, $2,500?"

"I will have to make monthly payments to you since I only get my paycheck from Moscow at the end of each month."

On their drive to Sheridan, Wyoming, via Cheyenne, Wheatland, Casper, and Buffalo, John told Lara, "I read an article in Wikipedia on Yellowstone National Park last night and found out there was a lot I did not know about the park. It was the first national park in the US, established in 1872, and is well known for its wildlife and geothermal features, especially the Old Faithful geyser. Half of the world's geysers and hydrothermal features are in Yellowstone. Yellowstone lake is one of the largest high-elevation lakes in North America and is centered over the largest supervolcano on the continent. Hundreds of species of amphibians, birds, fish, mammals, and reptiles have been reported in the park. Visitors usually see in the beautiful forests and grasslands many antelope, buffalo, deer, and elk.

"Although we got to see our own bear, hopefully, we can spot one from the car. As we drive around the park, we can also admire the lakes and waterfalls. I plan to show you Yellowstone Falls, the Grand Canyon of Yellowstone, Yellowstone Lake, and many other beautiful features of the park. Since we will be staying at the Old Faithful Inn for two nights, you will have several occasions to see the eruption of Old Faithful. The Continental Divide of North America goes through the southwestern part of the park. The origins of the Yellowstone and Snake rivers are near each other on opposite sides of the divide. The Yellowstone River is a tributary of the Missouri River that joins the Mississippi River that eventually empties into the Gulf of Mexico, while the Snake River joins the Columbia and drains into the Pacific Ocean.

"On my previous trips to Yellowstone, I flew from Denver to Jackson in the early morning, rented a car, and stayed one night in Jackson. In the afternoon, I usually took a nice stroll in the downtown area, looking at shops, then had dinner. Early the next morning, I drove to Yellowstone, with a stop to admire the beautiful Grand Tetons and take pictures. In Yellowstone, I always stayed at the Old Faithful Inn. After my two nights at the inn, I would drive through West Yellowstone to Idaho Falls to see friends and then back to Jackson."

"It appears this trip will certainly be a little different."

"Well, for one thing, I have a beautiful, intelligent, and fun-to-be-with professor to accompany me. I have only entered the park from the east side once, and it was years ago. To change the subject, as you know, I have been taking a class and studying how to fly a single-engine airplane. I would also like to parachute out of a plane strapped to a professional instructor. Would you like to join me in a tandem jump?"

"I will have to give that some thought since it sounds like one could have a heart attack jumping from the plane."

"We could find a handsome instructor to strap you to! Now I am reminded about a parachute story. President Nixon, Secretary of State Kissinger, and a boy scout were in a small government airplane. The plane developed engine problems, and the pilot told everyone to parachute off the plane. However, there were only two parachutes, so the pilot said the president must be saved, and Nixon took one of the parachutes and jumped. The pilot told Kissinger that he should let the young lad jump, but Kissinger said that he was the smartest man in the world and needed to be spared. Then Kissinger jumped. The boy scout told the pilot not to worry about him. 'The smartest man in the world just grabbed the backpack off my back and jumped. The second parachute is over there.'"

They both had a good laugh as they pulled into the Super Eight Motel parking lot in Sheridan. Following their arrival and check-in, they had a walk around the small town and ended the day with a Mexican dinner.

The couple left Sheridan after an early breakfast and drove to Burgess Junction, Lovell, and Powell via HY-14A. Lara was especially taken with the spectacular drive over a pass with beautiful mountains into a valley with the Bighorn River. After reaching Cody, they went back to Burgess Junction on HY-14 through Greybull and the Shell waterfall. Following a short visit to the Heart Mountain Barracks, which housed more than fourteen thousand Japanese Americans during WWII, they went onto Burgess Junction and then back to Cody on HY-14A. After checking into the Six Gun Motel for two nights, they went to the nearby dam above Cody that holds back Buffalo Bill Reservoir. The dam was built in 1905–1910 and was the tallest in the world in 1910. Later they returned to town for a walkabout. The town was very lively.

They left Cody early the next morning on HY-120, heading northwest out of town. Several miles later, they turned onto HY-296, which is Chief Joseph Scenic Highway. The drive was breathtaking, with beautiful snow-capped mountains and rolling green hills in view. After going through Cooke City, Montana, they entered the northeast gate of Yellowstone National Park and then to Tower Junction and Mammoth Hot Springs. On the drive to Yellowstone Canyon, they spotted a bear and took some pictures from the car. Farther on, they saw many buffalo roaming the hills and pastures. A little past Canyon, they parked Red and walked to the lower falls of the Yellowstone River and then drove to Yellowstone Lake to catch HY-14 back to Cody. The highway paralleled the Shoshone River and through a breathtaking canyon with weathered volcanic rocks that looked like towers and other interesting structures. The beauty lasted until the town of Wapiti and the Buffalo Bill Reservoir.

The next morning, they left Cody early and enjoyed the drive again through the beautiful canyon from Shoshone Reservoir, past the Sleeping Giant ski area, to the east gate of the park. Not surprisingly, a lot of cars were on the roads. Before reaching Fishing Bridge, they passed herds of buffalo and elk in the meadows. After lunch in the car, they arrived at the Old Faithful Inn. Lara especially liked the area. The discussion over dinner was mainly about what they did during the day and their plans for their last full day in the park. John asked Lara, "After seeing Old Faithful Geyser shoot off in the morning, how about heading to the western entry to the park and having a short walk around the downtown area of West Yellowstone. We can have a few stops to see some mud pots and maybe more buffalo and elk."

"That sounds great, John. I sure love this park."

After visiting West Yellowstone, they left the park and entered Teton National Park. John started making periodic stops for pictures of the beautiful Tetons. In Jackson, they stayed at the Snow King Resort next to the ski area. After a long walk around the downtown, they had dinner in a restaurant that was once a movie theater. Lara told John that someday she would love to come back in the winter and ski the slopes next to the lodge. John agreed. They ended the day buying some food to eat in the car the next day.

They left Jackson before the sun came up and took HY-189 to Hoback Junction. John stopped there for gas and told Lara, "Take a look at this Wyoming/Colorado map and see the route we will take back home. We will first take HY-191 to Rock Springs. There we will get on I-80 and go east through Rawlins. At Walcott, we will head south on HY-230 that changes to HY-125 at the Colorado border. We will continue on the highway through Walden to Granby. Someday, we can return to Walden and follow the highway that parallels the Poudre River to Fort Collins. It is a beautiful drive through the canyon. When we get to Granby, we will head east through Rocky Mountain National Park and stop in Estes Park for dinner. I think you will enjoy the scenery in the park and maybe see some wildlife. We will probably arrive home after dark."

V

After John and Lara left Red at a DIA parking lot and went through airport security, they boarded an Alaska Airlines flight to Seattle. In Seattle, they had a three-hour wait before their two-hour flight to Juneau. The Juneau airport is small with five gates, and the runway and taxiway are on the same road. At the airport, they were met by Joseph, a National Geographic representative, along with a dozen of their fellow passengers. He told the group, "You have four hours to explore the capital of Alaska. It was here in 1880 that Joe Juneau, Richard Harris, and Chief Keowa found gold in one of the small creeks descending from the mountains, touching off the first of the northern gold rushes. Today, Juneau is a small city of thirty-two hundred inhabitants dedicated to administrating the largest state in the nation. It is also the only state capital on the continent that you cannot directly drive to from the other US state capitals."

The group first went by bus to Mendenhall Glacier, where they had about a mile's walk to a large waterfall at the end of the trail. After about an hour's visit to the glacier and falls, everyone was bused back into town to spend about an hour walking around.

On the bus following the walk, John whispered to Lara that it was indeed enough time to see the older part of the capital.

After arriving at Juneau's main dock and boarding the National Geographic ship, *Sea Bird*, the group joined about two dozen other passengers who had arrived earlier for a safety drill, appetizers, and introductions in the lounge, followed by dinner. John and Lara's cabin was between the lounge and the staff dining room on the lowest level of the three-level *Sea Bird*. The small cabin had a sink between two single beds. There was a bathroom shared with the cabin next door. It had a toilet and shower that shoots water over the bathroom when one takes a shower. The water exits through a drain in the middle of the floor.

After cruising south from Juneau, the *Sea Bird* went out of Stephen's Passage and into Holkham Bay during the night. Holkham Bay is the entrance to the majestic Tracy Arm–Fords Terror Wilderness. This wilderness, established in 1980, is 653,180 acres in size and has Tracy and Endicott Arm Fjords in the center of it. Tremendous glaciers carved this spectacular fjord system deep into the heart of the coastal mountains of the mainland. It was here where the passengers spent the second day of the expedition, spending some time on shore and on the ship.

On the ship, John saw Felex, the Russian sailor who was aboard the *Akademic Abraham*. John walked over to say hello to him, but he walked away from John without saying anything. John told Lara about the incident, the problems he had with him in the past, and his suspicions that Felex tried to kill him. John asked Lara if she would mind going to Felex and finding out all she could about him since she could communicate with him in Russian.

After Lara met with Felex, she went back to their cabin and told John what she found out. "Felex told me that he got fired from his job on the *Akademic Abraham* because of accusations you made to the captain about him trying to kill you. He said that they were all false accusations but that he hoped that you would die on this voyage. John, I think you should beware of this big, mean-looking man."

John did not sleep well that night thinking about Felex. He thought that it was hard to dismiss three previous attempts on his life as accidents during his trips to the Arctic, Antarctica, and Iceland.

Following breakfast, some of the passengers saw about a dozen seals, many small and narrow waterfalls, a couple of big falls, and the glacier. Later the group received a briefing from Joseph about the day's activities, which included spending the rest of the morning cruising through this spectacular fjord, looking for wildlife, sailing by icebergs, and getting a look at the glaciers that carved this amazing scenery. The group also received a short safety talk on how to behave if they encounter a brown or black bear. Joseph first stated that you must always be in groups of five or more. If you see a bear approaching, do not run, but stay still and bunch up. A few minutes later, Joseph emphasized not to take any food along as it could attract bears from long distances.

After the meeting, Lara told John that he should have told everyone about the bear attack at Pine Shadows.

"You are right, during my bear attack, I should not have run but stood still and raised my hands. If that did not work, I should have dropped to my knees and prayed." Lara laughed.

"Lara, you heard Joseph advise everyone to be sure and not have any food with them. I wanted to say that everyone should be sure and brush their teeth before departing for the walk."

With a hug, Lara told John, "You are sure a comedian and lots of fun to be with. I love you so much."

"Lara, my dear, I also love you very much."

After lunch, about half of the passengers went out on zodiacs for about two hours to cruise the area while John, Lara, and the rest of the passengers went ashore for a walk.

On the walk, naturalist Macean was explaining to the group about each plant they came to for the first time. At one flower, he asked if someone would get down on their hands and knees and smell it. Of course, John volunteered and said it smelled like feces. Macean said, "Indeed, it smells like shit and is called an outhouse lily. Later the group came upon bear poop on the trail that was fresh. Macean told everyone not to worry as he was carrying along a spray can of turmeric to use on attacking bears.

After lunch, the *Sea Bird* made its way back out of Tracy Arm, with everyone enjoying the scenery that was missed in the early morning. Later in the afternoon, the ship anchored at Williams Cove. While most of the passengers were in their cabins resting, John was taking a stroll around the narrow lower deck, with Lara walking several feet behind him. As John was passing a doorway, a bucket full of soapy water was thrown in front of him, which caused him to fall and slide under the railing into the sea. Lara screamed. A couple of crew members who witnessed the accident came to Lara with a life buoy, a ring-shaped life-saving tube tied to a rope, and pulled John to safety. Lara said that she saw Felex throwing the water on deck. After John returned to their cabin and changed into some dry clothes, they went to the captain with their suspicion that Felex was trying to kill John. After Felex was summoned to join the three, he denied trying to kill John and said he just emptied the bucket of wastewater on deck, not knowing anyone was there, and returned to complete his work inside the ship.

At dinner, John and Lara shared a table with a spinal surgeon from Omaha and his wife, Grace. Dr. Mike Long was born and raised in Rwanda. He and John had a lot of talk about Africa, and the Longs had even spent considerable time in South Africa. Mike has a sister in Port Elizabeth whom he sees about every three years on his visits to South Africa. Originally, he got his MD in Cape Town and then went to Canada where he could not make a living as a surgeon. Then he and Grace moved to the United States. It was an enjoyable meal for the four of them.

The next morning, John and Lara woke up as the ship was in the beautiful little arm of Thomas Bay called Scenery Cove.

After breakfast, they went on a hike with about a dozen others to Cascade Creek. Living up to its name, Cascade Creek has a roaring waterfall. The short hike went to the base of the falls, where most of the group got baptized by the mist of the waterfall. John, Lara, and a few other brave souls went to the top of the waterfall. They had a walk along a steep, slippery trail, followed by crossing a nine-inch wooden blank across a ditch. One lady fell off and rolled over in the rain forest but was not hurt.

After lunch, the ship cruised over to Petersburg, while the group heard a presentation by Steve Macean. Afterward, most of the passengers went ashore and visited the picturesque community of Petersburg (population 3,100) on Mitkof Island, which was settled by Peter Buschmann at the turn of the century. This small town still shows off its Norwegian heritage. Fishing is the mainstay of the community, with approximately twenty million dollars of seafood processed each year. Most of the group went on a walk along the docks to learn about fishing and fishing boats and later explored the town on their own. On the couple's walk around Petersburg, they had several pictures taken of themselves standing in front of a small wooden sailing ship that was next to Bojer Wikan Fisherman's Memorial Park, a most unusual place in the center of the fishery town.

After dinner on the *Sea Bird*, there was a humpback whale sighting. The ship followed the large whale as it swam alongside, surfacing every five to ten minutes, with its tail flipping out of the water most of the time. Later the couple had some great entertainment in their cabin, watching a beautiful sunset through their cabin window, along with the whale putting on a great close-in show.

Later, Lara pulled back the covers on John's bed and screamed. John darted out of the bathroom to find a large brown spider, which he thought was a tarantula, on his bed. John captured the spider in a trash can, covered the can with a plastic bag, and took the spider to the bridge. The captain told the couple that they have never had anything like that on the ship before, no snakes, rats, or mice. He summoned Macean to come to the bridge to have a look at the spider.

After Macean arrived and inspected the spider, he said, "It is a wolf spider, the largest one I have ever seen, and it can be found anywhere on land. As you see, they are like a hairy tarantula, only maybe not so big, but still equally as scary. Their large size makes them generally feared. They are known to deliver a painful bite when handled, but their venom is not medically dangerous to humans. Given their size, one can imagine the fangs are also proportionately large, adding to the pain of a bite."

The captain said, "Macean, please take it ashore tomorrow and let it loose."

After returning to their cabin, John and Lara discussed the incident. They both agreed that Felex brought the spider aboard and put it in John's bed.

After traveling through the night, the *Sea Bird* arrived at Chatham Strait at first light. Before breakfast, the ship cruised by scenic Red Bluff Bay of Baranof Island, and everyone got to see a brown bear with two cubs on shore. During breakfast, the *Sea Bird* headed north, stopping at Warm Springs Bay to pick up Andy Sabo from the Alaska Whale Foundation. Andy traveled with the group all morning, answering questions about whales, while most of the folks looked for the beautiful creatures in the water.

In the afternoon, the ship anchored at Hanus Bay next to Baranof Island. There is a well-maintained scenic trail on the island that goes through the forest, and everyone had an opportunity to hike to Lake Eva. The forest on the island is particularly lovely, with a rich understory of mosses, ferns, and shrubs. The full cycle of forest life can be observed there, with fungi consuming dead trees, saplings rising from nurse logs, mature trees soaring into the canopy, and snags leaning over the small river. Everyone agreed it was a great walk.

When the couple woke up the next morning, the *Sea Bird* was sailing south into Idaho Inlet, a serene and lovely area, on the north side of Chichagof Island. The ship's anchor was dropped at a site known as Fox Creek, and the passengers spent the morning there. Before breakfast, most of the passengers received a grand show from several killer whales and humpbacks. John got a great picture of two killer whales together. Later, a hike along the creek and through the forest was taken by everyone. The trails were made by wildlife, especially bears. The visitors saw some fresh bear poop, bear prints in the mud, and some scratch marks on a few trees. They had to cross a couple of small creeks on the scenic walk. The flora and fauna were wonderful to admire.

On Wednesday morning, the group had another great hike through the rain forest. In the afternoon, they went on a two-hour zodiac cruise through an area known as the Inian Islands in rough waters. The Inian Islands are near where the Pacific Ocean comes into the northern end of the inside passage. It is a biologically rich area. Sea lions and seals are often plentiful there, as well as sea birds, bald eagles, and puffins The group saw quite a few sea lions, and one had caught a fish, and some others were trying to get the fish out of his mouth—it was quite a show. John got some great pictures. After dinner, the ship cruised in the area near Point Adolphus, just south of Glacier Bay National Park.

On Thursday, most of the group listened to a talk by one of the experts aboard about Captain George Vancouver who cruised by what is now the entrance to Glacier Bay in 1794; he found it to be filled with a tidewater glacier. In 1879, when John Muir visited the same area, the glacier had retreated about thirty miles north into the bay. Today, those same glaciers have retreated a total of sixty miles in a little over two hundred years and left behind a huge bay that is now protected as Glacier Bay National Park and Reserve. It is also designated as a World Heritage Site and a biosphere reserve.

The *Sea Bird* spent the entire day cruising the length of the west arm of the bay, stopping at places where the passengers got to view seabird nesting islands, beautifully exposed geologic formations, and of course, the faces of the glaciers themselves.

Along the way, they saw a couple of bears and mountain goats along the beaches, rocky headlands, and glacial outwashes. At the head of the bay, the ship lingered in front of Margerie Glacier, and the folks on the deck got to see some calving. Masaki Shima, a park ranger/interpreter, and Alice Hald, a cultural heritage guide from Alaska Native Voices, came on board to discuss the area with the passengers.

The endpoint was Margerie Glacier. Next to Margerie was the Grand Pacific Glacier that was covered in rock and was brown on top instead of white. After reversing course, the ship went back and stopped at John Hopkins Glacier. The passengers also got to see nine other tidewater glaciers in the park.

After glacier watching, the *Sea Bird* stopped at the small town of Gustavus with an airport. The dock is next to the visitor's center where most of the visitors had about a two-hour visit. John, Lara, and a few new friends took a walk past a nice campground and back to the lodge. Near the lodge was a display of a whale skeleton. The whale was named Snow.

On Friday, after traveling south through the night, the ship anchored during breakfast at Iyoukeen Cove on Chichagof Island. In 1902, this area was the site of a gypsum mine. The pilings along the shoreline are the only easy way to find remnants of the wharf that extended into deep water to load the ships with gypsum. Today, the forest has reclaimed the area. Their hike began on a tidally exposed beach and continued along a wildlife trail just inside the forest. It was not a well-maintained trail, so the hikers had a little exploration.

In the afternoon, the ship started working its way south toward Peril Strait and Sergius Narrows for arrival in Sitka in the morning. Along the way, most of the passengers kept a watch for wildlife, with some stops for viewing the animals.

At breakfast on Saturday, the *Sea Bird* docked in Sitka on Baranof Island. Sitka is the fourth largest city in Alaska, with a population of almost nine thousand. Originally inhabited by the Tlingit Indians, the name "Sitka" comes from *Shee Atika*, the

Tlingit name for the town. In 1804, Sitka became the capital of Russian America and was renamed New Archangel. In 1867, Sitka was the location for the transfer of Alaska from Russian to United States ownership. Most of the visitors took a tour of the Raptor Rehabilitation Center, the Sitka National Historic Park, and St. Michael's Russian Orthodox Cathedral. Lara especially enjoyed their time in the Russian church that was full of gold figures, crosses, and statues.

In the afternoon, most of the passengers took a flight to Seattle. In Seattle, John and Lara transferred to a flight to Denver. After their arrival at Pine Shadows, Lara gave John a loving hug and thanked him for a wonderful trip.

With a kiss, he told Lara that he would like to marry her once the threat to his life was managed.

"John, you are such a dear man. I love you, and of course, I want to be your wife as soon as possible."

"Lara, just be sure that you want to marry a guy whose last three wives were murdered because of him."

"I love you so much and would die for you."

After another long kiss, they departed for their living quarters. A minute later, John called out, "Lara, your cost of the trip is your birthday and Christmas gifts."

"Thank you so much, John. Good night."

VI

Early on Saturday morning, an Uber driver arrived at Pine Shadows in his black BMW to take John and Lara to Denver International Airport. The middle-aged driver did most of the talking on the drive. He told the couple that he works full-time for United Airlines as a baggage handler. "It is hard work, but I do receive free flights around the country. My next trip will be to Hong Kong and then Shenzhen, China."

The ride took about an hour. After the couple got through security, they went to the United Airlines lounge, where they had a free breakfast. Their flight was supposed to leave for Chicago at 10:30 a.m., but when John looked at the information display for departures, it was delayed several hours because of the hurricane in Houston. John then grabbed Lara, and they left the lounge in a hurry to try and get on a flight to Chicago that was boarding. When they got to the gate, John found out that the flight was full. They then went to the United Airlines business desk to try to get to Gothenburg another way. They ended up on a Lufthansa flight that was leaving for Munich at four instead of their planned route through Frankfurt that then went nonstop to Gothenburg. Thus, they spent about four hours in the United lounge where they had a nice lunch. While they enjoyed more free food and drinks, Lara told John, "I sent my folks an email when we would arrive in Moscow. I also wrote about our wonderful trip to Alaska. When will we arrive in Gothenburg?"

"We leave for Munich at three, and after our arrival tomorrow morning, we will take a two-hour flight to Stockholm, then another flight to Gothenburg, arriving in Gothenburg early tomorrow afternoon."

On the transatlantic flight, John watched a couple of movies, and Lara read more of John's travels in his diary.

Over dinner, Lara told John that she sure enjoyed reading about his trip to South Africa and Madagascar. "You were very brave in driving the rental car on the wrong side of the road."

"I suggest that you read about my trip to a couple of the Pacific Islands, where I also drove rentals."

Following their dinner, John resumed watching movies, and Lara read about some of his trips to the South Pacific Islands.

The Gothenburg airport was nice and new with ten gates. After John exchanged two hundred dollars for 1,500 krona, they took a taxi to the hotel for 550 krona. Everything in Sweden is expensive.

Gothenburg is a beautiful city surrounded by hills on one side and the North Sea on the other side. It has a population of one million. During John and Lara's three nights in Gothenburg, they stayed at the Radisson Blu Riverside Got, a nice hotel and only four months old. Their room was on the tenth floor of the twelve-story building with great views of part of the city. After unpacking, they walked across the street where the International Solvent Extraction Conference was being held. The building is large with offices on the upper floors and the conference center and several restaurants on the bottom floor. Next door is Chalmers University where John had given lectures in the past. A couple of blocks toward the river is a dock for the free ferry that takes mainly students across the Gota River to the older part of the city.

When they arrived at the conference center, they found out that the conference reception was already underway. The couple was met by the conference organizer, Professor Christian. Of course, he recognized John. After John introduced Lara, he explained to Christian that he did not register for the conference as all he wanted to do was see a few friends and not attend the meeting and banquet. Christian said that was okay and gave John two drink tickets. After getting some non-alcoholic drinks, John took Lara over to meet some of his friends. The first group of friends that he approached was from Brazil. His old friend Cecee gave John a hug and kisses on both cheeks. The other Brazilians were Ana, Camila, and Mitiki. After John introduced Lara to the four Brazilians, they started asking John a lot of questions about Deborah and his present activities. With tears in her eyes, Cecee told John how sorry she was about Deborah's passing. After fifteen minutes of discussions, John took Lara over to meet some of his other friends: Stefan (Sweden), Amares (Canada), and Bob, Bruce, Dean, and Sue, all Americans. Later John and Lara went over and thanked Professor Christian for the nice reception. As they were leaving, he gave John some bad news that their good friend Jan had died.

The conference began on Monday, but John chose to skip the talks and take Lara into the city via the ferry. After the short ferry ride, they had a long walk seeing the many wonderful old churches and buildings in the old city center. The old town was once surrounded by a wall, but now there is only part of the wall standing. Originally, three sides of the wall were surrounded by a canal or mote, and the fourth side of the wall faced the broad Gota Av River. In the afternoon, the couple took a two-hour boat tour around the city's canal, along with about a dozen other tourists from various countries. Everyone seemed to understand the guide's English. There were many low bridges on the trip, and their guide requested that no one stand up.

John and Lara took lots of pictures of the beautiful city that afternoon. On the walk back to the hotel, they stopped to admire a statue of Evert Taube, 1890–1976, next to the river and a tall Gaelic sailing ship. They did not know who he was, maybe a famous sailor.

That evening, the couple went out of the hotel to find a place to eat, but every restaurant that looked nice was closed. The only thing open was Subway, a terrible pizzeria, and a takeaway Thai restaurant that was housed in a shack. They finally decided to go back to the hotel restaurant for fish and chips. Lara thought it was funny that at dinner, they were served bread in a paper sack and water in a fruit jar.

John commented, "It seemed like everyone we came into contact with today spoke English."

"I agree. I was also surprised that all your overseas friends and their wives at the reception spoke good English."

After dinner, there was a fire alarm, followed by an announcement for everyone to leave the building. The hotel guests were allowed back into the hotel after firemen from two fire trucks surveyed the building for fire.

On Tuesday morning, the couple went over to the meeting hall during the morning coffee break, where John gave copies of his book *Separations Chemistry* to Cecee and Professor Christian. The Japanese Brazilian lady who works with Cecee got a copy of his *Actinide Separations* book. Now John could travel a little lighter. The couple returned to the hotel for a two-hour nap, and then they caught the ferry to the city and boarded Tram 1 for a trip to each end of the city and into parts of the suburbs. There were many high-rise apartment buildings, but only a few single-family homes. In the city, there were many pedestrian-only streets. They had an early dinner at McDonald's. There were at least three other McDonald's in the city, as well as a Burger King, KFC, and several Subways. It looked like there were 7-Elevens at every street corner.

The couple had to wake at four on Wednesday morning for a taxi ride in the rain to the airport for their KLM flight to Amsterdam at six. In Amsterdam, they got a flight to Newcastle UK that took one and a half hours and then an hour flight on Eastern Airways to the Isle of Man. They only had fifteen minutes between both connections. They arrived on the Isle of Man at 10:30 a.m. and went by taxi to the Palace Hotel and Casino in the main city of Douglas for a two-night stay; it was raining there just like in Amsterdam and Newcastle. Their taxi driver was from Transylvania in Romania and had been in Douglas for five years. His girlfriend was from Slovakia. They had a four-month-old daughter. He told the couple that the Isle of Man is a tax haven and unemployment is only 1 percent. He also told them that there had been world-renowned motorcycle races around the island that were founded in 1908. They were to race again on Sunday for the traveler trophy. The bikers were mainly from the UK. They had brought their bikes over on the ferry, with most of them there to only watch the races. As they were traveling near their hotel, they saw many motorcycles parked outside hotels, and the outdoor restaurants were full of bikers drinking and eating.

The hotel was quite old, and the adjoining casino was the only one on the island. The city is the largest town on the island, the Borough of Douglas, and it has a McDonald's, Pizza Hut, and two Dominos; however, the couple ate at the hotel restaurant and had fish both nights. During lunch, John commented to Lara, "I have a hard time understanding most of the Brits. Do you?"

"As you know, I have a slight British accent since I perfected my English at Oxford and, of course, have no trouble understanding them."

"I even had a hard time at Clemson University understanding some of the people who grew up there and spoke with a southern drawl. Of course, I also had trouble understanding a lot of the Australians when I worked there for three years."

Following lunch, they caught the number 1 two-decker bus that took them through town and the suburbs, past a few other small communities, and to the airport. A few miles past the airport is a small town called Castletown. It has the big and beautiful Rushen Castle located in the middle of the town. The couple took some pictures from the top floor of the bus. Then the bus continued west into Port Erin, turned around, and retraced the route back to Douglas. A steam train goes on the same route, but they did not have the time to take it.

In town, they took a walk on the curved boardwalk next to the large bay. Their hotel is on one end of the walk, near the start of the electric train and the end stop of the horse-drawn tram that rides on rails. The horse-drawn tram starts at the other end of the bay, about one mile away, and was built in 1876. The couple then walked over to the pedestrian-walking street where there were many shops selling everything, including lots of T-shirts and hats signifying the bike races. John commented that many cars had license plates with JJC, his initials, followed by three numbers.

The next morning, it was rainy and cold, but John and Lara borrowed umbrellas from the hotel and walked back into the shopping district so John could check his email at the library. Next, they caught the horse-drawn tram and went to the other end to catch the electric train to Laxey. After arriving in Laxey, they had a walkabout and a look at the Great Laxey Wheel, the world's largest waterwheel. It was used in the past for the mining industry. They were lucky that it had stopped raining on their arrival and the skies cleared.

After their half-hour Laxey visit, they caught the Snaefell Mountain electric train to the top of the highest mountain on the island, two-thousand feet above sea level. On the thirty-minute ride, the couple saw three rabbits and lots of sheep and horses. There was a twenty-minute stop at the summit station with a wonderful view of a beautiful reservoir surrounded by grass-covered hills. On the way back down the mountain, the engineer and conductor had to work the mechanical brakes on both cars to keep the train from speeding down the mountain. Once the train reached the bottom, the couple got on another electric train and continued north to Ramsey, the end point. In Ramsey, they stayed on the tram, taking more pictures, and returned to Douglas. The route was eighteen miles along the coast, over gorse-topped hills and Victorian glens. Back at the hotel, Lara tried her luck in the casino. The hotel had given her a five-pound coupon for a free spin at the wheel. She lost the coupon on the first spin.

John and Lara went to their room after dinner for an early night's sleep since they had another early flight the next morning, Friday, September 1. They left the hotel by taxi at 4:30. Their driver was interesting. Julie is the owner of Julie's Taxis and told the couple that she is fifty-two. She tried to guess John's age as fifty. She owns three taxis; is married with boys, fifteen and twenty-six; and has a large home on the other side of the island. They got to the airport in fifteen minutes and only saw three other cars on the road. The couple had a short wait outside the five-gate airport terminal since it did not open until five. John always liked to be early at the airport, and this time, they had a two-hour wait before takeoff. They had breakfast at the only restaurant in the airport and looked around in a gift shop during their wait for their plane to Heathrow. After landing, they had to go through customs, immigration, and security that almost caused them to miss their flight to Milan.

They arrived in Lampadusa from Milan midafternoon and were greeted by a driver with a reserved car from the Puesta De Sol Residence House. The airport is close to the center of the small town, and the couple could hear planes taking off and landing from their residence. The hotel is in front of a bay full of docked boats, and their shared room is large with a kitchen, two beds, and an adjoining bath. John was disappointed that there was no bathtub as they had at the Isle of Man. That evening, they ate at a nearby restaurant at the suggestion of the young lady at the front desk. She had an assistant, but neither one could speak much English.

The front desk lady had arranged a boat trip for John and Lara to take after breakfast. She said it was about all there was to do on the island. The lady told them that the shoreline of the small island has seven beautiful Caldor coves and two grottos that a boat could go into. Nearby underwater is a Madonnina or statue that can be seen only with scuba gear on. The waters near the shores are a beautiful green, and Cala Guitgia has one of the most beautiful beaches in the world. She said the interior of the island is much like the desert in North Africa. The island is only seventy miles from Tunisia and has a population of about six thousand, and its main industries are fishing, agriculture, and tourism. Since the early 2000s, the island has become a primary European entry point for migrants from Africa.

The next morning after breakfast, the boat owner/captain, who could not speak English, arrived at the hotel and took the couple to a nearby boat for a day of cruising around the island.

When they got to the small fishing boat that had a pilot house and a small second deck and two couples sunning themselves on the top deck, they met the captain's wife and daughter. John was very reluctant at this point to board since the small boat did not look seaworthy. After they boarded and left the bay, the boat entered the angry sea and started to be tossed about. At that point, John somehow managed to communicate to the captain using mostly sign language, with one hand on his stomach and the other hand pointing to the shore. The captain understood and kindly got the couple back on solid ground. They then had a short walk to the hotel to take a nap. Later they had a long walk and discovered nice pedestrian streets with various restaurants and shops. They had pizza for lunch at one of the Italian restaurants. Next, they found a shop where Lara bought a magnet and postcards. There were lots of people walking about, shopping, and eating. After their long walks in the shopping areas and by the beautiful coast, they had dinner, followed by returning to the hotel to watch a little TV before retiring for the night.

The couple slept in since their flight to Rome did not leave until midday. In Rome, they flew nonstop to St. Petersburg.

VII

On their flight to St. Petersburg, John told Lara about his first visit to Russia with Margrit. "I had been taking pictures from the plane. When the stewardess spotted me, she announced that no pictures were to be taken. Margrit laughed. The damage had already been done. We discovered later that the photos were not out of the ordinary. When we arrived at the Leningrad airport, we were full of suspicions about Russia and really expected a lot of trouble with customs and so on. We filled out the customs form declaring what money and valuables we had. Margrit listed her wedding band as her only valuable. We then proceeded through immigration, with only our passports being stamped, and then to customs. The customs officer was very Western in speech and manner. He appeared apologetic to have to ask us any questions and said he was sorry to have to confiscate Margrit's book, *The Russians*, that she was carrying. He did not check our luggage, just took our word for what we had, and ushered us on through. This only took at the most five minutes.

"We then went into the arrival hall and found the Intourist booth. We were informed that our reservations were in order, that we would be staying at the Leningrad Hotel, and that the hotel's driver would take us there. On the ride, we discovered that Leningrad must be one of the most beautiful cities in the world. We loved the wide tree-lined streets, the parks, the statues, and the beauty of the city. Our driver pointed out some of the sights to us on the way to the hotel and was most courteous and helped us with our luggage into the hotel. The hotel was immense, and we got a nice room. We found a lot of things to muse about in workmanship, but nothing to destroy our good time or to distract from what we were discovering. We found out that some of the Russian customs were strange to us, such as service, which was very poor since the Russian workers seemed more interested in avoiding their job rather than seeing to it that we were accorded every courtesy. We practically had to tackle the waiter to have him wait on us. But we enjoyed the delicious food once it arrived."

"John, that was before the wall came down. As you know, the people have changed a lot since those dark days."

"After dinner at the Leningrad Hotel the first night, we went for a walk by the bridge that crosses the Neva River. There we met three young Russian couples, and they invited us to join their party. We visited with them while they were drinking champagne. They offered us some, but Margrit told them in the little Russian she knew that we did not drink. I was amazed at how much her little knowledge of the Russian language helped us. We were enjoying the company of the young couples. We did not understand, however, what they told us. One young man stated that at midnight, the bridges would go up. Margrit and I briefly talked together and decided they were a terrorist group about to blow up the bridge. Further conversations revealed that the bridge would indeed go up at midnight, but that was to let the ships pass."

Lara chuckled. "Margrit sure sounds like a wonderful and fun-to-be-with lady."

"Yes, she gave me more than twenty-five years of marvelous memories."

"I hope I can do the same for you, John."

"Before we left the riverbank, they gave us several handfuls of Russian candy and said it was for our children. We gave them all the gum that we had with us. Then we went back to the hotel and went to our room to see the beautiful moon radiating on the ripples of the Neva River.

"On Sunday morning, we took the city tour and in the afternoon toured Pavlovsk and the Hermitage. We had a delightful Intourist guide, and we enjoyed her as much as the Hermitage. I had several photos taken with my camera of the three of us before we parted. We had dinner at the hotel before being transported to the train station. We loved the Russian food, the 'follies' show at the hotel, and the way the Russians sang together. It was a beautiful experience."

"I think we will be seeing the same things in the next two days, although there are many changes in the city besides a name change and a large increase in population. I have heard that the traffic is especially bad."

"Margrit and I got some sleep on the Red Arrow Express to Moscow that left at midnight and arrived early morning. At the Moscow station, we were greeted by my friend Misa and his wife, Sonya. We were treated to the absolute best while in Moscow and were not allowed to spend any money except for our hotel room and anything we bought or ate out of their presence. We had three lavish parties thrown for us, two at Misa and Sonya's flat and the other at the International Hotel, complete with a stage show, circus acts, dancing girls, gymnasts, and later a band playing both Russian and English music. The party was hosted by Misa, Oleg, and Dmitri and their wives, and the dinner was simply superb. We had plenty to eat and drink, and we danced and danced. We returned to our hotel via the subway, which I had read was the best subway system in the world. We were extremely impressed.

"We also attended the Russian Circus where we sat in the first row, wishing we had our children with us. We were entertained by the famous Popov the clown. The Friday night before we left, Misa and Sonya had a dinner party for us at their apartment. We again had a bounty of food and drinks, which Sonya had spent the entire day preparing. We danced to American music and just had a ball. We honestly had a fantastic time in Moscow. I am sure this visit will be much better since I am traveling with you, my dear lovely friend. I hope to call you my wife soon after I have assurances that Andrei's brother is no longer a threat to kill me so that you do not come into harm's way."

"It would be wonderful and romantic if we left Russia as man and wife."

During the next two days in St. Petersburg, the couple took an organized tour to visit the usual tourist places and spent a lot of time at the Hermitage. On their early morning train ride to Moscow, they shared a cabin.

Lara's parents and her brother Vadim greeted the couple at the Moscow station. After loving hugs with her parents and brother, Lara introduced John. After the wonderful welcome, the five went to the Mikhailovs' flat in Vadim's car. The two-bedroom flat is on the second floor of an apartment building a block away from the Mendeleev campus. John helped Vadim carry the luggage into Lara's two-bed room that John would be sharing with her.

After unpacking, they joined Lara's parents and Vadim in the living room, where John told the Mikhailovs a little about himself in a mixture of English and Russian. Lara's parents and brother could understand most of what John said, and they told him that they could understand written English completely. The conversation continued over a late lunch, with mostly Lara telling her parents about her sabbatical in the United States and their trip to Sweden.

Following their meal, Vadim offered to take John for a drive around Moscow. Before they departed, John said, "Thank you for a delicious lunch. Lara, you sure have wonderful parents and brother. I look forward to spending the next few days with you all and enjoying your wonderful hospitality."

On the tour, John discovered that Vadim's English was easy to understand. Later on the drive, Vadim commented, "Lara told me a lot about your traveling around the world and that you have visited every country except for Somalia and Yemen. What were your best three trips?"

"My number 1 trip was to Antarctica that included going over the Antarctic Circle. The second time I took the trip, it included visits to the Falkland, South Georgia, South Orkney, and South Sandwich Islands. My second-best adventure was visiting Greenland and the High Arctic. My travels on the train from Vladivalstock to Moscow were number 3. On that trip, I had a chance to visit Lake Baikal. I got my bug for traveling when I was about ten. I had an uncle who worked on a merchant ship and traveled the seven seas. During the summers when he would return to Denver, he always gave us an interesting slideshow of his travels the past nine months. Where have you traveled to, Vadim?"

"Well, since I do not make a lot of money as a high school chemistry teacher, even though I do not have a wife and children to support, I have only been to a few cities in western Russia and Eastern Europe."

"I assume your parents had an impact on your interest in chemistry."

"You are correct. Now we should head back to my folks for dinner."

After the three-hour drive, John gave his thanks to Vadim for showing him some places that he had not seen on previous trips to the city.

After a wonderful dinner, John excused himself for an early night's sleep. The foursome continued their conversations that started at dinner, and about an hour later, Vadim returned to his flat on the other side of Moscow. After Lara's parents retired, she got the volume of John's diary that he had brought on the trip and read about another one of his adventures. This one was his trip to Myanmar (Burma).

Following breakfast on their second day in Moscow, Lara took John to Mendeleev University to show him around campus and her office. She also introduced him to a few of her colleagues and the head of the department. She told her boss about her activities during the last six months in Colorado. After spending the morning at the university, they returned to the apartment.

After lunch, Misa met John at the Mikhailovs' apartment. Misa's driver, Alexander, then drove John and Misa to Misa's academy office for some technical discussions. Later they went to the academy's high-rise building for coffee at the top-floor cafe. Following their break, Misa offered John a chance to go to the building's roof for some picture taking. Misa told John, "Only workmen have been allowed to take the stairs to the roof where they are constructing an observation deck. Since they are not working today, would you like to have a visit there since you can get pictures of the city in all directions."

"Certainly, I never miss an opportunity to get the best shots."

After climbing the stairs and arriving at the deck, Misa warned John, "Be careful since the deck is still under construction and the hand railings have not been installed yet."

"Thanks, Misa, you were right about this being a great place to take some spectacular pictures of the city."

"I did not think the view of the city would be so great. Please excuse me since I would like to briefly return to my office to get my camera. I should be back in about ten minutes."

After John finished his picture taking near the edge of the platform opposite the stairway, a man quietly entered the platform and ran at John with the intention of pushing him over the ledge. However, John saw him out of the corner of his eye and jumped out of his way. The man then fell off the platform to the street below. A very shaken John went down the stairs and elevator to the street where he met Misa. John told Misa what happened and said, "I think this guy is Andrei's brother. And he tried to kill me, thinking I killed his brother and two nephews."

Misa advised John not to say anything to the police and that he would do all the talking. "I plan to tell the police we do not know the man or why he jumped."

They then walked over to join several other people near the body. One person said, "This man is dead. Can someone please call the police?"

Ten minutes later, a police car and ambulance arrived. Next, another police car arrived with the police captain. He searched the dead man's pockets and pulled out his wallet. After finding his driver's license, the captain asked the small crowd, "This man is Alexei Pushkin. Does anyone know him?"

No one answered the captain, but a few minutes later, Misa spoke up. "I do not know the man, but I saw him jump from the top of the Academy of Sciences high-rise. I work in the adjoining building. I assume he committed suicide."

The captain agreed, and as he was dispersing the growing crowd, the ambulance crew took Pushkin to the morgue. Misa and John, still unnerved, returned to the academy office. Misa made a call to Alexander and asked him to take John back to the Mikhailovs' apartment.

After John arrived back at the apartment, still shaken up, he asked Lara to come to the bedroom to talk. He told her about what happened at the academy, and she started crying. "Oh, John, I am so sorry this frightening thing has happened to you. What can I do to help you?"

"Thank you, Lara, but I will be okay, but it might take a few days to recover from this ordeal. The only good thing about Pushkin's death is that I do not have to worry about him trying to kill me. Now we can get married!"

Over dinner, Lara told her parents that she and John want to get married on Friday morning, the day before they leave Moscow. "We agreed not to have a traditional church ceremony for our wedding, only the required civil ceremony in the Department of Public Services. Following the fifteen-minute ceremony with the exchanging of rings, we would like to return here for the wedding party if you agree. We would also like you both to witness the civil ceremony as required by law." Lara's parents jumped up from the table and congratulated the two with hugs and kisses. Lara's mom said, "Of course, we will stand up for you both and host the party. Now we need to start making an attendee list and make a few phone calls."

John and Lara spent the next two days getting ready for the party as well as applying for the civil ceremony. Everything went according to their plans, and all the invitees could attend the party on Friday night.

Following the Friday morning ceremony and returning to the Mikhailovs' apartment, Lara's father gave crystal glasses to both the bride and the groom and were asked to proceed with the tradition of breaking the glasses. He told John, "The number of broken pieces is supposed to indicate the number of years you will spend happily together." John dropped his glass on the marble floor, breaking it into many pieces. The surprised group witnessed Lara's glass not breaking after she dropped it on the marble floor.

Later in the afternoon, the guests started arriving. Of course, Lara's brother was the first to arrive. Next, several of Lara's friends and relatives showed up, along with John's good friends, Misa, Oleg, and Dmitri with their wives. There was plenty to eat and drink with some music and dancing. Several toasts to the couple were also made during the fun party. Near the end of the party, a small group of guests asked Lara to tell them what they would do on their honeymoon.

"John and I plan on traveling to some of the countries in Europe that I have not been to before. Tomorrow, we will fly to

Vienna. After a couple of nights in Vienna, we will go by train for one-day visits to Bratislava, Salzburg, and Innsbruck and return to Vienna a different way via Graz. After one-night stays in Graz and Vienna, we will take the train to Warsaw, and after two nights there, we will visit Prague and stay there for several nights. We will then go by train to Chur, Switzerland, to see John's cousin and his family, followed by going to Munich for our flight back to the US. I think John and I will continue to live and work in Colorado, and hopefully, someday, I can get my American citizenship. Of course, we will come back here as often as possible that will hopefully permit John to perfect his Russian."

Later the guests slowly departed the apartment. After the guests and Vadim left, Lara's parents escorted an elderly friend back to his nearby flat and picked up a wedding gift from him for the Czermaks. John and Lara offered to put the leftovers away and wash the dishes.

After the newlyweds completed putting the leftovers away and washing the dishes, they went into the living room. John was standing in the middle of the room with his back to the entry door. Lara came over to John, put her arms around him, and gave him a loving kiss.

John said, "I am so lucky to have such a beautiful, intelligent, and fun-to-be-with darling wife."

"John, I am so happy to be your wife and to spend the rest of my life with such a wonderful man."

Lara then saw a man quietly enter the room with a gun, who shouted, "I don't want anyone to take my wife from me."

She let out a scream and said, "No, Ivan!" and quickly gave John a bear hug and twisted him around so her back was facing the door. At the same time, the man fired, and the bullet that was intended for John hit Lara in the back. Then the man quickly ran from the room. John franticly lowered Lara to the floor as he called out for help. While the man was running down the hallway, he passed Lara's folks, almost knocking them down. They recognized their former son-in-law. They heard John's screams and ran to the flat to find John trying to stop Lara's bleeding. Lara's father called the police and told them to bring an ambulance. A few minutes later, a hysteric John discovered that he was holding a lifeless body.

Chapter 4

I

On John's flight to Colorado from Moscow via Frankfurt, he was weeping every once and a while as he thought about losing Lara. *We had been married for only a few hours when her jealous ex-husband attempted to kill me, but Lara had quickly moved between him and me, and she got shot and killed instead of me. We both thought it was the perfect union of two people who had so much in common and loved each other so much. Besides losing her, I feel so guilty that she died instead of me, saving my life. I should have died in my car going down Black Canyon in California instead of Margrit. I should have been in my car instead of Ying when Andrei's older brother killed her by mistake. The bullet that Deborah took instead of me still haunts me. Now my fourth wife is dead because of me. I will never marry again.*

The only good thing about this tragic event was finding out, the day after Lara was murdered, that her ex-husband had committed suicide. I feel so sorry for Lara's parents. They loved her so much, and it showed at the memorial. I am sure that they will never want to see me again. Her brother probably feels the same way. Oh, the guilt is so strong, and I keep thinking of the mistaken deaths of all four of my wives. Please help me, dear Lord, to lessen my grief.

The flight seemed longer than eight hours since John kept thinking about losing Lara. After landing in Denver the next morning, John's renters at Pine Shadows, Randy and Gail, were at the airport to meet him. They gave John their deepest condolences. During the hour's drive to Pine Shadows, Gail brought John up-to-date on what had happened in Nederland during his absence. The only important event was the nice weather and now the threat of forest fires. John told the couple about his trip and cried at the end of his narration about Lara's death.

Right before they arrived at Pine Shadows, John asked them both if they would like to buy the property. He told them that he could not live in his home with all the wonderful memories of Lara. He planned to retire from his part-time job at the University of Colorado, move to Denver, and try to start a new life in full retirement.

The morning after John's return home, Randy came to his apartment above the garage and told John that he and Gail had agreed to buy Pine Shadows. John thanked him and started looking into property in Downtown Denver.

After spending the day looking for a place to live in LoDo (Denver's Lower Downtown area), he went to Amy and Dave's home for dinner in Aurora. Eric, Sylvia, and Lorrie also were at dinner. The five greeted their father and father-in-law with individual hugs, and they each told him how sorry they were about Lara's passing. Over the meal, they all got caught up on their activities since their last get-together.

John told the group that he had sold Pine Shadows to Gail and Randy and had put a deposit on an apartment in LoDo. "It is on the top floor of a luxurious new building rising thirty stories above the site where Denver was founded. It is adjacent to the convergence of Cherry Creek and the South Platte River and is an easy walk to the Aquarium, Union Train Station, Coors Baseball Field, Pepsi Entertainment Center, Elitch Gardens Amusement Park, and the college campus. As you know, near Union Station, I can catch the free 16th Street Mall bus to the capital, art museum, and main library. The light rail for the airport starts at Union Station, as do several other light rail lines to the suburbs of Denver, and of course, I can take an Amtrack train to anywhere in the United States. Everything indoors is equally exceptional. It has underground parking for owners and renters, valet parking for guests, a welcoming lobby with an attendant, a large workout room, sauna, hot tub, swimming pool, large conference/party room, and lounge with two pool tables. My two-bedroom apartment that I will call Three Thousand, or maybe TT, since the apartment number is 3000, is spacious, with bathrooms in each of the two bedrooms and living, dining, and laundry rooms, a kitchen, and a large balcony with stellar views of the front range of the Rocky Mountains.

I have a Wikipedia article about LoDo that I copied. Let me read the short article to you:

LoDo (Lower Downtown) is an unofficial neighborhood in Denver and is one of the oldest places of settlement in the city. It is a mixed-use historic district, known for its nightlife, and serves as an example of success in urban reinvestment and revitalization. The current population is approximately 22,000. Prior to European exploration of the area, Native Americans, particularly the Arapaho tribe, established encampments along the South Platte River near or in what is now LoDo. In 1858, after the discovery of gold in the river, General William Larimer founded Denver by putting down cottonwood logs in the center of a square mile plot that would eventually be the current LoDo neighborhood, making LoDo both the original city of Denver, as well as its oldest neighborhood. Then, like now, LoDo was a bustling and sometimes wild area known for its saloons and brothels. During the horrific Sand Creek Massacre, it was LoDo where the heads of the slaughtered Arapaho warriors were paraded in victory. As Denver grew, city leaders realized a railroad was needed to keep Denver a strong city, especially when the transcontinental railroad bypassed Denver for Cheyenne, Wyoming. In 1870, residents passed bonds that brought a 106-mile rail spur from Cheyenne. Union Station became the place most people traveled into the city and LoDo would be the first part of the city they would see. This section eventually became Denver's Chinatown in the 1870s to the 1890s, only to be torn down during race riots. By the mid-twentieth century, what was once a thriving business area had become skid row. As highways and air travel diminished the dominance of passenger railroad transportation, the importance of Union Station, LoDo's most prominent building, waned. In 1988, LoDo became the Downtown Historic District that was created to encourage historic preservation and to promote economic and social vitality. During this time, the neighborhood began its renaissance and new businesses opened. Gradually LoDo became a destination neighborhood. By the time Coors Baseball Field opened on the edge of the LoDo Historic District in 1995, the area had revitalized itself, becoming a new, hip neighborhood filled with clubs, restaurants, art galleries, boutiques, bars, and other businesses. Pepsi Center, located on the other edge of the neighborhood, opened in 1999 and further established the neighborhood as a sport fan's paradise. New residential development came to LoDo, transforming old warehouses into pricey new lofts.

"My grandfather Czermak told me that when he and grandma first came to Denver via Hamburg, New York, and Sterling, he worked in a wild saloon on Larimar Street. There were many fistfights there, and he always had to break up the brawls. Say, Amy and Dave, since you both work uptown, we need to start having lunch together occasionally."

"Dad, that would be great. How about on the Wednesdays of the first and third weeks of each month? Dave and I can meet you at the Brown Palace Hotel at noon."

"Okay. After I move into TT, I would like to have a housewarming party. It will begin at four a week from Saturday, and I hope you all can attend. Since I have two cars, Red, my Jeep, and Whit, my Smart car, and I only need one. How would you like Whit as a gift, Lorrie?"

"That would be wonderful. I like the white Smart car very much, especially the excellent gas mileage. As you all know, it will be my first car, and I promise Dad that I will continue to call the car Whit."

"I had the car appraised at three thousand dollars, so it is only fair that I give Amy and Eric three thousand dollars each as gifts."

All three young adults shouted, "Dad, you are wonderful and the best father anyone could have."

On the first Saturday following John's return to Colorado, Bob Stevens and his wife hosted a memorial party at their home in North Boulder for Lara. John's children and brother, a few faculty members, Gail and Randy, and a couple of John's friends attended the party. Following the memorial, John returned to his home in Nederland to start packing his personal things for the movers who would arrive the next morning. The day before, he had closed on buying TT.

Two days later, John went to his office at CU to pack his books and papers. During this time, he received a call from Kim Carn in Atlanta. She gave her deepest condolences to John in a weeping voice. John thanked her for her call. Before the call ended, she asked him if he would like to continue assisting the CIA. "John, let me warn you again that some of these assignments can be dangerous. If you agree, I will send you information on your first assignment by overnight mail since this phone and emails are not secure. I will need your new address."

Of course, John agreed to help her.

The following Saturday night, John hosted a housewarming potluck party at TT that his family and friends attended. Randy and Gail were present, as well as a few of John's former West High School classmates, some colleagues whom he worked with at Rocky Flats, and a few faculty members, including the Stevens. All of John's family were there, including his older brother, Bill, and his wife, Kay. Amy and Dave donated a vegetable dish, Kay made a wonderful potato salad, Lorrie purchased rolls and a vegetable salad, Eric and Sylvia brought the dessert, and John was barbecuing hamburgers, hot dogs, and steaks on a grill on the balcony. From the thirtieth-floor deck, everyone enjoyed the wonderful view of the Rocky Mountains.

During the buffet dinner, the conversations were mainly about everyone's activities. John was the last one to talk, and he told them some of his plans for retirement. "I have almost completed my flying lessons and hope to take my first solo flight in a single-engine plane out of the Longmont airport in a couple of weeks. I also want to prepare a second edition of my *Actinide Separations* book, work out at the gym, and explore Denver more. I also plan to make some trips around Colorado and attend conferences in the United States and overseas, mainly to see longtime friends. My next overseas trip is to Egypt next month to see an old friend."

After the meal, discussions, and several tours of the apartment, the visitors slowly left after giving John their thanks for a wonderful party. The young folks cleaned up the kitchen, and after more conversations, they left for home.

John's daily routine usually consisted of doing his stretches, weightlifting, and swimming at the building's gym; working at the computer, revising his book; continuing to learn Russian; keeping up with his French, German, and Spanish language skills; taking walks in various areas of downtown Denver; and every once in a while, taking one-day drives around Colorado. When possible, he would have a meal with friends and relatives as well as his neighbors.

On a few of his walks, he would visit his boyhood neighborhood near Speer Boulevard and Pearl Street, about a mile from LoDo. During these times, he would recall some of his activities before he started attending kindergarten. He had a tricycle that he would peddle around the neighborhood. One time, he tried to ride his bike off a two-foot wall to see if he could fly, but the dangerous event caused him to cut open his forehead. The scar was still visible today. He would also go with friends down to Cherry Creek to wade in the water and go to a nearby golf course to look for golf balls.

John also made some visits to the library, city park, zoo, and art and historical museums. He sometimes attended a few ball games. Of course, after his solo plane ride, he took flights over Denver and the suburbs at least once a month.

On one visit to see her father, Lorrie read about one of his trips to Hawaii in his diary since she planned to go there with a friend following graduation. John had promised to pay for the trip as a graduation gift.

II

John usually had meals with Eric and Sylvia every two weeks, either in Boulder or Denver. Most of the time, Lorrie joined them. She had started graduate school at CU Boulder. John also continued having lunch at the Brown Palace Restaurant every other Wednesday with Amy and Dave. Over lunch, the main topics of conversation were their activities over the past two weeks. John usually had the most to say since he had lots of free time for various things. He would always relate to Amy and Dave about his day trips around Colorado.

"Last Thursday, I got on HY-285 and drove to the road going to Pine, about halfway between Conifer and Baily. Just before reaching Pine, I stopped at Pine Valley Ranch Park, a Jefferson County Open Space, where I took a three-mile round-trip walk on the narrow-gauge trail where the train tracks used to run from Pine to Denver for a train transporting logs. It was a great walk with the wonderful sound of the North Fork of the South Platte River that parallels the trail. Following a drive around Pine, I drove on the dirt road that parallels Buffalo Creek to where it joins the South Platte River. There is an old, abandoned two-story hotel located there called the South Platte Hotel. After some picture taking, I continued the drive back to Denver via Foxton, Deckers, Woodland Park, Manitou Springs, Colorado Springs, and Castle Rock."

Dave commented, "My grandmother used to work at a saloon in Pine. That is indeed a lovely village with no more than two dozen homes. I will have to take you there sometime, Amy."

"On Friday, I took a drive to Greeley to HY-34 to Wiggins and then took HY-144 through the small towns of Masters, Orchard, Goodrich, Weldona, and Log Lane Village. Before reaching Fort Morgan, I stopped at the abandoned town of Dearfield so I could have a look at the deserted buildings and take some pictures. After going through Fort Morgan and Brush, I headed south on HY-71, past Woodrow to Last Chance, a town of one home and a deserted motel and Dairy King, not a Dairy Queen. From there, I got on HY-40 to home. It was a great trip."

"Dad, it amazes me how you can recall all the details of your trips, especially the highway numbers."

"You know I keep a diary, even of my day trips. Also, I have been on some of these roads before. For example, let me show you on this Colorado map the places I saw on a trip several years ago. I drove east on I-70 to Limon where I got on a side road paralleling I-70. Then I drove through a series of small towns: Genoa, Arriba, Flagler, Seibert, Vona, Stratton, and Bethune. The next town was Burlington, which could be labeled as a small city. I continued east past the Colorado border into Kansas and turned around at the small town of Kanorado. I then went back to Burlington to have a walk around the old part of town. Next, I went north on HY-385 to the intersection of HY-36 and then drove west. As you see on the map, the small towns I passed through were Idalia, Kirk, Jones, Cope, Anton, Lindon, and Last Chance. These small towns only had three to six blocks of deserted business buildings with several back streets of homes, some deserted. In a few towns, there were no gas stations or grocery stores. However, every town had a post office. I thought the abandoned motels once thrived until I-70 was built. Most of the areas between towns were farms with lots of corn and wheat fields. From Last Chance, I continued on HY-36 through Bennet and Watkins to home.

"Now I use the weekends for working at my computer, revising my *Actinide Separations* book and doing chores around TT. I usually see Eric, Sylvia, and Lorrie about every two weeks and periodically have meals with some of my friends. I have also made some new acquaintances. Of course, early most mornings, I have a workout at the gym and swim twenty lapses in the pool, followed by breakfast.

"On Monday, I went on an all-day trip that started on I-25 to Colorado Springs. There was construction on I-25 between Castle Rock and Monument, and this stretch of the highway was stop-and-go. South of the Springs, I got onto HY-115 and drove past Fort Carson to Florence. From there, I took HY-67 through Silver Cliff to West Cliff. Then I had about a fifteen-minute ride on a gravel road northeast out of Silver Cliff to Brother Bill's old home that he had built with no power tools. The cabin still looks great. Next, I took HY-69 through Cotopaxi to Salida where I had a nice walk around the lovely old town with many beautiful historic buildings. From there, I caught HY-285 to Fairplay and then went north on HY-9, over Hoosier Pass to Breckenridge. Following a walk on the main street and dinner, I drove home on I-70. On that day's drive, I had seen herds of llamas, antelope, buffalo, and deer.

"Yesterday's trip was unusual as I drove to Georgetown in moderate traffic on I-70 and made a short stop at a point above Georgetown to take pictures. There I heard what I thought was a bear in the bushes growling at me. Then I hurriedly continued the ride, between beautiful tree-covered mountains and past three lakes, over Guanella Pass, twelve miles from Georgetown, and Geneva Basin, two miles from the pass. There are still traces of two ski runs at the basin that now has a lot of trees on the trails. The ski area has been closed for many years, and all the buildings and ski lifts have been removed. As you know, this is where I learned how to ski in the mid-sixties. It was part of a required gym class at CU. The gym class in the fall was ballroom dancing. After arriving in Grant on HY-285, I headed back home, first through Conifer, then on the road to Evergreen. A little later, I stopped to take some pictures of a couple of abandoned cabins and spotted several deer nearby. I got some good shots with my camera and then proceeded on a nonstop ride to Denver via Evergreen and Morrison.

"Tomorrow, I plan to drive through Golden Gate State Park to HY-72, then at Rollinsville, I will turn off onto a gravel road that parallels the train tracks and South Boulder Creek and head west past Tolland to the East Portal of Moffat Tunnel. The only other route for train travel east and west is across Wyoming. A couple of miles east of the tunnel is a narrow rocky road to Rollins Pass. Thirty years ago, I could take the road over Rollins Pass into Winter Park. Back then, I had to drive through a tunnel and cross a narrow bridge that was very scary. Now only all-terrain vehicles and bikes can travel the narrow gravel road. After taking some pictures at the tunnel, I will drive to Eldora, a historic mining town. From there, I plan to drive home through Nederland, Boulder Canyon, and Boulder.

"I forgot to tell you at our last meeting about a trip I made a couple of weeks ago. Let me show you on the map. I went to Leadville via Copper Mountain ski area and over Fremont Pass and past Granite. I had a nice walk around the nice downtown area of Leadville and a short visit to the Mining Museum, then proceeded to Buena Vista. This time, I only had a drive around the small town, then went via Main Street to Cottonwood Lake that was fed by Cottonwood Creek. Uncle John used to take me, my brother Bill, and my cousin Don there to fish and camp out. After driving over Cottonwood Pass near Mount Princeton, I took a dirt sideroad to the small old ghost town of Tin Cup that had lots of old cabins with only a few people living there. There is a narrow gravel road that continued east out of Tin Cup over Tin Cup Pass to another ghost town, St. Elmo. However, the terrible washboard road had lots of sharp rocks, so I was afraid of a flat tire and turned around and headed back to Buena Vista. On the way back, I went by several deer and even saw a moose in a small pond. After I arrived back in Buena Vista, I went south through town and took a paved road west through a resort area called Princeton. The road changed to gravel and continued several miles to St. Elmo. I had a short walk around the small ghost town of a few old stores and cabins. There was no one there, but a block or two away were a couple of occupied homes. I then returned to Buena Vista and took HY-285 back to Denver. It had been a great trip.

"I now have a goal of seeing all the cities, towns, and historical places in Colorado. My dad used to ask me why I wanted to visit so many other countries when there are so many beautiful things to see in Colorado. He was right! Before you both return to work, let me tell you some jokes I recently heard.

"In the Garden of Eden, Eve says to Adam, 'Do you love me?' Adam replies to Eve, 'Do I have a choice?'

"'My ex-wife was deaf. She left me for a deaf friend. To be honest, I should have seen the signs.'

"'For Christmas, I gave my kid a BB gun. He gave me a sweater with a bull's-eye on the back.'

"Posted in the elevator at work is the usual warning sign: 'In case of fire, do not use the elevator.' Scrawled in pen beneath it is the addendum, 'Use water.'

"Anyone traveling on business for our company must fill out an expense report. 'A field on the form asks for the name on the credit card.' One Einstein wrote, 'Mastercard.'

"I was talking to my doctor about a weight-loss patch I had seen advertised. Supposedly you stick it on, and the pounds melt away. 'Does it work?' I asked my doctor. 'Sure, if you put it over your mouth.'"

As Amy was smiling, she asked her father, "Did you hear how they caught the great produce bandit? He stopped to take a leek."

"'A vegan said to me, 'People who sell meat are gross!' I replied, 'People who sell fruit and veg are grocer.'"

Both John and Dave laughed.

"Dad, it sounds like you are living life to its fullest by seeing some of the beautiful places in Colorado. Dave and I must return to work now. Love you."

John got a phone call, and the caller said, "Hi, John, this is Kim Carn. How are you?"

"Well, hello, Kim, it is great to hear from you. I have been fine living in Denver in a great apartment. The next time we get together, I will tell you more about my new life in Colorado."

Kim asked John to photocopy the summary of his trip to Egypt that he took last year and send it to her by overnight mail. She said, "I assume you received my package a couple of days after my last phone call outlining the purpose of this assignment."

"Yes, and I am looking forward to seeing a few of my Egyptian friends."

"The Penny Group will be sending you funds to visit that country and find out if they are starting a nuclear weapons program, that is, if you agree."

"As I have done in the past, Kim, I will serve my country in any way possible."

"This trip could be risky, so please be careful. After the trip, you can stop in Atlanta on your way back to Denver and give me a report of your visit to Egypt. This pay phone wants more money, so I will sign off. I am looking forward to seeing you in Atlanta."

III

After John's arrival in Atlanta from Cairo, he checked into a hotel near the airport. Following breakfast the next morning, he called Kim and informed her of his arrival. She told him that she would meet him in his hotel room at noon.

After their greetings, John told Kim, "Wow, you have lost some weight and look great, more like Marilyn Monroe than ever."

"And you are as handsome as ever and still could pass for a tall Tom Cruise."

"As I have told you in the past, Kim, we should go to Hollywood."

"I was thinking on my way over here that I have known you since you first came to Clemson University several years ago. I value your friendship and all the trips you have taken on behalf of the agency."

"I have also enjoyed working with you. However, I know you are busy, so let me give you a short summary of my trip to Cairo. I have also made a copy of my diary for your reading. I spent four nights in Cairo and was hosted by my good friend Hesham. As you know from reading about my last trip to Egypt, Hesham is retired from the Egyptian Atomic Energy Authority. I first met Hesham when he was a group leader. I was sent there twice for two weeks of consulting, sponsored by the IAEA. The work took place at the authority's research facility, about an hour's drive from Cairo, that housed two research reactors. Hesham took me there for a one-day visit on this trip where I gave a lecture and had a detailed tour of the site. From what I saw and heard from Hesham, they have no intentions of building a nuclear weapon. Their research reactors are not equipped to make nuclear bomb material. Of course, Hesham and I spent a day at the Pyramids."

"Well, that is good news, John. I really thought since Israel is reported to have nuclear weapons, although they have never confirmed or denied their possession of nukes, Egypt would want to have their own, especially since they were at war with each other in the past."

"Do you know what other countries have the bomb?"

"If you Google what countries currently have nuclear weapons, you would surprisingly read that Russia has about 4,500; the US 3,700; China 350; France 290; UK 180; Pakistan 165; India 160; Israel 90; and North Korea 20. Of course, one wonders where the authors of the report got their information. As you probably know, John, since 1970, 191 states, including the US, Russia, UK, France, and China, have joined the Treaty on the Non-Proliferation of Nuclear Weapons (NPT), an agreement to prevent the spread of nuclear weapons and promote disarmament. India, Israel, and Pakistan have never joined the NPT, and North Korea left in 2003. Iran started its nuclear program in the 1950s and has always insisted its program is for peaceful purposes."

"I recently read an article about Russia, the UK, and the US reducing their inventory of nukes, while China, India, North Korea, and Pakistan are producing more. In 2017, the UN proposed a treaty to ban nukes, but countries with them did not sign up because the agreement did not consider the realities of international security. The article also stated that while countries like the UK and US are reducing their nuclear stockpile, they are still modernizing and upgrading their existing armory. It also takes a lot of money to continue to maintain the bombs since the plutonium decays in time and makes the weapons less effective. Rocky Flats was where the plutonium triggers were renewed. Now other DOE sites are doing this expensive job.

"Nuclear weapons release huge amounts of radiation, which can cause radiation sickness, so their actual impact lasts much longer than the blast. For example, the neutron bomb that I worked on was designed to mainly emit deadly radiation while causing minimal physical damage."

"John, I think Truman should have never ordered the nuclear bombing of Hiroshima and Nagasaki in 1945. There was huge devastation and enormous loss of life. In Hiroshima, eighty thousand innocent men, women, and children were killed, and seventy thousand were killed in Nagasaki, not to mention the long-term suffering of the survivors who were exposed to the radiation."

"Yes, I agree. Truman should have ordered the demonstration of the bomb in an isolated area of Japan where there would have been minimal loss of life."

"John, sorry to change the subject, but Washington has ordered the upgrading of the files of civilians assisting the CIA.

So for the CIA's new records, would you please give me a short summary of your life, starting with your childhood? Let me turn my tape recorder back on."

"Kim, I am sure you know most of what I am going to tell you from my CIA and FBI files and what we have talked about at our other meetings, but let me start from the beginning. I grew up with wonderful parents and two brothers and two sisters in a two-bedroom home in West Denver. I attended elementary and junior high schools near our home and West High at the edge of downtown Denver. In high school, my grades dropped since I became more interested in cars and girls than education. I also worked at a supermarket part-time. I dropped out of high school during my senior year to work more but went back the following year and graduated. I then started college studies at CU Denver part-time in the evenings and began working full-time at Rocky Flats as a janitor.

"As you know, the Rocky Flats Plant was between Boulder and Golden off Highway 93. Parts for nuclear weapons were made at the plant for many years, but now the plant is no longer there. It was decontaminated and demolished several years ago. Now the area is a national wildlife refuge.

"During the next three years at Rocky Flats, I was promoted to laboratory technician and continued part-time studies at CU Denver, majoring in chemistry. To avoid the draft and being sent to Vietnam to fight, I joined the Army Reserve and took a six-month leave from Rocky Flats for active-duty training. Half of the training was for me to eventually become a chemical, biological, and nuclear warfare training officer. A year later, I took a two-year leave of absence from Rocky Flats and attended classes full-time during my junior and senior years on the Boulder campus. Following being awarded a bachelor of science degree in chemistry, I returned to Rocky Flats as a full-time chemist in the research and development department and continued going to CU Boulder full-time for my master's, doctoral, and postdoctoral studies. After my university studies, I was asked to teach an evening chemistry course at CU's medical campus in Aurora, a Denver suburb. I did that for two years. During this time, I was promoted to manager of a group in the department and later director of the department.

"I am sure you have noticed that I have a handicap. I am a stutterer. I have had a lot of embarrassing times as a stutterer, especially growing up. Some of my classmates used to make fun of me, imitating my stuttering. The worst time was when I was giving a seminar talk at CU when I was a graduate student. I stuttered through the whole talk. Margrit did not know I was a stutterer until a year after we were married. She had a calming effect on me. I have gone through several help sessions, and the flow technique works the best. When I get blocked on a word, I pause, take a breath, and slowly exhale as I say the word. Since my goal was to eventually become a professor, I joined a Toastmasters group and gave talks at high schools in the area. I also gave presentations at technical meetings and seminars whenever possible. Some well-known stutterers are Charles Darwin, J. Edgar Hoover, Jimmy Stewart, Anthony Quinn, Elvis Presley, Winston Churchill, Nicole Kidman, Marilyn Monroe, and Joe Biden. There are four times as many males than females that have the handicap.

"I met Margrit Hoffman when I was in graduate school. We only had a three-month courtship before we were married. She was a beautiful, wonderful lady, and we were lucky to eventually have three great children, Amy, Eric, and Lorrie. I am sure you will get to meet my adult children sometime. Margrit was killed in an automobile accident when we lived in California.

"Over two decades ago, I spent three years at the International Atomic Energy Agency in Vienna, Austria. In my previous work at Rocky Flats, I was a contributor to the development of the neutron bomb. In Vienna, KGB agents were trying to get information about the bomb from me via Margrit. She became romantically involved with Andrei Pushkin, thought by the CIA to be a KGB agent. Realizing the futility of their relationship,

Margrit told me about Andrei and how they unsuccessfully attempted to terminate their affair. Later Andrei committed suicide, and Margrit was beside herself with grief, but that event saved our marriage. Later I was to find out that Andrei had faked his suicide and left Vienna for Canada to start a new life. After leaving the agency, Margrit, our three children, and I returned to our home in Arvada, a Denver suburb. Margrit and I resumed a close, loving relationship that had been severely damaged in Vienna. I also returned to Rocky Flats as a manager of the Plutonium Chemistry Research and Development Group.

"About this time, I traveled a lot to conferences overseas and to Vienna and Moscow to have meetings with my two Russian coauthors on a series of books we were writing for the IAEA. Following more contacts with my Russian colleagues, I was informed that a background investigation had been conducted by the Department of Energy and the FBI. I was then subjected to several polygraph tests, but I failed all of them. I was puzzled by this, so I paid to have one performed by a private agency, but that test also showed that I was lying about a sexual encounter with a KGB agent. The FBI had received in the mail a picture of me and a lady I met aboard a Russian ship during a Russian Club of Art and Literature dinner. Margrit was a member of the club while we lived in Vienna. After the dinner, I was invited by this lady, whom I found out later was a KGB agent, for a tour of the ship. She took me to a room below deck and offered me a drink. Apparently, there was a drug in the drink that caused me to pass out. I had no knowledge of what happened next, but I am sure that is when the pictures were taken of the two of us without clothes on and in an embrace. I recovered about thirty minutes later. This investigation resulted in me losing my security clearance. I regret this whole episode in my life as it caused untold suffering to my family.

"I then went to Australia to teach for three years and later to work in California for three years. Andrei came to California and tried to renew his relationship with Margrit and kill me, but instead, he accidentally killed Margrit. I found out later that he committed suicide in Canada and told his son Alex in his dying breath that I had shot him.

"At that point, I wanted to start a new life and left California for a teaching job at Clemson University. As you know, I even started using my middle name, James. I enjoyed the academic life very much, supervising several students and teaching actinide chemistry. I even purchased the car and home that Margrit liked.

"Alex joined my research group using a different last name. I did not know that he was Andrei's youngest son. In early January, two years ago, I took him, another graduate student, and Ying, a postdoctoral student from China, with me on an expedition to Antarctica where we would do some ice sampling. By that time, I had fallen in love with Ying. We were married by the ship's captain as we crossed the Antarctic Circle. The following night, me, Alex, and a dozen other brave souls camped out on Hovgaard Island, where there was an attempt on my life. On the last night of the trip, as we were crossing the Drake Passage and heading past Cape Horn, the sea was very rough, and large waves were coming over the front of the ship. Alex met me at the stern of the ship and with difficulty admitted that his real name was Alexander Pushkin, that his father was the one who had a love affair with Margrit in Vienna, and that his father had cut the brake line on my car in California with the intention of killing me and not Margrit. I was shocked as Alex admitted that on the camping night, he was the one who had kicked the rock that was holding me and my sleeping bag in place. As I was sliding down the hill, Alex told me that he was immediately sorry for what he had done and ran, trying to stop me, but that I had managed to stop myself at the edge of the hill above the sea. He also said that his father shot himself in his home in Canada where he was staying and his father told him in his dying breath that I had shot him and that he should kill me. I sternly told Alex that I did not kill his father and have an alibi. Alex agreed and said he learned that morning that his father had committed suicide. Alex told me that he was extremely sorry that he had tried to kill me. At the end of our conversation, I informed Alex that under the circumstances, I forgive him. My last words were for him to come and give me a big bear hug. Alex happily jumped over and gave me a hearty embrace that caused both of us to accidentally fall over the back of the ship into the rough, freezing ocean."

John then told Kim about Deborah, a widow and retired medical doctor living on Navarino Island, saving his life; his time in Chile; falling in love with Deborah; getting his memory back; and returning to South Carolina. "Upon my return to the US, Ying and I resumed our lives together, and I went back to teaching at Clemson. But later, Alex's older brother arrived in Clemson trying to kill me but instead accidentally killed Ying in a similar manner as Margrit's death. A week later, he also attempted a second time to kill me but failed.

"In trying to get over my loss of Ying, I slowly renewed a loving relationship with Deborah, and we started traveling together. Several months later, while back in Clemson, I was invited to speak at an international conference in Moscow. I invited Deborah to join me, and we first went to Vienna where we were married. After our arrival in Moscow and my attending the conference all week, Deborah and I enjoyed the banquet on the last night of the conference. After returning to our room that night, Alex's brother surprised me and Deborah with a gun and shot both of us. Immediately after being shot, I jumped over to the brother and gave him a bear hug, trying to wrestle the gun from him. During the scuffle, the gun fired a third time, killing him.

"The police and ambulance came and took Deborah and I to the nearby hospital where we were operated on to remove the bullets and then placed in intensive care. I survived, but Deborah did not.

"After Deborah's passing, I had another attempt on my life in the hospital that nearly succeeded, but I had a good nurse that did an excellent job of CPR on me. I knew it was Andrei's brother that tried to kill me, and I told that to the police.

"After returning to Clemson, I had several email exchanges with Misa, my best Russian friend. He wrote that the police continued their search for the brother, but with no success thus far, and he would continue to keep me informed. I also arranged for a realtor to sell my two homes in South Carolina and, when I was ready, for movers to come and load my furniture and personal things for transport to Nederland. I then drove to Colorado so I could start a new life there.

"You know all the details about Lara and her death. Now I have started another new life in Denver and do not have any worries about any more attempts on my life. Kim, I know nothing about your personal life. Can you please tell me more about yourself?"

"I cannot tell you a lot because of my job. I grew up on Long Island, New York, and attended George Washington University for a bachelor's degree in criminal justice. Then I started working for the CIA after finishing my training at the CIA University in Chantilly, Virginia. My first post was in New York. After three years there, I was transferred overseas to our South African embassy. I worked for Sidney Carn, the station chief. He was not an especially handsome man like you but had a certain charm and captivating personality that romantically attracted me to him. Our relationship grew, and we were wed about a year later. Of course, the agency did not approve of our union and transferred him to our Ukrainian embassy. I remained in Johannesburg for a year before my transfer to Atlanta. Sidney and I have get-togethers every chance we get and, of course, spend our vacation time together.

"I am sure you can understand that I do not have any close friends because of my job, a lonely job, and only a couple of fellow workers have meals with me periodically. I have no relatives since I lost my parents and sister several years ago in a car accident. You are my only good friend. John, I need to return to work now. Thank you for your continued assistance to the CIA.

I plan to be in Denver in a couple of weeks when I will brief you on your next assignment." Kim departed after giving John a hug.

A couple of weeks later, John received a call from Kim telling him that she arrived in Denver the day before and would like to meet with him in the evening. He invited her to come to his apartment for dinner. Following their meal that evening, they enjoyed the view of the sun setting over the Rockies. The main conversation was about John's next CIA assignment to Venezuela. "We have reports that the country is preparing to support a terrorist group in the US. Since you have some friends at the University of Caracas, we would like you to see if you can confirm these types of activities."

"One of my friends has some relatives in high places in their government. He may be especially helpful for this kind of information."

"John, you know I spent some time in Africa, and I know you have made a lot of trips there. I have not seen much of West Africa. Could I borrow one of your travel diaries to read about your last trip there? I can return the book in the morning. And thank you for the wonderful dinner."

"You are always welcome to read any of my diaries. Let me see you to your rental car now."

IV

After John returned from his trip to Venezuela, he called Kim and told her that he had no luck in finding any of the information that she requested. She thanked him for his work and for making the cryptic phone call.

About a month later, Kim called John from a pay phone in Atlanta. She started to cry and told him that her husband was killed by a hit-and-run driver in Kiev. "You are the only real friend I have, and I needed someone to talk to."

"What happened, Kim?"

"All the ambassador could tell me is that they think the killing was no accident as a speeding car came up on the sidewalk Sidney was walking on, ran over him, and fled. I agree with the ambassador's suspicions that Sidney was murdered as I had received a letter from him saying someone had ransacked his apartment and he was worried about an attempt on his life. I plan to fly to Kiev in the morning and make arrangements to have his body shipped to Washington for a quiet funeral."

Kim arrived in Kiev the next day to settle Sidney's affairs and plan to have his body shipped to Washington. She discovered his flat ransacked a second time. Two days later, after Kim took care of her husband's personal things, she joined several staff members for a brief memorial at the embassy. Later that day, Kim took two suitcases to the curb and waited to hail a taxi to take her to the airport for her flight to the United States. As she was waiting for the taxi, a car came down the street at high speed, jumped the curb, and just missed hitting her and her luggage. Then the car continued down the street at high speed.

Two weeks later, John got another call from Kim. She told him she was in Denver and would like to meet him in his apartment. Of course, he agreed. Kim arrived midafternoon and told him that when she was in Kiev, a car almost hit her as she was waiting for a taxi to take her to the airport. "The car came up on the sidewalk, and I jumped out of the way as it sped by. I assume the driver was trying to kill me. After I returned to Atlanta following Sidney's funeral in Washington, I found that my apartment had been broken into and ransacked. I think whoever did that was looking for the papers Sidney sent me.

"Scarier though was what happened to me several days later. I went from my apartment on the tenth floor to the elevator on my way to work. Just as the elevator door was closing, a big, scary-looking man slid into the elevator and stood behind me. A few seconds later, the giant put me in a bear hug and started to strangle me. Just before the elevator reached the ground floor, I fell to the floor, unconscious. The next thing I knew was that a nice couple was attending me. Although I was shaken up, I told the couple that I was okay and thanked them for their help. They told me that when the elevator door opened, the evil man pushed them out of the way and ran from the building. They then moved me from the elevator floor to the couch in the entryway.

"I then went to the office very shaken up and told my boss about the incident as well as the car almost hitting me in Kiev. He suggested I transfer to the Denver office since a position is available there. It took a couple of days to finish my work, give my landlord notice, and arrange to have my furniture and belongings shipped to Denver. I then loaded my car with clothes and personal things and took the two-day drive here. I am staying at the Brown Palace Hotel until I can find my own place."

With a friendly hug, John said, "I am so sorry to hear about your loss of Sidney and the attempts on your life. You are always welcome to stay with me."

"Thank you, dear friend. My first assignment here is to get information on a terrorist group arriving in several US cities to disrupt our lives with simultaneous actions of putting poisonous substances in our water supplies and in public places to shut down hospitals and transportation systems. I received information that Colorado is one of the main targets because of the many government facilities located here, which include the North American Aerospace Defense Command in Colorado Springs.

"The CIA also received more specific information that terrorists had planned to steal some refined uranium to put in the drinking water of major cities. Usually, the water is not analyzed for uranium."

John told Kim about his Clemson student project of removing arsenic and uranium from drinking water for an environmental contest held each year at New Mexico State University. "My students' project was based on an actual incident in a South Carolina town. After numerous people got cancer, the authorities traced it to the town's drinking water. Further investigation revealed deposits of uranium ore in the same underground locations as the town's well water.

"One possible source of radioactive material is a uranium ore processing facility near Grand Junction. There has been a big problem with radioactive radon gas in some of the new homes built over uranium tailings from the ore processing. I suggest we visit this facility and find out what type of safeguards they have in preventing the stealing of processed uranium. We could fly there and rent a car or just drive. If we drove, you could see more of the beauty of Colorado."

"That sounds like an excellent idea, John. Let me tell my supervisor about your suggestion and see if he agrees with your plan."

"Would you like to have dinner with me at the Brown Palace? We could meet in the restaurant at six."

"That sounds wonderful, John. Now I need to return to work since I have a meeting to attend."

That evening, as the two were having dinner, Kim told John that her boss has approved the trip to Grand Junction. "When would you like to go John?"

"Why don't we leave next Monday in my car so I can show you some of the beauty of Colorado? We could stay in Glenwood Springs on Monday night and arrive in Grand Junction before noon on Tuesday for an afternoon visit to the uranium facility. I will contact the plant manager to arrange the meeting."

"Okay. Can you pick me up at six on Monday morning at the Brown Palace?"

"Certainly. But first, can you meet me for lunch tomorrow so I can discuss more of the details of the trip? I should also know if the plant manager is available for our visit on Tuesday afternoon. We could meet at the Civic Center Park at noon and buy lunch at one of the kiosks."

"That sounds great, John, and thank you for dinner. By the way, could I borrow another one of your travel diaries to read about some of your great trips. The stories are so interesting and educational."

"Thank you for your kind words. I will bring one to our meeting tomorrow at noon. Good night."

John arrived in the park and spied Kim sitting alone on a park bench. He joined her, and she thanked him for bringing one of his diaries to read. "You are welcome to borrow more of my diaries if you wish to read about a few more of my trips. I would also recommend reading *The Bare Essentials,* a book Margrit wrote. Here is a free copy for you. The story involves a University of Colorado chemistry professor who goes to the University of Vienna for a year's sabbatical. His friend, who is head of the analytical laboratory of Warsaw's Nuclear Energy Institute, asks him to analyze samples of natural gas to see if the gas contains mind-altering drugs. He suspects that the drugs are being introduced by the Russians to subdue the Polish people during the cold war. The professor agrees to perform the analysis but is unaware that by doing so, he will subject both himself and his Polish-born wife to acts of terror, including an attempt on his life.

"By the way, I have been invited to attend a dinner with my family at Eric and Sylvia's home in Boulder on Saturday. Would you like to join me? Please say yes as it may help you get your mind off the tragic events you have experienced recently. All my family will be there, and it would be a good time for you to meet them. I will just introduce you as a friend I met at Clemson and not mention the CIA. You can say that you have a government job at the Federal Building in Denver and have just been transferred here from Atlanta. I can pick you up at the Brown Palace at one so we can have a drive around Boulder and I can show you CU. It's funny that the initials are just like Clemson University."

After a short walk on the Pearl Street Mall in downtown Boulder and at the CU campus on Saturday afternoon, John and Kim traveled to Eric and Sylvia's home in South Boulder for dinner. Amy, Dave, and Lorrie arrived, and the five young adults spent some time exchanging information with Kim over a wonderful meal that Sylvia had prepared. There was also a discussion of everyone's recent activities. After dinner, John and Kim thanked their hosts for a wonderful time and returned to Denver.

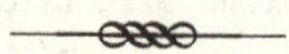

On Sunday morning, John phoned Kim and asked her if she would like to see Eliches Gardens Amusement Park in the afternoon. She agreed to meet him at his apartment at three.

After coffee and sweets at TT, John and Kim walked a couple of blocks up Little Raven Street to Eliches Gardens. They then strolled around the park and rode the Twister roller coaster, the Star Flyer, a high-flying swing ride, and several other rides. Later, on their walk back to TT, Kim thanked John for the enjoyable evening and commented on all the other scary rides that they took. As they were walking, a Tesla car slowly drove by toward the Eliches. John noticed that the driver looked like Felex, the Russian sailor who tried to kill him on several occasions. John commented to Kim that he was seeing more and more of the quiet electric cars. "I was recently on a short trip to California to see my other brother and got a Tesla at a rental place. I found it was easy to drive with lots of power."

At that moment, John spied the same car, but with its headlights off, coming toward Kim on the sidewalk at high speed. Just before the speeding car came upon Kim, John pushed her out of the way, but he got hit by the car and landed on the hood. He immediately grabbed the windshield wipers and got a good look at the driver. John hung on to the wipers until the car slowed down to make a right turn at the corner. When the car turned,

John rolled off onto the street. As the car was speeding away, Kim ran to John and helped him up. She assisted him back to his apartment. There she bandaged up a couple of bad scratches and put ice on his bruises.

Kim said, "I think that big, mean-looking man is the same monster that tried to kill me in the elevator in Atlanta. I think he is a hired assassin who killed Sidney."

John agreed and told her about the incidents of Felex trying to kill him aboard the *Akademic Abraham* in the High Arctic and Antarctica. "I always wondered why he would want to kill me. Of course, Felex denied the encounters when questioned by the ship's captain. Perhaps he was right as the attempts could have been accidental.

"Do you mind if we visit the nearby police station to report this incident? I will ask them to put out a bulletin to keep a lookout for Felex and warn them that he is a dangerous assassin. I did see that the car had New Mexico license plates. I also have a picture of Felex in Antarctica, and the ship's captain told me his last name is Frolov."

After John made a copy of the picture of Felex, they both prepared to go to Kim's car.

"I am sorry, Kim, that we have to walk to your car in the guest parking lot. The valet has gone home."

Kim drove several blocks to the main police station. On the way, John said, "We will have to postpone our trip to Grand Junction for a few days."

"That is okay. I will search the CIA and FBI files in the morning to see if there is any information on Felex. Maybe we can have dinner tomorrow night and exchange information on what we find."

"Okay, let's meet at the Brown Palace restaurant at six."

At the police station, John filled out a detailed report of the incident and left the photo of Felex with the report. The captain told them that he would put out an all-point alert for Felex and give John a report in the morning.

As they left the station, John asked Kim to drive to the hotel. "After I see you to your room, I will take a taxi to my apartment building."

After Kim left her car with the hotel valet, they went to her room. "Kim, please be careful tonight and tomorrow. I suggest you keep your door double-locked and watch out tomorrow for any sign of Felex. If you do see him following you, please seek a safe place and call the police. I am sure you have had some evasive training at the CIA Academy."

"I also have a black belt in karate and carry a revolver in my purse!"

"Wow! A gun. A black belt. Now I am not sure that I feel safer around you or scared if you get mad at me."

As John started to leave her room, she gave him a long loving hug and thanked him for saving her life.

Over dinner at the hotel restaurant the next night, the couple was seated at a table in the corner of the restaurant away from other occupied tables. John started the conversation. "I did not recognize you at first tonight. Your new look, short dyed black hair, fooled me."

"I got the new look after leaving the office early this afternoon. I am sure I will fool some of my office mates tomorrow, and I will have to get a new picture badge. I thought this would be easier than using your black wig to hide my long blonde hair or one of your suits and wearing a fake beard."

After John had a good laugh, he told Kim, "The police captain told me this morning that the car had been stolen yesterday afternoon from a couple here on vacation. The couple reported the car theft to police shortly after the car was stolen. The police found the car abandoned near Union Station about an hour after the attempt on your life. There was no information about Felex Frolov in their files. The captain told me he would keep me posted on what they find.

"After the incident with Felex in the High Arctic, I asked Tim Smith to find information on Felex in the CIA files, but at that time, I had no last name, photo, or fingerprints of him, so of course, Tim could not find anything. What did you find?"

"There was a small CIA file that listed him as a sailor, smuggler, and paid assassin. He was accused of killing a retired Canadian intelligence agent by the name of Don Cunningham, but the charges were never proven."

"Don was the same man that shared a cabin with me on the High Arctic trip. He was also with me when Felex shot at us during a hike. Felex denied the attempt on our lives and said there was a bear nearby that he tried to shoot. Apparently, he was trying to kill Don and not me."

"I think I will have to be more careful now and watch for anyone following me to and from the office. I will try and keep my new living location a secret once I find the right apartment to rent. I hope to rent one tomorrow. How about our trip to Grand Junction? Now would be a good time to leave town for several days."

"Why don't we leave on Wednesday morning at six? I can meet you in the hotel lobby."

"That is okay with me. If I find an apartment tomorrow, I will check out of the hotel before we leave town."

"I will call the manager of the uranium ore processing plant tomorrow and arrange a meeting for Thursday afternoon."

"I will tell my supervisor our plans. I told him today about the incident last night, and he also suggested precautions, including informing the FBI. By the way, thanks for dinner."

V

John and Kim left Denver at about seven on Wednesday morning in Red, John's Jeep, and headed west on I-70. After going through the towns of Idaho Springs, Georgetown, and Dillon and over Vail Pass, they stopped in Vail for a walk. "John, what a lovely drive so far. I am sure glad we agreed to drive and not fly to Grand Junction. I am happy that I found an apartment to rent."

"I hope this trip helps you forget about the evening visit to Eliches. Maybe on our return to Denver, I can show you Breckenridge. Now we should get on the road again. Soon we will leave I-70 and take HY-24 through beautiful scenery, take some photos of an abandoned mining town near Notch Mountain, and pass through the small towns of Red Cliff and Pando and Camp Hale to Leadville. Along the way, you will see that old, abandoned railroad tracks parallel the road. I took this exact drive earlier this year, and it was a great trip."

They had another stop, this time at Camp Hale. John commented during their short walk, "Camp Hale was constructed in 1941 to train soldiers in mountain climbing, Alpine and Nordic skiing, and cold weather survival. When it was in full operation, approximately fifteen thousand soldiers were housed here. It was decommissioned in November 1945.

"Our next stop will be in Leadville to have a short visit to the mining museum, that is, if you are interested. About twelve miles past Leadville, you will see several peaks above fourteen thousand feet. There we will head west on HY-82, past Twin Lakes, over Independence Pass, to Aspen."

Kim commented during their stop at the summit of Independence Pass, "This portion of the ride is beautiful, with great views of the leaves on aspen trees turning yellow, orange, and red. The stop at the mining museum was also worthwhile."

"Just before we go into Aspen, we will have a short detour to the ghost town of Ashcroft. Ashcroft was a silver mining town founded in 1880. At the height of Ashcroft's prosperity, over two thousand people lived there. High transportation costs, shallow silver deposits, competition from Aspen, and ultimately in 1893, the silver market crash destroyed the viability of the town. By 1895, Ashcroft's population plummeted to one hundred. In 1912, when the US Postal Service suspended mail delivery, the town's population went below fifty residents.

"Following a short walk around the ghost town, we will have a late lunch and a walk in Aspen. I would love to take you to see

Maroon Bells, but now one needs a reservation to visit. I will show you a picture of it when we return to the car."

After lunch, the couple went to Glenwood Springs, where they had a walk in the downtown area and a short round-trip drive through the beautiful Glenwood Canyon, which parallels the Colorado River. After they returned to Glenwood Springs and checked into separate rooms at the La Quinta hotel, they had dinner at the Village Inn next door to the hotel.

Over dinner, Kim asked John, "What hotel would you recommend that I make a reservation for on the night of our return to Denver? As you know, I checked out of the Brown Palace before we left Denver and placed most of my belongings in my car. The hotel agreed to my leaving my car parked at their underground valet parking level."

"I recommend TT. You are indeed welcome to stay in my guest bedroom until you can move into your own place."

"Well, thank you, John, that sounds like a wonderful idea. I can do all the cooking if you approve."

At six the next morning, they were back on I-70, going west to Grand Junction. They had a quick breakfast in Rifle and then continued the drive to Grand Junction. After their arrival, they checked into separate rooms at the Radisson Hotel next to the downtown four-block-long pedestrian mall lined with restaurants and various shops. Following lunch, they went to the uranium ore processing facility on the outskirts of the city to interview the plant manager.

Over dinner at the mall, they discussed what they discovered at the facility. "John, it appears like their safeguards of purified uranium, ore, and tailings from the ore processing are outstanding, and the tour of the facility with the plant manager certainly reinforced my conclusion that the plant is well guarded. He was surprised by the warning I gave him about terrorists possibly wanting some of their materials."

"I agree. Their safeguards are about what they were at Rocky Flats. All the employees must wear picture badges, and the barbed-wire high fence, guards, and guard dogs should be a deterrent for anyone trying to gain unauthorized access to the facility."

Early the next morning, following a quick buffet breakfast, the couple traveled southeast out of Grand Junction on Highway 50 that goes to Delta. Partway to Delta, they left Highway 50 at Whitewater and drove southwest on Highway 141 through beautiful canyons of red hills and rocks and the town of Gateway to Vancorum. There they headed west on Highway 90 and went through the towns of Bedrock and Paradox to the Utah border. "Here is where the highway number changes from 90 to 46. Take a look at the Colorado and Utah maps in the glovebox to see our route. At La Sal Junction, we will take the road to Canyonlands National Park and spend some time admiring the wonderful views from Looking Glass Rock and Needles Overlook."

After spending an hour in the park, they traveled to Moab on Highway 191 and then spent some time driving around Arches National Park. "John, I think seeing Devils Garden and Delicate Arch were the highlights of our visit to Arches."

"I agree. Now we will get back on Highway 191, drive to I-70, and head back to Grand Junction, with a short stop to see Sego Canyon Petroglyphs. Before returning to the Radisson, we will have a visit to Colorado National Monument with its beautiful sculptured red rocks."

On the way back to Grand Junction, John told Kim, "Now Monument moves the Grand Canyon to fourth place on my list of favorite places. Yellowstone National Park is still in first place, followed by Yosemite National Park."

"Well, I have not been to Yosemite, but I still have wonderful memories of my visit to the Grand Canyon and Yellowstone with Sidney years ago."

After another night at the Radisson and an early breakfast the next morning, they had a brief drive through part of Grand Mesa to see many beautiful lakes and forest-covered mountains. Then they returned to I-70 and traveled east.

On the drive, John told Kim, "As I get older, I see nature in a more puzzling and questioning way, such as the beauty of plants growing, the remarkable designs, colors, and smells of flowers, the variety of insects and how they know how to survive after being born, how young birds learn to fly, how animals know how to reproduce, ants working together to build an anthill and gather food, the many species of beautiful fish in the ocean, mammals in Africa, and much, much more. These things I just took for granted when I was younger. When I have more time, I would like to read more about these amazing things we have on earth and how they evolved.

"I have read a few Wikipedia articles on the chronology of the universe, history of the earth, human history, Charles Darwin, and even an article on the amazing ant. Did you know that there are about twenty-two thousand different species and that they evolved from wasp ancestors and are related to bees? Ants work together to support their colony and have colonized almost every landmass on earth, except Antarctica. Their success in so many different environments has been attributed to their social organization and their ability to defend themselves, modify habitats, and tap resources. They have division of labor, communication between individuals, and the ability to solve complex problems."

"One thing I do know, John, is that in the south, you do not want to get near red fire ants. Their sting is terrible. I think you know about these critters from your time at Clemson."

"To my knowledge, we are lucky in Colorado since no fire ants have been reported here."

"I believe in Darwin's work on evolution and that all species of life have descended over time from common ancestors in a process called natural selection, the basic mechanism for evolution."

"Well, I certainly believe that we evolved from apes. I see many people today that have facial features of gorillas. Felex is a good example, not that there is anything wrong with that."

"John, now you are starting to sound like Jerry Seinfeld. I think I have watched every episode of *Seinfeld*, some even twice."

"My favorite was the Soup Nazi. What was yours?"

"I liked the one where Elaine said with an Australian accent, 'The dingo ate your baby.' As you know, John, a dingo is a dangerous wild dog, reddish brown in color."

"That reminds me of the conference I attended on Frazer Island, off the coast of Brisbane, Australia. There were signs everywhere stating, 'Beware of the dingos' and 'Do not feed the dingos.' On the last night of the conference, a dinner was held outside, next to the hotel swimming pool. Sure enough, the dinner ended early because of a visit by several hungry dingos."

After going over Vail Pass into Frisco, they took Highway 9 to Breckenridge. Over a late lunch, John told Kim a little about the old mining town. "Breckenridge was founded by prospectors mining in the nearby mountains. Skiing and tourism are now the main attractions."

"John, this is indeed a beautiful town, with the main street lined with many old buildings housing a variety of shops and restaurants."

"From here, we will continue going south on Highway 9, over Hoosier Pass, to Fairplay. There we can have a look at the old town museum consisting of two blocks of old buildings. Finally, we will take Highway 285 to Kenosha Pass, where we can stop to look at the changing colors of leaves on aspen trees. After taking a few pictures, we can head back to Denver."

When they got back to Denver, they had a late dinner at TT. During the meal, Kim told John about the nice apartment she had rented. "The apartment is in a new building just a few blocks from the Federal Building. The one-bedroom apartment is nice and is on the twelfth floor. I plan to move in tomorrow when the movers arrive from Atlanta with my furniture."

"Congratulations on finding your own place to reside. If you need any help tomorrow, just let me know."

"Thank you, but I will rely on the movers to put the furniture where I want."

After dinner, Kim gave John her sincere thanks for a wonderful trip with a hug. "I will fix breakfast for us in the morning. Then tomorrow night, you are invited to come for dinner at my new place at about six. Here is the address. Good night."

"Good night."

VI

When John arrived at Kim's new residence, he pushed the outside buzzer for her apartment. Kim answered the buzzer and said, "Hello, John, I can see you on my security TV. The apartment entrance has a camera that shows who is wanting to enter the building. Please come up."

The door buzzed and opened, and John went to the elevator for transport to Kim's apartment on the tenth floor. Kim was standing outside her door and greeted John as he left the elevator. She welcomed him with a hug and said, "Please come in and make yourself at home. Let me take you on a quick tour of my new apartment."

"Thank you for inviting me to dinner and for fixing breakfast this morning at TT. You are an excellent cook, and your new apartment is sure nice. The movers did an excellent job of moving you in. I also love your new look, short black hair. You are still as beautiful as ever."

"Well, thank you, Tom Cruise. Yes, I like the apartment very much, especially the security camera at the front door. The fact that it is only a couple of blocks from work is also nice. As I mentioned to you after our trip to Grand Junction, I plan to walk to work and not drive to avoid trying to find a parking space."

Over a wonderful dinner, John warned Kim, "Please be careful and keep a lookout for Felex in case he knows where you live and work. I am sure he knows where you work, so be evasive on your walks to and from work. As you told me already, you were trained for that at the CIA Academy."

"You are right. Since tall, strange-looking Felex really stands out in a crowd, he will be easy to spot. I think my new short black hair should fool him. It will be interesting to see how long it takes for my coworkers to recognize me."

"I spoke with the Denver Police captain this morning, and he told me that they have had no luck so far in locating Felex, but his men will continue to watch for him. Your view to the west is great, and the sunset is sure beautiful tonight."

"Yes, it is, just like everything else I have seen so far in Colorado, thanks to you. Besides that, you are sure fun to be with. I am a lucky gal to have you for my dear friend."

"I am the lucky one."

"I was thinking this morning about the wonderful lunches we used to have at the Plantation House in the Pendleton Old Town Square after your return to Clemson following some trips. Of course, I had to debrief you on the trips and usually got a copy of your travel diary. Your reports were valuable to the CIA, especially your trips to Iran, North Korea, and Russia."

"Thank you for financially supporting some of these trips. Of course, other trips I took were funded by my research contracts so I could attend technical meetings and give talks on my students' research. My PhD advisor commented once that his students do all the work and he gets the fun part of presenting their results at meetings. Well, I must say I really enjoy traveling, especially to places I have never been to before. I think I told you about the Travelers Century Club that I belong to. Now I have platinum status since I have visited 320 countries and territories on the club list of 327.

"By the way, the couple that bought my home in Nederland has invited us for lunch next Saturday. I hope you can come with me. I could pick you up after breakfast so I can show you Nederland and more of Boulder. We can make a round trip, up Boulder Canyon and back through Coal Creek Canyon."

"That sounds wonderful, John. I look forward to seeing Pine Shadows."

"Sometime I would like to take you through some areas similar to the Flatirons in Boulder. Here, take a look at this Colorado map I brought so I can point out our route. We can drive through Red Rocks Park next to the small town of Morrison and then drive up Bear Creek Canyon to the town of Evergreen. Evergreen Lake is there where my grandfather Czermak used to take me, my brother Bill, and my cousin Don fishing. From Evergreen, we will go to HY-285, the highway we took coming back from Grand Junction. After a short ride southwest on 285, we will travel to Pine Valley Ranch Park and have a walk next to the North Fork of the South Platte River. From there, we will drive through the small towns of Pine and Buffalo Creek to Deckers. Next, we will go north to Sedalia and take Highway 85 toward Denver. On the way, we will make a short detour to see Roxborough Park that has red rock mountains like the Flatirons and in Red Rocks Park. From the park, we will travel through Waterton, past Chatfield Reservoir, and over to the entrance to Deer Creek Canyon. Then we will travel through another area of beautiful red rocks and take C-470 to I-70 to Denver."

"That sounds like a wonderful trip."

After John helped Kim load the dishwasher and clean up the kitchen, he said, "Well, it is getting late, so I am sure you would like to get ready for bed." With a loving hug, he thanked her for dinner and left for TT.

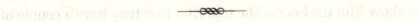

On Saturday morning, John picked up Kim for their ride to Nederland. After they started the hour's drive to Nederland, Kim said, "John, I had a very scary experience after leaving work yesterday. As I started my walk home, I saw Felex about half a block behind me. I then changed my route and took a short walk over to the Sixteenth Street Mall and got on the bus through the rear entrance. Just as the bus was about to leave, Felex entered the front door. Of course, the bus was crowded. At the next stop, I hurriedly left the bus with a group of passengers out the back door while bending down so as to hide from Felex. At that time, a large group of passengers boarded the front door of the bus that prevented Felex from exiting. After that bus pulled away from the curb, I was lucky that a bus going in the opposite direction arrived. I boarded that bus and got off at the nearest stop to my apartment and ran home. Then I called the police captain and reported Felex's location. He said he would dispatch some officers to the area to try to locate and arrest him. Later, the captain called and told me they did not have any luck in finding Felex. I plan to talk with the FBI in the Federal Building on Monday to see if they can help locate the monster."

"I am so sorry. I am sure you are being more careful now. I hope you enjoy the weekend that I have planned and that it helps you to get your mind off the brute. You are welcome to stay at my place tonight."

"Thank you, John. I told you about the papers that Sidney sent me that had some incriminating information on our relationship with Russia. When I was in DC for Sidney's funeral, I gave the papers to the director of the CIA. He reports to the director of National Security, who reports to the president. I was told that they had a formal inquiry underway into these type of activities. All I have now are Sidney's letters."

After their arrival at Pine Shadows, Randy and Gail were waiting on the porch. Following the introductions, Gail offered to show Kim the house. She told Kim that they have a couple of college students renting the apartment above the garage. Randy offered John a walk around the property. He first asked John, "Where did you meet this beauty?

"Back in South Carolina years ago. She was recently transferred to Denver and works for the government, handling research contracts."

"Well, I would have guessed that she was either a movie star or a stripper."

They both laughed.

After their visit with Randy and Gail, John took Kim to visit the colorful tourist town of Estes Park, followed by a drive through the eastern part of Rocky Mountain National Park. Following their return to Denver, Kim thanked John for the wonderful day. "I especially liked the park and seeing so many deer and mountain sheep. I was surprised by the small herd of elk in Estes Park, and the lunch we had at the restaurant of the Stanley Hotel was exceptionally good."

VII

John and Kim departed Denver on Sunday before the sun started to come up. Before they reached Colorado Springs, John pointed out the Air Force Academy next to the mountains. John suggested they drive through the Garden of the Gods to Manitou Springs. After going through Manitou Springs to Colorado Springs, Kim said, "I was surprised to see that the beautiful red slanted mountains at the Garden of the Gods are just like the Flatirons in Boulder, so beautiful and breathtaking."

"Now we will head southwest on Highway 115, past Fort Carson, to Canon City. I had two summer camps at Fort Carson when I was in the Army Reserve. From Canon City, we can have a stop at the Royal Gorge Bridge and Park, then a visit to Cripple Creek for a walk around the old mining town that now has gambling, just like Blackhawk and Central City. There are many beautiful old buildings there, much like Manitou Springs. We can also try our luck at the slot machines if you wish."

On their drive back to Denver on I-25, Kim commented, "I sure enjoyed this trip. The drive through Garden of the Gods was spectacular, but I am sorry I lost ten dollars in Cripple Creek. It is really the first time I have ever gambled."

"Sometime we must try our luck in Central City. I have always won more money there than I lost, mainly because after the first slot machine pays me some money, I go to another machine, then another. You might have noticed that I did win more money Cripple Creek than I played."

"I'm sorry, John, but I am not interested in doing any more gambling. In fact, I have never purchased a lottery ticket."

"I usually buy a Colorado Power Ball ticket once a week since some of the money goes for open spaces, parks, recreation, schools, swimming pools, trails, and wildlife open spaces for every county in the state. I have always played the same numbers. Let me see if you can guess what they are. Are they my Social Security number, the number they assigned me in prison, the number on my army dog tags, or my phone number?"

"I know you do not have a prison number, silly boy, so I would guess it is your phone number, not using the area code."

The following Saturday, John and Kim traveled north to Fort Collins on I-25 to have a stroll and a meal at the Austin Restaurant. After lunch and walks around downtown Fort Collins and Colorado State University, they headed south on Highway 287 to Loveland. There they had a visit to the downtown area of Loveland. They did the same in Longmont. On their return to Denver, they talked about what they saw. Kim commented, "Thank you for lunch, John, and for the wonderful visits to the main towns on the northern I-25 corridor. Longmont sure has some nice old buildings, and the walk around the Colorado State University campus was interesting."

"Eric attended CSU for his freshman year and then transferred to CU."

On Sunday morning, John picked up Kim, and they went west on I-70 and exited the interstate at Idaho Springs. After a short walk around the old mining town, they headed south to

Echo Lake. Over lunch at the Echo Lake Lodge Restaurant, Kim commented, "I sure liked our walk around part of Idaho Springs, and Echo Lake is sure beautiful with the surrounding snow-capped mountains."

"My grandpa used to take me and my brother and cousin here to fish. After we finish our nice lunch, we can visit Mount Evans. It is one of the mountains in Colorado over fourteen thousand feet and is the highest peak in the Front Range of the Rocky Mountains. It also has the highest paved mountain road in North America that goes to the summit. There we will have a breathtaking view of the Denver area and the plains. After some time on top, we can drive to Golden via Evergreen and over Lookout Mountain. In Golden, we can have a short visit to the Colorado Railroad Museum."

During the walk around the old steam trains, Kim said, "These trains are sure in good shape, and the views of Denver from Mount Evans and Lookout Mountain were spectacular. I also found our short stop at Buffalo Bill's grave interesting. He was quite a guy."

"Now I suggest we return to Denver and have a visit to the Denver Art Museum. Maybe next Saturday we can have a visit to the Denver Botanic Gardens, Museum of Nature and Science, the zoo, and the Wings Over the Rockies Air Museum. We can postpone visits to any of the places if we get tired."

"I hope you can join me for mass at the nearby Holy Ghost Catholic Church next Sunday."

"That would be nice. Even though I am a Catholic, I have not been to church since I was married to Margrit. I do say my daily prayers before I get out of bed every morning."

Over dinner in Kim's apartment, Kim said, "We may require your assistance on another CIA assignment. I will find out more this week at work if indeed we need to have you help us."

"As in the past, Kim, I am happy to help you out as much as I can. Thank you for dinner. Please keep me posted, and best wishes for a good and safe week at work."

VIII

Midmorning on Saturday, Kim picked up John at his apartment building for a drive around Denver and its suburbs in her car so she can get to know the city better. John first gave her directions to get on Speer Boulevard and head southeast, past the Denver Center for the Performing Arts on the left side and CU Denver on the right side. He pointed out the old tramway building that housed CU Denver when he went to classes there. Now the building is a hotel. They left Speer at Elati Street and drove south by West High School. As they drive by the school, John said, "On the left is Sunken Gardens Park, and as you can see, the school is on the right. It was organized in 1883, and the first graduation class numbered six students. In 1926, students started to use this building. My graduating class of 1960 had almost 500 students."

"It has beautiful architecture and is big."

"This is the street I got my first and only traffic ticket. I was driving around the school with my friend in my 1932 Ford hot rod and not going to class. He wanted me to show him how fast the car could go from a dead stop to the speed limit. Of course, I did not see Officer Buster Stiger nearby and took off laying rubber in front of the school until I reached about ten miles over the speed limit. The next thing I saw in my rear-view mirror was the police car's flashing light. My friend went to class, and Buster Stiger gave me a speeding and reckless driving ticket, the last one I have received to date. Buster was well known around the school since many other students had also received tickets from him.

"Since we are fairly close to the location of my folks' first home on Pearl Street, between Ellsworth and First Avenue, let's drive by where the house used to be located. Now there is an apartment building at the old home site."

As they were going south on Broadway, John told Kim, "Turn left at the next street, it's First Avenue. The Mayan movie theater is on the corner, where my friends and I used to watch many movies while eating popcorn and drinking cola that cost five cents. The movie that scared me the most was *The Wizard of Oz*. Have you seen it?"

"Yes, only once since it also scared me a lot."

"The botanical gardens are about a mile or two from here, so let's go over there and have a short walk around the gardens and then have some lunch."

After they got to the gardens and started their walk, Kim said, "What a fascinating place. So many different kinds of plants and trees. The flowers are especially beautiful."

"It is amazing if you believe it all started with the Big Bang. I am not talking about the popular TV show, but the theory of how the universe and earth were formed and evolved as it is today. I had a little trouble understanding the Wikipedia articles I read about it as well as the chronology of the universe and the history of the earth. The Wikipedia articles about human history and Charles Darwin were much easier to comprehend."

John then gave Kim a summary of what he had read.

"John, you have a remarkable memory."

"Thank you. I used to have a photographic memory, but now I am running out of film."

Kim joined John in laughing.

"Okay, let's head to Westwood now so I can show you the home on Irving Street where I spent most of my school years before high school graduation and moving into an apartment with my brother Bill and my cousin Don. First, drive south on University Boulevard to Alameda Avenue, then go west past Federal Boulevard to Irving Street."

When they reached Irving Street, John asked Kim to stop in a nearby parking lot. "The building across the street is where I used to work. Now the Millers Super Market building is some kind of a church. Now please drive about a mile south on Irving Street to Kentucky Avenue."

As they passed that intersection, John said, "On the left is where Irving Elementary School was located. It was demolished several years ago. Next door is Kepner Junior High. I attended both schools. A block farther south is the two-bedroom home where I grew up with my two brothers and two sisters. When I worked at Millers as a sacker, most of the time I had to walk to work and walk home at night. Sometimes the night walk was scary since Westwood was in the bad part of town in those days, and I had to walk past a housing project where a few thugs lived. The area demographics went from mostly Latino to Asian. I think I told you about the bike rides my friends and I used to take to Central City and Tiny Town and about the fun I used to have in my home lab.

"After we have lunch, let's go to the Museum of Nature and Science and have a walk around the zoo."

On the drive to the zoo after lunch at McDonald's, Kim said, "John, I know a lot about your traveling around the world and that you have visited every country except for Somalia and Yemen. What were your best three trips?"

"My number 1 trip was to Antarctica, which included going over the Antarctic Circle. My second-best adventure was visiting Greenland and the High Arctic. My travels on the train from Vladivostok to Moscow were number 3. I got my bug for traveling when I was about ten. I had an uncle who worked on a merchant ship and traveled the seven seas. During the summers when he would return to Denver, he always gave us an interesting slideshow of his travels during the previous nine months. Where have you traveled to, Kim?"

"Of course, I have not seen nearly all the places you have. I have been to most of the states and some countries in Europe and Southern Africa."

"What were the most impressive things you have seen or experienced?

"Well, I would have to say Stonehenge, the Tower of London, the Eiffel Tower, and of course, Red Square. How about you?"

"These things are not in any kind of order, but I would say seeing wild animals on African safaris, Victoria Falls, a polar bear on an ice float in the High Arctic, the Great Wall of China, Yellowstone National Park, Prague, thousands of stars while camping out in Antarctica, and of course, the things on your list."

"Since we will be going to church in the morning and have more plans to see things around Denver, I need to drop you off at your apartment now since I must prepare for an important meeting on Monday. Part of the meeting will concern your assisting us."

As John was leaving Kim's car, he gave her a thank you with a short kiss on her cheek. "John, I will pick you up in the morning at 11:30 for the noon mass at my church. Goodbye."

On Sunday morning, Kim picked up John, and they travel to the nearby Holy Ghost Catholic Church. She told John on the short drive that she is a devout Catholic and tries to attend mass every Sunday.

John did enjoy the mass since he was with Kim. At the end of the mass, everyone held each other's hands in a final prayer. After everyone released their hands, Kim hung on to John's hand. Then he looked at her and blew her a kiss. She returned the kiss with a smile.

Following church and lunch, they went for another ride in Kim's car. They saw more of the east side of Denver and Aurora and spent the rest of the afternoon visiting the Wings Over the Rockies Air Museum.

Before returning to TT, they stopped at a car wash so John could wash Kim's dirty car. John told Kim that she is an excellent driver and that he wants to take a quick shower and change clothes before they go to dinner at her new apartment. As soon as they arrived at John's apartment building, the valet was waiting for them. He took the car keys from Kim and told her, "I will be going home soon, so when you leave here, you will need to pick up your car keys at the front desk."

After the couple arrived at TT, they took their coffee to the balcony to admire the view. Kim pointed out her car at the far end of the guest parking lot about half a block from the building. She told John how much she has enjoyed being with him the past several weeks. "I am falling in love with you, John."

John then took her in his arms and gave her a long romantic kiss. He said, "I love you very much and would like to marry you someday."

"I think we need to know that Felex is in police custody before we get married since you may also be in harm's way.

"While you are showering and getting dressed, I will read about another one of your trips. So please take your time.

After John finished showering and getting dressed, he went into the living room where Kim was still reading about one of his trips. "John, do you mind going down and getting my car since I would like to finish reading about your trip to India and Pakistan? I will meet you at the entrance to the building in about ten minutes and will be sure to lock your apartment before I join you.

"No problem, Kim."

As Kim finished reading about John's trip, she heard a loud explosion, and the building shook. She ran to the balcony and saw that her car was blown apart and on fire in the parking lot. She screamed, "No, no, John was in the car." She frantically ran to the elevator. After it arrived several minutes later, she took it down to the ground floor. As the elevator was slowly descending to the next floor, she was hysterically thinking that the car bomb was meant for her. "John, I am so sorry. I love you and want to marry you." She knew that it was probably Felex who placed the bomb in her car since he was the one trying to kill her and certainly the same one who assassinated her husband in Kiev.

Chapter 5

I

There were three elevators in the thirty-floor apartment building, each serving ten different floors. After making a second stop at the twenty-ninth floor, the elevator was full. Kim got more anxious as the crowded elevator made eight additional stops without any of the curious apartment occupants boarding the fully loaded car. As the elevator was slowly descending, Kim was frantically thinking to herself with tears in her eyes despite the other elevator occupants talking about the explosion that shook the building. "Why did I let John get my car out of the parking lot? It should have been me that was killed in my burning car. I know it was the assassin Felex who planted the bomb. Without John, my life is now over. I so wanted to spend the rest of my life as his wife."

While Kim was in the crowded elevator, firemen arrived at the car and quickly put out the fire. As Kim was leaving the elevator, the firemen discovered the burned remains of a man in the demolished car. Kim ran outside to find John with cuts on his head talking to a police captain. He took her in his arms as she cried out, "John, I am so, so happy that you are okay. I thought you were killed in the explosion of my car."

"As I was walking to your car, I saw Felex under the car. I called out and asked what he was doing. Then the bomb exploded and knocked me to the ground. Apparently, Felex had accidentally set off the bomb by mistake when he heard my call. The ambulance has just arrived to bandage me up, so please come with me. I was asked to go to police headquarters to make a statement. I hope you can join me in telling the police the whole story of Felex trying to kill you."

II

A couple of weeks later, John and Kim resumed somewhat-normal lives. Kim received an assignment to confer with the FBI in DC on how to reduce the number of mass shootings in the United States that have taken place to date. The day before the meeting, John accompanied her to DIA so she could catch her flight to Washington. They walked to Union Station and caught the light rail to the airport. It was midmorning, so there were a few passengers in their car. They started discussing the mass shootings that have taken place recently in the United States.

"John, I have been reading a lot about the mass shootings the last couple of days to prepare for my meeting in Washington. At least a dozen people were killed and more than sixty injured in at least ten mass shootings the past weekend in our country. In Philadelphia, at least two people were killed and eleven others hit by gunfire at a bustling entertainment district. In Chattanooga, Tennessee, two people were killed, and fourteen were wounded at or near a nightclub. One person was killed, and at least seven others were wounded at a graduation party in Summerton, South Carolina. In Phoenix, a fourteen-year-old girl was killed, and eight others were wounded at a strip mall. In Mesa, Arizona, two people were killed, and two others were wounded. Five people were wounded in Socorro, Texas. In Omaha, Nebraska, one person was killed, and three others were wounded. In Chesterfield, Virginia, one person was killed, and five others were wounded. One person was killed, and three others were wounded in Macon, Georgia. In Saginaw, Michigan, three people were killed, and two people were wounded.

"America's deadly weekend of more mass shootings raised stakes for more Senate gun control talks. The bloodshed comes as our nation grieves for these killings this past month, including a massacre at an elementary school in Texas, a deadly assault at a medical facility in Oklahoma, a racist rampage at a supermarket in New York, and an attack on a Taiwanese church service in

California. America has recorded at least six hundred mass shootings in 2022 and sixty at K-12 schools. The Buffalo shooting suspect showed signs of violent behavior. Experts say troubled youth like him need long-term support."

"Yes, Kim, something needs to be done. In the aftermath of mass shootings, other nations have tightened restrictions on gun ownership that slowed or nearly eradicated such massacres. The last time I spoke with my old boss at the University of New South Wales, he reminded me about Australia's gun law reform that included the buyback of assault rifles and stringent limits on the availability of high-risk weapons. As a result, there were fewer firearm-related homicides overall and a much greater reduction in mass gun homicides. Semiautomatic long guns were prohibited, while all gun owners were required to prove a genuine reason to possess a firearm. As a result, in the decade before gun law reform in Australia, there were thirteen mass shootings. During the twenty-two years that followed, there were none.

"What can be done to prevent mass shootings in America's schools? Keep guns that can kill dozens of people a minute out of the hands of potential shooters. Improve the security of school buildings to stop intruders from entering and respond quickly when threats arise. Increase mental health care for troubled young people."

"I agree with you, John. I will bring up what you said at my meeting with the FBI tomorrow. We have arrived at the airport. Please come with me to the United Airlines desk so I can get my boarding pass and check my bag in."

After Kim was finished at the United counter, they walked to the nearby escalator that would take them down to the departure hall. Just before they boarded the escalator, John took her to a nearby area that had a view of the hall full of people waiting to go through airport security.

"Kim, every time I come to this place, I think of a potential mass shooter who could come here with two golf bags containing assault rifles and a backpack full of high-capacity magazines with hundreds of rounds. I think he could kill hundreds within a few minutes before he is shot down."

"That would be terrible, John. What is the solution?"

"Perhaps airport security could be increased with police stationed at places like this. Of course, a terrorist could always steal a truck and run down arriving passengers outside or come in here with a knife and start stabbing people. Please let us think of more pleasant things as I escort you to airport security."

"By the way, John, I plan to inform my boss next week that I want to take early retirement in two weeks."

"Kim, what great news. Then we can get married and take an around-the-world cruise for our honeymoon!"

John departed for the nearby light rail station after he gave Kim a long loving bear hug and kiss.

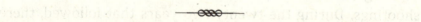

Three days later, John drove to DIA to pick up Kim. After he parked his car in a waiting area, he received a call from Kim that she has arrived in the arrivals hall and will meet him in a few minutes outside the first west-side door of the airport. John arrived at the airport and stopped his car behind a car that had just parked. He saw Kim coming out of the exit door and at the same time saw a man get out of the car in front of him with two AK-47s in each hand. The man started shooting at passengers coming out of the airport, and John saw Kim get shot, along with several other people. John immediately drove up on the curb and ran over the armed man as he started shooting at him.

Epilogue

The next morning, television stations and newspapers around the country were informing their watchers and readers of the tragic event the previous day at Denver International Airport. All the stories were about the same. A retired Clemson University Professor was a hero. With his car, he ran over and killed a terrorist who was about to go into the airport and gun down many arriving passengers. The assassin did manage to shoot several arriving passengers with two AK-45s that he had in each hand, but the only ones killed were the professor and a CIA agent. The gunman was identified. He was a TSA agent who had been fired from his job at DIA just two days ago for unprofessional and careless work as well as harassing and making threats to his fellow workers and supervisors.

Summary

The story begins with John James Czermak and his wife, Margrit, returning to their home in Arvada, Colorado, after spending three years in Vienna, Austria, where John worked for the International Atomic Energy Agency (IAEA). John is a world-renowned nuclear scientist and contributor to the development of the controversial neutron bomb. He returns to the job as manager of Plutonium Chemistry Research and Development at the Rocky Flats Plant (RFP), where parts for nuclear weapons are made. In Vienna, Margrit was romantically involved with Andrei Pushkin, thought by the Central Intelligence Agency (CIA) to be a KGB (Committee for State Security, foreign intelligence, and domestic security agency of the Soviet Union) agent. Realizing the futility of their relationship, Andrei and Margrit had on several occasions unsuccessfully attempted to terminate it. But Andrei suffered continual agonizing self-debasement and eventually left Vienna for Canada after faking his suicide.

Following their return to Colorado, John and Margrit resumes a close, loving relationship that had been badly damaged in Vienna. About this time, John is recruited by Tim Smith of the CIA since John travels to conferences around the world and to Vienna and Moscow to have meetings with his Russian coauthors on a series of books they are writing for the IAEA. Following more contacts with his Russian colleagues, John is informed that a background investigation had been conducted by the Department of Energy (DOE) and the Federal Bureau of Investigation (FBI). This inquiry results in John losing his security clearance.

John is then granted a three-year leave of absence from Rocky Flats management to teach in Australia. Tim continues to keep in contact with John and asks him to visit certain countries to find out if they might be producing nuclear weapons. During John's travels, there are several attempts on his life. After his return from the leave of absence, John starts work in California. It is there that Andrei surprisingly contacts Margrit to try to renew their love affair. Margrit rejects him since she has a good relationship with John and tells Andrei she might go with him if she were a divorcée or a widow. This statement prompts Andrei to try and kill John, but instead, he accidentally kills Margrit. Back at his home in Canada, Andrei learns of her death and commits suicide. In his dying breath, he tells his son Alex that Czermak had shot him.

John wants to start a new life and leaves California for a teaching job at Clemson University in South Carolina and even starts using his middle name. Andrei's son Alex joins James's research group using a different last name. James takes two of his graduate students and Ying, a postdoc from China, on an expedition to Antarctica that the CIA supported to see if one of the Russian crew members is passing nuclear weapons information to a group of Argentinian scientists.

On the expedition, a loving relationship develops between James and Ying, and they are married by the captain. Alex tries to kill James on an island campout but later finds out that James did not kill his father. On the last night of the voyage, during a violent rainstorm, Alex meets James at the stern of the ship and makes amends to him, which ends with Alex giving James a big bear hug that causes both to accidentally fall into the rough and freezing ocean.

The morning following the violent storm, a man and two ladies discover James washed up on the shore of Cape Horn. They take him back by fishing boat to Deborah's home on another island. The couple is Deborah's neighbors, and she is a widow and retired medical doctor. Deb assists James in recovering but finds out he has amnesia and does not remember anything prior to being washed up on land. Deb agrees to let James help her around her small farm. Several months later, the two start to travel to different parts of Chile together, and a loving relationship develops. James's memory slowly returns after an accidental meeting with a friend in Peru and returns to Clemson to have a reunion with Ying, his family, and his friends. The university appoints James as chairman of the chemistry department. During this time Ying gets killed in a hit-and-run accident that is meant for James. A week later, another attempt is made on James's life in his university laboratory, but he manages to escape the Molotov cocktail fire.

James is then contacted by CIA agent Kim Carn, who requests him to go on certain trips to collect intelligence as he had done for agent Tim Smith when Cermak worked in Colorado and Australia. James attends a technical conference in Moscow, and he asks Deborah to accompany him. On the trip, they spend a few days in Vienna where they get married. The Czermaks then go onto Moscow so James can attend the conference. On the last night of the meeting, the two are confronted in their hotel room by a man with a gun who identifies himself as Nikolai Pushkin, Andrei's son and Alex's older brother. Before he shoots Deborah and then James, he says, "This is for killing my father and brother." Gravely wounded, James jumps over and gives Nikolai a bear hug, trying to wrestle the gun from him, but it goes off, putting a bullet into Nikolai's heart, killing him.

The Moscow visit concludes with Deborah dying and James recovering. However, Andrei's brother, Alexei, is determined to kill James since he is convinced that James was responsible for the deaths of his brother and two nephews. However, Alexei is unsuccessful in killing Professor Czermak. James then returns to work at Clemson University.

Czermak wants to start a new life because he was responsible for his third wife getting murdered. He retires from Clemson University, sells his two homes in South Carolina, and moves to Nederland, Colorado. John then starts working as a part-time professor at the University of Colorado (CU) in Boulder and shares an office with a visiting professor from Moscow. Lara Medvedev and John start traveling together to meetings, and a loving relationship develops. They attend a conference in

Sweden, and later fly to Saint Petersburg, followed by a train ride to Moscow so John can meet Lara's parents. After their arrival in Moscow, John visits a good friend at the Academy of Sciences, where they go to the roof of a tall academy building so John can take some pictures. Then Alexei shows up and tries to push John off the building, but instead, he falls to his death. Since John now thinks no one is trying to murder him, he asks Lara to marry him. She happily agrees. A few days later, they have a wedding reception at Lara's parents' home. After the party ends and everyone has left, Lara's ex-husband arrives to kill John but accidentally kills Lara. The next day, Ivan commits suicide after he hears of Lara's death.

John returns to Colorado, sells his home in Nederland, retires from his part-time job at the CU, and moves into a luxurious thirty-floor apartment building in lower downtown Denver. CIA agent Kim Carn continues to request his help on a few missions to gather intelligence for the CIA. Kim is also on the lookout for the person who murdered her husband, the CIA bureau chief at the US Embassy in Kiev, Ukraine. She knows he was killed because he had obtained strategic military information concerning the Russian government. Kim now has the information and narrowly escapes being killed by a hired assassin who had murdered her husband. The second attempt by the assassin involved Kim's car being blown up, apparently with John inside the car instead of Kim. However, it turns out that the assassin gets killed instead of John.

Kim and John take some time to unwind from the attempts on their lives and make plans to get married and take a trip around the world. Meanwhile, Kim gets an assignment to assist in ways to reduce the number of mass shootings in the United States. John accompanies Kim to Denver International Airport so she can attend a meeting in Washington. They discuss the subject on the way to the airport. A few days later, he drives to the airport to pick up Kim. A mass shooter also arrives at the airport and is confronted by John.